KING'S COMMISION

A HIGH FANTASY NOVEL

JAMES M. WARD

Cover design by James M. Ward

ISBN 978-1-960016-18-8

ALSO BY JAMES M. WARD

Wolfoid

CONTENTS

PROLOGUE
ORDERS FROM THE KING

"Even a blind sow gets an acorn once in a while."

— JIM KREMS

WALKING THE SAME STREET FOR THE TENTH time that evening, Captain Corbyn Cauldron of the King's Own 25th Lancers couldn't believe the orders in his hand. The Captain cut a dashing figure in his green, perfectly tailored lancer uniform. Six foot, eleven inches tall, massively broad shoulders displayed corded muscles running down his arms; the Captain was the perfect example of the best type of officer. While the uniform bore the rank of Captain on the shoulder lapels, the medal insignias filling his chest spoke of a warrior having seen many successful battles.

The Captain fumed at his Sergeant, shaking the orders in the Sergeant's face. "I realize we must obey our commanders. By the high moon above, why in this world or any other is a lancer regiment off their horses, searching like madmen through the basements and attics of every ducal manor in the royal quarter of the city? Are there no infantry divisions to tread into people's homes?"

Sergeant David Wise, hiding a smile behind a military expression, nodded sagely at his commanding officer. He took the crumpled orders from his Captain's hand and gave them off to Private Donont for the fifth time that night. Wise was almost as tall as his Captain. While his green uniform wasn't as neat as his leader's, he bore almost as many medals on his chest. As an officer, Cauldron had to be clean-shaven, but a Sergeant could sport a thick beard and long hair, and that's what Wise liked to do. A few gray hairs coursed through the beard, but Wise was fond of saying, "I've earned every one of those hairs in the King's service."

With the moon high, irritation at silly orders forced Cauldron into a nervous pacing. Wise stood back, waiting to carry out orders and remembering many a time when his leader rode into the thick of battle, displaying not the slightest bit of tension. The good Captain showed himself to be a coiled spring of irritation now.

For some strange reason, unknown to the normally in-the-know Sergeant, his leader displayed more power and deadly capability when the moon was full and high. The Captain's magical ability proved itself greater during the times of the full moon as well. Magic-using battle leaders weren't that uncommon in the King's regiments, but his Captain was something special.

Corbyn proved himself a deadly swordsman and a crafty spell-user in the service of the human empire of Dulse. In past conflicts, Wise witnessed Corbyn's eyes glow the color of the moon and saw moon-colored lightning leap from Cauldron's hands to burn enemies massing in front of their battle position.

Known as a lucky officer among his men and the other cavalry regiments, there wasn't another leader in all the armies of the King that Sergeant Wise would rather follow. "I can see you don't like what we're doing. Begging your pardon, Sar, but this work detail is easy as details go. You could look at it this way: we're saving the lives of servants in these manors who would be forced to fight and die at the talons of zombies."

"True, I'll give you that, Sergeant," Corbyn replied. "The zombies are crazed things; their best attack seems to be a charge straight ahead with talons extended. So far, troopers with a good blade in their hands have been able to down such monsters with practiced strokes."

Wise munched on the last of the pastries he

grabbed from the manor kitchen they had just inspected. His Captain was relaxing so the Sergeant could as well. "Besides, there are excellent kitchens in every rich man's home, and everyone knows zombies often hide behind freshly baked cream puffs," Wise said with a mouthful of food.

Both men laughed, and the lancer regiment continued searching.

In the hours that followed, they found several zombies on Gold Street and dispatched them. The head of a zombie had to be cut off, or the creature rose again, no matter how many wounds it suffered in a battle.

"Sergeant, what do you think is causing all of these zombies to rise?" Corbyn asked, knowing the answer but wanting to discover if his Sergeant knew as well.

"There are several ways to make a zombie," Wise replied. "An evil priest can raise the dead. Some powerful wizards skilled in death can make them. Those that we're killing are from a demon. Common knowledge dictates when a Nevil Demon feeds, it sucks the life out of a person, leaving an enchanted corpse to rise and search hungrily for its lost life essence. Zombies in their hundreds, appearing all over the rich quarter of the city in the past few weeks, speak to an unusually powerful Nevil Demon doing its evil mischief."

On this pleasantly warm summer's evening,

with the full moon rising in the sky, the regiment marched onto Silver Street. Corbyn turned to the long column of men and shouted his orders. "Corporals, each of you take ten men and search these manors. Don't take no for an answer. When servants try to stop you, mention the orders from the King and proceed. Sergeant, you and the remaining men and I will take the White Goose Inn for ourselves."

The squad walked to the end of the street. Porters and city watch roamed the area with weapons ready. This White Goose had been left alone in past searches, more orders from above. This time, Corbyn was going to search it as well.

The good Captain snorted, noting night watchmen going by. "These streets are guarded better than some of the forts we've been in." Corbyn gestured to the many mansions all around them. "I see night watchmen. I see Ducal guards at every mansion gate. Some of them armed and armored better than we are. By the gods above and below, was there ever such a waste of time?"

Then, the Captain's eyes fell on the inn. Famed all over the city, the White Goose Inn presented the best in food and entertainment for the elite of Sanguine. The inn was also a place reserved for the rich and royal of the kingdom to play and have fun away from the lower classes. Normally, a Captain and Sergeant couldn't get near the establishment.

"Sergeant Wise." Corbyn turned toward his Sergeant with a gleam in his eye.

"Sar!" Wise said, coming to attention.

"In the last nine times, we've searched this street. We haven't gone to the White Goose Inn, have we, Sergeant?"

"No, Sar!" Wise rolled his eyes, knowing the look and tone of voice. The massively muscled Sergeant enjoyed a good scrap as much as the next man, but he didn't enjoy dealing with royals. His big, calloused hands clenched tight as he dreaded the orders he knew he was about to hear.

"I think it's time we obeyed the orders we have to the letter. Follow me."

Wise would normally have cautioned his Captain about the folly of entering a royal establishment. The set of his leader's square jaw and the look of pure bedevilment in Cauldron's gray eyes told Wise not to bother. *We're in for it now.*

Smiling, Captain Cauldron stepped lively to the double doors. The inn was a huge, two-story stone structure more than five hundred years old. A sign displaying a white goose in a copper kettle proclaimed the name for any passersby. The connecting stable had long ago been converted into a gambling den and theater for the rich. The fresh white paint on the stonewalls and the many stained glass windows displayed an elegance not found in most inns.

People in the know claimed the current King

loved this place, but Cauldron doubted it. He thought the King would never be able to fit through the double doors of its entrance.

Dressed in white, the doorman stood beside the large portal. With a disapproving grimace, the lackey walked in front of the inn doors. An impressive, well-used mace appeared in the livery-man's hand. The powerful weapon's handle displayed wear; the business end clearly showed lots of use. "Why are you at our door, lancer Captain?"

There was a smile on Corbyn's lips as he shifted position so that the porter would have to take a wide swing to hit him instead of a short jab. It would be a very long swing to reach Corbyn, and the lackey would be dead long before the mace landed on its intended target.

Corbyn tried to defuse the situation with a bit of humor and goodwill. "We're on the King's business, don't you know. My orders are to search every house for zombies and their like. My men and I will disturb your guests as little as possible. Please, won't you let us inside?"

"I'm sorry, Captain. Only military Colonels and above, with their retinues, are allowed to cross this threshold. There are no zombies in here, I can assure you," the lackey answered.

"The nerve of the idjet." Private Stonefist shouted, his blood up. "It's been a long night already.

I've been ripped by a zombie claw a street back. Let me at 'em, Captain. I'll soon . . ."

"Steady on Private," Sergeant Wise interrupted. He shifted to his Captain's right, brandishing his nine-foot-long halberd. The weapon was a twig in the big man's hands. "Our Captain's up front doing his job. You remain in the ranks and do yours."

Suddenly, with a hand signal from the Sergeant, they all drew their curved lancer sabers, the hiss of steel sounding deadly.

The eyes of the door steward grew wide. "Ahem, I see. I'll tell the mistress you are here. Please wait outside."

The lackey went in. Corbyn turned to his men. "Sheath your blades. There'll be no waiting at this door. Who knows how many zombies are escaping out the back of this place right now?" The huge grin on his face showed he wasn't serious.

"Left column, search this floor and any basement or wine cellar you find. Be discrete. Right column search upstairs--if there's roggering going on in a room, it won't have zombies, so leave them to their fun. I don't want any Duke complaining to the King that one of my men rousted them from their important royal endeavors. Sergeant Wise, you come with me."

Corbyn pushed open the door and walked into a riot of light. The front entrance to the inn dazzled the senses. Blazing hearths sparkled with firelight.

Blindingly reflective copper kettles hung from the ceilings everywhere, each holding an ivory goose. The place clearly deserved its silly name.

"Never been in a room where I've sunk in the carpet like this," Corbyn said.

The place smelled of flowers, without a single flower in evidence. Corbyn cocked his head and sniffed. "Magic or clever architectural design, I wonder. Most inns smell of beer and sweat. This place smells like Teka roses."

"I thought only elves could grow Teka roses," Wise mused.

"You know, David, a hundred years ago, I favored sleeping under an oak covered in Teka vines." Corbyn shook off the memory, indicating he was back to business.

A gorgeous longhaired blond and her companion, the famous Duke of Tens, rushed to confront Corbyn. The Captain's men ignored the Duke and filtered up the stairs and into all the chambers off the first-floor landing, seeming ignorant of the wealth and nobility around them. All the troopers in the King's armies knew the Duke of Tenn. He'd served for years in the King's regiments in the cavalry and was the commander of all the infantry armies. The Duke grew famous for his love of being in the thick of every action. Retired now, he still commanded respect.

"Captain, I must protest," the fair lady at the Duke's side spoke in an excited rush.

Corbyn silenced her with his hand and a winning smile. The worried lady strained the Captain's eyes as he drank in her beauty.

Her ample bosom overflowed the dress, and her long blond hair spilled onto her bodice in curly waves. The lady's cheeks shone bright crimson from her irritation. Her fan, studded with gold and gems, was easily worth more than Corbyn made in ten years on a Captain's pay. It moved with stunning swiftness across her bodice.

Corbyn offered a courtly bow to the lady and the Duke. His eyes never left the Duke's face.

The Duke was a swordsman, evidenced by the well-used grip on his expensive rapier. Corbyn moved to the unweaponed side of the Duke, a move the Duke acknowledged with a turn of his body and the shifting of his stance.

"Is this search really necessary, Captain?" the Duke asked. "Surely this inn, filled with the Dukes and Counts of the land, harbors no zombies."

"I'm positive you are correct, my Lord," Corbyn's tone was polite. "The men will be in and out as quickly as possible. I'm sure you realize when the King orders every building in the city searched, his wishes must be obeyed."

"Err, well, hurmph," the Duke replied. "You are jolly well correct, sir. I served in the King's regiments myself and know a good officer when I see one. Lady Eve, we must let the men do their work. Come, Captain, and sit with the Lady and me at our Blood & Guts table while your men go about their business."

"But Percy, there are delicate negotiations upstairs. What of them?" the hostess protested.

Corbyn took her tiny white hand and kissed the tips of her fingers. He noted the red of her cheeks increasing somewhat. That was all right with him because he liked what he saw.

Corbyn found the innkeeper far too lovely to keep distressed. "The lancers are following orders to be discrete, and they will be. You have my oath as a gentleman and King's officer on that dear lady. No one wants to interrupt spirited negotiations."

The Duke put a protective arm around her, and she rapped him with her fan to show she didn't want protection.

"There you have it now," the Duke told her. "When a king's officer gives his word, you have nothing to worry about. Come, come, Lady, and bring the good Captain and his capable-looking Sergeant some of the house biscuits. I wager they haven't had their like before. Searching houses is hungry work, what?"

The gambling chamber of the inn held ten large Blood & Guts tables. The huge room showed itself lined with tables heavy in food and drink. Kettles of all sizes, covered in gold, hung from the ceiling and walls. The gold brilliance of each light-shedding kettle stunned the eyes as each increased the illumination given off by the lanterns and fireplaces. The food smelled wonderful, and servants constantly removed cold platters, replacing them with warm ones. The jewels and wealth displayed on the ladies and men in this chamber could pay the salaries of entire armies for years.

Corbyn was sure there wasn't royalty less than a Duke among the fifty men and women playing at the tables. He recognized several court Earls and Counts among the throng.

Naturally, the Duke led them to the center table. Three other lord types played there. One of the lords was massive, easily as tall as Corbyn with plowshare, handle-wide shoulders, and a deep booming voice.

Corbyn noted the man's weapon was an unusual axe. The weapon's long handle rested against the gambling table at the side of the Duke. Corbyn's moon-enhanced powers sensed magic about the weapon. Axes were not the usual weapons of choice among royals. As Corbyn looked at the axe, his magically enhanced vision showed it to have a dark mist all around the blade. He could also smell a bitter odor of dark magics on the weapon. Whatever it was, the blade was dangerous. All the rest of the Lords wore swords at their hips, even the older players.

The other two men at the table were local Earls, men who followed the King and helped collect taxes.

They smiled politely at Corbyn but clearly dismissed him as unimportant.

"Will you play a few hands, Captain?" the Duke of Tenn obviously tried to be charming, and Corbyn appreciated it. Blood & Guts was one of Corbyn's favorite parlor games, and an offer to play with such powerful men wasn't something to refuse for a Captain of the King's lancers.

"What's the buy-in, my Lord?" Corbyn asked.

"Oh, we like to keep things simple here. It's a hundred gold for the red and two hundred for the white. If you can't afford it, we'll understand. I'd offer to take whatever marker you wished to give, but as you know, that's forbidden at a Blood & Guts table."

The buy-in was a lot for a Captain in the King's 25th Lancers. For some reason, Corbyn didn't want to appear any less in the eyes of these men. He also wanted to observe the big axe-owning Duke during the game. Corbyn twisted his hand, causing a large moon opal to appear in his palm with a slight of hand trick, and threw it to the dealer. The opal was easily worth two thousand gold. The dealer gave him a red and white token, a silver round player marker, and seven hundred gold in seven sliver-thin gold bars. He was shorted a thousand gold but expected nothing less in a gambling establishment. Corbyn wouldn't be in for many hands at this rate.

Blood & Guts was a kingdom-wide popular dice

game with many strategies. Each player bought into the game getting a red marker (blood token), a white marker (guts token), and a colored player marker. Each player had their own particular color to mark them from the rest of the players. The gold was spent on tokens collected at the center of the table for the winner of the game. One of the players rolled two dice into a bladder at the center of the table. The bladder prevented dice cheats, allowing the dice to tumble down a long tube and out onto the table. The number rolled out determined what the roller could do at the table.

Corbyn loved the game because he was a lucky roller. He also liked to see how others handled the roll of seven. One could tell a lot about a person by how they played Blood & Guts.

Corbyn was introduced to the Duke and Earls, but the big axe man, the Duke of the Eastern Forests, held his attention the longest. The Captain instantly took a disliking to this Duke. Corbyn acted on his deadly hunch. He motioned for Sergeant Wise to come over and whispered: "The good Duke over there, the one with the bloody great axe, stand a bit behind him. If and when I dance with him, I'll signal you and the dance will start with you ripping that axe away."

Not blinking or showing his surprise, Sergeant Wise nodded and slowly moved about the room, getting into position.

Corbyn's dislike was just a soldier's hunch. Still, there was enough evidence in Corbyn's mind to make him wary. Dukes were rarely as heavily muscled as this one was. Generally, as a group, they didn't have time to do physical things, being too busy governing their lands or enjoying themselves. The magic on the axe was another sign. The humans of the empire didn't generally like magical weapons. Magic put intelligence in the heart of a weapon. Often, that intelligence demanded a price for service. Finally, there was a deadly look about the Duke of the Eastern Forests. Even as he smiled at Corbyn, the Captain could sense death and danger hanging about the man like a black cloak.

As the new player, he rolled the dice first. He picked up the two wooden cubes, hesitated for a heartbeat, and tossed the dice into the top of the bladder. Smiling, he watched a seven come out at the bottom. The others sighed, not liking the roll and what would happen next. He pushed four of his gold bars into the tiny circle, thus doubling the wager amount.

"Everyone roll."

Corbyn, senses on high alert discovered something when he picked up the dice. The cubes were magiced in some way. Without careful study, he couldn't figure out how the enchantment affected them. He reached for the dice on the table, needing to sense their nature with his own magic. Closing his eyes so that no one would see them glow, he held the dice for a heartbeat in his fist and coated them in the invisible essence of the moon. It was a minor mirror magic preventing anyone else from adding magic to the dice. He passed the cubes with his eyes closed to the Duke of Tenn.

Eyes open again, he watched the Duke roll a five.

"Damn it all." The Duke forcefully tossed in his blood token.

"Bad luck, Percy." The axe Duke picked up the dice, and as he rolled them, he grimaced. There was the slightest puff of smoke as he hurriedly tossed the dice into the bladder. The Duke stared at the red cubes as if they were his enemy. He'd rolled an eight, forcing him to toss in his blood token. The other two Earls rolled nines and tossed in their blood tokens as well.

Corbyn felt moonlight on his shoulders and looked up to see the full moon from a large transom in the ceiling. Welcoming its energy, he knew he'd need all its power tonight if his suspicions were true. He noted his Sergeant well positioned behind the Duke of the Northern Forests.

When it was Percy's turn to roll, he made a ten, forcing him to throw in his guts token as well.

The Forest Duke picked up the dice with his fingertips and flipped the cubes into the bladder as if each was a blazing thing. Corbyn thought he noticed a darkening of the Duke's flesh. It was very possible the moon enchantment burned his fingertips.

A roll of double fours allowed the Duke to make the wager eight hundred gold. Everyone but Corbyn turned in his guts token. Poor Percy threw in his all-in-marker and was out of the game. Corbyn threw in his blood token.

On their turns, the other two Earls rolled a six and a five, forcing them, according to the rules, to throw in their player markers.

"Lady Eve, could I have a large flagon of wine, please?" Corbyn asked.

The chamber was filled with punch bowls and tiny cups. Corbyn could see by the looks of the men around the table that he was thought incredibly boorish to order Lady Eve about like a tavern wench.

"Of course, Captain, I'll see what I can find for you," she graciously replied.

Before he rolled his next play, there was a large tankard of dark wine at his elbow. He rolled a nine and was forced to throw in his guts marker.

The Forest Duke smiled as he still had his last token. He reached for the dice and quickly tossed them into the bladder. There were clear burn marks on his fingers. A large cockroach crawled out on his sleeve. Such things were common everywhere. No one thought a second about the bugs, but this time, in the intense action of the game, the Duke slipped up. With tables full of food all around, he shouldn't have reached down smiling as he picked up the cockroach. He bit into the bug with great relish, and Corbyn beheld a Nevil demon.

A seven came out of the bladder.

Corbyn raised his heavy tankard as if to salute the Duke and signaled Wise by balling his other hand into a fist.

The Sergeant pulled the axe away from the table and the Duke's reach. Corbyn threw the entire contents of the large tankard into the Duke's eyes.

Lady Eve screamed in shock. Corbyn rose, beginning the dance of death. Corbyn drew his sword and, in one smooth and perfectly timed lunge, sheathed it into the heart of the demon.

That didn't end the matter, as his worst fears were realized.

The room filled with screams as chairs flew back and weapons were drawn. Those with common sense rushed out of the gambling hall.

The demon-Duke sat there laughing. With a sword in its chest, it slowly wiped the wine out of its eyes, and its body grew larger as it transformed.

"Well, it was fun while it lasted." The deep base of its expanding throat revealed deadly menace. The creature's voice rasped into a barely understandable growl. Tusks erupted from its mouth. Its manicured fingers turned into huge razor-sharp talons. Inhumanly large muscles burst through its silk shirt and pants. "Little human, you and I must dance for a bit.

I really need to take your soul since you took away my fun."

Corbyn stood his ground as the creature rose and reached for him. Using the essence of the moon, light streaming down on him, he cast a deadly spell. A huge crash of lightning erupted from his hands and smashed into the demon. The creature flew back twenty feet into the wall. Hitting it with a bone-crunching smack, the demon rippled down the wall to the floor.

Laughing, it got up and grew even taller and broader.

"You can't kill me, little human." The creature's growing voice was terrifying. People around the demon froze in fear at just the sound of the monster's words. "You don't have a demon dagger here. I can sense those, and they're all at the palace. I'll be eating you, and there's nothing you can do that won't make me grow larger and stronger."

Corbyn mentally sorted through his options, noting his sword still in the monster's heart, not slowing it down at all. His deadliest spell made the creature grow more powerful. As the demon moved toward him with its talons outstretched, taking its time and enjoying itself, Corbyn signaled to Wise to try the axe.

With a huge swing, the tall Sergeant smashed the blade of his newly acquired weapon fully into the neck of the demon. A small weal of blood appeared on its throat, and the thing grew even more massive with the axe bouncing off its hide.

Dukes, Earls, and Counts rushed for the only door and jammed it up so that no one was leaving the chamber. Suddenly, intense fire bathed the demon from head to foot. Trying to protect a lady behind him, a Duke used a potent magical ring on the demon. While Corbyn respected the effort, all it did was make the monster grow even larger.

Corbyn's only option seemed to be running, and he didn't like the chances of getting away from an eight-foot-tall demon from the pits of hell.

Some of his lancers cleared the press of the entrance and rushed into the room with their swords drawn.

Corbyn shouted at them. "Men, throw wine in its face. David, to me!"

Corbyn jumped onto a food table and tried unhooking the largest cauldron in the room. It was a huge thing, coated in gold.

Sergeant Wise helped him get it unhooked; the weight of the thing required two strong men to move it. "What in the world are we doing with this thing?" Sergeant Wise asked pulling the china goose from the pot.

There was lots of wine in punch bowls all over the room. His men splashed the head of the demon with gallons of the stuff.

"Owe, that hurts!" The demon whined as it constantly opened its eyes, was dashed with wine, and squeezed them closed again to shed the stinging liquid. The demon blindly picked up two of the lancers and bent them in half. The sounds of their spines breaking were lost amid the shouts of fear as the last of the guests dashed from the room. The alcohol raised puffs of grape-colored smoke from the eyes of the demon, but the creature blinked the liquid away.

Corbyn and Wise rushed forward with the heavy cauldron and threw it over the demon's head. The kettle barely fit.

Corbyn pulled his sword from the heart of the creature with a twist.

"Stab it! Chop it! Kill it!" Corbyn ordered his stunned men into action while he repeatedly lunged his blade into the creature.

His men chopped and cut as well. Wise used the magical axe. The weapon started screaming a battle song. The attacks failed to kill the monster, and the demon grew and grew. In seconds, the inches-thick kettle became wedged tight around the head of the creature. Its talons raked the metal and gouged grooves in the cauldron but didn't penetrate all the way through the thick metal.

The size of the monster grew to fifteen feet, but the kettle held the massive head of the creature in a deadly vice the monster couldn't tug free.

Wounds would close magically, but the lancers put hundreds more into the creature. The massive monster finally fell to the floor, twitching its last. It took thirty minutes of constant stabbing for the creature to die. At death, the demon turned to dust, and the dust vanished back to its demonic plane of existence.

In the quiet of the chamber, Corbyn looked around to see Duke Percy standing over Lady Eve with his sword drawn and a deadly look on his face. She'd broken her leg and fainted at his feet.

The mountain Duke, who used the magic ring, checked his still unconscious lady and rose up to shake Corbyn's hand.

"It's the damndest thing I ever saw. I'll make sure you're nominated for a King's Commission for this, damned if I won't. You've saved the lives of hundreds of royals. Damned clever, choking it in that pot. How did you ever think of that one?"

Corbyn wasn't going to tell the Duke; he only wanted to put it on the demon's head so that he could gather everyone up and retreat. "The King's training, of course, sir. We're supposed to think clearly in any situation. I was just lucky the effort worked."

Percy handed him a large leather bag with a white goose emblem on its side. Later Corbyn would discover several thousand in rubies and diamonds, and his moon opal.

"The sack is just a remembrance of the good lady Eve and me. Well done, Captain. I, too, will make sure the King knows of your effort and considers you for a King's Commission."

Corbyn took his command and left the inn smiling. He treated his men to many rounds of drinks at a much friendlier inn. Corbyn Cauldron's star was clearly on the rise.

1

THE MAKING OF A KING'S COMMISSION

"Do not put your trust in Kings and Princes;
Three of a kind will take them both."

— ROBERT C. SCHENCK (1880)

RACING QUICKLY DOWN THE GOLD-GILDED hall of the greatest palace in the world, Lord Anwardentine of the High Passes felt in his bones that a nasty, nasty day lay before him. Rushing up the stairs to the throne room, his fifty-two years didn't slow him down a bit as his hands checked each of his tools of the trade. Magical rings, bejeweled armlets, and fresh herbs decorated his clothes and protected him from all sorts of magical and unmagical effects.

Lastly, pausing on the wide black marble stairs, he took out his small personal notebook in a ritual done every day before entering the throne room. The first page opened to four tiny hand-painted images. His lady, Delsenora, and his three sons looked up at him. *By the gods, he loved them dearly, and he would see them and his empire safe at any cost. Hopefully,* he sighed as he put the notebook away; *the costs would only be measured in gold today.*

"The King is having thoughts," he muttered to himself. "Why today would the King have thoughts?"

Anwardentine tried to concentrate on the last of his enchanted items. His mistletoe brooch was fresh, and there were oak coins in each of his pockets. The juniper leaves under his lapels were a little old; he'd replace those this afternoon. Two more steps took him to the small side entrance to the throne room.

"Morning Thomas, how goes the court today?"

"Chancellor, good to see you this morning. The King's having thoughts today, he is. The nation's already changed some holidays, and it looks like we might be planning to build a bridge over the Swanee again, imagine that." Thomas, the king's enchanted door guard replied. Looking like a huge China statue of a warrior, it stood eight feet tall if it stood an inch. Its magical spear could punch through the thickest plate mail or demon hide at need. It was arcanely protected from illusions and destructive charms, and it had worked for the rulers of this empire for several centuries. Golem guards of this type were common in the royal palace as they could not be bribed or filled with fear.

The sarcastic smile on Thomas' face clearly foretold of very bad news for the day. Thomas was an able doorguard, like all the enchanted throne guards. This fact hooked it into the web of information surrounding the King. When Thomas was sarcastic, Anwardentine would be spending thousands of the Kingdom's hard-earned gold pieces on useless projects.

The chancellor threw open the door, not waiting for Thomas to open it. He took several long breaths to survey the throne room. This chamber was the heart of the empire he loved, and Anwardentine adored every moment he worked in this focus of the empire's power. He noted the chamber's scent was still morning pine. The magical chandeliers lit every corner during the day and dimmed their diamond lights at night for the many grand dances held for this or that holiday or because the King was in the mood to dance with a pretty Countess. The four chamber corners held large alcoves where court administrators processed the business of the Dulse Empire.

He glanced at the north alcove to see his people hard at work. Lord Anwardentine was rarely there, but his court officials picked lords, and ladies knew their tasks well. He smiled to see Lady Marsh enter from another side entrance. *Hopefully, she would be bringing in the tax revenues from the northern mountain provinces.*

Military types in gleaming armor filled the south alcove. That was not a good sign. Dulse had just finished another disastrous war with the elves. The size of the army had to be increased, fearing a counterattack from the elfin territories. He could not blame the elves, really. His people had invaded the elfin nations six times, each campaign an utter failure.

The east alcove only had a sprinkling of merchants and guildsmen today. He breathed a sigh of thanks for that small favor. Life was hard enough dealing with the King without having to smooth over the ruffled feathers of the merchant class.

The seven magical Sars mirrors on the west wall were all in use. These wonders allowed instant communication with officials all over the empire. They were one of the reasons the government was so strong. He frowned, noticing several of the court ladies gossiping at mirrors with ladies of the court elsewhere in the empire of Dulse. *That wouldn't do at all.*

What's this? The west alcove is empty? Normally, there were ten to twenty clerics and bishops working on holy missives for the temples of the empire in that alcove. *There must be a high holy day today. Which one was it? It was impossible to keep all the holy days straight. Oh, never mind, on to business.*

Anwardentine had to get in there and put a stop to something! He sprinted the one hundred yards to the throne, noticing there were few courtiers around the King this morning, another clear sign of trouble. No one wanted to be associated with some of the King's more dangerous or stupid thoughts. The chancellor arrived just in time to hear the latest of the King's royal ideas.

"I think an elfin brooch would be nice for Princess Talyn's birthday. What do you all think?" the King asked no one in particular.

The King sat slumped on his throne in irritation. King Hamel came from a long line of slumpers. He'd taken slouching to a new kingly art. Although he was six feet tall and almost that wide, he looked about four feet tall as the huge gold throne engulfed his body. As usual, his long hair was pasted to the sides of his giant jowls. There was something magical about his clothing. The King could put on brand new clothes, especially tailored for him, and instantly wrinkles appeared everywhere, and sections of the cloth, normally more than wide enough, pulled tight against his body parts. The magical effect was not pleasing to the eye. Small piggy, unkind eyes and tight little lips served to pinch up a face that rarely smiled. It didn't really matter what those around King Hamel the thirteenth thought. As ruler of the vast empire of Dulse, his every word was law.

Anwardentine muttered as he reached the

throne, "It's a good thing laws were made to be broken." He took a louder tone to make himself heard over the rumble of the court. "Well Sire, there is a slight problem."

Lord Anwardentine was forced many times to tell the King what was and wasn't possible. That didn't mean he liked to do it. "Magical elfin brooches are difficult, if not impossible, for humans to get. Elves and their brooches being the way they are, you understand."

Lord Anwardentine presented everyone in the immediate area of the throne with a strained smile. Many of the King's courtiers found other places in the palace to be just then, knowing full well what was going to happen next.

"Blasted elves!" the King snarled. "Insufferable creatures! No, I don't understand!"

His throne trembled with the strain of holding his bulk. Even solid gold throne parts had their engineering limits when put to massive stresses. "Are you telling me someone can't take a bag full of gold into elf lands and buy me a simple brooch? Furthermore, are you telling me one of my more loyal lancers can't just kill an elf and take the creature's brooch?"

"Well sire, to answer your second question first, the brooches magically vanish when the elf brooch owner dies. Buying a brooch from a friendly elf would be almost impossible as we have, after all, unsuccessfully invaded their country six times and finding a friendly elf is going to be dashed difficult." Anwardentine held his hands out in a pleading gesture with his King.

A burst of blinding light erupted in the throne room.

It seemed in sensing the extreme anger of the King, young Commander Janon's ancestral magical armor suddenly burst into a protective magical glow under the redirected glare of the King.

"We aren't at war with them now, are we?" The King's voice filled with sneering disgust as he twisted his head sideways away from his court. This little infamous gesture told everyone the King was in one of his moods. For the next five hours, it didn't matter what anyone said. Every word, every idea would be wrong. In the past, at times like these, lords were sent to the headsmen's axe for the most trivial of comments.

Commander Janon felt the need to answer this charge, as guilt at the loss of the war was driving him to an early grave. An imposing man sporting powerful magical armor, Janon's well-muscled frame never seemed to tire of wearing the heavy enchanted plate mail. "Well, no. But we have only just gotten our troops out of their lands in the last month. Even though we lost the. . ."

"That's quite enough, Commander." Lord Anwardentine liked Janon and didn't want to see another high Commander lose his head for speaking undiplomatically to an angry King. "An elfin brooch is what is needed; does anyone have any ideas on how to get one?"

"Princess Talyn, just the other day, said she really liked dwarven harps. Maybe we should get her one of those instead." Lord Cortwin, titleholder of the Rill lands, wasn't watching the King when he made his stupid suggestion. A tall, lanky man with long, dark, greasy hair and a thin mustache he was constantly fond of twirling with his fingers, Cortwin was new to the court. He'd taken over the Rill lands from his recently dead father. Mincing about and trying to be friendly to everyone, the term country bumpkin was often used to describe him behind his back.

Not only had King Hamel turned his head away from the group, he was tapping his fingers on his kingly stomach. It was a huge stomach, and tapping his fingers on it showed any fool who had been at court more than two weeks that a nasty rage was building in the King.

Commander Janon's armor glowed even more brightly now. It knew, even if its wearer didn't, that the King was about to blast at him as the closest target. The magical essences alive in the armor considered the current problem of its owner. The armor would do its best to stop a headsman's axe, but it was not sure its makers had that sort of chopping in mind when the armor magically rolled off the creation anvil. The good Commander turned to leave in a glowing haste when the treasury chancellor's words stopped him.

"Janon, may I have a moment of your time? With your leave, my King, we will be presenting you with an elfin brooch in thirty-one days."

Turning to the cringing servants at the far corner of the court, Lord Anwardentine waved them closer in a jovial manner. Muttering under his breath, he said to no one in particular, "I don't believe in miracles. I rely on them."

To the people of the throne room, he called out, "Minstrels, jugglers, attend the King while lunch is served." It was an hour before lunch should have been served, but eating was one of the things the King did best, and that damn head turning was impossible when the King stuffed his jowled face with food.

Stepping off the dais, Anwardentine put his arm around the young general and led him away from the king's group, "Janon, why don't you send a brace of lancers to the towns along the edge of the border between the elf lands and ours. Maybe someone there has an elf brooch."

"Won't work," Cortwin chimed this up, even though he wasn't asked as he followed the pair. "There's no way to tell if it's a true brooch. What would happen if a false piece of jewelry were presented to the King?"

Janon's armor broke into a magical sweat at the very thought of those words.

Lord Cortwin slapped Janon on the back in a friendly manner and walked off.

Janon appreciated the gesture, so his armor allowed the physical contact. The enchanted armor also noted the magical listening scarab Lord Cortwin placed on his wearer's back. It didn't hurt the master, so the armor allowed it to stay. There was something odd about the hand or talon that placed the scarab, but the armor wasn't bright enough to decide what it was. It made a magical note to itself to not allow Lord Cortwin near its wearer from now on.

Anwardentine really liked this young Commander of all the empire's armies. "Err, humph, quite right, quite right. Calm down, Janon, calm down. The next thing you know, that sword of yours will start singing its enchanted battle songs."

Commander Janon held on to the pommel of his sword to prevent it from doing just that. Battle magics reacted to the fear of their user. The good Commander was completely unruffled on the battlefield with hundreds of swords turned against him but wasn't made for political maneuverings at court against a single unarmed King. The sword really wanted to belt forth with a rousing battle chant to calm his owner's fears, but the huge grip Janon held on the pommel prevented any rousing music from happening just then.

"What are we going to do? The King wants this bloody elfin brooch! After what we have been doing in their lands, chopping and raiding and the like, there isn't an elf in the world that would give us one!"

In seconds of conversation, the two planned how to get a brooch at any cost and whom to send to do the job. A King's commission like this didn't come along every day, and although it wasn't important to the safety of the realm, it was a clear order from their King.

Little did anyone know just how important this simple brooch-finding task would be. . .

———

In another alternate dimension, an entire underground world existed made of brimstone, lava, and dark enchantments. At the heart of this world, there came a deafening crash!

Lord Cortwin of the Rill lands, transformed into its true ten-foot tall Nevil demon form, hit the hot stone floor of the pentagram. All spikes, talons, and massive muscle, this unexpected teleportation might have ruined all the Nevil demon's plans if any court human saw it vanish in a burst of sulfur and brimstone. The creature roared its anger, looking for the fool who summoned it back to the under-dimension.

"How, by all the evil deities past and present, can

a creature get its work done if it's constantly being called back to its home interdimensional plane?" the demon roared.

As the demon gingerly stepped out of the gold dust summoning pentagram, it noted its surroundings. The outer pit cavern delightfully displayed the usual number of delicious Nevil larva crawling around on their bellies, avoiding lava flows. The worm-like larva with human heads mewed their pain and agitation at existing in their larva form. The cute little demons often took thousands of years to transform into the more humanoid demon-kind, and they were all naturally upset at their lot in life until that change. Briefly, Talonten shuddered at his own memories of larva life. There was a difference in the cavern, however. A half-mile section was fenced off, and glowing humans milled around inside. By the strength of their glows, watching demons could tell there were several different human gods angry at having their clerics stolen and placed here. There was no natural way those humans could have found their way to this dimension. Their gods held little power here, but any deity could lend some magical support to their worshipers. The brighter the glow, the more angry the god and hence the more holy power the god lent his or her cleric. Two of those humans were beauties in power, glowing with sun-like intensity. The ugly mass of humanity represented a new feature in a cavern unchanged in millennia.

"Calm down, Talonten. 'The It' wants you, and you know how it gets when it's in a state," Tailstinger tried to explain.

Talonten picked up a larva and munched on its wormy side. No demon liked having his true name spoken aloud. Tailstinger was 'The Its' cavern-spokes-demon. The title gave the powerful Nevil demon certain speaking rights, but Talonten didn't have to like those rights. He crouched on his haunches, munching and pleasantly listening to the larva's screams as the unwanted spokes-demon approached.

Talonten thought about ignoring political conventions and ripping one of Tailstinger's heads off, there and now. Talonten's position as the only demon currently with free will and able to travel to the ancestral dimension at will gave him a certain amount of push among the Nevil demons. He just wasn't sure if it extended to killing the current ruler's favorite lackey.

Tailstinger raised its three right talons in an effort to calm down the obviously agitated Talonten. The uncaring Talonten continued to munch on the larva worm, knowing larva breath was unusually rude for any demon to endure.

Tailstinger had centuries before changed its form in favor of multiples: multiple hands, multiple legs, and multiple heads. "I know what you're going to say, and it's not anyone's fault. 'The It' wants you to report in person, and that's what you must do. I'll tell you that for sure."

The munching demon nodded over to the new enclosure.

"Oh, that. Those are obviously holy humans. You must be noting the glows. Suddenly, there seems to be a devilish need to study them and their hellish, holy effect. Tricking them from the ancestral dimension proved difficult; I'll tell you that for sure," Tailstinger gloated. "Now that they are here, we have to keep them penned like larva pets. I locked them up so we all didn't have to put up with their painful glowing in the power cavern. 'The It'd tried eating one just a bit ago, and the human burned our master's forked tongues so bad the master couldn't talk until healed. Let's get you into the power cavern so you can get back to the ancestral dimension as soon as possible. Demon gods, I hate their glow, and it never shuts off or dims; I'll tell you that for sure."

Talonten always liked teleporting into the power cavern. The miles-long lava flows meandered attractively around the cavern into special pools of boiling plasma. Every once in a while, one or two larva would accidentally fall into a lava stream, and their burning flesh would fill the cavern with wonderful scents. Many considered it bad form for an adult demon to toss a larva into the molten streams, a feeling not shared by Talonten.

Nevil demons seeking favor filled the cavern.

Pushing one of them into a plasma pool also made the cavern smell delightful, but most of these fun spoilers made that activity difficult. Talonten was one of the few there who had successfully pushed over one thousand Nevils into the plasma. The honor wasn't lost on any of the demons as they all crowded away from plasma pool edges when he magiced into the area.

As 'The It' noticed Talonten, the summoned demon fell to his spiked and crusted knees. "I'm truly sorry I couldn't bring a human skull to add to your throne. My summoning was quite unexpected."

The twenty-foot-tall ruler of all demons shook with its usual anger on the mountain of human skulls it called its throne. "You've been summoned here for a history lesson. Grovel and learn spratling," It commanded. The demon lord's head tentacles plastered themselves to its wide-tusked face. Fleshy layers of scaled hide flopped from side to side all over its weighty body as the demon ruler moved.

The demon lord stood up from his skulls and began pacing around the cavern. Demons packed wall to wall started falling into the lava flows, much to the amusement of watchers farther out in the masses. Several of the fallers hit plasma pools, instantly killing them but making the cavern more flavorful. Size did count when it came to demons, and 'The It' was the only demon allowed to grow to a height of twenty feet. Most of the demons here were in the ten-foot range, and so they were flung like ten pins as their ruler shuffled about the cavern in deep thought.

"In the ancient times, before even I was spawned, our kind roamed freely in the ancestral dimension. We were supreme overall save the elves, but we cared nothing for their foul forests. Then came the humans with their tainted gods!" This last said as 'The It' stomped on part of his throne, crushing several hundred of the human skulls. Skull dust lay thick on the edges of the bony mountain.

Talonten noted there was an unusual amount of bone dust floating about the ruler today. He shook his head in mock sympathy for his lord and master. Demon life was so hard for those in charge.

"They cast us out! Humans with their god-given powers forced all of demon kind away from our true home!" roared the It.

The long-suffering Talonten began mouthing sentences, mocking his not-so-beloved ruler, "While this dimension is pleasant, it's not the ancestral dimension."

"While this dimension is pleasant, it's not the ancestral dimension. You, Talonten, are the only demon currently able to move about freely. It was clever of you to trick your human summoner into giving you free will. The only other demon to achieve your status recently returned to us dead. You must continue to work toward keeping elves and humans apart. You must also work toward turning those silly humans away from their gods. Tell me what you have done so far. Rise, you idiot!"

"Um, yes, well, I've become the minor ruler of a rather nasty section of hills and swamps called the Rill lands. I've tricked the humans there into believing their temple clerics have been stealing from them for years. I've also talked the King into the last of several foolish wars with the elves, in which the humans suffered great losses. Summoning me here has disrupted several of those plans. I was wondering if you could leave me there for a few hundred years so that I could get my work done?"

Splat! Magical essences covered Talonten, smashing him to the rocks of the cavern floor.

"There, I've given you the ability to summon a few of our kind in case of need," the It said. "They won't be there long, but they will do as you order. Go and get my work done."

'The It' plopped back on the throne of skulls, turning its head sideways and ignoring everyone, never a good sign in any ruler.

Talonten teleported happily back to work with the pleasant scent of the caverns in its nostrils. The Nevil demon briefly considered growing a little taller. It was really sick and tired of its boss, and among demons, there was only one way to rise in the company of demons. It wondered for the thousandth time how 'The It' would taste.

2

THE MAGIC OF CORDELLIA

"Throwing down a gauntlet in challenge means one of your hands is cold."

— COMMANDER JANON

SEX WAS A GREAT DEAL LIKE CASTING A magic spell, Captain Corbyn Cauldron of the King's Own 25th Lancers observed, gently moving the lady Cordellia onto his bed. As her shapely legs came into view, Corbyn smiled, pleased that her ample breasts weren't her only amazing feature.

Planning a spell beforehand made its casting much easier. Planning to bed, Cordellia also made that task easier. Lunch in his chambers proved magical in its success. There was just the right amount of tender and perfectly prepared food. The heady wine, chilled with mountain ice, was also perfect, and the vintage brought the enchanting Cordellia to a rosy, almost mystical, glow.

A sexy giggle escaped her lips as the last of her clothing was flung to the end of the large canopy bed. She was a true redhead all over, as her long, curly hair cascaded over her creamy white shoulders all the way to her ample hips. Corbyn, being the consummate soldier, charged ahead, lance held at the ready, mind moving in one direction while his hands moved in quite another.

Cordellia was polite enough to give a moan of encouraging pleasure.

Spells required a great deal of a person's inner force. Cordellia, as he shifted above her, was getting a great deal of his inner force as well.

The best magical spells erupted quickly and with satisfying force. While the same thing could be said for Corbyn's current activity, he liked to savor this type of magic for as long as. . .

BAM! BAM! BAM! "Captain Corbyn, are you there? Corbyn, open up, damn it all!"

Cordellia revealed amazing strength as she twisted away and threw the covers over her head, disrupting a very enchanting moment. "Corbyn, I mustn't be found here."

The lady had a flair for the obvious. It was good

to know that her legs, hips, hair, and breasts perfectly matched her amazing sense of the ridiculous.

Calmly rising, he closed the heavy curtains of his bed. Grabbing his shirt, he mused for the hundredth time--nay the thousandth time--how silly it was that humans should think curtains around a bed good only for keeping the heat in and the light out.

"Corbyn, damn it all, man, I know you're in . . ."

Cauldron threw open the door and bowed with a flourish while at the same time totally blocking the entrance to his chambers. "Commander Janon, damned decent of you to come to my door. How may this simple swordsman help you?"

"Captain, you just received the King's rank of Royal Commissioner, did you not?" Janon sniffed the air, a curious expression filling his features.

"Yes, Commander, and it was unusually difficult to pass those tests, as you well know. That smell you're catching is lilacs, sir. The court is all in a rage for lilacs, and I just started using the stuff myself. Damned silly for a fighting man, but court fashion is court fashion, don't you know."

"Yes, indeed, I do know. The court picked up that fragrance from my lady and fiancée, the Countess Cordellia."

"Fiancée? I had no idea. Congratulations! Have you announced your marriage to the court?" Corbyn asked.

"Well, err, no. Damn it all, man, I haven't really

asked her yet. What with Dukes and Earls constantly buzzing around her, I haven't been able to get a word in," Janon replied.

"Well, Commander, when you ask, I'm sure she won't refuse you," Corbyn exclaimed.

"Humph. Well, to matters. You are the latest to receive the King's commission rank, so it's up to you to carry out the latest of the King's orders. He wants an elfin brooch for Princess Talyn. Take twenty hand-picked lancers, a bag of emeralds, and anything else you need in the way of supplies. Race to the lands of the elves and bring back one of their magical brooches within thirty days. You'll have to hurry, as it's a good six-day ride to elfin lands, but there's sufficient time. Have you any questions?"

Corbyn had thousands, but he also had Commander Janon standing there thinking of lilacs and fiancées.

Janon's brows drew closer and closer together as he noticed Corbyn was only dressed in a lacy dueling shirt.

"I will attend to it instantly; long live the King!" shouted Corbyn, closing the door.

"And the empire with him!" The Commander turned and left, expecting his orders to be accomplished with haste.

Turning, Corbyn mentally recalled his magic and sex analogy. He wasn't pleased at Janon wanting to marry the target of Corbyn's attention at the moment. Corbyn wouldn't be seeing and dining with the countess after today. However, if magic spells weren't finished to their conclusion, all sorts of ugly aches and pains occurred within the caster's body. The amazing Cordellia was a spell needing finishing and Corbyn was just the caster to do it. Sixty minutes of brooch-searching time could be spared to finish a project well worth doing. Even as the good Captain opened the curtains to see the still-amazing Cordellia, his mind was in the armory gathering supplies for the impossible task of securing a magical brooch from an elf who would rather die than give one to a human.

———

Deep in another section of the palace nestled the rooms of a certain wizard. Wizards being who and what they are, these chambers seldom attracted human visitors. Even the shouts of pain heard down the corridors by the distant guard posts didn't move the guards there; after all, the shouts came from a wizard's chambers.

"Argh! It takes time!" gasped Disingen. "I can't cast the spells you want in seconds!"

Long ago, he magically placed his heart in a heart-stone ring. At this moment, that ring twisted in the talon of the dark lord tormenting Disingen. The pain forced the wizard down on his knees.

"Stop. If you want any of the things you've ordered, you must allow me to live."

He shuddered in agony and failed in his efforts to rise. His thick dark robes spilled spell components and magic items by the dozen. His enchanted skullcap of black Tarnen metal fell from his head, and his bristly black hair spilled out, showing the oddest patches of bare flesh in circle tattoos around his skull. Black piggy eyes pleaded with the holder of his ring to not twist it anymore. Several vials broke with his new fall, and the chamber filled with the smell of death and decay as green goo ate its way through the black marble floor tile. Skeletal thin arms poked through the rapidly rotting cloak as the effects of the gas destroyed Disingen's clothing. The wizard, normally priding himself on his appearance, could do nothing about his robes in the throws of the torment the demon worked on his body.

The magically cloaked lord stopped twisting the ruby ring on his talon. "You're being well paid. I expect results from the most powerful of wizards. I want this ridiculous empire to have no successful dealings with the elves. It would be bad for business, shall we say? What have you been able to do so far?" This last question came as a shriek through a magical aura, transforming the speaker into the demon he truly was as green mists coated its body from horned head to taloned hoof. Its anger blocking its concentration, and the human disguise spell kept turning on and off as the magical gooey gas filled the chamber and touched the body of the demon.

The three-hundred-and-ten-year-old wizard rose unsteadily to his feet. His claw-like hands swept his spectral staff in a defiant circle and enchanted images appeared out of thin air all around him.

The first image appeared to be a floating parchment map of the roads from the castle to the elfin lands. "I've cursed all the routes this Captain of lancers could possibly take. Bad luck will plague his cavalry troop from beginning to end. Actually, bad luck will plague everyone on those roads. Brigands will appear where none were before. Monsters of unusual power will attack in the night. Bad weather of all types will strike every day."

The second image was of a hooded daggerman finding his way onto the castle rooftops.

"I've hired the best of daggermen to kill the lancer's leader. These assassins have never failed me in the past and they won't fail now."

The last image was a faerie mound with its ring of poison mushrooms. The hill rose from the middle of an ancient forest glade.

"At the risk of my own power, I've made arrangements with the Fey elves. They've been alerted to the lancers and even now spin their magics trying to stop the troop of riders."

The images vanished.

"You only gave me until sunset to get all this accomplished," whined the wizard. "No other wizard in the world could have done as much."

"Maybe so," the demon admitted. "When these lancers are destroyed, others will try to do things with the elves. You'll be on your guard here in the castle. I'll travel to the border and work more magic there," the demon growled.

"As you wish, Dark One," the dark wizard bowed humbly.

The false Lord of the Rill Lands vanished in a cloud of demonic brimstone.

The eyes of the spectral wizard glowed as the rage and hate pulled at his mind. For the thousandth time, he wished he never placed his heart in that ring. Reaching over for the arcane volume on demon lore, he continued his research on demonic destruction. The wizard briefly considered sending off a few helpful spells to the lancers as well as the curses. After all, any enemy of his enemy could be a friend. He shuddered at the thought of what would happen to him if the demon found out. Life could be so cruel. He continued to turn the human skin pages, looking for more answers to his problem.

Hmmm, there seemed to be some possibilities in the blood of ten-year-old virgins. Note to self: I must start looking into what this Cauldron is doing to prepare for his King's Commission.

———

Corbyn found himself deep in the armory. This set of dozens of chambers was better guarded than the King's throne room. The good Captain was in the middle of bartering for things he needed for the King's Commission.

"Captain Corbyn, I realize this is a King's Commission affair," explained Quartermaster Arullian. "But I don't think a Nightwing Dirk is really necessary. There are only seven of these blades in the entire Kingdom, and five of them are being used to guard the King, night and day, against demon attack."

On display in their black jade case, the two blades could barely be seen, even with the full light of the sun shining down on them from the barred windows above. Nightwing Dirks were evil things spawned by demons to kill other demons. The sacrificial magics going into their making were terrible to contemplate. With an intelligence all its own, the weapon's mystical power had been known to take control of a lesser-willed holder of its handle. The dirks warding the King rotated every day between a squad of fifty strong-willed knights guarding his majesty. The carved, human bone handles held the faces of those sacrificed in the weapon's making. Every few minutes, one of those faces would writhe in anguish and adjust its painful position to a different location on the dagger hilt.

"I'm going into elfin territories where demons and devils are common. As the Quartermaster of the army, Baron Arullian, do you have anything else that would serve me better against those types of foes?" Corbyn knew the answer to that question before he asked, but the Baron and he had played this game since Corbyn was a Sergeant in the ranks of the cavalry.

Corbyn would come in requesting the moon, stars, and lesser planets full of items for his troop. The Baron would try to give out as little as possible from the King's vast stores of enchanted and mundane supplies. Even getting in to the King's Development Chambers, inside the armory complex, was difficult, but Corbyn could charm his way into most places; getting out of some of those locations often proved to be a problem.

His early days in the lancers taught him to use the names of his Commander and King to open guarded doors. They were almost like command spells and rarely was he called to question for using royal authority. The King's Resource Center was the first place where evoking the King's name meant little or nothing to the guards watching over the special resources of the kingdom. Baron Arullian stopped Corbyn that first day, years ago, when the new Sergeant wandered into the Resource Center. In those days, they had developed a fast friendship even though one of them was a Baron and the other was a lowly lancer.

"Is that special saddle I ordered done, Baron

Arullian?" Corbyn hoped he knew the answer already.

The old baron's eyes twinkled at the thought of the new saddle Corbyn suggested two months ago. He absent-mindedly handed over one of the highly magical dirks to Corbyn. The weapon twisted itself in Corbyn's hand, but he sheathed it in a special elfin-made sheath hidden under the top of his ornate sword scabbard. He knew the enchanted blade wasn't finished with him, but he wasn't going to let any demon-made weapon get the best of him. What would people say if such an unthinkable thing happened? He followed the Baron deeper into the maze of the King's Supply Chambers.

"Your saddle idea was a marvel, and it turned out very well. I can't imagine why we didn't think of it sooner. I've had several more made for the commanders of the other lancer regiments. Each part of this saddle was an amazing delight to build. Where did you get so many good ideas? I think, just from the thought you placed in the creation of your new saddle, you should consider joining my branch of the service," the Baron said positively beaming.

The idea of being cooped up in the bowels of the palace filled Corbyn with a tension even battle did not give him. "No, I'm sure I'm not talented enough for the work you do. I have an occasional idea that I'm more than happy to share. Somehow, I long to be in the front of a battle and not twenty miles to the rear of it. No offense meant, Baron."

"None taken, my boy, none taken. Maybe you'll change your mind in a few years after you've stopped an arrow or two," the Baron was actually smiling as he said this.

"Hmmm, not a pleasant thought. Are the rest of the special scouting supplies being delivered to my troop?" Corbyn asked.

"All of the standard materials have already been sent over." Baron Arullian walked to a black marble table filled with lancer equipment. "We had no trouble with the healing potions, magical cloaks of swift movement, and the standard magical quivers of arrows. The night vision salve proved to be a problem. The last elfin troubles depleted our stores of that. We only had enough for one full night for each of your men. I hope that will do."

"What about the shields?" Corbyn said as he looked at the strange shields on the table.

"Oh, I'm glad you mentioned them, Captain Corbyn. Your people are going to try a new type of shield," replied the Baron. "We've incorporated the undead magics of the clerics of Caliginous, the bloodless god, with the protective magics of Arcania, the white goddess. We're fairly sure these shields should force most undead creatures to flee--or, at the very least--hesitate before attacking."

"Have the things been tested?" a very unsure Corbyn asked.

"Well, no," admitted the Baron. "But they have every chance of working well. You should be pleased to be given the first chance to use them."

"We're facing elves, not vampires. We'll take the things, but they bloody well better stop arrows and sword slashes," Corbyn stated.

"Well, err, yes. I agree. Now, to the last thing on your list: this bag full of emeralds, are you sure the King said exactly those words?" The Baron didn't sound like he wanted to hand over a King's ransom in jewels.

"A bag full is what I was told to take, and that's exactly what I want," Corbyn honestly answered back. "You know elves don't value gold or anything we humans make. Emeralds hold an important place in their religion. If I have a chance at all of getting the brooch the King wants, I'll need all the luck in the world as well as those emeralds."

Baron Arullian took out a doeskin bag from an iron chest. "Captain Corbyn, I've taken the precaution of having a special bag made for these emeralds. It's quite magical. It won't burn, be torn, or open to any who don't know the command word. Touch it on its magical seal."

Corbyn reached out, grabbed the seal, and jerked his hand away. "What was that sting?"

"Part of the magic," the Baron explained. "Now,

the bag won't allow itself to be more than fifty feet away from you. You can transfer this effect to whomever you wish by having them touch the seal and saying the command word. If that's all, I wish you a speedy trip and the King's own luck. You're going to need it, I should think. Do try to bring back the magical equipment, more intact than not."

Corbyn walked out of the chambers with a smile on his face at a job well done. He had gotten more than he had planned from old Arullian. The demon dirk alone was worth all the time it took to talk the Baron out of his supplies.

The Resource Center's head lord smiled at the back of the young Captain walking away. "I'd have given you two of those dirks, my good Captain," the Baron muttered. "That boy is like a son to me. He's a young hellraiser, but mark my words, he's going to make history with his actions. That trick saddle is going to cause some enemy of his to be very unhappy." The Baron laughed at the thought and turned back to work. Crossbow bolt-proofing windows were proving amazingly difficult.

———

Sunrise the next morning found ten of the King's Own 25th Lancers standing at parade attention in front of their mounts. Light armor gleaming in the sun, each trooper appeared blindingly bright in the polish of their metal. At attention, each cavalry trooper waited, ready for inspection by their Captain.

"Sergeant Wise, front and center!" Corbyn bellowed as he arrived on the parade ground, walking briskly toward his troops.

Corbyn appeared dressed in forest greens; he and his mount were prepared for quiet movement through forests. His metal equipment was wrapped in green felt to prevent the risk of clanking and alerting the enemy. A set of long, dull silver mirrors hung from bridle to tail of his light warhorse. A small matching silver set of mirrors was in evidence on both sleeves of Corbyn's battle tunic. The mirrors would lessen and often totally disrupt magical spells thrown at the rider. His tunic's front material was thick enough to stop many types of arrows. A silk fencing shirt with long sleeves peeked out from under his battle tunic. The silk of the shirt would go into the flesh with any arrow strike, making an effort to pull out a wounding arrow much easier. Each lancer in his command wore the same expensive silk tunic. These were gifts from him to them and not part of the normal military equipment. The shirts had proven themselves hundreds of times in the elfin wars of the recent past.

Sergeant Wise marched to the front of the unit of men. Standing six foot ten, he was an inch shorter than the Captain. Wide as two men, there wasn't an ounce of fat on the Sergeant. Specially made, his battle gear perfectly fit his powerful frame. The expensively tailored armor was worth every copper as far as Corbyn was concerned. In a fight, you wanted this Sergeant beside you or behind you because no enemy was getting past him.

"Who ordered parade dress for my troops?" Corbyn asked.

At the same time, Corbyn and the Sergeant said, "Lieutenant Arnt."

"And where is the good lieutenant right now?" Corbyn asked.

"Why he's sleeping in Sar! Just like good lieutenants all over the palace, Sar!" Wise stiffly answered.

"I get your meaning, Sergeant Wise, and now we will see just how good a soldier you are," Corbyn said, reviewing the men. "Are the ten other men of this detachment moving out as ordered?"

"Yes, Sar!"

"Did Lieutenant Arnt order parade dress for them as well?" Corbyn asked, knowing the answer.

"Yes, Sar!" Wise answered in military style.

"Did he inspect them before they left?" Corbyn found it difficult to get to the bottom of things sometimes with the wily Wise.

"No, Sar!" Wise explained further. "It seems you sent him and the other lieutenants a cask of brandy last night, ordering them to drink to the King's health. The charge for that cask has mysteriously appeared on your tab at the Inn of Smiles, Sar! Seems the good lieutenants weren't up to the predawn inspection duty, so I took care of it, Sar!"

Corbyn's eyes grew large for a second. "How much does a cask of brandy cost these days, Sergeant Wise?"

"I think I dickered it down to fifteen gold, Sar! It was a bargain if you ask me, Sar!" Wise answered, smiling now.

"Remind me not to ask you to buy my next horse, Sergeant," Corbyn quipped.

"Yes, Sar!" Wise answered.

"So, you inspected the men as they left the castle. Did they have the baskets of Winters Bark to spread on the trails?" Corbyn asked.

A strange questioning look filled the face of the good Sergeant. "Begging your pardon, Sar, may this Sergeant speak freely?" Wise asked.

"At ease!" Corbyn shouted to the detachment. Nine men spread their legs and crossed their hands behind their backs. It didn't look like a more relaxed stance, but it was. All of these men could fall asleep in that stance for hours on end and never stagger.

"Speak your mind, David," Corbyn said this in a much quieter tone; no one but the Sergeant could hear his words.

"That spreading of that Winters Bark makes the men uneasy, it does," Wise responded. "You're the only officer in the whole bleeding army, begging your pardon again, Sar, that orders that bark spread. Magic is magic, but doing that is blooming odd if you don't mind me saying Sar."

"David, we've had this talk before," Corbyn showed his impatience in his face and tone. "How long have you been soldiering with me?"

"Five good years, Sar, five good years, bless you, Sar," Wise answered back.

"None of that; you've been an able trooper, hence those Sergeant's tabs I've put on you four different times," Corbyn replied. "Now, in all that time, tell me some of the unsuccessful and unlucky things that have happened to the troopers and officers of the 24th lancers and the 26th lancers."

"Begging your pardon, Sar," Wise asked. "You mean like supply wagon wheels bursting, the chill hitting all the men at once, losing horseshoes every mile or so, or the rum turning to vinegar after a hot day. Things like that?"

"Things like that and fifty other things stopping them from being successful," Corbyn said. "Would you say we've had our share of luck in those five years?"

"Luck and then some Sar. Why, we weren't made the King's Own until after you took command and .. ." The Sergeant's face lit up in understanding. "Is that Winters Bark all it takes, Sar?" Wonder filled his voice, and there was a new respectful look in his eyes.

"David, between you and me, I don't know," answered the Captain. "We've had our share of retreats and losses, but I have several uncles swearing by Winters Bark spread at the beginning of every duty and along every soldier's path. They've each lived good, long military lives. In fact, you would be amazed at how long they've lived. Catch my drift, David?"

"Me and the boys will collect a ton of the stuff, Sar!" Wise said in full understanding.

"Don't overdo on anything, David," Corbyn advised. "Now, did the ten lancers go out in their battle greens like they should have?"

"Every mother's son of them went out dressed just like you are now Sar," Wise replied. "I wouldn't let no fool; wet-behind-the-ears officer send them out looking like toy soldiers. Each is ready for battle except for those baskets of Winters Bark they're carrying and spreading along their paths. I'm afraid most of them will be dumping their baskets within ten minutes of leaving the city gates, begging your pardon, Sar."

"Not a problem, as long as they dump it at all, David," Corbyn's tone grew more brisk as he wanted to get a move on. "Now, let's finish inspecting the men, shall we?"

"Ready when you are, Sar!" Wise, snapping to attention, caused the rest of the command to do the same without the spoken order of the Captain.

He walked the line of men inspecting their equipment.

"Jelston, your silver mirrors are dragging," Corbyn spoke in a tone everyone could hear. "What happens on the march if the mirrors aren't attached, right?"

"Magical attacks will hit me first, Sar!" Jelston replied.

"That's correct, fix those mirrors." Corbyn moved to the next man. "Private Kaledon, that's good fresh mistletoe on the barding of your mount. Well done!"

Walking a bit further, he stopped once more. "Private Sunston, did you sell your Pennyroyal again?"

The eyes of the private grew wide. "Sar, how did you know? My wife and kids needed . . ."

"Quiet in the ranks, you idiot," Wise growled. "Quick march to stores and collect some more. It's coming out of your pay it is! Now move, you daft, bloody fool."

Corbyn looked at Sergeant Wise with a gotcha look. Both knew the Sergeant should have caught the missing equipment. In the end, he found the rest of their turquoise amulets, bloodstone bracers, and moonstones in perfect condition.

"Men, we'll discuss this duty on the trail," Corbyn ordered, taking his horse's reins and walking slowly away from the group. "I am going into the officer's mess for a drink and will be out here in thirty minutes. By that time, I want every one of you dressed in elfin battle gear and ready to ride. Dismiss the men, Sergeant Wise."

Walking away, the Captain knew they would all be redressed and ready to ride in twenty minutes. He led good men, and they wouldn't let him down. Moving across the cavalry green, he gathered his thoughts, mentally blocking out each leg of the trip. Looking at the morning sun peeking through the front gate, he felt it was good to be a Captain in the King's Own 25th Lancers, even if he had fool orders to follow and an even more foolish duty to perform.

The shadow of the deadly missile struck him before the crossbow bolt did. Lightning swift, he slapped his mount in one direction and rolled away from the angle of the missile in another direction. The deadly bolt passed an inch from his neck and thudded into the soft grass of the parade ground.

Raising his new undead-repelling shield, he rather doubted the crossbow-using daggerman was a vampire. His voice filled the huge castle parade ground. "Alarm! Assassin!"

Some of the guards on the outer walls turned to see Corbyn pointing in the direction the crossbow bolt came from. One of the tower wizards saw the dark shape in the shadows of the distant tower where a shadow shouldn't be. Lightning burst from his fingers and crossed the parade ground to bathe the killer in deadly energy. The daggerman fell from the roof.

His body burst into green magical flames, and ashes hit the ground instead of a body.

Corbyn could only shake his head as he viewed the area of black dust. The lancer Captain couldn't believe what he'd just experienced. A man tried to kill him and died for that effort. Assassins tried to kill people all over the empire. Who would bother to hire one to kill a Captain in the King's lancers? The odd jilted lady or irate husband would not be spending the type of gold it took to hire a Caliginous dagger-man. The type of assassin was clear to Corbyn as it was only the followers of the dread god who turned into dust when they failed in their missions.

3

WINTERS BARK, THE HERB OF CHOICE

"Getting your enemy to throw down his gauntlet in challenge means you only have to work half as hard to steal the other one."

— ASH THE REAVER

AN HOUR BEFORE SUNRISE, CORBYN'S TEN youngest lancers carried large baskets of bark as they moved out of the city. There were no parade drums or trumpets sending them off in pomp and circumstance. They appeared to be just one more unit of brave men on the King's business. Each of these advance troopers dropped moss-covered pieces of bark along their entire route of departure. Each of the ten took different roads out of the capital. In minutes, the Sanguine capital disappeared behind in the dust of their horse hooves. The bits of Winter's Bark scattered unseen along the roads drew on the energy of the earth and stars for a special magical effect.

The herb bark glowed with an arcane power all its own, and the dropped bark began pulsing with a warm radiance. Unnoticed, dark clouds left all those paths as the bark did its warding work. Small evils and bad luck situations vanished as the magical power of the bark forced dark enchantments from the roads. Certain plans of fey elves and powerful highwaymen became unusually complicated and required more effort than first planned to accomplish. Several scrying attempts failed completely, and the brows of a wizard, a demon, and a fey elf all drew closer in consternation. Just who was this Corbyn anyway, they were all asking themselves. Bit by bit the lumps of Winters Bark shrank to dust as more and more evil power unknowingly exerted force against the herb's effects.

After a day's hard and uneventful riding, a blazing campfire warmed the second element of Corbyn's troop. A warren's worth of unlucky, fat rabbits roasted in the fire's heat. Guards peered outward from well-concealed positions around the camp. Special magics twisted in and about the area and extended to several hundred paces outside the light of the fire. These eleven men of the King's Own 25th Lancers were able to relax for the first time that day.

"An elfin brooch for the princess; surely you are joking, Sar. What kind of orders would send good fighting men after such a daft thing?" Wise asked.

"Why, the King's orders, Sergeant Wise," said Cauldron. "All we have to do is beg, borrow, or steal an elfin brooch from an elf without killing him. The magical brooch must appear in the hands of Lord Anwardentine before thirty days are up. The order seems fairly clear to me."

"You and I've been fighting those demon-loving elves for five years!" Wise exclaimed. "I know what would happen if one of them came up to me and asked for something of mine. They'd get something all right. They'd get the edge of my saber, they would. All this effort for an elf brooch, every good soldier knows you kill an elf, and all its magical jewels turn to green dust. How are we supposed to get the thing?"

Stuffed with bits of roast rabbit, the other men nodded their heads in grim, smiling agreement. All of them had lost friends to elfin warriors.

"I know what you're talking about, Sergeant Wise, I do," Corbyn said, smiling to everyone. "On the other hand, fortunes and land grants occur on a King's whim. My intention is to give our current monarch his brooch and anything else he asks for as long as it's honorable. I love this empire and intend to live a long and happy life here. Therefore, we'll travel to the elfin borderlands and get this damn fool brooch. On the way, we'll drink and eat at a few fine inns, on the King's orders, of course."

The men all smiled big rabbit-grease smiles at that thought.

"Let's raise our mugs to King and empire, eat our fill, and get some sleep," Corbyn raised his tankard. "I'll be up at dawn, which means my good Sergeant Wise here will be up before dawn. This probably means all the rest of you will be in your saddles, ready to ride by the time I've eaten the last of the cold rabbit. To King and empire!"

"To King and empire," everyone roared.

Six sleeping troopers rested easy, knowing other members of their troop protected their bodies. The large fire still burned brightly, shedding warmth over all the sleepers. The sliver of a bright moon rose to its highest point in the midnight sky. Corbyn woke with his usual gasp. It didn't matter how hard he'd worked during the day; he could be totally exhausted, and every night, as the moon rose to its highest point, he would wake. Magical energies filled his body, the strength of them making him ache in places he didn't know he had. He rose with his usual sigh. Although he woke every night, he didn't like it. He was a morning person. He enjoyed the dawn. Something about the night and the moon called to his magical soul but didn't make it any easier to get up.

Buckling on his sword, he moved about the area, inspecting his camp. The picketed horses were calm and resting. His magical wards twirled undisturbed and continued to flow about the camp. Corbyn attempted to sneak up on each of the stationed guards. It was a trick he'd tried for years, but his men knew him too well. Each of the first three were wide-awake and watching for him. Private Kaledon even had a ring of dry leaves and twigs about his watch post that Corbyn hadn't noticed as he noisily came upon the Private. That earned Kaledon a gold piece and a pat on the back.

Corbyn found lance Private Sunston fast asleep. Corbyn's gut turned cold, and he summoned up several protective magics with a snap of his fingers and a few thoughtfully chosen arcane words. He knew Sunston was far too good a soldier to be asleep. Something was very wrong. Corbyn was about to bellow the camp awake when he saw the white wolf, an unnatural creature wrapped in glamour. The beast, standing at least five feet tall at the shoulders, had moon-white fur. The creature also glowed with enchantment of its own as it stood panting in front of Corbyn. Its head looked able to bite a man in half with one slash of huge fangs. The worst thing about the monster was that it was standing bold as brass in the middle of Corbyn's magical wards, as if those wards weren't even there, wards that were supposed to warn him of just such creatures.

"*Un tanen sortem, attol on opt, genn tal?*

I would know your name before we dance, elf lord?' Corbyn asked the question in the high elf tongue, but he didn't really want his conjecture answering back.

"Grr rr, we shall speak the human language." The wolf shape-shifted into a fey elf lord of aching beauty. The elf stood seven feet tall, a perfectly proportioned warrior with long blond hair shaped into a war braid. His gray eyes and smooth, sharp, lined face marked the elf as coming from the royal clans. Rich courtly clothes cut in the dark Fey style with many sharp edges and dark jewels on the cuffs and throat showed the powerful elf to be rich and fashionable to an elf standard. The Fey elf's left arm, covered in arcane combat bracelets, revealed to those who knew the style of jewelry that a powerful fey elf from the royal clan was ready to do battle. The age and enchanted energy broadcast from the jewelry also declared the elf a being of great power among his evil kind. Fey elves were outcasts within the elfin nations. They lived in magical strongholds under the ground because their woodland cousins would kill them on sight if they knew where they made their homes.

A rune-covered rod of immense power lay strapped in a sheath at his belt. A living, rune sword of equal magical power hung on his other hip. Either weapon had the arcane potential to magically level the land around Cauldron for a mile with just one arcane word of power.

"We're already dancing, human. Your trick of Winters Bark was subtle, appreciated, and very unusual for a human, but you aren't all human, are you?"

"Un salat corunden eshen talupson, genn tal."

"I'd know your name before one of us dies, elf lord," Corbyn said the words slowly as he drew his cold steel sword. The touch of steel anywhere on a pureblood elf's body was deadly poison to one of its kind. It was the only thing leveling the playing field in the human wars against the elves.

"Please, let's speak your tongue. We need the practice. Out of respect for your knowledge of our ways, we vow to keep this part of the dance between just you and our royal self if you'll agree. This way, none of your men will have to die in the magical backwash."

"But of course," Corbyn bowed low, sheathing his sword, but kept his eyes on the elf. "I'm at your service. You say we've begun the dance. I would understand how you have a concern with me before one of our blades finds the other's heart."

The elf walked around Corbyn. He hadn't drawn his sword yet. "Most humans are so very droll. Some of your fellows know of the great dance, but none would try it with the likes of us. All the best dances have beginnings, middles, and ends." Stopping, the elf started walking around the other way, all the while looking Corbyn up and down.

"The very best dances have something of a taste of what the dance will be like even before the dance begins. These dances also have a lingering after-effect as the music ends and the remaining dancer leaves the dance floor. We imagined with your Winters Bark; you presented our royal self with the prelude of a very great dance." The elf stopped again. "Did we imagine in error?"

Corbyn moved ten paces to the right and further away from his sleeping troops. "You won't be allowed to spin around me a third time. I haven't your skill with magic, but I do know something of the rule of threes."

The elf laughed with a taste of disappointment in his chuckle. "Excellent. We would expect nothing less. So, it would seem you are a worthy opponent. We had to come and see for ourselves before we danced in earnest. In all honor and respect, we offer you the first name of the dance. We are called Lord Cimmerian Nix by the few mortals who lived to see and talk to us." He bowed, more a nod of the head than a bow. The action presented itself as a gesture of a King to someone a King thought worth noticing.

Cimmerian Nix was a thousand-year-old legend among mortals and elves alike. This elf of the shadows was a creature with a name used to frighten small children into their beds. The human lands knew this fey creature for a leader of armies, wizard of a thousand spells, and one of the most powerful enemies of humans in the world. The King's lancer Captain tried hard not to let his fear and curiosity show. Corbyn, this time, bowed low and kept his eyes downcast. It was the gesture of a noble to a visiting King and one of respect to a more powerful being. Averting his eyes was dangerous in front of an enemy. A sword could easily be unsheathed and take his head in an eye blink. Not averting his eyes was equally dangerous now that the elf had named himself of the royal line. If the elf grew tired of their verbal sparring, he could effortlessly cast a rain of fire, destroying Corbyn and all his men in an instant.

"Lord Cimmerian Nix, you do me great honor. I am known as Captain Corbyn Cauldron of the King's Own 25th Lancers. If it pleases you, lord."

"Marvelous, simply marvelous. You clearly aren't human. You know many of our elfin ways. You've given me a name but haven't proclaimed it a first name. We vow we must make this a very special dance, just between you and ourselves. The plan was to kill all your men as well as you, but that's no good now, of course. We would dance the dance of three gifts with you, Captain Corbyn Cauldron of the King's Own 25th Lancers, if it pleases you?"

Corbyn couldn't help himself. His hand half drew his blade once more. When an elf, fey, or otherwise offered another intelligent being three gifts, they were paying them the highest compliment and the most deadly threat at the same time. Corbyn and Cimmerian Nix must now exchange three gifts. Each gift would be of ever-increasing excellence. After the last gift passed hands, there would be a no-holds-barred duel to the death. The winner would own all the possessions of the loser.

"Naturally, who could refuse such a polite offer? I am at your service." Corbyn did not intend to give this powerful elf lord even one gift. No attack could happen if he didn't present a gift. Postponing the dance indefinitely seemed a good possibility. Corbyn Cauldron thought himself a powerful being of action. He went to great lengths to hide his real skills from others. The human world often misjudged him for an incautious scoundrel. This error, in most people's judgment, was a mistaken impression he worked hard to cultivate. While he was powerful, he knew the potential of a several thousand-year-old evil elf, filled with the magical powers and abilities of the shadow elf clan. The thought of avoiding a fight with such a being brought a smile to his face.

"We will long remember this day," the elf said, bowing.

A huge black oval appeared behind the elf lord. It hurt Corbyn's eyes to look at the thing. A wave of brimstone and corruption hit his nostrils and flesh. With an almost friendly wave, the elf stepped backward into the oval. The thing shrunk to nothing, leaving a feeling of death and decay after itself as the elf vanished in the magical backwash.

A black pile of ash-withered plants lay underneath where the oval disappeared. The oval could be nothing less than a necromantic spell of great power. Corbyn didn't have the slightest idea how the oval appeared or what it did. That lack of knowledge of the spell ability of his foe bothered him a lot. His necromantic studies were slight, as the concepts were extremely repugnant to him. His moon magic skills were the antithesis of necromancy.

"One can't know everything, can one?" Corbyn clucked to himself. He woke lance Private Sunston with a small thrown stone. For another hour, Corbyn circled the camp three times, making sure the elf lord hadn't left any surprises for his lancers. Cimmerian Nix and he were now in a duel to the death, but Corbyn wasn't going to have his men hurt in the backlash of a blow aimed at him. The Captain was sure the duel would not begin until both sides had exchanged three gifts. For his part, that just wasn't going to happen. "Score one for the King's Own 25th Lancers," he whispered to himself. Sleep came easy to him for the rest of the night. He made a mental note to order silver mirrors around every guard post from now on. The silver would at least stop elfin sleep spells. He should have ordered that from the beginning.

4

TO THE HEART OF THE MATTER

"Once the bridge is burned, it's a bit late to worry about the owner's feelings."

— FINN OF THE HIGH REACHES

THE INNER SANCTUM OF THE DAGGERMEN assassin cult was not a place to inspire hope. Blood-red marble columns held up a black marble ceiling. The floor was white to better show the blood stains of past victims. There were a lot of stains from just yesterday to centuries ago. The chamber dimly showed illumination by magical, eerie green fires floating about the room, creating sinister shadows where cult members could hide if they wished. There were no obvious outer doors to mar the surfaces of the chamber's walls. Known as the death chamber, assassins worldwide boasted of their achievements only in this most secret of rooms.

The head of the cult lounged on a pure gold throne of immense size, twice as large as the King's throne above the ground, of course. The throne made a statement to captives brought in for killing or torturing. Wealth meant little to the death god and his followers. Using it as a simple chair was their way of scoffing at the riches used above in the city.

At the moment, a messenger lay on his belly in front of the throne, waiting for his leader to speak.

The messenger prayed to all the gods; he knew that she wouldn't kill him for bringing his ugly news. He would never tell anyone that he was praying to other than the death god. After all, if you did not want to die, you had to hedge your bets somehow. Praying to the death god for life seemed a bit absurd to the assassin. There were great rewards for being a member of the daggermen guild, but there was only one penalty—and it was applied liberally to any error.

She clearly had heard a bit about his news as she seemed to appear out of the shadows around the throne. "He missed? Ibon Alzum never misses."

The little Caliginous daggerman tried to fall even deeper into the white marble floor of the audience chamber. He noticed an unusual number of old bloodstains by his head. "Leader of us all! I'm sorry if my news is not to your most noble and generous liking. In all things, your word is law, but fate and the unkind gods plotted against our cult and its deity. I humbly offer more details, oh deadliest of mistresses. I used the spirit magics of our glorious dark cult to verify the deed. Ibon Alzum's ghost described his death in baneful detail. He said his crossbow bolt was ducked with supernatural ease, and castle wizards threw lightning at him, killing him. May his spirit haunt the palace he died in for a thousand generations."

"Do we know where the mark, this Corbyn Cauldron, has gone?"

"Our spies report he has been sent on a fool's errand to secure an elf brooch for the King. He and twenty lancers have gone east to the elfin lands."

"The contract still stands. Send three of our first daggers toward the mark. Send a bodyguard to Disingen as a gift.

- from us until the mark is destroyed. Rothal has wizard-killing skills. Send him to the spectral sorcerer who hired us with our compliments. We will need to create a sphere of silence around this mission if we fail again. It wouldn't do for news of our mischance to spread among our clients."

"So you have said, so it shall be," the little daggerman said, his heart beating faster with elation at surviving. He'd killed hundreds with his own hands but knew he wouldn't last an eye-blink against the head of his death cult.

After the daggerman left, the leader of the assassins sat contemplating the cult's next set of actions.

Aliesha, former slave girl, now head of the most deadly assassin's cult in the world, waved the ten shadow watchers away to their normal guard posts. Shadows moved in the darkness. No one was allowed to speak to the leader of the assassins in their own center of power without shadow guards ready to kill the instant she motioned for death. She moved from the chamber, taking off her killer's judgment hood and robes. Standing six feet tall, she unpinned her black hair, allowing it to flow to her waist. Her clear blue eyes constantly marked the shadows in every chamber she went through. Her muscles rippled, displaying taunt arms, legs, and wrists as she traveled lower and lower into the assassin catacombs.

She didn't like her best man missing his mark. Ibon had also been a splendid lover. She owed Ibon a parting gift, and killing this Corbyn seemed like just the thing.

She mulled over the fate of the wizard. *It didn't really matter how powerful Disingen was. He might prove just as much of an inconvenience as the missed mark. Should she end his life immediately? No, Rothal was a good man, and there would be no need for killing if the mark died. Besides, the guild couldn't go around killing everyone who wanted to hire them; that was just bad business.*

Smiling, her perfect body began moving through her morning exercises. The thousand twists of the daggerman pattern always put her mind at ease; maybe she would do them twice today. Large, well-defined shoulder and leg muscles corded up with the first killing move of the twists.

———

Ash Greenwood was not having a good day. There wasn't a man alive who knew the lands around Sanguine City better than Ash. The big man dismounted and tethered his horse for the fifth time that day. Dressed in forest blacks and browns, Ash blended seamlessly with the surrounding trees and brush. His dark eyes looked over the forest trail, noting the wagons and horses that had recently passed. None of the trail signs showed military mounts or wagons. He kept nervously shifting his quarterstaff from his left hand to his right. Ash liked the weight of the weapon. Although he was skilled with a sword, he was even more deadly with his staff. Battle scars on his face and bear arms told of his military history, but he was a reaver now and fought against the King's law.

His main stomping grounds were the woods on the edge of the elfin lands, but there were only three trails from the city to the elf forest country. The lancers couldn't hide from him and should have been easy to find. *So far, this Cauldron was unusually difficult to track.*

Thrown down, Winter's bark turned to dust under his feet as he contemplated his next move. As leader of the reavers, he liked to work the beginnings of a plan out all by himself. He'd set out to trail this Corbyn Cauldron and see if attacking him was even possible.

Several years ago, Ash was the leader of the King's Own Guard infantry company. He'd seen the injustice done by the new King and realized he would have to take justice into his own hands as he saw this King heap evil on innocent subjects.

In the beginning, Ash started out doing little acts of rebellion. He'd purposely let innocents escape. He'd dropped tax monies back into the hands of those paying too much then. Ash had been ordered to hang an entire small village as a lesson to others, and that order decided his actions for the rest of his life. He'd gone outlaw reaver and never looked back. Stealing only from those he deemed rich and evil, he'd managed to grow a band of 100 trained reavers who struck fear in the hearts of the lords of the country. He moved about the forests and river lands, keeping two or three steps ahead of the guards who now constantly chased him. Peasants and small villages helped him, but it was the elves giving him the most aid. He was sure they did it just for amusement, but he didn't care why it was done. Their magics protected his main camp and kept it from being discovered. He owed them, and both sides knew it. Long ago, Ash had saved the lives of a band of elfin females. This garnered him a special elf amulet, allowing him to move safely through elfin lands.

Ash didn't have anything against this Corbyn Cauldron, but the gold offered for his head was just too good to refuse.

Taking half the night, he'd finally found the lancer's camp. As he watched from a distance, he thought about the wizard and the ten bars of gold back at his camp, half his payment to kill this Corbyn before he reached the elfin forest. Ten lancers protecting Corbyn shouldn't be all that hard to take out in an ambush. Maybe even one well-placed arrow could solve his problems. He could put forty good forest reavers together for several nights hence if he could just figure . . .

Then, the white wolf appeared. It was the biggest wolf Ash had ever seen. It just trotted up to the lancer camp as calm as you please. When it turned into a fey elf, and Corbyn started talking to it, Ash knew he needed more than forty men. This Corbyn was special and consorted with powerful evil. Ash didn't stay there to watch the whole scene. He'd work to do, and the thought of ten more bars of gold was just too much for the leader to resist.

"Whew!" The smell of something long dead filled his nose after he'd been traveling for a few minutes.

"Ahem."

Spinning in the dark, Ash's iron-capped quarter staff came up to guard point as he faced the very same elf who had talked to the lancer Captain.

The elf spun his finger around several times, raising a purple mist. Twirling in the air above the elf, the mist stretched a tentacle out for Ash.

Suddenly, Ash's staff twisted in his hands and spun itself around his arms and chest.

In the seconds as he was being crushed into unconsciousness, Ash felt only sadness. He thought of the silver mirrors back at the camp that could have prevented this squeezing death from happening. He thought of his band of men and what would happen to them without his guidance. He also didn't like the thought of dying at the hands of a fey elf.

"Human, it's never a good idea to spy on your betters. Also, and this is just a thought when you're dealing with fey elves in the future, perhaps using a wooden weapon against them isn't the best of ideas."

The elf placed an enchanted purple finger across Ash's cheek and easily overbalanced him. Burning pain filled Ashe's brain, and he fell to the ground senseless.

———

Dawn's light touched the palace of Sanguine. Few people or things moved about the corridors. Some late-night revelers tried dragging their bodies back to their rooms. Some guard posts changed troops from the night squad to the day squad. One spectral wizard flew invisibly home on the wings of ghosts after a long night of successfully robbing royal tombs. In any city the spectral wizard lived in, he loved to break into the tombs of the kings and queens and take the bones of such people for his spells. He thought it fitting that the spoiled rich of the past should pay in spirit energies for his magics of today.

Disingen moved about his chamber, extremely pleased with himself as he set his latest collection of skull bones and heart dust on his workbench.

At first, Rothal had put him off when the dag-german came to act as a bodyguard. Then, after a brief discussion, it turned out this Rothal knew a great deal about demons and their killing. What a capital fellow Rothal seemed to be. For the last twenty-four hours, they'd been working on several anti-demon magics and artifacts. Rothal was even now on a quick mission to bring back demon texts from the daggermen's very own libraries. This was turning into a. . .

All Disingen's protective magics went dead. Sulfur gas swirled in the middle of the chamber. Pain clutched at Disingen's chest where his heart used to be, and he fell to his knees.

"Wizard! Idiot! What are you doing to kill Cauldron?" snarled the demon. The demon's disembodied head floated in a sulfury mist inches from Disingen's head. The wizard couldn't help squealing in fear.

"Eep! Master demon, if you would just leave me in peace to do my work, all would be as you command," Disingen implored on hands and knees.

"Human!" the demon head made of magically summoned sulfur horrified the normally powerful wizard. "Your weakling race makes mistakes every hour of your miserable lives. Now tell me how my plans are proceeding."

Disingen, who could blast away entire castles with his magics, couldn't think straight. Huge glowing demon eyes as large as his fists glared at him, withering his will. The sulfur mists surrounding the head took his breath away and gagged him with every gulp of air. Closing his eyes, he worked a minor cantrip allowing him to not draw a breath. Worst of all, the twice-blasted head kept floating right in front of his own eyes, no matter where he turned his head.

Twirling, Disingen caste a lesser force field about his body. The spell pushed the demon's head and choking gas a few feet away.

Summoning up the spectral clairvoyant spells he

needed, he caused images to appear for his hopefully temporary master.

The first image showed three black-clad daggermen of Caliginous flying through the foggy dawn forest on a magic carpet.

"As you can see, failing their first attempt, the assassins have sent three more of their best killers to find and stop Corbyn. The leadership of the cult even sent a bodyguard to help me. I thought that gesture amazingly thoughtful of them," sobbed the wizard.

Shaking its head, the demon belched fire and brimstone. "Just make sure the bodyguard doesn't assassinate you before you finish your task. There's a reason they get paid for assassinations and not bodyguarding."

A sudden chill hit Disingen's spine. It never occurred to him that the knowledgeable Rothal could turn from bodyguard to killer at need.

"Of course," the wizard moved to his worktable and thought about the assassin. *The guild couldn't have it said they failed in killing a mark. When the first daggerman missed, they must have been concerned that he would tell someone of their failure. He would only live if these three killed that blasted Corbyn. If they failed, his life would end soon after that. Rothal knew far too much about wizards and wizard things.* "Something must be done about my bodyguard."

After the demon left, spells would have to be cast to safeguard him even further. Then again, spells might not work.

Sighing at the life of a poor, struggling wizard he moved to the next image of the woodsman lout he hired. The image he summoned was particularly disturbing as other magical essences surrounded the woodsman.

Ash was talking to his reavers in the middle of a forest setting. A purple glow that hadn't been there before coursed around and around his head. There was a mage's mark on his cheek that wasn't there the last time Disingen spied on the reavers. In the wizard's viewing spell, the mark was a brightly glowing purple scar across Ashe's face. With a wave of his hand, Disingen removed the magical effect. The reaver leader fell to the ground in terrible pain, but at least whoever cast the mark wouldn't be listening in to whatever Ash said from now on.

"As you can see, the outlaw is preparing his men for the attack," the wizard told the demon. "If the daggermen don't get Cauldron, then these outlaws should do the trick."

The demon head said nothing and continued to gaze at Disingen.

In the last image, a hundred fey elves all glared at Disingen.

"Human, why do you spy on us?"

Surprised, Disingen viewed Lord Cimmerian Nix

sitting on his throne of living humans. Disingen could tell powerful purple-tinged magics kept the human slaves alive and immobile as the fey elf lounged on their bodies. He shivered at the power that spell must have taken.

"Excuse me, great lord. I only called to ask if there was anything I could do to help in our bargain. I'm only a humble human wizard, but I have some skills, and they are all at. . ."

"Silence," the fey lord didn't look pleased.

"We will be sending one of my own to collect the artifact you offered in payment. We have begun a great dance with this intriguing Captain Corbyn Cauldron of the King's Own 25th Lancers. We thank you for introducing him to us. If you ever spy on us again, your eyes will turn to dust. Do we make ourselves clear, human?"

"Perfectly," Disingen whispered, ending the viewing magics.

"Elves, bah, dealing with that last one was a mistake, mark my demonic words. Continue on, and I will converse with you in three days time." With a flare of bright magics, the demon head turned into a solid chunk of sulfur and landed with a thunk on the floor; all animated life gone out of it. Disingen took great pleasure in grinding the entire head to dust under his boot, not minding at all the irremovable sulfur stains cutting into his boot leather.

———

In a faerie mound several hundred miles to the east, the royal fey elves slept away their lives during the day. Magic filled the cavern, making scenes underground indistinguishable from the above-ground forests of the day elf lands. Mystical energy made the stone columns appear as great oaks. Elfin glamour turned cavern ceilings into the open night sky and stone floors into pleasantly fragrant wooded paths. Every one of the thousands of chambers appeared to be forest glens and vales. A great deal of magical effort went into the numerous illusions for this woodsy effect. That effort was inconsequential, as appearances must be observed at all times, traditions being what they were.

No fey elf liked living underground, but they had no choice. They were outcasts from their own race and killed on sight if they appeared in any above-ground elfin community. Over the millennia, they'd grown powerful and developed new magics, but the stain of banishment would never allow itself to be erased from their minds. They made the night their time, riding their enchanted steeds into the real forests, avoiding large elfin communities, and pretending they didn't mind their underground faerie mounds. Each mound grew in and around a pool of enchanted forest magic. Normal elves couldn't get in or even see the mounds. If truth be told, they didn't want to get in. These fey lairs were allowed to exist as things a civilized day elf just didn't discuss in polite society. The fey were allowed to roam the night forests as long as they didn't try to interact with normal elves during daylight times.

When an elf was banished from the high elfin court, they were always welcomed with open arms among the fey.

Lord Cimmerian Nix turned from dealing with the human wizard, moving to get more comfortable on his human body throne; he remarked, "Humans, they really only have one use."

The rest of his court smiled politely and continued to watch their lord as they stood in and around the royal chamber. When an elf became an outcast and fey, there was a moment of sadness at being cut off from family and friends, but there was a certain pleasant freedom granted to them as well. Lord Nix was considered the freest of all the fey elves. High-day elf society prided itself on following many traditions and rules. Some elves just couldn't conform and became fey. The society of fey elves was characterized by a distinct lack of rules and order, except for the royal court. The court served as the head, directing all the rest of the fey elves. Bedeviling day elves was the fey elf's favorite pastime, but tricking humans would also do in a pinch.

"We've begun the dance with this Captain Corbyn Cauldron of the King's Own 25th Lancers, and it's so delightful," Nix exclaimed in glee. "He isn't human; we know that for sure. If we aren't mistaken, we believe him to be the Unicorn Lord."

His court gasped with this tasty bit of information. The Unicorn Lord was infamous among all elves for turning his back on their community and joining the human cause.

"Yes, yes, we know." The elf rocked back and forth on his throne. "We've already worked out the first two gifts we plan to give him. But that third one must be very special. It's been centuries since we've had so much fun with a project. We know this will be an epic dance. It will take most of the Unicorn Lord's lifetime to finish." There was a polite twittering at this small jest. "Speaking of projects, Tornalal, do you have some time in your schedule?"

The elf Duke in question moved from the crowd and approached the throne. He bowed low, averting his eyes. He was eight feet tall and elegantly dressed in hunter-green silks. The hilt of his sword held glowing, trapped demon eyes that constantly watched his back for him.

"My lord, I'm ever at your service," smiled Tornalal.

"Yes, Tornalal, that's what we like about you. Please mist into the land of the humans. We know how dreary that will be for you. We want you to go to the lair of that upstart human wizard, Disingen,

we think he names himself. The one who just

tried to spy on us." Lord Cimmerian Nix teetered behind his hand, enjoying himself immensely. The rest of his court also laughed at the thought of a human wizard using any type of magic on them. "He has an artifact owed to me. We want you to collect it and leave him a little present. We're sure you'll come up with something delightfully appropriate for a human wizard."

"I've just the thing, great lord. I will be back in days." With a wave of his hand, the elf lord turned into a gray mist, wafting up and out of the cavern.

5

FORTUNES TOLD AT NIGHT

"The manner in which a man chooses to gamble indicates his character or lack of it."

— WILLIAM SAROYAN

THE DUST LAY THICK ON THE LANCERS AS they rode into the village of Five Corners. Thunderclouds filled the sky behind their trail, but bits of bark still prevented rain from falling and slowing them down. A few miles behind them, rain smashed down on their back trail, making movement all but impossible. The air was thick with the energy of the storm, and the men couldn't help but wonder when the rain and lightning would hit them. Cauldron didn't wonder, however, as he watched a piece of Winter Bark vanish on the trail in front of him. The men had stopped talking among themselves long ago, their bone-dry throats hurting from the dirt and hard ride. These men were the elite of the King's cavalry troopers and none thought of complaining. Late on the third day of their journey, the sign of the Red Dragon Inn was a welcome relief. The village of Five Corners was a hole-in-the-wall place with no more than ten thatched houses, but it had one of the most famous inns in the empire.

Only one story tall, the stone inn spread out into several acres of the surrounding countryside. An outer high wall of granite surrounded the inn, much like a castle's outer defenses. In the two times Corbyn had been here, he'd been amazed at the number of rooms and special chambers the inn offered. There was a huge library in the place as big as the King's own book reserve. In another set of large chambers, several strange water pools bubbled with hot water at different temperatures, and some of the guest rooms had smaller versions of these baths. Several large rooms featured games of chance running night and day. There was even a wizard spell-casting chamber for guest wizards. Corbyn hadn't liked this last place because it reeked of dark magics.

For many, the Red Dragon inn was a place more out of dreams than reality. He could sense no magic in its creation, but there was clearly an odd enchantment to the place.

Many thought dwarves built the inn. Dwarves always presented a very poor attitude toward mankind, so there was some doubt to that claim. Corbyn didn't care, as it had the best food he'd ever tasted--and the other inn features weren't half bad either.

"Sergeant Wise!" Corbyn called out.

"Sar!" Wise came riding up from the tail end of the column.

"You will post a guard outside the inn," the Captain commanded.

The troop groaned at the thought of a long guard duty outside an inn with amazingly good food inside.

"That guard will have double portions of food and ale while on watch," Corbyn said.

"Yes, Sar!" Wise answered

Dusty smiles covered the lancers' tired faces.

The Red Duke threw open the double gates of his inn, and a squad of stable hands poured out to help the lancers. The innkeeper was a short man with wide shoulders; some could mistake him for a dwarf. Others pointed out a dwarf would rather die than be clean-shaven with short-cropped hair, and the Duke sported both of these. His thick red hair and eyebrows marked him with dwarf blood sometime in his past, but no one dared ask him to his face what his lineage might be. He wasn't really a Duke, but the old King had been there on several occasions and insisted that the Red Duke cooked so well that he was clearly a Duke among all the cooks of the land. The title stuck, and from then on, everyone called the innkeeper the Red Duke.

Corbyn flipped a large emerald into the huge palm of the innkeeper.

"Through the course of this night and tomorrow, another ten of my lancers will be riding up. I trust that emerald covers expenses for tonight and as long into tomorrow as we need for food and lodging. I expect that gemstone to also cover any breakage and ladies smiled tonight or tomorrow morning by the men?" this last Corbyn posed as a question.

The gem vanished from his shovel-sized hand. "More than fair, Captain," the Red Duke's voice boomed out over all the troopers. "Two of your men are already here and ready to report to you. Come in and enjoy the fire, food, and fun. We just happen to have roasted a whole pig today, and the meat is even now falling off the bones."

Corbyn handed off his horse to Sergeant Wise. As he entered the inn, a lovely, redheaded serving lass handed him a thin tankard of elfin Spring wine. Corbyn had long ago stopped wondering how the servants of the inn knew what customers liked to drink as they entered the inn.

The nine visible serving women were all breathtaking as they moved about the huge feast hall. The one in front of Corbyn curtseyed, naming herself Detania. The name proclaimed her a woman from far to the South. She dressed as all the women of the inn did in a short fur vest and a pair of long, shimmering silk pants. The pants were delightful to watch, as passing by any firelight made the material transparent when light passing through them. She swayed away, looking back and smiling at the effect her hips had on the inn's latest guest.

"I know, I know," the Red Duke said, waving Corbyn into his establishment. "They're all pretty as pictures. Friends and former guests send attractive young ladies who are down on their luck to me as young things. I hire them and pay them way too much. In a few years, they're gone, married or homesick, but more always come to work at my inn.

"Your lancers told me to expect you, and I have. Room five is ready for you whenever you wish to rest. Hot food will hit your table within a minute of your sitting down. Come, relax, and feel safe, even if you did feel you had to post a guard outside. My people will watch the directions your guard can't see. Few enemies have dared walk into my inn, and when they have entered, they never walked out, if you get my meaning."

Corbyn looked up at the ceiling, into every corner of the chamber, and all around the feast hall, noting everyone and everything. He did this as a custom when entering any chamber for the first time. As the leader of his men, he made it a habit to check out any new camp. It didn't matter that the camp was a comfortable inn or a deep dungeon cavern. The checking always went on. This time, it was an unusually pleasant inspection, what with ladies giggling all over the inn's feast hall.

"Duke, please tell me about the guests you have here tonight," Corbyn asked.

"Normal travelers mostly," the Duke answered. "Those three young bucks over at table ten arrived this morning and are from the North, out on their coming-of-age journey. Our two minstrels have been here for about two weeks and are very good. Don't sit too close to the stage; however, they like throwing pies at guests every once in a while. The other ten men over at table nineteen are merchants from Sanguine. They come here every year at this time to talk privately about business and try to get some of my cooking secrets. Maybe this year I'll tell them how I make my spiced potatoes; as I recall from your last visit, you liked that recipe a lot."

Corbyn shook his head, amazed. "That visit was three years ago. How in the world do you remember that?"

"Oh, Captain, that's my job," the innkeeper said, smiling from ear to ear. "Now sit down, get your report, and enjoy the evening. I must get back to my cooking."

The Red Duke wandered off in a direction totally opposite from the kitchens, but Corbyn was too entertained to complain.

His two lancers stood at attention when he walked up to the table. The remains of a large meal spread out in front of them.

"Take it easy, you two. Sit down," Corbyn motioned to their bench. "Finish what you've so well started, and tell me of the road ahead."

They were veteran troopers and good fighters. They fell to the remains of the food as if it would be their last. Between mouthfuls of fruit pie and glazed donuts, their trip unfolded.

"King's bridge crossing is suffering high waters from the mountains to the North."

"And thar been lots of reaver attacks along the King's road. I saw me some recently burnt wagons, I did."

"I rode out to the Blinding Light monastery and something's got monks all stirred up. They were praying and carrying on all over their hill. It seems two of their order vanished in the night, and thar are dark warnings in the skies, whatever that means, begging your pardon Captain Cauldron."

Detania placed a tray of raw vegetables and spiced partridge in front of Corbyn. He gave her a huge smile and didn't stop to think how she knew he didn't eat pork. Another longhaired blond brought a pitcher of well water and a tall, thin glass.

"I'm called Sparkle," she said as she poured the water, her white fur vest parted in a most appealing manner. "The Duke tells us you and your men are to be well-treated. If I can do anything else for you, please let me know." She curtsied low, and her smile spoke a thousand very pleasant thoughts.

"Aren't they amazing, Sir? They are all like that. Dressed like doxies from the Red Hill quarter in Sanguine, but always with a pleasant smile and quick wit. I've never seen the like, have you, sir?"

A gaggle of serving lasses suddenly moved from the bar to the large front doors, only to be parted by Sergeant Wise. He tried hard to keep his hands out of dangerous territory, but it was next to impossible as serving lovelies pressed him harder than a troop of raging goblins.

"Back off, my beauties," The voice of Sergeant Wise boomed out in the large hall. "We'll have none of that now. Order is the way of the lancers."

One lovely, black-haired beauty followed the Sergeant to Corbyn's table. She held a huge tankard in her hands. The frustrated look on her face told Corbyn his Sergeant was letting duty get in his way again.

As Wise came up to the table, he frowned at privates Stonefist and Gateway.

They rose to attention again.

"Are you two done reporting to the Captain?" Wise asked, knowing the answer.

"Yes, Sergeant," they both said at the same time.

"Well, move over to yer mate's table and be leaving the good Captain to his own dinner. Quick march now," snarled Wise.

"Yes, Sergeant."

Turning to Cauldron, Wise stood ramrod straight. "I'm ready to report, Sar!"

"And I'm ready to report as well!" griped the serving girl. With a stamp of her tiny foot and tears filling her eyes, she slammed the huge tankard down on Corbyn's table. "This is my first day here, and all I wanted to do was give this huge lout a drink, and he won't . . ."

"Here now!" The Duke came bustling out of his kitchen over fifty yards away and bore down on the trio.

Corbyn thought it very interesting that the Duke had sensed there was a fuss. Cauldron shook his head with a smile at his Sergeant and the new server.

"I'm trying, I'm trying so very hard. I'm carrying this Red Berry Ale in more of a pitcher than a tankard. Who would have thought a man could drink so much ale?" the wench whined.

At the mention of Red Berry Ale, Sergeant Wise twitched from his parade ground stance. Red Berry Ale was his favorite drink, but it was too expensive for a Sergeant's pay. He moved back to attention. Corbyn gave him a bottle of the ale once a year on his birthday, as it was a bit expensive for a Captain's pay as well.

"Starbright, you have to let the good Sergeant report to his Captain," the Red Duke's tone was stern even if the smile on his face wasn't. "Sergeant David Wise of the King's Own 25th Lancers won't drink or eat until he reports. Your little outburst will end instantly."

She stopped crying and stood there with her head bowed, looking miserable.

"You will wait until the good Sergeant is finished reporting. Then, you will work very hard at apologizing to the Sergeant for doing his duty. Do you understand?"

"Yes, my Duke," a very meek young lady stood waiting.

"Please forgive Starbright," the Duke explained. "This is her first day, and she has a little bit to learn yet."

"Not a problem, Duke. Please don't let us keep you from making the white grape pie. I'm sure it is in the oven even as we speak," Corbyn said, smiling back at the innkeeper.

"How did you . . ." The innkeeper laughed, nodding his head. He left.

"Well, Sergeant Wise, this little lady will be miserable until you assure her everything is all right. So, report, please?" ordered the Captain.

"Sar! The horses are bedded down for the night,"

Wise replied. "The stables have excellent forage, and a ration of grain has been given to each mount. They have a blacksmith here, and he's checking all the hooves. I'm well pleased with his work. Private Sunston is on guard duty till the moon rises, when I'll replace him with Private Kaledon."

"Excellent as usual," Corbyn complimented his sergeant. "Now take your ale and assure the young lass you don't hate her."

David grabbed the tankard; the thing looked tiny in his huge hand. He took a thirsty man-sized pull on the drink, displaying obvious relish at the taste. "Starbright, my name is David, and this is the best ale I've ever tasted. Thank you. I'll be eating with the men as soon as you bring me some of that fine pork; I smell roasting and a whole loaf of white bread. Now, get along with you."

He patted her on the behind; she went giggling and all smiles.

"David, did you notice how the Red Duke knew your name and the fact that you were from the 25th Lancers?" Corbyn asked.

"I did find that a bit strange, Sir," answered Wise.

"It's also a bit strange that he came bustling out knowing there was a problem from a bow shot away. Tell the men there will be no talking about our mission or the direction we travel. Is that clear, Sergeant?"

"Sar, yes, sar!" Wise said, coming to attention.

"Oh, and Sergeant, make sure you sit close to the stage. I hear these minstrels are very good, but it's best to be close. You and I will not be drinking much this evening. It might be a good idea for us to have clear heads, even if our men don't end up in the same condition," Corbyn said, winking at Wise.

The little conversation told the Sergeant to be careful and to make sure the men were careful no matter how much the lovely ladies of the inn might ask questions. With any luck, it would also present David with a pie in his face, but that was neither here nor there.

Time passed most pleasantly at the Red Dragon Inn. Three more lancers rode up, reported nothing of importance, and joined their mates. Sergeant Wise did indeed get a pie in the face, much to everyone's amusement. Lucky for the two bards, the Sergeant was amused as well. Corbyn called him over after he cleaned up. The Red Duke, Sparkle, and Starbright hovered as well, undoubtedly to make sure a fight didn't break out.

Still laughing, David sat down.

"Begging your pardon, Captain," the Duke said, grinning as Starbright cleaned the last of the pie from David's face, managing to nuzzle him in the process.

"There's an old lady in the village who happily comes into the inn to throw the luck bones and predict the future for anyone with a copper bit. It's not real, of course, but the area people love her, and she's great with herbs and whatnot. Would it please you and the Sergeant to have her toss the bones for you both?"

"Don't bother for me, Sar. Nothing good comes from such things. But if you've a mind, I'll soon as watch what happens to you," David said.

"Bring her on, Duke," Corbyn said, feeling in a very good moon. "A last bit of entertainment would be welcome before I turn in."

"I thank you for the invitation," came a voice behind him.

Corbyn turned in surprise. All night he'd sat with his back to the same wall. He'd constantly surveyed the front doors and the other three entrances to the hall. The crone's appearance five feet away startled him as she had no way to come upon him unannounced.

The Duke didn't seem surprised.

David leaped up and dumped the pretty Starbright on her unmentionables. She yelped but didn't complain because it put David between her and the crone. Sparkle gave out a short shriek, rushing behind the Red Duke.

Corbyn looked at the crone, "You're a shadow mover, aren't you?"

"With your permission, this poor old woman does have that ability. May I throw my bones for you and the good Sergeant? It'll only cost you a copper bit each," the crone asked.

She couldn't have weighed ten stone soaking wet. The hump on her back bent her over almost in half. She was clean and smelled of elderberries and cats. Dressed in old gray from head to toe, her clothes were mended many times but still serviceable. Her eyes weren't the old, rheumy eyes of the aged. They were bright green and sparkled with a magical fire all their own. Corbyn liked her smile and noted that she still had all her front teeth. Her life couldn't have been that bad or hard with a smile like that.

"Please come and sit with us," Corbyn said. "Duke, she is most welcome at my table, and my thanks for summoning her. Please bring her drink and food at my expense. Here, old mother, are two silver pennies for the telling of the Sergeant and I." Corbyn knew his friend was keenly interested in such fortune-telling things but didn't like to admit it. The Captain couldn't sense any evil in the woman and didn't want to be unmannerly and use stronger magics to determine her true power.

"I thank thee, good sirs," the crone said. "You are both too kind."

Sparkle brought her a small meat pie and a glass of elfin spring wine. "While I quickly eat and drink, Captain, would you please place the dagger you have hidden up your sleeve on the table in front of me. And you, Sergeant, who is also a shield to this good Captain, please place that strange head-basher thing you have not so well hidden in your boot on the table as well."

David's eyes grew big as he put his hidden head knocker on the table. Corbyn wasn't smiling now as his favorite dagger went on the table. He'd foolishly thought no one could notice that particular dagger and didn't like being wrong.

"I'm called Agete by the good people of this tiny village. You've paid me well, and so I will do my best by you." Her old hands reached out every once in a while as she delicately sipped and ate to touch the dagger and the club.

As her hand touched the dagger for the third time, there was a small spark of light from her touching finger and the tip of the dagger. She cackled and jerked her handpack in pain.

"Your blade resents my touch," remarked the crone. "You have many arcane secrets, my brave Captain. Don't worry, I won't reveal them to your friend or these doxies. But now I can throw the bones for you and tell you your three future events."

She looked long into the eyes of David as she put her hand on his weighted head basher. He finally couldn't take her penetrating gaze and looked away.

"And you, you big rock. By this silly thing, I know you for the great lout of a fighter that you are. You know, you shouldn't be a doing all this battling. You know if fate hadn't introduced you to this good Captain, where you'd be even as we speak."

David was clearly in awe at the power of this little crone, but he had the courage to speak up in an angry tone. "Now, don't you be bringing up my past and the should-ofs and could-ofs. I can see you are a lady of power. Do your job and entertain my good Captain. Get on with ya now!"

"All right, you big mountain of flesh," the crone smiled back at David. "As you wish it today. As you come back to this inn time after time in the next few years, we will speak of other things, you and I."

"If I ever come back, then we'll speak," David said, wanting to put an end to her probing.

"I'll throw the bones first for this big Sergeant of the King's Own 25th Lancers if you don't mind, Captain?" the crone asked.

Corbyn shook his head. He wondered at the little exchange between the crone and David but said nothing.

Most of the lancers had come over to watch the crone. Several of the other serving girls were there as well.

An old gray leather bag was produced from somewhere on her person. As she opened it up, the inside of the bag spread to make a circle of dark crimson leather on the table. There was a six-pointed star drawn in gold on the inside of the bag. Lots of strange little skulls and thin bones spilled forth from out of the bag as well.

Picking up all the bones, she waved them several

times above the star. Corbyn could sense some type of slight enchantment spinning between David and the bones. He knew it to be divination magic, and for a moment, he wondered at its effects. Snapping his finger once, he activated personal protections spreading over himself and David. The crone's eyes grew big at this change in the air, but she was the only one to mark the action. The Red Duke and his ladies were all smiles in anticipation and seemed to notice nothing unusual.

The crone closed her eyes and let the bones slip through her hands onto the star. The enchanted pieces fell into three different sections. Each of the piles made patterns on the well-oiled leather. One pattern made a small heart. Another pattern formed a long line of thin bones trailing just to the edge of the star. The last was a pile of all the tiny skulls.

The crone laughed. "Well, we have what one would expect, my brave giant. In the near future, I see lust ending eventually in marriage."

Starbright blushed bright red and buried her head in David's shoulder.

"The second is the chance for a good long life. That's a tad unusual for a man in your line of work. Don't go getting cocky in your next few battles. All these bones say is that if you are lucky and continue down the right path, you can live a long time."

"What more can a man like myself ask for?"

David said. "I be thanking you, old mother. That's quite enough telling for me for one night."

"Not a bit of it, you over-grown giant," the crone smiled back at the sergeant. "I must do everything in threes, as you very well know, and your third is not good, my boyo, not good at all. A great battle looms in your very near future. It's in the next thirty days, and it's going to change your life for better or worse. When that time comes, don't shrug off the training of your youth. Do you understand me, man mountain?"

"I hear you, old mother," David said in a worried tone. "I know exactly what you mean. I've marked your words, but you won't mind if I be concentrating on the lust part."

She cackled again. "No, I'm not too old to remember a bit of that part myself."

Looking at Corbyn, she turned serious. "My brave young royal lord, please place the bones in my old hands. My ancient ways won't work well on you, and I'll need all the help I can get. Usually, I don't let anyone touch my bones, but you're different, aren't you now?"

"I'll do as you ask since lust, long life, and battle seem like fairly good things to see in a warrior's future." Smiling, Corbyn placed the bones in her old hands. Each one tingled in his fingers, but he paid them no mind, confident in his protective magics.

As the last bone filled her hands, she gently

tapped his retreating fingers and, without any waving, cast the bones high into the air. Just that quick, the bones and her leather turned milky white and began to glow with the color of the moon. Sparkling with what seemed like moonlight, the bones slowly and unnaturally floated down onto the table like feathers. One by one, they assembled themselves into three tiny forms. The red leather and the golden star turned so white it hurt everyone's eyes to look down at the table. The bones formed little beings and began moving about the star pattern.

The crone gasped and began whispering so quietly that all had to strain to hear her. "I see you are ruled by the moon. I see also that you are, well, we won't talk of that in front of these others. You've put a new life in my casting bones, and I thank you for that."

The Red Duke stood there with his mouth open. "Agete, are they supposed to do that?"

Laughing, she folded her arms, resting them on the table, and leaned her chin against her arms, watching the dance of the three figures. "Oh no, my casting bones were never meant to do what they are doing right now."

Three tiny bone figures circled around and around different sections of the star. Clothed in moonlight flesh, one could almost see three very different forms. The first and smallest was clearly a woman. She moved tightly around the very center of the star pattern. Her moonbeam naked flesh showed a perfect feminine figure. Her movements suggested a sensuous dance of clear lust as the tiny figure twisted about the star. The second moonbeam figure of bones shaped itself into some type of demon with demon horns and demon talons. It moved around the middle of the star. Its slashing talons cut the empty moon-glowing air in a deadly pattern of death as it seemed to strike out with every swipe of its tiny talons and gnashing fangs. The last figure moved about the outside edges of the star. It was some type of thin warrior. A tiny bone sword wove a deadly pattern of thrusts and parries round and round the outside of the star. Every few seconds, its other hand would make some type of magical pass, and tiny purple sparks would fly from its hand and outline some other unseen figure inches away.

All gasped when they could finally make out the figure; it was a tiny image of Corbyn outlined in purple flames with a sword in his hand.

Suddenly, the tiny bone warrior stopped its dance. Sheathing its bone sword, it folded its tiny arms and looked straight up at the crone. It shook its head, and the entire figure turned to dust. The other two figures turned back into the bones they were made of, and the moon glow vanished.

Everyone took a long breath. They'd all been totally captivated by what they saw.

"Does that happen often when you throw the bones, Crone?" Corbyn asked.

"No, noble lord, in fifty years of casting those very same bones, that's the first time that's happened. Each of those figures fills your life. The first is lust. I'm sorry to say love isn't in your near future, but you will know lust in all its forms."

"That's not so bad," David and the ladies were all smiles at the crone's words.

"There is a demon on your trail. It means to kill you. It's powerful for one of its kind. When you face it, don't spar with words and magics as is your usual want. You must kill it quickly, or you might not survive. I also sensed something very strange about it. I think it cloaks itself in the guise of a human. Now, I've never heard of a demon wanting to do that, but this one is very different. I get the feeling it walks with the lords and ladies of the empire's court."

The Nightwing dirk moaned and vibrated softly in its elfin sheath. Corbyn paid it no mind but took the words to heart. The next demon he encountered would die as quickly as he was able to make it happen.

"That last figure is a being of great magical ability. At the last, it sensed my foretelling and ended it. No one is supposed to be able to do that," said the crone with awe in her tone. "The being and that battle are far in your future. That's why it danced at the outermost circle, but an unwise word or deed on your part could bring that deadly battle much closer. One other thing, that being is a deadly swordsman but will try to trick you with magics to finally kill you and end the duel you two have begun even now."

Corbyn laughed as the others drank in every word. "Well done, old mother. You've given us wondrous entertainment. We will go to our beds quite pleased with this night."

The others still sat around the table, wanting to talk about the crone as she left the inn. Corbyn got up, shaking his head at the night's recent events. He knew that last swordsmen, but there would be no gift-giving to make that happen, and the further in the future that deadly duel was the better.

Entering the long corridor of inn rooms, he came to number five. On the door was a strange hooked latch. On the latch was a knotted cord. The idea was clear to Corbyn, but only because he'd been here before. From the inside, you tied the door shut using your own idea of a knot. Just before leaving the room, you tied the knot on the outside, if the knot wasn't exactly as you tied it when you came back, someone had been in your room. He liked the idea.

Opening the door, he looked up, and in all the corners, his eyes instantly touched on the figure by the large hearth fire. Her beauty astounded him.

Standing up sensuously, the woman smiled and began taking buckets of water from the edge of the fire and pouring them into a large sunken tub.

As she worked, she boldly glanced at Corbyn still in the doorway. Her figure was unequaled. Her raven black hair cascaded down her back to her perfect backside. The muscles in her arms and legs showed a sexy strength. Then, there was that amazing feature of her silky pants. Every time she neared the fire for a new bucket, her pants turned transparent in the firelight.

"If it pleases you, my lord, I'm called Leaf. I'm assigned to warm your bath water and help you bathe."

"Of course you are, dear," Corbyn said as he entered the room and quickly tying a few knots in the door latch to make sure they weren't disturbed. It was going to be a very pleasant night.

A few hours later, as the moon reached its height in the night sky, Corbyn filled with his usual energy and this time he put it to very good use.

"A fourth time?" Leaf asked the question with a great deal of admiration in her voice.

———

In another part of the inn, the three daggermen rose from their three different rooms and entered the corridor in exactly the same heartbeat. Magic rings allowed them to move invisibly from torchlight shadow to shadow. They advanced on chamber five.

Poisoned and enchanted weapons were drawn

and ready. Daggerman magics protected their bodies from spell blasts. Enchanted cloaks allowed them to move quietly past all human eyes. Each was a master of weapons and death. Each had killed hundreds of dangerous marks in their years of cult assassin work. It had been child's play to follow the lancers, figure where they would stop, and fly ahead to convince the stupid innkeeper they were three youths from the North. Ready with ring spells to make chamber five magically silent, nothing would stop them from their mark.

Stilling for a second, three of the serving wenches and the fat innkeeper came at them from far down the hall. Invisible in the shadows, the daggermen waited for them to pass on whatever fool's errand they needed to accomplish. Magically invisible, the killers knew they had nothing to fear from trollops and the doddering owner of this crazy inn.

Laughing and making teasing comments, the ladies followed the Red Duke. As the group came abreast of the hidden killers, they turned with lightning swiftness and struck at the necks of the very surprised and clearly not-that-invisible-killers. The three death dealers fell like chopped meat at the hands of the pretty serving women, who just proved, by seeing the three assassins in the arcane shadows, that they weren't quite human.

The Red Duke shook his head and waved special dwarven clerical magics at the still twitching forms.

"Daggermen in my very own inn, what is the world coming to? No, my three dead boyos, your god will not claim you in his green dust, not in my dwarven inn. You coming here is just wrong, and we will have to make a clear example of you three. Detania, Sparkle, you get the boys to prepare the large wagon."

While talking, the Red Duke easily picked up the three bodies and, with obvious dwarven strength, hefted them all on his shoulder. "I'll be cutting off their hands and putting those little gifts in a bag with my Chop on it. I want the boys to drop these three and the bag of hands on the front door of the assassin's cult at dawn, at least three days hence, and no sooner. Have the boys generate a little mischief of their own against the guild while they're there. The mark on the sack should be enough of a message that tells them not to conduct their business in my home again. Arlan, you go wake up the good Sergeant and Starbright. I know he'll want to be changing the guard they've posted. If he's up already, just make sure he doesn't come into the kitchens for a snack. Get along with you all now."

The dwarf prince hummed a digging tune from his youth as he moved to the back of the inn to prepare the bodies. He didn't like assassins, and he shuddered to think of the mess it would have caused to have a Captain of the King's lancers killed in the middle of the night in his inn. It had taken several hundred years to get the dwarven outpost up and working the way he wanted it done, and he was not going to let some silly human daggermen spoil the plans of the Dwarven Empire he so loved.

———

Corbyn rarely dreamed. That night, he found himself surrounded with images of a giggling Cimmerian Nix. Normally, a laughing elf, no matter how deadly, wouldn't have disturbed Cauldron at all. In this dream, he found those giggles terrifying, and he didn't know why. Waking, he deliberately didn't open his eyes as he could sense the lush woman moving about his chamber. *She had been amazing in bed.*

"My lord, my lord, please wake for a moment."

Sensing only affection for him, he hadn't minded her moving about. His eyes opened at her urging, and the face of his lovely bedmate greeted him in the firelight. She didn't look at all mussed from their partial night's sleep.

"Great lord, my Master thanks you for the gift you've given him."

Smiling, he watched her gracefully dress into a different set of clothes from the vest and pants she almost and briefly wore last night.

"Gift? I enjoyed myself greatly," Corbyn told her, "but I haven't yet given you anything for last night. You're worth a fine gift. If you'll bide awhile, I'll be even more generous." He lifted the sheets, inviting her back to bed, even if she was all dressed in forest greens and seemed ready to leave.

"No brave Corbyn Cauldron of the King's Own 25th Lancers, you have given my Master a most noble gift. In a little less than nine months, I'll be birthing a son, your son," the woman claimed. "Lord Cimmerian Nix will raise him as his own in the court of the Fey elves, and I will have a much higher standing among them as well. For that, we thank you." The minor glamour fell away, revealing a lovely elfin woman with flashing green eyes and hair. In a rush, she untied the cord on the door and left with a parting smile.

His stunned look turned to laughter as he fell back to bed. "Well, that was smartly done. It seems I've given the first gift of three without even knowing it. What a lout I am," the good Captain said, shaking his head. "Well, nothing for it, but to be more careful even in dalliances. There will be some way to get my son back from the fey court. Sons need to be raised by their fathers."

He weighed sleeping a bit more, but his disgust at giving the first gift kept him wide awake. He rose and dressed, shaking his head for the thousandth time at the power a lovely woman could have over him. He'd better learn a lesson from this, and it wasn't that all beautiful women needed his special attention, or was it?

Moving silently through the inn, he started his Captain's rounds with the guard at the front gate. "Private Jelston, how goes the dawn?"

"All's quiet, sir. The last of our lancer detachment arrived. They've fed their horses. They reported a lot of reaver action on the trails, but nothing we can't handle. When do you think we'll be leaving here, sir?"

"I'll give the boys a chance for breakfast, and their horses will be needing a good rest," Corbyn said. "We'll leave with lunch in our saddle bags. Go off and tell the innkeeper that for me."

Corbyn knew nothing was going to happen to his troop this morning. He could always sense imminent attack. He went to check on the mounts. The company would head for the lower river ford. It was a bit longer ride than he planned on, but there were old friends at the border outpost just past that old ford. It would serve as a good jumping-off point for the difficult task ahead. For the hundredth time he shook his head at his quest, barely able to imagine what he would have to go through to get this silly brooch for the princes's birthday.

6

RESPECT IS A ROAD TRAVELING BOTH WAYS

"Stay out of battle kid, or all you'll ever have is fun."

— COMMANDER JANON

IN ALL MONASTERIES OF ARCANIA, THE white goddess looked the same. Although this forest retreat was the smallest of her sanctuaries and the newest, its construction mirrored the other monasteries. The large outer walls were tall and tilted inwards to make storming them more difficult. Proportionally large towers stood at every corner and at the front barbican. These were bristling with white catapults and liquid fire throwers. Carved in images of smiling children at play, the crenellations at the top of the monastery walls seemed almost alive. Each sturdy statue had an iron gauntlet for its right hand. The gauntlet made the statement that even if Arcania was a kind, protective goddess, she was not one to be trifled with.

Every Arcanian monastery held three inner towers with their complement of outbuildings. At every high feast day throughout the year, each of the towers was painted in white and cleaned by the monks of the order. The central tower rose high above the others and the outer wall. It served as the lookout center for the fort-like monastery. The goddess smiled a lot, known for her kindness, but she wasn't going to allow even her smallest of monasteries to fall by force if she could help it. The fort was more in elf lands than human holdings, built two years ago in the middle of the forest at the conclusion of secret negotiations with the elves. The elves and the human clerics of Arcania started trading information and magics a hundred years ago. Arcania was very akin to the elfin goddess of nature, and both deities shared similar tenants.

Unknown to the forces of the human empire, this outpost established healthy relations between the clerics of both races. This fact didn't stop the creation of a killing ground cleared of trees for three hundred yards all around the holy monastery. The goddess was friendly, not stupid.

At the edge of the forest, Lord Cortwin, in human form, contemplated his next move. He'd spent the last two days laying a huge false trail of Winter's Bark for a deadly hunter to find. The elemental forces were tricky at best to try to use, but Cortwin thought his efforts would bear fruit of a nasty kind with the rising of the full moon.

The holy glare of the building made the demon seriously consider changing its current plans. Still hidden in the forest, the fake lord could ride on and not trouble with this foul place.

Hours earlier, Cortwin had summoned a lesser demon and forced it to assume the form of a horse.

"It hurts my eyes," the demon-looking warhorse whined as they approached the monastery. Talonten summoned the demon for the effect it would cause as he rode the forest trails. In the form of a huge war charger, everyone would be appropriately cautious when dealing with this clearly powerful lord and his mount. Now, he regretted having to manage the cowardly creature.

"Be silent!" Cortwin, the demon ordered. "Horses on this plane of existence do not talk. You're supposed to look menacing and impressive. We'll ride up to this monastery of Arcania's, I'll subvert its leader, and we'll ride on. If Cauldron comes this way, he'll be poisoned, stabbed, or ripped to pieces, and I'll have won. The simple plans are always the best. If and when we are in battle, you breathe fire every once in a while and summon thunderclouds over our heads. I'll do the rest. So, I order, so you will obey."

"Yes, great and powerful master, but the glare still hurts," moaned the demon horse.

The goodness of the monastery hurt his eyes as well, but he wasn't going to admit that to a lowly Net demon. The twice-damned holy glow spread out from the monastery and covered the countryside for miles and miles. That was the problem with human religions; they tainted the land around each center of their clerical power and holy places, increasing their taint so that it was almost impossible for demons to move unblinded about their own world. Some of the cities glow bathed in a blaze of holy blinding light so strong demon-kind couldn't see ten feet in front of their fangy faces. It had taken Talonten all of his two years here to get used to the glow. Luckily, the capital city of Sanguine was so despoiled with different forms of evil that its human temples showed only a mild illumination.

"A demon's lot is a hard one, make no mistake." Talonten settled his magics around him and rode ahead toward the center of goodness in this area.

It was a bold and handsome Lord Cortwin, ruler of the Rill Lands, who rode to the closed barbican gate of the monastery and politely rang the guest bell several times.

In full plate armor with his helm pulled back off his face, he looked every inch a perfect human warrior of the age. The hilt of his chain sword set across the back of his saddle in easy reach. The banner of the Rill Lands waved in the breeze and proclaimed him from the farthest northeast reaches of the empire. His war charger appeared richly appointed in the black and gray colors of the banner. Its own barding shone like the sun in a pleasantly blinding glare. Each of its huge hooves thudded against the ground with a heavy tread and kicked up a pound of dirt with every strike of the earth.

Lord Cortwin laughed deeply in pleasure, seeing the portcullis already up and out of the way. The cold iron bars could be hard to deal with at times. He put on his best human smile in preparation for the timid friar who would answer the door. His mighty steed shifted nervously underneath him. He patted its neck with a reassuring hand, hoping that gesture might make him seem an expert horseman to any casual observers.

He waited and waited some more. The morning sun beat down on his flashing armor. The sun's scorching heat was nothing to his arcane flesh.

This wait is odd. He rang the bell with more enthusiasm, still smiling but now using a forced smile. *They must be busy with foolish Arcania things. The heavens and nine hells alone knew what monks of Arcania did with their time. He was sure it was disgusting, whatever it was.*

Dismounting, he ordered his horse to stand firm.

Walking to the front of the large double gate, he used the huge knocker on the door and bashed it so hard-wood split underneath the brass.

"What is it?" an exasperated voice, out of thin air, asked in magical tones.

"I'm high, Lord Cortwin, ruler of the Rill Lands and on the King's business. I would see the head-mistress of this monastery. Open the gate!"

He tried to sound official and polite, but his patience, never very good, was at its thinnest at the moment.

"All in this holy place know who you are," the disembodied voice sneered. "Your banner is easily read, so we also recognize you as the lord of the Rill Lands. Your expulsion of our friars in those lands is also known. Go away."

"Go away? Go away!" Cortwin couldn't quite believe what he was hearing. As he stood in front of the doors, Cortwin reviewed everything he knew about humans, thinking he was doing something wrong. The human-appearing lord began talking to the Net demon horse.

"I've appeared at their gate, a lord of the realm. This is a lowly, nothing monastery stuck out in the woods on the edge of contested lands between the elves and humans. These friars should be hungry for news from anyone."

The enchanted demon horse nodded as horses have nodded since the beginning of horsedom.

Painfully, the Demon Lord continued speaking. "I've announced I'm on the King's business. That's supposed to open doors everywhere the King rules. What am I missing here?"

The demon heard the voice that was speaking from the air, laughing. Clearly, whatever magic conveyed the voice to his ears was still working.

Talonten turned to his horse once more. "Now I understand. I haven't met a lot of this type of human before; that's what confused me."

His horse cocked its head to one side in a clearly questioning, horsy stance.

"We're being held up by an officious bastard. Kick the gate down."

"Yeah, like that's going to happen," the voice sneered.

The oak planks of the double gate must have been at least a foot thick. The wood was fire-hardened and braced with huge brass plates embedded into the wood to give it more strength. Sensing behind the gate, the demon knew there were only two thick beams across the back, preventing the portal from opening for anything less than a battering ram.

With a squeeze of magical talons aimed at the stone groove above, the portcullis froze in place. The gate might be made of iron, but the stone grooves on either side were subject to earth magic. Lord Cortwin gave a very demon-like smile, knowing the friar would be surprised when he tried closing the portcullis in the Lord's face.

The war charger backed up to the massive gates. Its hind hooves began glowing with a swirl of amber magics. Rising up, it kicked out and smashed both hooves into the gates. Each twenty-foot-wide portal blasted back into the killing corridor space behind the barbican as the doors flew from their hinges. Lord Cortwin and the charger walked in; they saw the crushed body of the friar, who must have been talking to them from just behind the portal.

Lord Cortwin shook his head sadly, thinking it would have been nice to lesson this friar himself. "Oh well, there are hundreds of other friars to teach lessons in respect for their betters."

As he walked the fifty paces of the killing corridor of the barbican, he noted the hundreds of archer slits on the sides. Looking up into metal bars, the ceiling reeked of oil.

"What's the sense of making great defenses and then not using them when they're needed? I've always suspected Arcania was very crafty and very stupid all at the same time."

The Net demon horse could only nod its head sagely as they walked through the second gate and portcullis, standing wide open. A few friars and nuns dressed in white stared at their passing as the two entered the walled-in area, but since they got past the porter friar, they must be needed inside and none of them stopped the pair's progress.

Two friars dressed in white robes were applying coats of whitewash to the large oak door of the center tower. The structure was so large it could be nothing but their main hall and gathering center.

Talonten made a mental note to look into buying the franchise selling the friars the white paint. *There must be some way to make the paint appear white, and then in a day or so of constant sun or maybe even if it rained, the color would turn red.* He laughed for the first time in months at the thought of Arcanian monasteries turning from white to red with one rainstorm.

"I need to see your headmistress on important King's business," the knight shouted.

Both of the friars turned to look at this impressive lord by his war charger. Then they recognized the Rill Lands heraldry and frowned.

"Oh, that won't be possible. I'm surprised friar Arnt didn't tell you at the front gate," the oldest of the two said.

"Friar Arnt was more interested in laughing at me than telling me anything," the demon knight said. "The good friar has become indisposed with other weighty matters. Let me offer you the kiss of Arcania peace, and we will talk further."

The two friars walked to the dismounted Rill Lord. "You know of the kiss of peace. That's amazing; we thought only inner circle Arcanians knew of that most holy of acts."

"Oh, I know all about Arcanian ways and a good many other lawful religious myths," the demon in human form said. "One must know all about the competition to deal with them on an even talon, as it were."

As Lord Cortwin's demonic lips touched the necks of each friar, he sucked the life and souls out of them. The magic of a Nevil demon was powerful and almost impossible to counteract. As fangs penetrated each throat, the life force of the human thus touched, left their body, and empowered the demon. The Nevil filled with increased strength and speed; this aura of newfound strength would only last a few hours, but there were many friars in this place. Each human thus touched turned into a zombie, whose only concern was the capturing of some of the life force the undead thing had lost. Most zombies were unintelligent, but those taken from holy places held a spark of evil knowledge. Friars and nuns turned into zombies were the most deadly of all zombies. These two had freely offered themselves to his touch after all. They thought he was going to do something quite different from what he did. Two cunning un-dead things stared up at him with soulless, hungry eyes.

"Let's find the soon-to-be-dead headmistress. Shall we? Along the way, I'll be happy to deliver more kisses of peace, Nevil demon style. I have just decided to take a little more time here. I was remiss in trying to get away quickly. If you are going to do a thing, you should take the time to do it properly."

———

At another time and in a distant place, the dawn mist burnt away with the heat of the newly rising sun. The forest filled with sounds as jumpy birds chirping warnings and nervous squirrels chattering from tree to tree. The wide trail was used by many to get to the Arrow Heart river crossing, but it was early yet for travelers to come this way; not too early for a troop of the King's lancers, however.

"They've passed us by, or they ain't coming," the reaver's second in command said dryly.

Turner Blockwood, a former sergeant in the infantry, was a dangerous man. Ash respected him a lot, but his second-in-command was often too smart for his own good. Ash carefully moved over to Blockwood's hiding place along the forest trail; at the same time, he crushed some Winter's Bark that briefly glowed a last time before turning to dust.

Since early dawn, seventy-five archers hid along the trail. The spot they picked was a perfect killing ground as thick trees blocked all but the cut trail; unfortunately, there was nothing to kill.

"I know they were headed this way. I heard them

talking yesterday. We'll wait till noon. If they don't come, we'll pack it in here and move deeper into the forest toward the elf lands."

"Mark my words," Blockwood was in a foul mood as his old bones had set too long in one place. "I know we're being paid well, but this is an unlucky business. We should take our gold and run, if you ask me. I know it's hard to run from a wizard, but no good is going to come from this. I'll send some of the riders to the trails above Axe Head Crossing and Princess Crossing. We'll pick up their trail at one of those places, and then we'll try to get them before they reach SouthSword fortress. We don't want an outpost patrol coming up to spoil things."

The disgusted Ash could only nod his agreement. He moved back to his hiding place and loosened the tension on his bow. Reavers were good at waiting, and he was the best of the lot.

———

The spectral chambers of the wizard Disingen appeared not to be the most pleasant place to be at the moment. Even the undead spirits forced to stay in the chambers wanted nothing more than their cold graves as they watched their master throw a temper tantrum. Just then, a five-thousand-year-old enchanted elf skull of immense value and power hit the floor and broke into a thousand pieces. The air spirit trapped in the skull's eye sockets escaped into other ethereal regions, taking its magical effects with it.

For the tenth time, Disingen failed to form a clairvoyant image of Corbyn and the other lancers. The evil wizard could tell where they were in the forests as there was a huge blank spot in his picture of the lands. He couldn't get a clear, single image of any of them. He could tell his spectral thunder magics hadn't slowed the troop a bit. They were moving ahead of schedule on their way to the elf lands.

"Great, I'm the greatest spectral weather wizard and clairvoyant of this or any age, and I can't spot one human rider."

Rothal looked down at the pieces of the assassin's magical artifact Disingen had just destroyed in a fit of temper. The daggerman was really going to enjoy ending this idiot's life. "I'm sorry, great enchanter, that the artifact my guild supplied you couldn't give you what you wanted to see."

Disingen looked up from his black mood and couldn't help but smile.

The daggerman stood tall and powerful in his black leather armor. Sets of magical daggers hung on his chest and legs. Other arcane equipment hung from boots and belt, but none of it bothered the wizard in the slightest. Unknown to Rothal, two Fetchins hung suspended invisibly over the shoulders of the spectral wizard.

Fetchins were highly magical creatures Disingen discovered in his travels to other planes of existence. Invisible to human eyes, Fetchins were deadly monsters made mostly of fangs and talons. If Rothal did anything dangerous to the wizard, the Fitchins would rip him apart. Once, a pair of ogres had tried to kill Disingen, and a single Fitchin had ripped the creatures into tiny pieces in seconds. The Fitchin fought invisibly to most eyes. The creature's talons and fangs were awesomely powerful and quick. In less than a minute, the ogres were body parts outside the wizard's castle gate. Unfortunately for the wizard, after their killing spree, the creatures returned to their home plane of existence.

Disingen sighed; these two were his last ones. The other nine vanished one at a time after killing Disingen's foes. He'd have to seriously consider visiting the Fitchin dimension once more. The trip was a bit dangerous, but the creatures were so useful that the trip was worth the time.

"Fitchins are a little heavy-handed, aren't they?"

The gray mists swirled in front of Disingen and moved back several paces to allow for the wizard's pentagram.

"Human pentagrams, how very droll. Oh, and I'm sorry, but several of your guardian spirits really needed to be released from their bondage." The voice still hadn't identified itself.

Disingen could only sputter in amazement. His

defensive magics were supposed to be proof against surprise entry.

"Please allow me to introduce myself," the now-visible elf said. "I'm Lord Tornalal, and I come on behalf of my Master, the great Cimmerian Nix. I believe you have an artifact of his and I'm to collect it. Maybe you should tell the quaint human with the lethal daggers that Fitchin loves elves, just a thought."

Disingen didn't know how to act. There was an eight-foot-tall elf in front of him where no creature should be. The elf, dressed all in gray, had strange swirling mists moving all about its body. The wizard's senses could tell some of the mists were decidedly deadly, but the gods only knew what the mists could do to the unwary.

None of Disingen's magical defenses appeared broken. The wizard sensed each one as threads always connected to his wrist by the power of his magic. Several of the enchanted guards were gone, but all the human ones were still at their posts, none the wiser.

"How did you get in here?" Remembering whom he was talking to, he added, "Elf Lord."

"It's a Fey thing. You really wouldn't understand. The artifact?" questioned Tornalal. Tornalal flicked dust from his sleeve and looked around the room with a bored expression on his face.

"I was under the impression that our agreed-upon target had to be removed, and then I would surrender the artifact," said the wizard.

Tornalal waved a hand at the magical human. "Please, Lord Cimmerian Nix isn't a common laborer. You have offered a gift, and my Master has consented to do you a favor. If you see it any other way, I must leave and report that, once again humans have lied to the elfin nation."

Rushing to a small cupboard, Disingen opened the magical portal to another dimension and pulled out a glowing emerald rod. He was breathing so heard he almost couldn't think. These elves showed such amazing power; Disingen vowed if he lived through this experience, he would never again strike a bargain with an elf.

"Lord Tornalal, you're absolutely correct. Here's your Master's gift. Please convey my deepest regards to the Elf Lord. Also, thank him for his efforts on my behalf," clinched teeth spat out this last sentence.

"Your thoughts are already known to my Master. Good day, and may you always have the sun at your back."

The elf turned into gray mist and vanished.

Rothal walked the room with one of his daggers out. The blade of the weapon burst into sparks every few feet. "Did you know that last was an elfin curse? They tell you they want you to have the sun at your back because they want you buried face down in the dirt. As the sun rises and sets, you always have the sun shining on your back, but you can't enjoy it."

"What's that all about?" Disingen pointed at the assassin's sparking dagger as he asked the question.

"Elves are deadly magical creatures, but they're terrible assassins. This one filled the room with Anntoon fungus," replied the assassin. "They use it a lot, but even the King's army knows how to stop it. The fungus takes about three weeks to get into your system, and then it burns out your eyes from the inside. Nasty stuff, but I'll bring you the cure right away. It's all part of the assassin cult's services; otherwise, you would have been dead in a month. We couldn't have that now, could we?"

The smile on Rothal's face made the wizard sick to his stomach. Elves, assassins, demons, he really needed to get away from all of this.

7

SACRIFICE IS THE DUTY OF COMMAND

"To deal well with everyone is a sign of misspent youth."

— LORD ANWARDENTINE

FAR, FAR IN THE DISTANCE FROM CORBYN'S camp, enchanted lightning cracked over the heads of the Hunt pack. Finally, they'd found the real trail. The first part of the night wasted itself as the Hunt pack chased blind lead after blind lead into dead ends. Winters Bark thrown down everywhere, tricked up the scent, and expended magical protective energy on behalf of someone or something. The Hunt Master loved following Winters Bark trails. In four hundred thousand years, it had only found seven of these trails, and anything different was welcome in an eternity of hunting. These enchanted bits of bark always meant a formidable foe lurked at the end of the hunt.

The first trail it followed held the trait of a demon. Hours later, the demon element was gone from the trail, and humans and their horses filled the scent trail. The demon was forgotten. The Hunt Master had killed many demons in the past; it was glad its prey was free of their taint.

For half the night, the pack roamed over the human-held lands looking for who had spread the Winters Bark. The trail took the Hunt Master past one dangerous pool of elemental power. It didn't like the wild energies centered on the dwarven-built stone structure. It was able to go around this place to pick up the trail in a new location. Shivering, it remembered the hunts made on dwarves and didn't like any of those memories. Dwarves were much like it. The Hunt Master was an elemental force taking power from all the hunts going on around the planet. The dwarves took part of their strength from the elemental force of the earth itself, and this made them wild and dangerous opponents. Most of the Hunt Master's permanent scars were from dwarven hunts. However, this time, it hunted humans on horses and there was a taint of something elfin as well in the mix of smells to be tracked down. By the time the thin crescent moon was high in the sky, the Wild Hunt would be upon the prey, and there would be a wonderfully satisfying feeding of souls. Cracking its yellow whip of life-essences, the Hunt Master urged pack and chariot steeds to a faster pace.

———

"By the moon, that hurts!" Corbyn sat up with a stab of pain deep in his skull.

The pressure on his brain forced Corbyn painfully awake from his deep sleep. The foreshadowing ache of deadly danger settled around him like a cloak. His spirit-eye filled with the moon-granted image of the Hunt, the Wild Hunt. Corbyn's mind filled with the night-vision of a charioteer and its horrific pack of beasts searching the land for what could only be Corbyn and his lancers. The good Captain did not know how he knew this was so; he just knew the Hunt chased him tonight. The light and magic of the moon granted him visions sometimes. This time, he could see the Wild Hunt in all its glory. The Hunt Master, supporting huge elk horns on its head, not bowed in the least by the massive weight, stood tall in Corbyn's chariot-filled vision. This manlike beast, hugely muscled, wore little in the way of fur clothing. Its skin almost seemed like tree bark, with jagged edges showing here and there on its dark body. Its eyes glowed with a wild yellow fire, and its head constantly moved back and forth, obviously trying to sense something. That something was Corbyn.

As the Captain looked at its face, the Hunt Master looked back, laughing a deep, dangerous laugh. "Yes, I'll find you this night or know the reason why."

Corbyn's vision pulled back to see the entire Hunt. Giant bone spears bristled from quivers along the side of the chariot. The chariot itself, equally horrific as its creator appeared made out of the bones and skulls of long-dead victims.

The Hunt Master flicked a yellow whip of pure energy, spurring its pack of hunting creatures forward. The lightning and thunder the whip made could be heard by Corbyn in his vision and very faintly in the distance to his ears. The four demon horses pulling the chariot whinnied in fear with every crack and leapt ever faster through the night forest. Their hooves struck sparks of yellow fire with every contact of the earth. Corbyn thought he recognized the land the Hunt trod as ground his lancers traveled yesterday.

The hunting pack appeared as terrifying as their master. A mixture of huge hound-things and terrible lizard-things, each of the creatures appeared larger than the horses pulling the chariot. The hounds howled their thrill of the chase; their massive canine bodies flowed through the thick underbrush like it wasn't even there. Each one of the lizards ran bent over with huge tails, balancing the rest of their massive bodies. Their heads, all fangs, and glowing yellow eyes, bent low to the ground. One brushed a piece of Winters Bark, causing it to magically become dust at the attention. These lizard-things made no sound, and the thorns and thick underbrush rebounded off their scaly hide, never making a scratch.

The moon, rising in the night sky, filled Corbyn with its energy, giving him magical clues and foreshadowing the fate of his lancers if he didn't do something instantly. The Wild Hunt searched for his men. A wild, elemental force, legend told that to be the prey of the Hunt was to be assuredly dead. Moving to where Wise slept, he grabbed the man's shirt and lifted him out of his bedroll like a rag doll.

"It's the Wild Hunt, David. We're all dead men if you don't do exactly as I tell you."

Sergeant Wise blanched in the firelight. His eyes wide and full of fear; his first thought was easy to read. The Wild Hunt destroyed entire armies in the field. No one survived the Wild Hunt.

"Mount the men up as quickly as you can and get them moving toward Arrow Heart Crossing. Take my horse as well. The Hunt hasn't picked up our scent yet. I can feel them casting about over the land, far in the distance. It's been raining on our back trail, but the gods only know if that's going to slow the Hunt down. I'm betting they'll be here in less than an hour. I'll stop them somehow for a bit; if I'm not with you by the time you get to the crossing, continue without me. Here is the packet of emeralds and the command word for the magic bag. It's your only hope of getting an elf to give up their brooch. Now, get moving. I know you would stay and fight by my side, but it's the time for running now, my friend. Go. You're all in deadly danger until the dawn, so keep moving until then."

In seconds, the men were rushing about in wild abandon. As the lancers swirled around him, mounting up in confusion, Corbyn ignored them. Concentrating on the challenge ahead, he sliced the palm of his hand and mashed the bloody cut into the earth at his feet. His freely given blood would serve as a challenge to the Hunt. Standing, he backed up several paces and raised his bloody hand into the air. Glowing with the light of the moon, a beam of lunar enchantment flowed down from the sky, covering his palm and then his body with a luminescent glow.

With stern discipline, Sergeant Wise hurried the men away through the moonlit forest so fast they didn't have time to see the eerie magics playing out behind them. The trail through the woods was easy to follow, and an hour from now, the men would be long gone from the area.

Whispering in the wind, Corbyn called on his oldest friend in the telepathic language of the unicorns, *"Moonborn, I need you."*

The answering whinny barely touched his mind,

but that was enough to light a happy grin on Corbyn's face.

The Wild Hunt, still many miles away, approached, and Corbyn planned on being their only prey tonight. For untold thousands of years, the Wild Hunt roamed where it wanted in the world, hunting dragons, elves, dwarves, and humans. The Wild Hunt was the stuff of legends. Mothers of every race scared their children into obedience using the deadly Hunt's name. Normally, the Hunt stayed away from civilization and roamed the untamed places of the world. It was one of the ten wild elemental forces known by scholars and wizards alike. Anything was possible with the Hunt, and now it was on his trail and drawing closer with each heartbeat.

His stalwart ally, Moonborn, hurtled from another dimension into the glade. A unicorn stallion, its blinding white main flashed in a gust of cool lilac-scented wind, announcing its presence to the Captain.

The creature reared high in salute to its friend. The unicorn stallion appeared as a powerful and commanding presence. Humorous thoughts filled Corbyn's mind. *"Sure, an what have you gotten us into this time, my moon-struck brother?"* The thoughts of the unicorn were like spoken words to Crobyn.

"The Wild Hunt approaches," Corbyn said in hushed tones. "If you and I try to travel the dimensions as of old, the Hunt destroys all my men. I can't allow that, so we seek to bargain with the Hunt Master. Stalling for time, maybe my men can get free of the Hunt with the dawn's light."

"Bargain with the elemental force of the Hunt. Well, if they do not start calling you Lord of Fools and Chance Taker from tonight's actions, they never will. No one gambles like you do, moon brother. In thousands of years, none have thought to bargain with the Hunt. Sure, an if we live, we'll have an interesting story to tell our young."

Corbyn slapped his horse blanket and saddle on Moonborn. Cinching the straps, he muttered to himself and the unicorn all the legends he'd heard of the Wild Hunt. None of his memories were helpful or reassuring.

"During the light of the moon, the Wild Hunt searches out prey all over the magical lands of the planet. An elemental force having no respect for wealth or race, it scents out victims, rides them down, killing them for sport. It's said only the wildest miracles can stop the Hunt as it searches out its prey. One legend holds that a griffon fleeing through the night went through an elfin army marching on its way to a battle. The army sought to stop the Hunt, thinking it was an attacking foe. All through the long night, the creatures of the Wild Hunt battled thousands of elves. At the dawn, the elfin army lay totally destroyed to the last elf. The Hunt rode in the light of the next full moon, sporting the heads of the leaders of the elf army on the front of the Hunt Master's chariot. To the good of that story, the griffon was never hunted again. Some legends speak of heroes and wizards who would become prey and defeat the Hunt Master in one-on-one combat. Those legends always give tragic ends to the victors as fate and ill luck plague them till their dying days. So, even if we win out this night, bad luck might follow us until we're dead. Now that's a comforting thought."

"We unicorns have a story of a lone unicorn stallion hunted to its death. The unicorn galloped all night through the dimensions, as is our power. The Hunt traveled to these wild places as well and never lost the trail. One of the Hunt Master's bone spears sports a unicorn horn for its tip. None of the legends among your people or mine talk about running being the best way to win over the Hunt Master."

"Bide with me in my moon circle," Corbyn said. "We'll wait the coming of the Wild Hunt. I thank you, Moonborn, for standing with me in this time of great danger."

"Sure, and I still owe you a few from the time of trolls. Work your magics, and I'll lend you what energy I can."

The unicorn moved behind Corbyn, and its horn lightly touched Corbyn's shoulder. The legendary magic of the unicorns flowed through the horn and strengthened Corbyn with added unicorn magical power.

Once more, Corbyn raised his now moon-healed hand into the air and gathered the protective energies of the moon to himself. He snapped his fingers, and a bright beam of power flowed from his other hand, and he used it to burn the earth in a large circle around their position. As the beam from his hand hit the earth, it boiled, turning the dirt into shiny glass. In ever-quickening heartbeats, the moon glass circle, now complete around man and unicorn, glowed with the same light as the orb in the sky.

"Would you mind, my moon brother, if I ask you a question while you work these magics of yours?"

"Not at all. I've a few I would ask of you as well."

"Sure, my two-legged brother, you do some amazing things with the magic of the moon. I can see the power of the first circle you've created. Now I'm seeing that you've put a strange set of lacy web energies behind the first one. I don't understand why you're reinforcing the circle with webs of magic defenses instead of putting all your energy into that first moon circle barrier you've enchanted?"

Corbyn added web layer after web layer of protective spells to the inner circle of the moon barrier. From the inside of the circle, the energies looked like fancy laces intertwining a thousand times on top of each other.

"I've seen the creatures of the hunt. All I want to

do is stop them until their master and I have a chance to talk. Not all the protections in the world could stop what's coming for us when they marshal all their strength. I spin many levels of protection around us because each one supports all the others, and many layers are much stronger than just one. It's just something I've used before, and if it doesn't work, then we're both eaten, and I'll have learned an important magical lesson as the last of me is gulped up by the pack we'll be seeing in just a few heartbeats."

"Sure, and I'm so glad I asked."

"Now, my turn. Why is it that when I ask you to come, I'm always smelling lilacs around you?"

"Female unicorns are shy creatures and loners as well. That's why there aren't a lot of my unicorn kind about. I learned as a young one that the pretty females of my race love the smell and taste of lilacs. I often rub through a bush or two, and many's the time I make my resting place in a lilac hedge just to interest the females of my kind with my scent. This saddle you've put on me feels funny and has some magical taint on it. What's wrong with it?"

"Nothing's wrong with it," Corbyn replied. "I've a few surprises packed in that saddle, which is the sum total of all of our chances of surviving the night. We're going to do a little testing of the good Baron's work this evening. There, the last of the barriers is up. It should be very interesting to see how my work holds against the elemental forces of nature. Life is full of little mysteries, and one is about to hit us in the face, like as not."

Corbyn's head throbbed, and his jaunty manner was all an act for his old unicorn friend. Corbyn, the planner, didn't like unexpected surprises, especially deadly ones. He stood at the center of his magical circle, having done all that he could to survive the next few hours. He'd hoped it would be enough, but there were too many unknowns.

Leaping out of the darkness, a hound bigger than any hound had a right to be bounded right at Corbyn's throat.

After seeing the brutes in his vision, Corbyn expected just such an attack from them, and he'd totally prepared for it.

"Awrow!" The dog-monster bounced off Corbyn's magical protections and sat on its haunches, howling in pain a few feet away. Then, the night filled with the baying of hounds.

Three more of the dog-things rushed in to have their noses bashed as well.

"Not very bright creatures, are they."

"They don't have to be bright; they have very intelligent fangs." Corbyn felt the magical strain of maintaining his barriers against the smashing force of the canines. As long as they hit it one at a time, he was sure he could hold out. Then the lizard-monsters rushed in.

The monsters were massively powerful now that

Corbyn got a closer look at them. Reptiles of some type, as each came into view, they circled the glade always looking in toward the protective moon circle. Huge reptiles, their scaly flesh, looked greasy and silver in the nighttime forest. There was something unclean about these creatures, and their yellow eyes moved with deadly intelligence. Sniffing and har-rumphing the ground, they circled ever closer, and more of them joined this strange dance. Soon, there were twenty lizards all circling closer and closer. These monsters never rushed the circled or tested its strength. Hounds were continually pawing or noshing at the circle and howling in pain at the ef-fort, but not the lizards.

"Moon brother, they work the ring of threes on us."

"We can't stop them. I know it means trouble, but our defenses will hold long enough, I hope."

The unicorn constantly shifted his position, watching one way and then another. *"I can probably kill two or three of those scaling things, but I'm leaving the rest to you. By the way, you have all the dogs as well. Sure an I just thought I would mention that before we begin what promises to be a very ugly and short dance."*

There was an amazing amount of doubt in the thoughts of the unicorn.

Suddenly, the smallest of the lizards dug into the ground close to Corbyn's moon circle but never touched the circle edge. Clods of earth flew up and out with each talon strike. All the other lizards watched to see what would happen to the digger.

The unicorn had to ask, *"How deep did you make your protections?"*

"Deep?" Corbyn said in amazement. "Who would have believed a ten feet tall monster would dig to get at its prey?"

"Well, that's reassuring, and it's a good thing I have a few sons and daughters to live on after I'm eaten. One can only hope these digging devils find the flesh of a unicorn tough and stringy."

Several of the lizards looked up from their digger-watching and glared right in the eyes of the unicorn.

"Oh great. Sure, an you think they might be able to hear my thoughts? The gods wouldn't be cruel enough to make them read minds as well as be big and ugly, do you think?"

Suddenly, the Hunt Master and its chariot stormed into the glade, spilling hounds and lizards to the left and right as they hurtled themselves to the sides to avoid getting run over. A ten-foot-long bone spear flashed from the hand of the Hunt Master and bounded off Corbyn's protective circle in a shower of moon sparks.

A deep laugh filled the glade. The chariot stopped with the Hunt Master leaping off its vehicle. With a bone spear in each hand, the Hunt Master walked up to Corbyn and his unicorn, stopping at the moon circle edge.

In a deep booming voice, like rolling thunder, the Hunt Master announced itself and its intentions. "I've thrown down castles. I've torn apart mountains. Prey can't hide from me. Your little moon barrier can't stop me if I want to get past it."

"My name is Captain Cauldron of the King's Own 25th Lancers," said Corbyn, defiant to the last.

"No, your name is Prey," snarled the elemental force in front of them.

The Hunt Master sniffed the air and knelt on the ground, sifting the bloody dirt with its fingers.

"I gave of my blood freely to give you the scent of me. That surely allows me a few words," Corbyn asked.

"No," the Hunt Master snarled. "Prey, you gave your blood so I wouldn't hunt the twenty other humans and thirty horses you sent away from here an hour past. Why should I not kill you and continue this excellent hunt?"

Standing, the Hunt Master's elemental power washed over Corbyn and the unicorn in a wave of force. Stabbing one of its spears deep into the earth, the Hunt Master raised a shovel-sized hand up to the barrier and pressed the barrier. Sizzling sparks and fantastic heat met the hand. The smell of burned flesh filled the glade.

"Moon magics fill this barrier," the creature said. "That was a mistake, Prey. Let me tell you what few know. The moon's own light is part of every night hunt. It grants me power and gives me life. In the thousands of years of my existence, I've been killed seven times, and each time, the hunter's moon draws my spirit back to this world as all creatures of the world hunt, lending energy to my being. Your magics, Prey, are powerful, but I've used the light and power of the moon for eons."

Stabbing the earth with his other spear, he clapped his hands together and then pushed at the magical moon shield. All the magical barriers Corbyn worked so hard to set up sparkled into moon dust and vanished.

Corbyn drew his main gauche and long sword. "If you'd bide a heartbeat before killing me, I have a proposal to make."

"Prey that talks and stands to fight with a smile on its face," acknowledged the Hunt Master, "now that's something new. You seem to be a pleasant diversion. Divert some more." There was humor in the manthing's voice. Just the stance of its body kept its hunting pack from rushing in. All those deadly creatures waited on their master's command.

Corbyn could sense the massive elemental power of this mancreature.

Ignoring the tips of Corbyn's sword and dagger, the Hunt Master boldly walked up to Corbyn. Standing eight feet tall, the manthing glared down at Corbyn with its wild yellow eyes.

"I've offered my blood in a challenge," Corbyn

said boldly. "My life is my wager. I mount my unicorn, you give me twenty-one heartbeats, and the chase is on. I'm wagering you won't catch us."

"I've hunted unicorns before. If I allow this to happen, you may not walk the dimensions using the unicorn's powers," snarled the now-interested elemental creature. "You stay on this plane of existence, and I will think about allowing your twenty friends to escape me this night and forever. As you must know, once I give up a hunt, I'm not allowed to ever hunt that prey again."

"Then it's a wager?" Corbyn asked.

"You know my pack is faster than your unicorn, don't you?" queried the Hunt Master.

"I don't doubt it," Corbyn answered, and in those few words were volumes of unspoken acknowledgement of the futility of his effort.

"If you've lied to me and the unicorn walks the dimensions, I will not only hunt you to your death; I'll hunt the entire unicorn herd that spawned this creature and all of your relatives to their deaths, including the elfin ones I can even now sense," the Hunt Master warned.

Corbyn sheathed his weapons, showing the creature before him that he wasn't afraid of the huge spear in his face. "We've a bargain Hunt Master."

Corbyn mounted the strangely silent unicorn and waited for the Hunt Master to begin counting.

The Hunt Master released the binding magic of

threes his lizards cast over the unicorn and Corbyn and held up its spear, holding Corbyn back. "You're barely human. Humans don't usually ride unicorns. Humans also don't shape the magical energies of the moon. Prey, what are you really?"

"I'm a proud Captain of the King's lancers," Corbyn shouted in defiance. "You've unjustly come to hunt me down and kill me, and I've honestly struck a fair bargain with you. This night, we contest against each other, and you'll find me a bold enemy. You call me prey; I call you fool. Catch me if you can!"

Ignoring the spear, Corbyn gave the mental urging for Moonborn to race into the night. The unicorn was ten hoof beats away before the surprised Hunt Master thought to start counting. It was a minor victory but a win nonetheless for Corbyn.

"One, two, three!" shouted the Hunt Master, and then it stopped counting.

In the opposite direction from Arrow Crossing and his men, Corbyn directed the galloping Moonborn.

The unicorn raced on, but there was a great fear in his thoughts. *I won't walk the dimensions bringing that deadly creature down on my females and young, my Moon Brother, even if it means our deaths.*

The unicorn strained every muscle to speed away

as fast as possible. The sound of the held-in-check hounds filled the forest behind them.

Reaching down, the elemental force that was the Hunt Master scooped up the bloody earth left by the unexpectedly interesting Prey. A creature of strict habit, it would use the blood as a last resort in case the Prey proved to be as tricky as the Hunt Master thought the rider and unicorn could be. It shook its head, smiling as it mounted the Hunt chariot. Never in thousands of years had Prey challenged it. It had fought and died against Prey in those years, but the Prey had always battled in trapped desperation. This new one was pleasantly different. The strength of the moon flowed in its veins as the moon's hunt strength flowed in the Hunt Master. The rider wasn't an elemental force, but it was powerful. After hundreds of heartbeats, it sent the hounds after the Prey. Holding the raptors back to follow the chariot, the Master snapped at the reins. It hoped this would be an eventful hunt and smiled a deadly smile of death.

Further in the forest, lancer and unicorn moved quickly along the trail.

"Is there a plan to your madness, or am I just galloping along until their fangs pull me down and they rip out my bloody heart after I've killed nine of them for their effrontery, of course?"

"By the moon that made me, I haven't a plan, exactly. I've got some very good ideas. I even have some solid thoughts. There was no real time to form a plan. Are you getting tired already?" Corbyn amusedly asked.

"Sure, and I could race the wind like this all night. On the other hand, the pretties behind us seem better at running than I am. Imagine that of creatures having run for eons."

"Well, before they see us and begin ripping your legs off for a light snack, let's try idea number one." Corbyn reached behind and felt among several saddle tabs for the tab with a raised number one. He yanked this one, ripping open a long pocket along the back of the saddle. The up-and-down action of the unicorn's backside threw hundreds of bright bits of metal high into the air and in all directions behind them.

"You can't see idea number one in action. Let me tell you in just a few minutes, I'm hoping we'll be hearing the effects of caltrops cutting into the paws of those rather quick-moving hounds of the Hunt Master."

"Caltrops? You mean those three spiked metal things your human friends use to slow down horse charges? That's a nasty thought. I'm very glad I'm not following you right now. Are there more bright ideas like this in their future?"

"Unfortunately, there is only one blast of that type of idea. We have a few others ready when. . ." Corbyn stopped when he heard the sound of the hounds in pain.

Arro, Arro!

Riding through the night, forest branches whipped at the pair. It was easy for Corbyn to imagine the hounds getting their paws caught in the razor-sharp caltrops. The only thing he couldn't count on is how many of those beasts he'd slowed down. The howls fell far back in the distance. Corbyn started counting the gallops to measure how long of a lead they had when compared to the howling behind them.

After several counts of a thousand, he could hear nothing from the wounded beasts. All that meant was that the reptiles were assuredly on their trail now.

"Those metal spikes won't get them all, you know."

"Right as always," the Captain answered. "It's time for idea number two."

Reaching back, Corbyn pulled packet number two. Red powder flew into the air in all directions.

"Whew! What's that stuff? Even moving away, it burns my nose?"

"When I was thinking of the things I wanted in this saddle, one of the possibilities occurring to me was that I would be tracked while riding. That red dust is dried talen root. It's not only going to make sniffing us out impossible, it's going to make them lose breakfast, lunch, and dinner all at the same time. Take the first deer trail you run across. We can't keep following this straight merchant's road North. They'll surely move up it for miles in hopes of picking up our spoor again. I want to generally head back the way we came for the last several days, but I don't want to use the main trail to do it unless speed is our last option."

———

The Hunt Master wasn't pleased. The Prey employed an evil trick to ruin the paws of some of its hounds. Six were rolling in pain with metal slivers tearing up their paws. The rest of the hounds howled in anguish and confusion at the suffering of their brothers and sisters. Stupid but loyal creatures, they didn't know whether to continue following the Prey or stay to protect their wounded siblings. With a wave of its hand, the Hunt Master sent the wounded ones back to their elemental homeland. They healed with the rise of the next moon.

With a mental command, half of the raptors rushed off on the trail. Their scenting abilities were stronger than the hounds, and their talons would be affected by these tricky bits of metal. This Prey was proving worthy of the Hunt. The Hunt Master gathered its life essence and caste the magical elements of the earth and the moon out before him. Taking it slow, it made all the bits of sharpened metal glow with the light of the moon. Then all those located bits rose up and joined into a ball at the center of a moon circle. The Hunt Master had his steeds use their demonic fires to melt the slivers. This Prey trick wouldn't work twice if the quarry decided to back track on the trail. The Hunt Master sent protective magics to cover all the remaining members of the pack. More of these slivers of metal would now glow with the light of the moon and wouldn't catch his pack unawares.

Looking up, the Hunt Master could hear gagging in the distance. By the forces of nature, what was happening now?

Riding up to the next disaster scene took many minutes, its four horses began rearing and refusing to go further. This reaction by the horses had never happened before! The trail was wide here, and in the distance, it saw all of the raptors sent ahead. They were on the ground dead. Springing from the chariot, the Hunt Master carefully approached, snapping its fingers caused elemental protective magics to surround it.

Scenting the air, its nose started to burn. Poison! The Prey had somehow managed to poison the trail. Raising its hand into the air, the Master summoned the forces of the moon into itself. Foggy mists began streaming from its nose into the surrounding area. Every time the mist touched some of Corbyn's red dust, the dust glowed with the pulsing heartbeat of the Hunt Master. The dust was everywhere along the trail. The powder thickly crusted the dead noses of the raptors. Detecting every effect of the red root, the Hunt Master knew it would make his raptors sick. Raptors couldn't regurgitate their food, and so each had died gagging to death.

"Ripper, Talon, my strong beasts. You both first gave me life all those long years ago. I thought you and I would go on through the ages forever. Rest well, my brothers. I will avenge your souls," wept the Hunt Master for the first time in its long life.

Raging at the moon and its fate, the Hunt Master gathered even more energy from the moon.

This was not to be born! Over half of its pack was ruined, and the moon was not at its zenith yet. There had never been a Hunt like this. Mentally cautioning a hound and a raptor, the Hunt Master sent only a pair ahead on the trail to find the prey. The rest of the pack stayed behind the Hunt Master's chariot. Moving far around the red glowing poison area, the Hunt Master gained a new respect for this Prey.

Galloping through the night, the unicorn raced along deer trails and often followed creeks to hide its scent. In less than two hours of travel, all the effort was for naught as the baying of a single hound began dogging their trail. Far too quickly, the hound and raptor closed on the heels of Corbyn and Moonborn. The hound howled its thrill of a quarry found once more.

"How many more good ideas do you have?"

Looking back, Corbyn could see a hound and raptor gaining on their trail.

"I've only one more thought, and I really wanted to save it for more of the pack. It seems a waste to use it on just two of them."

"You're right. If the Wild Hunt is only going to send two of the pack after us at a time, we should turn and kill them? You take the lizard; I'll take the hound."

"Your idea has definite possibilities. Let's do it."

Turning, they clearly surprised their two pursuers. The unicorn used its hooves to crush the skull of the hound before it even knew the Prey closed to meet them. Corbyn thrust his longsword into the mouth of the raptor and pierced the creature's brain. It stopped dead and tumbled over.

Magical moon-bright sparks struck Corbyn in the chest and hand. He clutched his heart in pain and hit the ground.

"What's wrong? Did the lizard fang you?"

"No, someone or something is tugging at my insides. I've never felt anything like this before. The pain is terrible." Corbyn fell from his saddle, clutching his stomach.

The unicorn licked Corbyn's face, tasting a new magic circling him. Now that the unicorn held Corbyn's essence on his tongue, he could sense a strange white thread. It came from his friend's chest and went out into the night.

"The Hunt Master has some type of spell connecting it to you. Saddle up, we'll try to get past the limits of whatever spell is being cast on you."

Corbyn weakly got in the saddle and Moonborn shot forward.

In heartbeats, the Hunt Master came across its two dead pack members. Shaking its head the Master called itself a fool for sending more of the pack to their deaths. The Master loved each pack creature, and it should have known this Prey was too deadly to send just two out after him. Holding the bloody dirt in its hand, the Hunt Master used the essence to sense the pair in the distance. The Master hadn't liked using this tactic for the hunt. The blood magic would allow the Hunt Master to catch up to the Prey wherever they went, but the effort was an admission of weakness. The spell tainted the Master's sense of honor.

The Hunt Master wasn't pleased to feel the blood connection cut. The Prey used lunar magics to shield itself from the blood link the Prey had with its own essence. Closing its eyes, the Hunt Master used ancient moon magics of its own to try to sense the Prey. Ah, yes, there they were racing down a deer track in the distance. The two had made a mistake. The Prey used moon magics to shield against the blood magics used against it. The

Hunt Master was also a creature of the moon. The lunar spells called to the Hunt Master, and suddenly, the trial was clear. The Hunt Master whipped its horses forward to full speed. As long as the Prey used the moon, they would be easy to locate.

———

"My magical shields seem to be holding the tugging at bay. Change direction once more and fly as fast as you can along the main trail. We must rely on speed now. Let's see how fast you can go. I have one good idea left and then there is another forming in the back of my skull if this idea fails.

Moonborn's night vision easily copped with quick movement through the trees and brush of the ancient forest. In minutes, the unicorn raced on the main trail running north and south. Heart pounding, the unicorn put on a rare sprint of speed and fairly flew up the trail heading north.

Both groups raced through the long night. The speed of the unicorn amazed the Hunt Master. Many hours after the chase began, they were only now within several spear-throw lengths of the Prey. To the Master's questing senses, they were a brightly outlined moon glow image just ahead. Now that it was close enough to see them, the Master let the pack pull ahead of the chariot. The baying hounds and deathly silent raptors would rip them down. The pack surged forward, thirsting for the kill.

———

"I'm sorry, I just wasn't fast enough." Growing tired, the unicorn asked for Corbyn's forgiveness as the pack gained on them.

"Don't say that," Corbyn answered. "There's few in the world that could keep up with your speed and they had to be supernatural to do it. I've one more little surprise for these bastards. Just as they close in, we'll try my final thought. Start moving from side to side along the trail. I know it'll slow you down a might, but I have to wait until they're almost on us anyway."

Hearts pounding, the two heard the pack gain on them. The hounds baying for the kill filled the pair with terror. A feeling of helplessness sunk into their bones and numbed them. There were too many of the pack to fight. They weren't moving fast enough to escape them. The Hunt Master and its demon horses were right behind. The forceful magics of the Hunt made the two just want to stop and surrender.

Courage from a thousand successful past battles allowed them to continue on when all their senses and their very spirits cried to surrender to the chasing death and end the horror of being hunted by an unstoppable foe.

As the pack rushed to biting distance, Corbyn pulled his last tab. The ripping sound faded in the fizzling bang of the huge gas cloud erupting from the back of the saddle. In seconds, the smoke engulfed the pack. Howls of pain and gasps from the raptors filled the night.

"Well, I hear them back there. What's happening to them?"

"It's a special gas blinding them and causing them to choke," Corbyn said grimly, smiling. "The gas-only lasts a minute or two, but anyone closely following us gets a lung full, slowing them down a lot. With any luck, none of the pack will be any good until dawn. That's all the tricks the Baron's saddle is giving up tonight. My only other thought is to run for the Red Dragon inn. There's something strange about that inn and its master. I think it's a good place to make a last stand. It's going to be a race now between the sunrise and the Hunt Master recovering in time to get after us."

———

Choking and gasping for breath, the Hunt Master dragged his sick horses out of the cursed fog. It had sent all its choking hounds back home. All of this pack's raptors lay dead on the ground. Never had Prey destroyed all its pack in eons of years of hunting. Using healing water magics, the Hunt Master cleared up most of the effects of the fog on his elemental horses.

The Master threw its whip to the floor of the chariot in disgust. Trying to drive the horses to a quicker pace was useless. The healing magics could only do so much. These were faithful beasts and would give their all to catch the Prey ahead of them. The sun would soon rise, and it was up to the Master to reach the Prey before that happened, or the quarry would be free, and that wasn't something to be born!

Traveling in hours, what had taken the lancers three days, the unicorn stopped in front of the huge gate of the Red Dragon inn. Amazingly, the double gates opened, and the Red Duke greeted the pair with open arms.

"Captain, my Captain, how good to see you again," the happy Duke said. "Look at this wondrous unicorn. The ladies inside will be impressed. Come, come in, and we will talk."

Looking back the way he came, Corbyn had to tell the truth. "Duke, I've a bit of bad news. The Wild Hunt is chasing me. I probably shouldn't come in, but I'd like to make my last defense here in front of your gates if you wouldn't mind?"

"Come on in," the Duke said. "We'll meet that old bastard with a drink and a song. Come in, my boy, and bring your unicorn friend."

They hadn't taken two steps into the inn when the Hunt Master's chariot rode up. Horses rearing, the Hunt Master leapt from his chariot with a spear in hand.

"You're mine!" shouted the hunter, leaping from its chariot.

Corbyn drew sword and dagger. The Red Duke stepped in front of him. Mysteriously there was a huge stone chalice in the Duke's hand where there was none before.

"Hunt Master," the Duke smiled. "How proud I am that you've come to my little establishment. It's so good to see supernatural beings like yourself. I seem to have a flagon of good Ergont tea in my hand, just for you. Please come in and sit a bit."

"Ergont tea," the Hunt Master sounded amazed. "I haven't sipped that in over four thousand years. How did you know?"

"It's a gift, like growing plants or casting moon spells," replied the Duke. "Please come in."

"The Prey and I must have a little talk," said the creature. "I'll be with you in a few heartbeats."

"Oh, I'm so sorry," replied the Duke. "You see, the dawn comes early to these parts. It's one of the reasons I picked this spot to build my inn. Look."

Turning to the east the Hunt Master glimpsed the first rays of the sun and sighed the sigh of defeat.

"I'll take that drink now," said the creature. "It would seem Captain Corbyn Cauldron of the King's Own 25th Lancers has thwarted me this evening." Politely bowing to Corbyn, the Hunt Master walked into the inn, calm as you please, ahead of the other two.

A stunned Corbyn sat and drank elfin spring wine with the Red Duke and the Hunt Master. After an hour, the creature faded to nothing in its chair. The Red Duke just sat there smiling. The good Captain thanked the tavern keeper, who was clearly more than an inn owner, and left soon after the dread Hunt Master.

Corbyn and the unicorn used the dimensional ways to return to Arrow Heart Crossing. His men hadn't gotten that far yet.

"Moonborn, you saved my life this night, and I thank you," Corbyn praised his friend's efforts.

"Sure, an please, it's all in a night's work for a unicorn. Always call me at your times of great need. There's the matter of a few hundred dead trolls that I'm still owing you for. It's an impressive story you and I now must tell. I think the females will be flocking around me for miles just to hear it. We'll probably forget to mention about that trick saddle. We unicorns don't like saddles much, if you get my meaning. So, goodbye until the next horrible monster comes calling."

Rearing high, the unicorn raced off into the forest, and Corbyn smiled at the best friend anyone could have.

8

REPORTING AS ORDERED

"Time will often place a severe limitation on your pleasure."

— LADY CORDELLIA

AT THE ORDER OF THEIR CAPTAIN, THE squad rode all night to reach Arrow Heart Crossing.

The twenty tired lancers riding foaming, exhausted horses found their Captain calmly waiting on the riverbank with the crossing barge and bargeman. Corbyn told his amazing story to them all while they crossed the river.

The bargeman and his wife, happy for the company--and the emerald Corbyn gave them--stood ready to do whatever the Captain asked them to do. He informed the two that the King's lancers expected to cross for a year free on that gemstone payment. They just shook their heads in wonder at the green gem, a King's ransom to them, and started cooking up eggs and bread for the men.

"We'll camp on this side of the river until noon," Corbyn ordered. "I'm beat right down to the ground and need some sleep. I sense we're going to be safe here, so only post one guard. We'll head for South-Sword fortress and should be there by sunset. I know the Major commanding that fort and we'll have a good night's rest when we reach it. Make sure I'm up a little before noon."

Wise shook his head in wonder as his Captain gave orders as calm as you please. Most men, after the night's ride the Captain experienced, would be shaking from the near-death experience. He left his Captain to his rest. Moving out of Corbyn's earshot, he began giving orders in soft tones.

"The Captain risked his own life to save us from the Wild Hunt. We're all going to be quiet now and let him get some sleep. After all the horses are seen to, we'll all take a wee bit of a nap. Sunston, you take first watch and keep that crossing barge on our side of the river no matter who comes a calling. We'll only deal with visitors from one direction until noon."

Veterans all, none of the lancers refused a chance to sleep the morning away after taking care of their mounts. Curry brushes and leather buckets swung into action as each horse, and the extra mounts were tended. Brushed and well fed from the grasses along the riverbank, the horses needed rest from their hard ride as well as the men did.

Sergeant Wise went to talk to the river man.

"I'm Sergeant Wise of the King's Own 25th Lancers. What's your name?"

"They call me River Tom when they call me anything at all. Is that story your Captain told about the Wild Hunt true?"

Wise pointed to the bargeman's log dwelling. "Now, it wouldn't be a good idea to be calling my Captain a liar, don't you know," Wise advised. "Just the thought of you bad-mouthing him would cause me to think about burning your fine cottage there to the ground if you get my meaning."

The bargeman's eyes became like saucers in his fear at having said something stupid. "No, no, I didn't call anyone a liar, but many a folk would say your Captain tells an amazing story. What can I do for you, my good Sergeant?" River Tom moved nervously about his barge, brushing off the mud and sticks on the far planks, not daring to look the Sergeant in the eye.

"I'm thinking me and the men would like a fish lunch. Be there any fish in this river?"

"The river's filled with silver trout," replied the bargeman. "If you'll help me, we'll take my river net out and catch a few baskets full. By the time the sun's high in the sky, my wife and I will have them all cleaned and cooked for you. It's the least we could do after your Captain paid so handsomely. How does that sound?"

"A wee bit of fishing sounds good to me. Let's get to it," Wise said, his mouth watering already at the thought of the fish meal.

Many hours later, Corbyn woke to the smell of fish cooking over an open fire. The sun was high in the sky and warmed his tired bones. He'd spent a lot of energy last night and needed the rest. Now, he needed the good food he smelled near at hand.

"Captain, I was just coming to wake you," Sergeant Wise said, holding half a loaf of fresh bread in his hand and offering it to his Captain. Melted butter covered the top of the still-hot loaf. "We've fish on the spits, and all the men are just finishing their lunch. I thought a bit of fish would hit the spot. What do you think?"

"Sergeant, we need to talk about promoting you," Corbyn said with a hungry smile. "At the very least, I think a medal is deserved for the fish idea."

Sergeant Wise laughed at his Captain's jest. "They don't make a medal for serving fish, but maybe they should."

———

A few hundred yards away, with a river between them and their target, Ash Greenwood and his band of men could do nothing but hide in the forest and smell the cooking fish. Ash felt the harsh stares of his men as they crouched hungry in the brush on their side of the waterway. He was starting to look foolish to them. They'd risen well before sunrise to set up another ambush along the trail. When the dawn sun rose in the sky, their best trackers found the torn-up earth on the trail. The lancers must have passed before them in the night. There was no way to tell what caused this unusual behavior from the military troops. This band of cavalry rode when a normal troop would have rested and they rested when all other lancer regiments would have been on their way. Cavalrymen in Ash's experience, rarely rode hard through the night. If this mystery wasn't enough, he now saw there were twenty lancers instead of the expected ten. The battle would be much closer, and Ash's men didn't like that either.

Complicating the matter was the fact that the reavers now moved into the southern most part of the kingdom. They didn't know these forest paths as well, and it was making them all edgy. Turner was the only man who'd been down in this area of the kingdom before.

Turner used a stick in the earth to mark out SouthSword fortress and the river west of the outpost, where they were now.

"The lancers are going to reach SouthSword no matter what we do. From there, it's just a few hours to reach the edge of the elfin empire. If we don't get them coming out of the outpost, we'll never get them."

Turner appeared in a rare good mood. Ash thought Turner must be enjoying Ash's rash of bad luck.

"Well, I'll give you a choice, my fine Mr. Turner Blockwood," Ash snarled. "We can move past the fort and set up one more trap, or we can wait for them to come out of the elf lands and kill them then. What's it to be?"

"Oh, I'm not one for liking any type of waiting," Turner replied. "Let's ride past SouthSword and try to kill them when they first enter the forest of the elves. We'll pepper them all with arrows, and the world will think elves did it."

This was a modification of his own thoughts, but it was a good plan. He gave the orders, and his men spent the next few hours sharpening their weapons, for the third time in as many days.

———

With the warm sun high overhead, Corbyn's troop quickly rode down the open trail. While they rode, Corbyn gave Sergeant Wise a little history lesson because he didn't want to talk about the Wild Hunt at all, and he knew his good Sergeant had many questions about last night.

"All of the forts along the border between the elf and human lands started out the same way. An army came in and chopped down the surrounding trees while elves ambushed them from the edges of the forest. Eventually, after thousands of troopers died in action, the forest was cut far enough back, so the elves had to come into the open and battle the empire's armies. More often than not, the elves lost in those battles. There are now four human forts along the borders. SouthSword fortress is by far the biggest and oldest. It's a star-shaped fortification with cold iron placed throughout the outer walls to resist elfin spells. The fortress sits atop a hill. Its black granite outer walls came from quarries far to the north. That type of rock is extremely resistant to magical effects. The black stone gives the fortification an evil appearance, and I'm sure the elves agree about how evil the place is.

"I haven't been down here in a while. I'm told that below the hill and only to the west, away from the forest, a large community has grown up. With all the wood from the forest, I'm sure it's easy to raise many different buildings. When the elves came in the night to burn the town down, the people of the community rushed to the fort for safety. The next morning, the very practical inhabitants of the town chopped down more trees, with the troopers of the fort searching the forest for elves. The elves hated getting their forest chopped down and eventually stopped attacking the town."

Sergeant Wise rode enthralled at what his Captain told him. He didn't know any of this history, but he knew what facing elvish arrows was like. Taking a firmer grip on his shield, he listened on.

"The heartwood of each elfin tree is perfect for carving," Corbyn said. "There's an enchantment to each piece of elvish heartwood. When this wood appears in an object, that object is better than normal. If the wood is used for beds or furniture, those beds are the most comfortable imaginable. Products from the community, in the early days of its building, became highly prized in the rest of the empire for their quality and durability. That's when the elves changed their tactics. They started attacking only humans who chopped at the trees.

"Over the years, the elfin influence fled the trees within several miles of the outpost, making the forest's heartwood unmagical. I'm told there's an uneasy truce between elves and humans down in this area," Corbyn said.

Wise's imagination ran wild with his Captain's words. "I've heard stories myself, especially about this part of the empire. Is it true that the forest is having an affect on the humans living nearby? I've heard it told that every once in a while, a human baby's born with green skin or pointed ears. The poor wee babies become shunned in the communities, and the new borns are put out in the forests to die. They always disappear at night, and it's assumed the elves pick up the crying children."

"I've heard rumors of those children," Corbyn answered, "but there's not a thing anyone can do about them. It's what happens when humans choose to live in or near magical elf lands. There isn't a lot of that talk going about the empire, is there?"

"No, but I keep my eyes and ears open," Wise said. "One can't get too much information about the enemy or things happening around the lands of the enemy. Do you think our going into elf country will be spelling us and making us turn into weird ones?"

Corbyn laughed at the fear in his Sergeant's voice. "There's not a chance in the world of that happening. We are all too set in our ways for magic to change us. Now, from what I'm hearing in the weekly reports, SouthSword enforces the peace, and it's been quiet during the last human/elf war. The fighting you and I took part in was all to the north in the making of the newest fort, Red Fort. With any luck at all, we'll ride into these elf lands and find an elf that won't kill us on sight."

Wise rolled his eyes at that thought.

"And," Corbyn continued, "We'll get our brooch and get back safe and sound."

They rode on in silence after that, each thinking

thoughts of the elves they've fought in the past. None of those thoughts was very comforting.

———

In the late hours of the afternoon, with the sun setting below the tree line, the forest trail opened suddenly into a wide valley. Lush farms dotted the far western edges and an oddly shaped town flowed away to the west from an imposing fortress setting high on a hill in the middle of the valley.

"I've never seen a town shaped like a cone before," noted Wise. "And that great black fort rising up out of that hill is a deadly-looking place if there ever was one."

"Yes, Sergeant," Corbyn replied. "It's almost as if the town doesn't want anything to do with the east side of the fortress valley. That's the elfin edge, of course. I'm sure every elf attack hit anyone foolish enough to build on that side of the fortress first. Look how they've turned that entire area into farmland. Elves worship plants of all kinds. They would like that growth and leave it alone."

"For an outpost, there are sure a lot of cottages in the town," Wise said, looking at all the hovels.

"I bet these people have learned to build and rebuild quickly. There's no shortage of wood, and with the troopers helping them when they cut it, they could harvest a lot of planks from the large trees around here. Halt the men, Sergeant, we've official company wanting to talk to us."

Wise didn't see anyone nearby, but he naturally did what he was told and raised his left fist into the air. The entire column of troops halted their mounts.

"Dismount and be recognized!" a voice rang out toward the troop.

With that shout, ten infantrymen popped out of the tall grass on each side of the wide road. Each stood in a grass uniform, blending perfectly with their surroundings. Crossbows politely aimed away from Corbyn's lancers but presented unspoken words about the deadliness of the hiding soldiers. The tactician in Corbyn realized most of his men would have been dead in the first volley of crossbow bolts these hidden troops could fire. It was as neat an ambush as he'd ever seen. Corbyn looked at the one soldier still hiding, and the man rose from the grass, knowing he'd been seen.

"I'm Lieutenant Stonebridge. We guard this side of the valley. You are?"

Dismounting, Corbyn put out his hand and offered the Lieutenant a smile.

"I'm Captain Corbyn Cauldron of the King's Own 25th Lancers, here on a King's Commission. We'll need supplies and beds for the night. We're heading into the elf realm tomorrow. Is Major Stonewall still commanding the fortress?"

At the phrase, King's Commission, the young

Lieutenant stood at attention and signaled his men to parade rest. King's Commissions were the most important orders of the empire, and every trooper, from the lowest Private to the highest General, was to do everything they could to help the troops carrying out such a commission.

"Yes sir, he is," answered the Lieutenant. "We'll all be glad of news from the capital. I look forward to buying you a drink at the Inn of the Three Coins tonight. I'll signal your arrival and needs, and all will be ready for you when you reach the fort. It's been quiet here for six months, but you're on a dangerous errand if you're going into elf lands. The password today is 'Dulse forever.' That will get the gate opened for you right away. Major Stonewall will be notified of your coming and expect to see your commission and hear your report."

"Thank you, Lieutenant. Carry on." Corbyn saluted and waved his detachment forward.

Sergeant Wise hadn't liked being the prey of the infantry's trap, even if it was sprung by empire troops. "What in the world were those strange uniforms? I can see that they helped the men hide in the grass, but wouldn't the grass armor slow them down in battle?"

"Sergeant, you're right," Corbyn noted. "The woven suits would slow them down in battle, but the troopers fight a different war down here. For battling with elves, troops want to strike from hiding and strike hard. Troops firing in volleys from hiding can win battles just as well and even quicker sometimes than a massive cavalry charge. If I know Major Stonewall and the type of troops he commands, I'm sure they can take those woven suits off in a heartbeat. Elves have been using their skin and clothing to conceal themselves for generations. It's past time; humans started doing the same thing."

———

Down in the valley, Corbyn and his troop entered the bustling town of Oakdale. The Captain liked everything he saw there. Small stone towers poked up all about the village; these appeared manned with troops. They would be perfect for defending the town in elf raids.

"Well, this place is far from a troop camp," Wise noted.

"You're right, Sergeant," the Captain observed as well. "This village doesn't look like a temporary military camp. The people look happy as well. They appear to have a good life here. There's discipline here as well. Notice how the villagers all get out of our way?"

"I did," Wise remarked. "People getting out of our way wouldn't be happening in most of the towns we normally ride through," Wise smiled. "Moreover, this road through the middle of the town is wide enough for a full troop of cavalry to charge across it. I'm sure some good design went into its building."

The fortress loomed up as they moved to the bottom of its hill. A typical star fortress, the main entrance was between two of the star wall formations. As enemy troops rush in to try forcing an entry, they would find themselves between two forces of catapults and archers on the walls to either side of the open road to the entrance. This feature allowed for constant crossfire from the wall sections.

The fort was surrounded by a large moat of constantly moving water. Razor-sharp stakes pointed up on both sides of the trench, making it impossible to rush the walls easily.

Even though mirror signals proclaimed their arrival, the heavy drawbridge and portcullis weren't open until they gave the password. The drawbridge cranked quickly down to let them enter.

A lone man stood at the far end of the killing ground under the portcullis.

The troop rode in with Corbyn. He noted the gate at the other end of the killing field remained shut tight. They might have passed muster with the young Lieutenant in the fields far outside the town, but they still hadn't cleared the officials at the fort. If they weren't who they claimed to be, they would die in this wide tunnel entrance. Corbyn could smell the hot oil above them and see several troopers with crossbows loaded and ready to fire.

The Captain of the Engineers wasn't tall, but he had huge shoulders and big, beefy hands. His sword showed a worn grip of much use, and there was a very nonregulation stiletto in his right boot sheath. His rosy cheeks and red nose spoke of a love of drink, but Corbyn didn't see an ounce of fat on the man. The lancer Captain took an instant liking to him.

He dismounted again and offered his hand to the Captain of Engineers he saw there. In his other hand, he held the King's Commission orders with the seal of Commander Janon on them. "I'm Captain Corbyn Cauldron with a detachment of the King's 25th. Who do I have the honor of addressing?"

The other Captain noted the seals of the King and Commander Janon of all the armies on the commission, then offered his own hand and a smile.

"Captain Andren Norval of the King's 10th Engineers, I and my Engineers had the pleasure of battling alongside your lancers last year at Red Fort. We had a couple of close calls in that little scrap together, didn't we?" He waved his hand, and the rear portcullis and barred gates opened up. The two men walked into the fortress, turning to travel in the direction of the horse barns.

Star forts of the empire showed the same design from fort to fort, allowing empire troops to know their billets in every one of them. As a visiting unit of cavalry troops to a major fortification, Corbyn and his men were to go to the horse barns to the right of the first gate, and their barracks were beside those horse barns.

"You and I must report to Major Stonewall, who is expecting you. Your men can handle your tack, of course."

Corbyn waved Sergeant Wise and the rest of the troop away, then followed Norval. As the two men moved through the various halls and towers toward the center, the interior of the fort appeared well-run and filled with active troops. Corbyn noted the constant bustle of busy men and was pleased to see the Major kept tight rein on all his infantry command. Some of the forts in the interior of the empire were not as efficient, encouraging a different brand of trooper. Soldiers who lacked spirited discipline were a danger to themselves and everyone in their battle group.

"As you can see, the Major runs a stout fortification, what. He's been here for three years," Norval said. "He took it over from a lout who let the elves constantly push our troops round and round the forest. There's none of those goings on with Major Stonewall in command. We've pushed back the elves, taking more and more of their territory in the last three years, and never lost a skirmish. This fortification is constantly being updated and has all the most modern siege equipment and defenses."

"Ten years ago, the Major and I served together,"

Corbyn said. "I learned a lot about the cavalry from him. I look forward to seeing him again."

Norval had been able to simply wave his hand at the checkpoints encountered before the center tower of the fortification, but it wasn't that easy to get into the heart of the fortress. It took the showing of the King's Commission documents to open those final doors. After several guarded checkpoints, Norval and Cauldron entered the command chamber at the heart of the fort.

Corbyn gasped in surprise.

Norval chuckled, noting the Captain's awe. "Yes, it is quite something, isn't it."

The entire chamber appeared made from elfin heartwood. There was a king's ransom in enchanted woods covering the walls, floor, and the furniture of the chamber. Corbyn knew several king's ransoms could be taken from the gold made by the sale of the wood in the desk alone.

Major Stonewall came around his desk and warmly shook Corbyn's hand. "That will be all Captain Norval."

Norval handed over the King's Commission, leaving with a salute.

Dan Stonewall was a muscled man of forty. Scars filled his face from elf arrows and sword cuts, giving it a dangerous appearance. His duty uniform was crisp and unadorned with the usual medals an experienced Major earned after many years in the wars for the empire. The lack of medals was in keeping with the Major's no-nonsense style of command. He had them in plenty; he just didn't think it was necessary to flash his medals to impress anyone.

Finally, Corbyn found his head, his senses filled with the magic aura generated from the wood all around him. "Sir, I'm reporting as ordered."

"None of that, Corbyn. We were friends when you were a Private in the King's 2nd lancers and I was your wet behind the ears Lieutenant, and we're still friends now. When it's just us, I'm still Dan to my comrade in arms, and you've saved my life too many times for me to forget what we've done for each other over the years. Can I offer you some elfin Spring wine? It's chilled with mountain ice just the way you like it."

"How in the world can you get elfin Spring wine?" asked Corbyn.

"The grapes for it grow wild along this border," replied Dan. "I've had the men plant some of the onions and potatoes the elves like in the glens far from the fort. Then I have our troops harvest the grapes they find wild in those same glens. As long as the elves see us planting things, they never attack the column. I'm trying to convince the elves our two peoples can trade as well as kill each other on sight. Naturally, I don't let my superiors know about what I'm doing. I think the elves down here might be warming to our presence. I've actually had some of them come to ask for some of the healing salves we make that they can't."

The Major noted the smile of pleasure on Corbyn's face as the Captain smelled the heady scent of the wine in his glass. "I have several barrels of the wine here. I'll be happy to send one back in the next supply caravan going to the capital.

"I can see you are impressed with all the heartwood in my office. It's one of the few luxuries I allow myself. I figured since we were cutting back the trees anyway that I would use some of that wood for the office. The effect of the magic wood makes me think clearer and feel great. I feel ten years younger than I should, and I now know one of the reasons elves live so long."

"I can well imagine, Dan, how good this place must make you feel. You could buy your own empire by selling the wood out of this office."

"You and I know we already live and fight for the best empire in the world." He raised his own glass. "To King and empire!"

Raising his glass, Corbyn rested easy for the first time in many days. "To King and empire!"

Dan sat Corbyn down and reviewed the Commission. Corbyn enjoyed his wine and the expression on Dan's face.

Finally, the Major tossed the King's Commission papers down on his desk. "These orders are a joke, right?"

"No, I think not," Corbyn answered. "I've been ordered by the King, and then Lord Anwardentine of the Exchequer, and then Commander Janon of all the armies of the empire to boldly go into elfin lands, approach an elf, and secure by any means possible an elfin brooch for the princess' birthday."

"This is a daft thing, isn't it? What good can it possibly accomplish?" Dan Stonewall was growing more agitated by the minute, and Corbyn was enjoying his old friend's response to the orders he was duty-bound to carry out.

"I understand foolish orders, Corbyn. Of course, I'll help you all I can. There isn't a chance in the world of you completing this assignment, is there? I mean, when you kill the bloody elves, all their magical equipment turns to dust, including their brooches. We don't really know what those enchanted brooches do for the elves. What if the princess puts the bloody thing on, and it turns her into an elf or something equally foolish?"

The aroma of the wine filled the room. Corbyn would normally have refused the wine, being on duty, but there was no refusing if friend and former commander drank as well. Corbyn took the chilled glass to his lips, tasting the crisp, tart liquid. The first blush on his tongue suggested sunshine and springtime to his senses. He didn't allow himself to daydream back several hundred years ago when he first tasted this brand of wine. Those were days best left forgotten, especially now when he'd thrown aside his ancient family traditions and made traditions of his own. He hid his troubled thoughts of the past with a smile and a quip, underplaying what he'd managed to accomplish so far in the past few days.

"The orders have caused a bit of excitement as I've already escaped the Wild Hunt," Corbyn said. "I have a sack full of emeralds at my belt, and I think I can get two or three words out before arrows hit me. For another glass of this wonder I'm drinking now, I'll tell you the story of how I got away from the Hunt. Neither one of us will worry about tomorrow, and a few thousand elves bent on killing every human they see."

He handed his empty glass to his old-time friend, and the story telling began.

"There's lots more where this comes from, and there will be no officers mess for you and I," the Major explained. "I plan to retire down here, and I own the largest inn in the town below. The Inn of the Three Coins has become quite the popular little spot, and this week, it's filled with foolish merchants from several caravans. We'll take a carriage down and enjoy the food and the show."

9

A MATTER OF THE NAMES OF FLOWERS

"When gambling with your life, that final bet isn't at all modest."

— CAPTAIN CORBYN CAULDRON OF THE KING'S OWN 25TH LANCERS

THE CARRIAGE DROPPED THEM OFF IN FRONT of a large stone inn on the outskirts of town. Once again, Corbyn couldn't believe his eyes. The inn was made of the same black granite as the fortress.

"Dan, please don't tell me you had your army engineers take stone meant for the fortress and turn it into an inn for your use," Corbyn asked.

"Not a bit of it, old son," Dan smiled. "I had the empire's army of engineers make a bloody great officers club from left over stone the fortress would never use. Then I waited the mandatory, by the book, don't you know, one year for evaluation of the place. After careful thought, I found this club too small for the fort's needs. In my own judgment, as the commander of the fortress and considering the needs of the good officers serving the empire, nothing would do but to make a change. I had those same engineers build another, better officers club, this time inside the fort. Legal as you please, I put this great stone shack up for bids as the military code of conduct says I must. The only bidder just happened to be myself. Imagine the amazing luck of that. Then I named it the Inn of Three Coins, and it's been a going concern with the caravan trade ever since."

"Dan, we both know luck had nothing to do with any of this," Corbyn said. "Your actions aren't quite a hanging offense, but Lord Anwardentine would be shaking his finger at you."

"Well, when the good Lord Anwardentine comes this way, I will be sure to take his concerns into consideration," Dan chuckled.

Laughing, they both left the carriage.

The sign on the outside of the inn showed three huge gold coins with the face of the King on everyone. The black walls of the three-story structure seemed to absorb the moon and starlight, making the darkness fold in on all sides of the inn. Even the lanterns the carriage used didn't shed light more than a few feet from the carriage. Designed to resist attack, the iron shutters on the windows allowed no light to escape. The ones for the upper levels were all closed tight. As the large doors swung open, the well-lit inside displayed a marked and pleasant contrast from the darkness outside.

Corbyn looked up at the ceiling, down to the floor, and toward all the corners of the outer chamber, as was his practice when entering any new building or room. The common room was huge and bustling with people. Military round stoves heated sections of the chamber; the large cooking hearth couldn't reach with its heat. The bar at the back was huge, and bottles and barrels lined the space behind it.

"Half the town and most of the fort must be here tonight," Corbyn speculated to his friend.

Several large men stood at attention when Dan came in, and he waved the bouncers down to their benches. "No, not even close. There are two caravans in town this week, and many of the local men and women come here to talk with them. I strongly suspect the caravans do some trading with the elves, but I'm not inclined to stop it. I like the elves buying our human products. We'll go to the back room where there's a new game I want to show you. I think it will test even your skills as a gamesman."

At first, Corbyn didn't want to leave the common room. All the serving maids were wearing the oddest clothes. Each was dressed in work clothes of a different color. They were wearing what first seemed like typical inn fair. Each sashayed in a modest long dress, sporting lacy full sleeves and a high collar. There was nothing modest about the front of each of those dresses. The cleavage on display was amazing, and not one of the women had anything less than a full hourglass figure. Each was so busty. Corbyn didn't have the slightest idea why many pleasant things weren't spilling out into public view with every serving of a drink or a tray of food. There wasn't an ugly one in the bunch, and all smiled at Dan and Corbyn as they passed.

"Flowers, they are all named after flowers." Dan showed his glee at the looks his ladies were drawing from Cauldron.

"What in the world are you talking about?" Corbyn felt like a kid in a candy shop with way too many pleasant decisions to make.

"I knew you would find the ladies interesting," Dan grinned much too wide for Corbyn's taste.

Even these lovelies couldn't prevent Cauldron from studying the gambling tables. Gambling of all types was a passion for Corbyn, and he liked to think he was good at all the games the humans of the empire played. The center of the common room had ten tables, all filled with players. He noted blood and guts games as well as the common dice games found in every inn of the empire. There was something odd about the tables, but he couldn't quite put a finger on the oddness.

Dan kept talking as they moved past the gambling tables and toward the back of the common room. "I've named all of the serving wenches after flowers. It didn't matter what their names were before they came to work for me. Every sleeping room upstairs has a flower name as well, and these bar maids come to serve the guests upstairs as well as downstairs. People are filling the inn every night. I might open up another one of these places at the capital after I retire. Corbyn, you won't believe the food served here. I've found the best cook in the world.

Let's go to the tables in the officer's room," Dan suggested. "You must see this new game."

The second chamber they entered was almost as large as the main chamber. A much quieter crowd of gamblers played in here. At least thirty men played games of chance around several round tables. More of the lovely flower women served them food and drink on trays setting beside each chair. The furniture and attention paid to each of these gamblers marked them as bigger spenders than the people in the common room. Suddenly, Corbyn heard wolf howls from the center table. He shot a questioning look to Dan.

"The game is called Red Wolf, and one of those

men just lost a big pot," Dan explained. "Two of my Captains are waiting for us at the other Red Wolf table; come this way."

Coming up to the table, Corbyn shook the hand of Captain Andren Norval, the officer he met that morning.

"Good to see you again, Corbyn," Norval said. "This other Captain is Darren Dragon of the King's 84th regiment of Grenadiers."

A slim, tall man with shifty eyes rose to shake Corbyn's hand but didn't look Corbyn in the eyes very long. He was of the grenadiers.

Cavalrymen and grenadiers didn't get along in the empire's armies. Grenadiers constantly vocalized their irritation at the cavalry being able to ride everywhere. Cavalrymen, on the other hand, complained about grenadiers commonly getting the best of food and equipment.

"The fort whisperers say you are on a King's Commission," Norval said. "Well done that; I've always wanted that honor for myself these past nine years I've been a Captain."

Corbyn took the measure of the man, noting the calluses on his hand. These were signs he was a competent swordsman. His weapon was clean and had a handle that had seen a lot of use. Corbyn heard the words of praise, but there was a sly tone to the voice, making the words far from praising. This man would be one to watch and wouldn't soon be a friend of Cauldron's.

Sitting down, Corbyn started at the metal of the table. "Dan, are these tables made of cold iron?"

"Right, you are my good Captain," Dan replied. "I've seen Captains use far too much magic in my time as commander to allow such going's on at my gaming tables. It cost a pretty silver piece, let me tell you, but all of my gaming tables are made of cold iron. I have three maids spending every morning just keeping the rust off each one. Lots of the town men come in just to watch those ladies at work. No one can perform magic and cheat on my games, as the iron stops any spells from working. It's almost fool proof."

Corbyn looked up to see a vision walking up to the table dressed all in red. Corbyn took the initiative and guessed what her name might be. "Rose, would you please bring Dan and I some spring water and whatever the inn's serving tonight. Let me buy a round of whatever my fellow Captains are having as well."

Both Darren and Andren took out large money purses and tossed a gold coin to their Major. Corbyn gave Dan a questioning look as Dan sported a huge grin.

"It's a little game we always play with people new to the inn," Dan explained. "I've wagered you'll guess right on the name of every serving maid coming to our table tonight without being told their names. These two doubting Captains of mine didn't have the faith in you that I have. Now, let's get to the game, shall we."

Dan took out a case of thin wooden cards. He flipped over several of them, revealing numbers in different colors and four other cards with wolf head images. Corbyn picked up one of the cards. The wood was iron oak. The tooling showed no grain on the backside, and that appeared heavily stained and varnished. Even a razor-thin card made out of iron oak would be unusually sturdy. Someone must have used magic to work it as thin as each card showed itself to be.

"There are four colors of cards: red, blue, white, and black. Eleven of each color, and the cards numbered one to ten. An eleventh card in the set has a wolf image in the same color. So, you see four wolves: red, blue, white, and black. We shuffle up the cards, and every player receives four of them. The remaining cards go in the middle. Each of us puts in a gold coin at the center of the table, and the winner of the hand gets all the coins. In each hand of cards, you have a choice. You look at your cards and decide if you want to play or not. If you don't play, you stand to lose only the single coin you wagered. If you play and lose, you have to equal the pot of whatever is in there at the time, and we continue playing new hands till only one player wins the pot."

Dan threw four cards up on the table. He revealed a red 3, red 9, white wolf, and white 2. He flipped up the card at the top of the deck at the center and showed a red 6.

"If the card I would have flipped up was white, the white wolf of this hand would have beaten all the other white cards that could have been flipped up," Dan said, explaining the rules. "These four cards in front of us is a winning hand because I've flipped up red 6 at the center of the table. The red 9 in the hand is higher than the red 6. If someone would have played in this game with a hand of cards containing a red 10 or a red wolf, they would have beaten this red 9 and the red 6 at the center and won the game. The losing person with the red 6 would then have to match the value of the pot and everyone would be getting a new hand of cards to play for that new pot.

"Sometimes the number flipped up is higher than all the player's cards. Then, all the players who said they were in the game lose, and they must equal the pot. When a wolf turns up as the card to beat in the middle, everyone who said they would play loses, and we often howl like wolves, especially if we don't equal that pot. We just play for single coins, but as the night goes on, we might up the stakes if we feel like we can afford it. Let's play."

Corbyn liked the game right away. Placing a gold coin in the center, he received his four cards. A tavern maid dressed in bright yellow brought his drink and a strange cup made of bread. Corbyn tossed his hand in the center to say he wouldn't be playing this round and picked up the bread cup.

"Thank you, Daisy. What do we have here?" Corbyn asked.

Andren chuckled and tossed one of his gold coins to Dan. The grenadier wasn't laughing as he handed over his gold coin.

Dan acted the good host and explained the bread cup. "I told you my cook is a genius. Its bread shaped in the form of a tankard. He hollows out the center and fills it with the soup of the day. In honor of your coming tonight, I had him make white bean soup. I remembered it was the only soup you ever liked from the mess cooks of the regiment back in our days serving together. With this bread tankard, we can eat to our hearts content and still hold our hand of cards. What do you think?"

Corbyn took a big sip of the thick soup. The white beans had that same meaty tang Corbyn re-membered enjoying as a child long ago. He loved the taste and the invention of putting it into a bread-shaped container. He knew if he left it too long, the soup would soak through, but that would never happen with a hungry man, and he was very hungry.

"It's brilliant," Corbyn answered. "I don't know what you're paying your cook, but he needs a raise."

"Done," Dan replied. "If I win tonight, that's what he's getting."

Corbyn was in soldier-heaven as the game progressed. Well-fed, in the middle of pleasant company, and with a game he was just starting to learn, he couldn't ask for more and enjoyed himself more than he had in a long time.

This new game intrigued him like no game he'd played before. Red Wolf had a mathematical style to it that Corbyn quickly picked up on. If he had a white wolf, he knew he had a twenty-five percent chance of winning the pot. With a white wolf and a red wolf card in his hand, he had a fifty percent chance of winning the hand. Hands with several high-number cards in different colors were strong hands and worth a risk. Even a hand with one wolf card was worth a risk when no one else was playing the hand against him.

Corbyn looked at his current hand to see a black wolf, red wolf, a blue 10, and a white 9. He finished biting through the last of his soup cup. While he was still hungry, he was much more interested in playing the game than eating. Any distraction from the game lowered his chances of winning. His current hand had an eighty-four percent chance of beating everyone else. The pot was twelve gold, and he said he would play. Andren opted out with four low-number cards. Darren said he would play.

"Ah, your first real test of the night." Dan folded his hand and pointed at the two maids approaching the table. One was dressed in light purple, and the other in dark purple. One held deserts on her tray, and the other held cigars.

Corbyn didn't really want more food, but he was also enjoying the spirit of the serving maid naming game.

"Lilac," Corbyn smiled at both attractive females. "I'll take two of those wonderful-looking desserts. Violet, I don't want one of those fine-smelling cigars, but let me buy one for each of my friends.

"Right, and right again!" Dan was very pleased with himself.

Andren, still smiling, handed over two coins. "Remind me to never again underestimate the cavalry and especially this fine Captain of the King's lancers."

"This is getting a little old." Darren showed his ill humor at losing his ninth and tenth coins of the night to Corbyn's correct guesses. "Up until this night, I had been the best guesser in this little game of our Major's. You are showing a remarkable talent for flowers, that's rare in a real fighting man. Thank you for the cigar."

Corbyn caught the taunt the Dragon was making. He chose not to take offense at the slight suggesting he wasn't an able fighting man. The stinging words would make beating this infantry Captain all the sweeter in this and future hands.

Dragon showed his cards. He stayed in with a

black 10, white 10, blue wolf, and a red 4. It was a strong hand.

The card turned up was a white wolf. They had both lost. Andren and Dan began howling in pleasure. Startled, Corbyn joined in the fun with his own howl. Darren didn't howl as he poured in his twelve gold coins. The pot was now 36 gold, and the four men each had a new chance at trying to win it.

Two ladies dressed in white came to the table. One of the ladies was short with long white hair. The other was very tall with short red hair. Both displayed a great deal of the same pleasant cleavage Corbyn had been admiring all night.

Dan whispered in the tall one's ear as the others waited for Corbyn to figure out their flower names, even when both were the exact same color.

Even Dragon was smiling at this test, clearly thinking, from his expression, that Corbyn would never be able to solve this feminine puzzle.

"I'm assuming there are no two ladies with the same name?" Corbyn asked.

"You would be correct, sir," Andren, having too much fun at Corbyn's puzzlement, burst forth with that clue.

Dan also seemed inordinately pleased at the growing puzzled expression on Corbyn's face. "These are the wolf maids. When they hear howling, they come to the table to see if the sportsmen need anything, including a little bit of comfort. When the pot is large, like this one, they also provide free drinks on the house."

The red head moved to kiss Darren, as she could see he lost. He would have none of it and pushed her away with one hand. Her pout touched Corbyn's heart, as he wouldn't have minded kissing her at all.

The blond came up to Corbyn and kissed him full on the mouth. He tasted and appreciated the mint she'd placed on her tongue. He enjoyed the attention greatly but remembered a certain female elf. The memory of that experience, although pleasant, caused him to politely refuse further advances.

"Well, it's an interesting and puzzling pair you have before me, Dan," Corbyn told his friend. "I'm able to notice, after looking past their clearly exposed charms, that they are wearing the exact same color, and I don't think there is a flower named white. I must assume since you are a careful man, that their size might have something to do with their names. Lily, run and get me some more spring water, please."

The redhead gasped in pleasant surprise when directly addressed by Corbyn and went to do as ordered.

"Well, that leaves this likely lass." Corbyn put his arm around the blond maid and took her in his lap, once again noting her small size. The other three men were holding their breath, waiting for his guess.

"At first, I wanted to call you Carnation," Corbyn noted. "That wouldn't take your size into account. Here is a gold piece for Lily and one for you; now go on with you, Baby's Breath."

The serving maid clapped her hands with glee at the coins and the correct guess. Giving him another quick kiss, she left as Andren and Dan pounded the table in pleasure at Corbyn's cleverness. The two Captains paid up once again.

More hands passed back and forth. Suddenly, a murmur of surprise flowed from one end of the room to the other. Dragon saw her first. Then Dan and Andren looked up and grew quiet. Corbyn tossed in his hand and turned to see a green vision.

She was a King's ranger. Their uniforms were quite distinctive. This one wore forest green. In the winter, they all wore white. The tight military cut of the supple leather armor couldn't hide the generous figure underneath. The leather of the uniform glistened with magic. Rangers were an elite fighting force skilled at moving through any type of forest. The empire's Ranger's claimed they could match the elves for woods skills.

She moved much like a lioness through the crowd, displaying power and assurance with every step. The leather armor didn't hide her muscle tone. Her thick arms and legs perfectly balanced a muscled torso, speaking of great strength and displaying perfect curves. Ignoring everyone and everything until she reached their table, she threw down a messenger tube; the seals on both ends declared it a message straight from the King's hands. She stood stiffly at attention.

"Ranger Red Slash reporting to the fortress commander. Sir!"

"At ease, Ranger, pull up a chair and join us," Dan ordered. "Why didn't the watch Commander take care of you at the fort?"

She pulled up a chair and rested easy in it; Slash went from strict military posture to an attractive lounging position. "The King and Commander Arrow told me only to report to you, sir. I've been riding hard behind a Captain Cauldron and his troop. I've orders to assist him in any way I can. I've missed him every step of the way so far. I'm hoping he isn't far ahead of me now. With your permission, I'd like to get some more supplies and be off quickly after him tonight."

Major Stonewall scanned the orders from the leather scroll tube and noted the King's seals on the document. "I really don't think that's going to be necessary, Ranger," Dan said. "My lucky, flower-identifying friend over there is your Captain Cauldron." Dan handed the orders over to Corbyn.

All branches of the military had their pride. Rangers were proud of their skill in the forests. For the last twenty years, a great deal of the wars of the empire played out in border woods. For some reason unknown to Dan, Corbyn had always been one to scoff at Rangers and their ways. Rangers made

Corbyn bristle, for no reason Dan could understand. The thought of the King sending a Ranger to help Corbyn was amusing to Dan, knowing his friend's attitude about such people. The fact that this Red Slash was an outstandingly good-looking woman would make observing Corbyn's unease even more enjoyable for the Major.

Unknown to the others at the table, the orders and the Ranger uniform were fake, but they were the best imitations gold, and the assassin's cult could buy. She sat up straighter in her chair, taking note of Corbyn for the first time. Boldly, she held out her hand to shake his. "It's a pleasure to meet you, sir. I hope I can be of service to you."

Still reading the orders, he shook her hand and noted the calluses. Those marked her as an expert dagger thrower with long practice in the art. There were also hand creases telling him she was good with a sword. All these details presented unremarkable traits for a Ranger in the King's Scouts. One crease along the small finger on her right hand bothered him, as he couldn't identify its cause. Corbyn knew it was significant and that he would remember its cause with more thought, but right then, he just couldn't place it.

"These orders say you're attached to my troop by order of the King," Corbyn noted. "They also say you're an expert in elfin ways. Does Commander Janon know you've been assigned to me?"

"I don't have the slightest idea, Captain," the Ranger replied. "Ranger Commander Arrow put those orders in my hands and told me to get going. I've been on the gallop ever since. You and your men have been moving amazingly fast, sir. I'm impressed."

"*Talen thunon, onburrow apt soloton.*" In high elf, Corbyn asked her how well she knew the elves.

In high elf right back at him, but with a vicious accent, she answered. "*Cralenshaw soon all undun.*"

"I hope I know enough to get by," was the translation of her words.

"We leave an hour before first light tomorrow," Corbyn advised. You can retire to the Ranger barracks at the fort or stay and eat here your choice. Be ready to leave with my troop. I'm sure the good Major can get you any supplies you might need."

Dan tried to be both a proper commander and a good host. "We can feed you here, or you can bed down after your hard journey. What do you wish?"

"I'll eat here if it pleases Captain Cauldron," she replied.

"Carry on, Ranger. I wouldn't stop my worst enemy from eating a good meal before a deadly mission." Everyone noticed the irritation in Cauldron's voice.

Pleased with what he was hearing, Captain Dragon ordered food and drink for the Ranger. "How long have you been in the King's service, Ranger Slash?"

She shed some of her leather travel armor to reveal a fulsome figure barely hidden under her silk combat blouse.

Pleased to see the silk shirt, Corbyn knew from its presence that she planned ahead for the danger of combat with elves and their arrows. She was scoring high marks for being a capable Ranger. Catching up to his troops from the capital would have been a difficult thing at the pace they moved in the last few days. He'd been impressed with her elfin language skills as well. Nevertheless, he had never liked Rangers since his early days in the armies of the Empire. He tried hard to put his bias aside.

"Captain, I'm hoping I'll never be considered your worst enemy." Her sexy smile radiated warmth, turning on everyone at the table.

Dragon bristled as she clearly ignored him for the moment.

The maids in the room turned sulky at the sight of Ranger Slash. Each one knew they couldn't compete with a woman who was as sexy as they were and a fighter. The action at the tables resumed. The Ranger quickly picked up the rules of Red Wolf, and the game play began anew with the addition of her gold as well.

The hands of Red Wolf went back and forth for an hour, with each player winning a hand or two. Corbyn was thinking of calling it a night when a pungent scent reached his nose.

Dan spoke up. "I know you have to turn in soon, Corbyn, my old friend. I thought I would stand a round of Elfin Spring Wine to say how good it's been to see you once more. Old comrades in arms are seldom seen and very much appreciated."

The serving maid brought up a large pitcher of the heady wine and glasses for everyone. She was all dressed in black. Besides her pert figure, she had re-markable bedroom eyes. They were dark gray and very wide. She was a dark-skinned beauty. Dusky-col-ored people were very rare in the Empire. They only came from one portion of the Empire, far to the east and south. There were many myths about these peo-ple. Some said they were all fierce warriors. Others said the dark-skinned females could charm the heart right out of a man. Corbyn didn't believe anything he hadn't experienced himself.

He watched her serve the wine. Her hands were not the hands of a warrior. The satiny skin she showed was flawless, with no fighting scars. Her warm smile lit up the chamber brighter than any of the lanterns about the room.

An obviously irritated Dragon spoke up to break the mood set by the beauty. "Major, I'd like to up the stakes on this last guess if you please. He's done amazingly well all night, but this one is going to stump him. I'd like to wager a ruby dragon ring worth a thousand gold; he doesn't guess her name."

"He's been guessing the flower names of the

maids of the inn and doing a fine job," Adnren praised Corbyn. "All night long, he hasn't missed once. Considering all the tests put before him and their obvious distracting charms, Corbyn's done amazingly well. This dark-skinned beauty dressed in black is the last one of the lot. Our good Corbyn here won't be able to turn in until he drinks his wine and makes this last guess. I don't mind the larger wager if the good Major doesn't. I'll toss in a moonstone ring worth Dragon's wager."

Corbyn raised his hand, not wanting the night spoiled by these larger wagers. All the fun of the evening could be ruined by the boorish behavior of Dragon trying to get more than even.

The Ranger shook her head and pulled out an expensive pearl ring with an amber pearl-shaped counter stone set beside the pearl. "There are no black flowers found in nature. If the Major and the Captains don't mind, I'd like to be part of this wager as well. I don't think any man could make this guess."

They all picked up her ring and agreed it was worth the price of Corbyn's guess.

Corbyn looked at the Ranger, astounded by her boldness. Dan was a boon companion, but now the Ranger had made the game a personal test, and Corbyn wouldn't mind another chance to prove a Ranger wrong.

Dan held the three rings in his hand. "Corbyn, this is going to cost me a great deal if you guess wrong, but I still have faith in you, old son. I'll stand the wager and give a ring to each of these betters if you are wrong. Don't be wrong, old son. The Ranger's right; there are no black flowers, yet my lovely serving wench stands in front of you with a flower name you haven't used tonight. If you guess right, I'll be giving you this moonstone ring, as I know you are fond of that type of stone. I'll also toss in Dragon's ring as well as your part of the prize. I'm sure there is no one here boorish enough to think I won't pay off if he guesses wrong, is there?" The Major looked right at Captain Dragon when saying this, and the Captain had the good sense to shake his head no. "What's your guess, Corbyn?"

Corbyn sat with the glass of wine gently swirling in front of his nose, enjoying the bouquet of the vintage. He wasn't pleased that his friend was now standing a very large wager at a guess he was making. The Dragon fellow was wagering a great deal on this guess but wasn't risking a lot because of the difficulty of this puzzle, making the odds strongly against a correct guess. It would be very bad form to refuse to guess since all night Corbyn had been making correct guesses. He took a sip of the wine, realizing there was no graceful way out of this encounter. He set the glass down on the table.

Standing up, he moved to the dark-skinned serving maid. "Please permit me to be a bit boorish, but this is for high stakes."

"Of course, Captain. Do with me as you wish." Her sultry tone made it clear he could have her body later if that was his desire. He wouldn't be taking her up on her offer, but parts of him instantly became more than ready. He stood behind her, closing his eyes and taking in her scent. She wore a perfume he'd never smelled before. An expert on ladies' scents, he was intrigued.

"She comes from very far away," he said.

Filled with mirth, Captain Norval chuckled. "Oh really, who would have thought that from looking at her." His irony wasn't lost on anyone at the table or the large crowd developing around them as the news of the wager spread through the inn.

Corbyn's hands ran up and down her arms. The good Captain could feel her tense muscles. His hands went to her hips as he kept his eyes closed, letting his senses take her all in. Everything else around the pair forgotten; he totally concentrated on the puzzle in his hands.

Slowly, he caressed her hips, feeling the material of her dress as well as her womanly body. He noted the hot warmth of her being. Corbyn stalled for time, trying to think around all parts of this naming puzzle. His hands traveled up her waist, slowly moving to encircle her neck.

Corbyn's lips were near her ear, but he spoke for everyone to hear. He badly wanted to sense any reaction in her. "As the bold Ranger said, there are no black flowers found in nature, so this one must be named after some imaginary flower."

He could feel her pulse quicken under his fingers. Slowly, he stroked down the open front of her dress. He wasn't interested in her in a sexual way at that moment. Nevertheless, he was very interested in her quickening heartbeat. He opened his eyes and looked straight at Dan for any clues his old friend might reveal with his next words.

"She's black-skinned. Just as the lovely Baby's Breath was small, the color of this one's skin must be a clue. She is a black-skinned woman in a night black dress. There are few imaginary flowers talked about in song and story, and there's only one black one that I know of. To solve this puzzle, only part of the solution lies with this lovely serving maid. My good friend the Major over there, who names all his ladies, loves hearing bard's tales. Dan, you made every bard who even got close to our regiment spin their tales deep into the long nights when we served together."

The lovely serving maid took a quick breath. His hand half on her breast, he could easily feel her heart beating even faster. He had it, and she knew he'd solved the puzzle as well. Instead of going into territory that would be even more pleasant and stringing everyone along for a few more minutes, he lightly kissed her on the cheek and took his seat. He tossed her three gold pieces from his pool of winnings.

"Well?" They all said it at the same time as he downed his glass of wine.

"Black Orchid, please refill my glass."

The crowd, who already knew the answer, roared its approval.

"Drinks for everyone!" Dan bellowed out.

The Ranger leaned back, shaking her head. "Black Orchid, of course, famed in bard's tales for its magical nature, but not a real flower at all."

Dan relaxed, all smiles. He tossed the moonstone and ruby rings to Corbyn. The Major of the King's fortress had just won several years of pay with that one wager.

Andren tapped the table, acknowledging the cavalry Captain's cleverness.

Darren Dragon stood stiffly to attention. "I must attend to other duties, my Major." He left without a word to the rest.

Black Orchid filled his glass, and her eyes told him he could have other things if he wished them this night. He politely shook his head no.

The party broke up as the moon reached its fullest for the night. The carriage took them all back to the fort and a good night's rest.

10

DANGEROUS ARCANE MATTERS

"I have set my life upon a cast, and I will stand the hazard of the die."

— WILLIAM SHAKESPEARE

WIZARD'S CHAMBERS WERE DANGEROUS places to navigate in the best of times. Even the crudest of wizards could bespell their doors with life-threatening curses and their floors with deadly spells to attack the unwise intruder. Naturally, there were rules placed on wizards living in the palace of any empire so that simple King's messengers and various lords and ladies couldn't be turned into bats or blackened husks just for delivering a message or coming by to get their future told. Just as naturally, the more powerful and evil wizards generally ignored those rules. This wizard-caused condition led to few people wanting to be Palace messengers.

Disingen's chambers were in the furthest and deepest depths of the King's castle. Like most wizards, he didn't like company much unless that company turned useful as a sacrifice or was a cheerless undead companion. In the three years he'd been living there, at the permission of the court, he'd paid his tithes faithfully and never received a message from the King. This was a good thing for the palace messengers because they wouldn't have enjoyed the magics on the door to his chamber. Cursed and turned into an ant in the palace was never a good thing. Right now, the wizard wasn't thinking much of his door protections.

Disingen thought he'd go crazy in frustration from the orders of his master, the demon who controlled his heartstring. Nothing Disingen tried in his attempt to obey the commands of the nine-hells-blasted demon was working, and the powerful wizard, who wasn't used to failure of any type, paced with worry over the torture the demon would be inflicting.

Briskly moving about his spectral spell-casting chamber, Disingen muttered constantly to himself. "What's a poor wizard to do? I have power greater than most wizards in this dimension, yet I can't seem to kill or even find one mortal rider."

To prove his power to himself, he used massive amounts of magical energy to cast a spell he'd only used one other time in the last century. From memory, he repeated the ninety-seven arcane words of destruction and location. He forced his spectral hand into his crystal ball and through to a distant mountaintop a thousand miles away. The greatly enhanced hand proceeded to casually knock off the top of a random western mountain. For the first time that day, a grim smile filled his worry-ridden continence; he'd gained some personal satisfaction with his latest effort and its success. Withdrawing his hand from the crystal ball, he shook mountain dirt from it and went back to pacing, convinced he was still powerful.

––––––

Unknown to the wizard, Dwarves living peacefully under that now peakless western mountain became highly agitated as they noticed the top of their home vanishing in a mist of spectral power. The Dwarven Empire began taking instant action to find the mountain top destroyer. Dwarves, being the way dwarves were, every individual of the hundreds of thousands living there took such mountain bashing personally. The doom they planned for the culprit would take years to unfold. After all, it had taken millions of years for their favorite mountain to develop.

Dwarves not known for their magic tracking ability had world-class clerics serving deities who loved and cherished them. Those deities, at that exact second, were casting about for the fiend who crushed their worshiper's mountain. Spectral magic was rare and left many different types of indicators of who cast such a spell. There would be an accounting, even if it took a thousand years to accomplish.

———

Back at the palace, Disingen felt much better after his little display of pique. True, it did sap most of his magical energy for at least a week, but he proved to himself that he was still as powerful as he thought he was. He mulled over the mystery of this Captain of the King's cavalry. "What's the good of power if I can't use it? Nothing's worked right since I started this task. My storms haven't stopped Cauldron. My road curses seem not to have cursed anyone but the ones I sent after that fool cavalryman. I paid the elves to work their magics and kill this puny mortal, and all they seem to want to do is dance with him. Those same tree-hugging bastards have tried to take the eyes from my head for my trouble! How wrong is that? I must ask myself."

Looking into his crystal ball, it showed only his

reflection. He chided himself for being spectrally foolish, remembering he'd just cast a mountain-crushing spell through it. The spectrally enchanted orb wouldn't be ready to use again until he made the proper undead sacrifice over the top of it. He made a mental note to capture a few vampires this evening so he would have spares ready if he needed them. It was never a good idea to be without proper communication and viewing devices. "Damn, what's a master spectral wizard to do?"

Turning, he noticed the smirking form of Rothal. The wizard shut up then, knowing he was ranting in front of the blasted assassin.

Briefly, Disingen considered killing his new-found guardian. The presence of Rothal, knowing there was a chance the assassin might try to kill him, made the spectral wizard uneasy. Mind you, Disingen didn't think there was a chance in this or any other world that an assassin could kill him. That's what heartstrings and other spells of protection were for, but this Rothal fellow seemed unusually learned in magical ways. Disingen knew from experience there was always another way to perform a spell if one thought long and hard about it.

The little wizard stood still for a moment, really concentrating on killing the assassin. Disingen noticed the dull mirrors that were almost unnoticeable on the killer's shirt cuffs. Spells would bounce off the assassin so that avenue was closed to the wizard. He could just order the Fetchin to do the work. *There couldn't be that many more assassins that the wizard would have to deal with after this one died could there?*

The wizard estimated the cult couldn't have more than five to twenty more members back wherever the cult called home. Call it thirty tops; surviving attacks from those numbers was very likely. Deep in thought, he started clicking his tongue in an odd nervous habit he didn't even know he had. He put away his own death thoughts for a bit. There still might be demon information he could get out of this one and Rothal's cult.

The wizard used his mystical senses to feel the two Fetchin on his shoulders. Magically controlled, those creatures had no choice but to protect the wizard. Disingen calmed down a bit with the comfort they gave him. *No,* he thought to himself as he began moving about the chamber again; *killing the assassin wasn't the best of ideas. The assassin did have his uses, having just recently brought over some highly instructive scrolls on demon freezing.*

The spectral wizard thought he would take a break from his killing Corbyn Cauldron labors and read more on the destruction of demons. While demonology wasn't his strong point, lately, he was becoming quite an expert on the topic if he did say so himself.

As the wizard fumed in his corner of the laboratory, Rothal, the Caliginous Assassin, stood in another corner of Disingen's chamber guarding and, at the same time, considering how to kill the wizard as the spell caster moved about his room. The assassin had already abandoned five death plans but mentally worked through four others as the wizard muttered to himself.

Rothal still hadn't given up the cold iron dagger to the heart plan. The concept was quick and easy, with lots of plusses for its directness. The only way it wouldn't work was if the wizard had placed his heart in a magic ring. Such a spell could easily be beyond the range of this wizard. Stabbing the heart was a tried-and-true method, sadly now thought old-fashioned by the current death cult and most of its 9,999 members, but Rothal considered himself a better workman for his classic methods. Other assassins might hire a golem to crush the wizard's skull or fill the wizard's rooms with poison gas. Shaking his head at those methods, he once again shifted his eyes and used his second sight. A minor wizard with certain natural skills, Rothal kept his arcane talents hidden from his assassin brothers. He didn't want his comrades in death thinking any less of him for his magical abilities.

Shaking his head at what he saw, he gave up the dagger plan. With his second sight, Rothal could barely make out two strange creatures resting invisibly on the wizard's shoulders. The assassin was fairly sure if he physically attacked the spectral wizard, those creatures would attack him back, and that would never do. It wasn't impossible to fight invisible opponents; after all, he practiced just that at the cult hall every Tuesday night with some old cronies of his, but it was twice-damned difficult. These creatures seemed to be mostly jaws with razor-sharp teeth. Rothal thought to himself that he really needed a refresher course on attacking and killing interdimensional creatures. His last course was three years ago, and one should never let important skills go fallow.

Disingen ranted on. "I've got to kill the demon. It's the only way to free myself. What to do? What to do?"

Rothal wasn't pleased about the demon and its control of the wizard. The assassin's cult had a "no-demon" policy. It was rule 666 in the assassin handbook. He had already passed the demon information on to the guild masters. Aliesha wasn't at the guild right now, but when she got back, he was sure his orders would allow him to mark the wizard for death; that was the hope, anyway. Contemplation of the doing-in part was the only thing putting a natural smile on his face. Once again, he took up considering plans six through ten. Rothal briefly wondered how long it would take him to acquire the fresh scent gland of a Nor skunk; such a gland became a vital component in every one of the death plans he contemplated.

The monastery of Arcania, nestled in the elfin forests, was peaceful once more.

After days of back-breaking work, in which the demons broke a surprising number of Arcanian friar and nun backs, the two demons were not happy with the end result of their labors. It was true; all but one of the members of the holy order were now highly intelligent zombies pleasantly dedicated to evil and darkness. Granted, some of them moved awkwardly now, having to work around some unusually broken backs, but on the plus side, each was at the beck-and-call of the two demons. It was also true the blinding glow cursing the monastery was removed from all but one chamber, the chamber they sat in front of, high atop the center tower. Ticking off in their minds what had been accomplished so far, there was a lot of very pleasant evil roaming about the now-cursed monastery. The pair could be proud of a job fairly well done.

Then they thought again about the door. The thoughts stopped being pleasant at that point.

The demon bellowed his rage and desperation, "For the love of your whorish goddess and the salvation of my dark god's tufted ears, stop caterwauling woman!"

The droning prayers of the abbey's head mistress floated, easily heard, through the inch's thick door.

Her prayers had been the same for two days. She didn't ask for salvation. She didn't ask for protection against the demons she felt outside her door with plans to rend her into pieces. She just asked for peace for her followers.

Sighing heavy sighs, Talonten and the Net demon sat on either side of the very bright door. The holy, glowing portal led to the inner sanctum of the monastery. Both demons were showing their true demonic forms, having dropped their horse and human appearance in the good fun of yesterday as they killed hundreds of monastery humans. Scaly black skin appeared shiny from their demonic perspiration. Two huge demonic bodies, normally rippling with strength, showed total exhaustion right now in every bend of their forms. Their body language displayed their sadness in their present plight. Each knew if they left this single human alive, she would spoil the trap set in the monastery to kill Corbyn Cauldron.

"Two days; who would have thought a little old human lady could hold out for two days!" snarled the fake lord.

The Net demon ducked for the twentieth time that day, responding to the anger of its current highly unreasonable master. A night and a day ago, the Nevil demon ordered it not to speak for any reason. Just before that order, Allen tried advising its master that the demons should attack the inner sanctum of the monastery first. Every demonic tactic tome the

Net demon had ever read about fighting holy humans detailed the need for inner sanctum attacking right at the top of the things to-do list. Those tomes and many other texts all agreed clever humans always tried to hide in their holy sanctums. Such sanctums were extremely difficult for demons to enter in the best of times. Holy places being the way they were, demonic strength and magic had little effect on them. All would have been well if his master had listened to Allen, but no, the tired creature thought to itself, *Nevil demons know everything.*

The much smaller Net demon liked to call itself Allen, a very undemonic name. Allen was the name of the first human the Net demon ate four hundred and ten years, seven months, and eleven days ago. In honor of that highly enjoyable occasion, the demon started calling itself Allen. The evil creature quite liked its distinctive name. Most other Net demons named themselves after demonic body parts and sometimes after demon waste. It might be small, but it had a human name, and that was something special and to be. . .

Two friar zombies came into view at the other end of the long corridor, facing the pair of demons, interrupting Allen's thoughts. They signaled Allen to come with them. On the first day of the attack, just after it was allowed to change from its horse shape to its true demonic form when Allen could still talk, the Net demon ordered all the zombies of the monastery to look for signs of battle and bring the Net demon to such places. Every time a splash of blood was found from some dashed head or ripped-off arm, Allen, with permission from Talonten, could clean up the mess any way it wanted. To Allen's way of thinking, licking up the blood had to be much more satisfying than sucking souls from humans like the big lummox of a Nevil demon seemed to like to do. Everything about the spirit of a human repelled the Net demon, but human blood tasted remarkably fine.

The Net demon and the two zombies walked to an out-of-the-way spot in the third tower of the monastery. Allen thought he had been this way several times before and was pleasantly surprised to see the mass of brains, skull bits, and blood on the floor. His long, forked tongue began working the tasty blood splatter, saving the brains until last, of course. The life history of the human came into Allen's mind, presenting increasingly more information with every lick of her blood. The Net demon could sense all the past days of this human and much more.

The human leaving this wonderful meal called itself Eleanor. Her life essence tasted great, and her spiritual memories told of her life and the Abbess cherishing her as a daughter. Now, there was a useful thought. The tomes on subverting humans were always talking about this love concept as a useful tool for demonkind. The little demon summoned the zombie formed from the death he was cleaning up.

The cleaning process had been necessary so that other humans coming to the blasted holy place wouldn't know a battle occurred here. It wasn't a trap for the cavalry and Cauldron if they saw smashed bodies all over the monastery. It wouldn't do at all for humans to know their danger until the zombies were ready to strike. Now the effort would be well worth it if kindly little Eleanor could be the key to ending their trials at this slut goddess' inner sanctuary.

The zombie Eleanor arrived in a bright new robe. The Net demon stripped off the heavy robe with a rip of his talon and inspected the zombie body. Eleanor stood immobile, waiting mental orders from the demon. Allen shook his huge demonic head, thinking to himself that he didn't like the undamaged look of the human female's body. Only the crushed back of her head marked her cause of death; everything else was perfect. *This will never do,* he thought. His talons cut several large slashes into the flesh of Eleanor. He wondered if he should break an arm or leg, but no—that could wait until he got the zombie back to his master. Hopefully, the big lug would like Allen's new plan.

Back at the inner sanctum portal, tired and as unhappy as a demon could possibly be, Talonten stood up on his sore hooves. He smacked a huge talon against the door, charring an already burned talon for the tenth time, happening every time demonic flesh touched holy wood. "Come on, old human. You know what's going to happen. Why don't you just let it happen?" The demon's taunts roared out, echoing in every tower of the monastery. Even the zombies milling about the place were embarrassed at the sound of desperation in the powerful Nevil demon's voice.

In irritation, the demon started pacing the hall. Talonten gave his heartstring two twists just to send numbing pain through the body of the stupid human wizard Disingen, hundreds of miles away. After all, if the fool had done his job properly in the first place, the demon wouldn't be standing in front of the painfully holy door of an idiot cult. The pain the demon knew he was causing to the human wizard didn't give any comfort at all. He had to get back to finding the human Corbyn Cauldron. "I've clearly spent too much time here. Also, though I'd never tell that imp of a Net demon, I should have come to these nine hells blasted chamber first before this stupid old witch of an abbess could close this door and drone on and on with prayers to her slut goddess, keeping the pair of us out."

Hearing footsteps, the Nevil demon looked up to see his servant throw down a naked human body at the far end of the hall. "What are you doing, larva idiot?"

The demon could sense the human body was a zombie. It couldn't help wondering why it was lying there naked and looking dead when it should be up and dressed in fresh robes. Talonten remembered ordering all the zombies to prepare for the possible coming of Corbyn and his troop. The Net demon waved for his attention and motioned to his mouth. Allen wanted to speak.

Talonten strode to the end of the corridor, hoping to get away from the noise of the prayers behind the blasted door. The effort did little to clear the painful buzzing in his skull. "All right, you can talk again. I had better not hear anything that displeases me, or there will be a zombie demon added to this mix of Arcania losers. What is it?"

Trying to appear humble, the Net demon whispered. "Great lord, most majestic of all demons, this tiny follower has an idea. You actually inspired this thought." The last bit was an attempt at not receiving another beating in the hopes praise would win some demonic favor points. "All you want is to kill the human in the chamber. I know it's a chamber we can't enter right now because of the actions of the human. However, I also know that she can leave it whenever she wants. We just have to make her want to leave. When she dies, we can continue our quest. It really doesn't matter to our quest if we despoil that final shrine or not. I have just the idea to make her die."

Ducking, the demon expected a talon to rip at his head, but there was now a puzzled look on the demonic, tusked face of his master.

"Go on, you little larva, tell me this plan of yours," the fake lord ordered.

The plan unfolded to the hearing of Talonten. He liked every single part of it. In fact, he was amazed at the cleverness of it. The Net demon appeared to be right; Talonten must have inspired this idea.

Taking a few minutes to set up the concept trap, both demons ended their new plan, standing painfully in front of the holy door.

"Old witch, you've won. I swear by your foolish white goddess that I'm leaving this place instantly, and if I ever come back to this monastery, Arcania may blast my body to cinders," the fake lord shouted.

Any goddess worth her salt would be aching at this very moment to blast the two despoiling demons. The goddess would be taking any chance to use divine power and the oaths of the demons would allow her to do just that if they ever came to the monastery again.

Allen spoke up as well, "I also swear by your goddess to leave instantly and never to return here, and if I do, I ask your miserable excuse for a deity to strike me dead as well."

The demons turned and quickly left, not knowing how fast the slut deity might decide to act against them.

Eight hours later, the prayers of Abbess Gwendolyn stopped, and she waited, resigned to her terrible fate. She naturally heard the binding oaths of the two demons outside the door and knew of the power of those oaths. Her goddess would indeed destroy the demons if they ever came back to this place. There was an Arcania blessed chance the two were done with their foul acts in the monastery. Maybe she could lead whoever survived their attacks and rebuild once more.

Opening the door, she saw Eleanor lying naked and broken at the end of the corridor. "Oh no, not Eleanor!"

Abbess Gwendolyn loved young Eleanor like her own daughter. She rushed to the side of the body, gasping in horror as she saw the bones sticking through the flesh on the young girl's legs. The poor nun's entire body displayed terrible bruises and talon rents. The Abbess spread her hands to cast spells of healing in the hopes of bringing life back to this poor young girl.

At that same moment, masses of zombies hiding in the corridors on either side of the wide hall rushed out to grab and tear at their former leader. Twenty talons ripped at the Abbess, sending her spirit up to her goddess, who waited with open arms.

———

Fifty miles away, back toward the human capital of Sanguine, Lord Cortwin of the Rill Lands reached out and patted the neck of his noble war steed. Both steed and man arcanely looked through the eyes of zombies devouring the flesh of the Abbess. With any demonic luck at all, Corbyn Cauldron would be receiving some of the same attention in a day or two. Zombies were always hungry, and the dark demonic gods they served once in a while answered even zombie prayers.

———

The city of Sanguine was a bustling human metropolis of almost a million souls. This didn't even count the thousands of individuals of other races filling out the ranks of workers and business-creatures needed to keep the sprawling cities' people fed, clothed, and watered.

At dawn every day, the gates of Sanguine opened to the throng of rural wagons and caravans of merchants waiting to enter the city with goods and supplies from all over the empire. As the sun sent its first light over the horizon, a large wagon, pulled by four work-horses, could be seen a mile down the road by anyone paying attention.

No one was paying attention.

Not even the gate guards, whose duty it was to watch for contraband, cared what a large wagon pulled by old workhorses might carry. Guards, whose duty it was to check wagons, were only interested in keeping away from the dung plastered all over the sides of this wagon. It smelled terrible in the hot rising sun. The Commander of the gate looked over the two young boys- *clearly farm hands guiding the wagon team- and* determined the farm vehicle must be of little or no consequence. After all, the Commander thought to himself--*if evil intent were meant, boys wouldn't be driving the wagon.*

The high-walled wagon rolled into the city, and people got out of the way of the large horses, as the beasts didn't look bright enough to not crush any passersby unwise enough to stay in their path.

No one questioned the wagon's drivers as the vehicle, and fifty other wagons much like it, but generally far less smelly, threaded their way down the wide streets of the city. The high vehicle had a tarp over the huge back box, so even the spectators on the upper floors of the city buildings couldn't tell what the contents of the wagon might be.

Secretive spells from gate wizards, hidden in the towers making up the wide gate, scanned the drivers, horses, and wagon, and the spells revealed simple people on a simple errand. Naturally, it is impossible to magically scan dwarves or dwarven horses. The wizards knew this, but their check wasn't for dwarves. Such humanoids were known to be squat, thick, and massively muscled. In a hundred years, the two dwarven teenagers driving the farm wagon would be massively muscled and wide, sporting huge red beards instead of the boyish clean faces they had now, and so would the four dwarf teenagers in the back of the wagon. Dwarves really didn't come into their size until they were much older, but humans didn't know or care about that. Maybe they should of, but today, six young dwarves were on a mission, and no human at the gates stopped them.

The wagon moved from street to street, with the two drivers never asking directions. Coming to the merchant's quarter of the city, one of the drivers hopped off the moving vehicle and silently walked to a large warehouse owned by a small merchant house with headquarters at the other end of the long merchant-lined street, two hundred yards away. Swiftly moving along the side of the warehouse, the young dwarf placed Tenda mushroom caps on seven different sections of the wooden warehouse wall. The caps stuck with a squishing noise. On the other side of the mushroom-covered wall were hundreds of bolts of cloth stored for future sale. In seconds, the air reacted with the enchanted mushroom caps and burst into bright flame. Glancing at a job well done, the young farm hand started running back to the wagon, all the while screaming, "Fire! Fire!"

As the shouts of fire reached the wagon, the vehicle came abreast of the front doors of the Tindel and Sons Merchant House. The Tindel's were the smallest merchant house in the city. Most merchants thought little of the Tindel family and its sales of cloth.

As people began coming out of merchant doors between the Tindel's and the warehouse fire, no one was paying any attention to the south end of the street. The tarp of the wagon flew up, and three handless assassin bodies erupted out of the wagon to land on the front doorstep of the Tindel merchant house. The driver of the wagon took special delight in throwing a leather sack on top of the bodies. The finely made black sack had the dwarven chop rune of the royal house of the dwarves of the North Mountains boldly burned into the leather. The young driver didn't think there was a chance in the world the humans of this city would know what that chop meant. Mainly, this was a gesture politely informing a certain assassin's cult that they needed to be more careful around dwarves.

Satisfied at a job very well done, the dwarf spy clicked the horses faster down the road as his brother remounted the wagon, and the warehouse burnt down to the ground. There was still work to do, as there were all sorts of supplies needing to be collected before they rode back to the inn.

At that exact instant, the wagon horses clopped their hooves on the cobblestones of the street above-- a thousand assassins practiced their craft in the well-lit caves below. Hundreds of daggers flew out at different types of targets, from horses to plate-mailed warriors. Garrotes flashed out to stone and wooden statues in fifty different poses so that the assassins could get used to garroting bent bodies, prone bodies, and bodies with hands up by their throats. Assassin-in-training climbers worked catacomb rock faces, and hundreds of others climbed dressed castle stonewalls built in other parts of the area. There were brick mansion walls of several different architectural styles as well, with each testing the abilities of the climbers. All of these perfect model walls represented real buildings somewhere above ground in the city. Darkness covered some of the walls, others were wet as if a rain soaked them, and even others had guards at the top throwing down blunted javelins at the climbers.

In another huge corner of the catacomb, a festive royal ball played itself out in an exact duplicate of the throne room of the palace far above the cavern. Hundreds of fake Earls, Barons, and Dukes and their ladies danced to the latest court music. Assassins all each had a mock kill assigned to them. These assassinations were supposed to happen so that others at the royal dance wouldn't be able to tell who committed the murder. An exact look-a-like for the King sat on the throne with his head turned sideways in irritation. This King was the leader of this practice and chided assassins for weapons he could see hidden under their ball gowns and courtly robes. The music played on.

At the center of the huge catacomb, ten-experienced daggermen moved through the thousand twists of the daggerman pattern. At this time of day, only experienced assassins with more than 100 kills could practice the twisting one thousand-move pattern of death. One man led the others. Each of the ten was a finely tuned killing machine, but they were all hard-pressed to keep up with their fit training leader.

Callum Darksoul moved cat-like through the 819th move of the thousand twists of the daggerman pattern. As second in command of the 9,999 assassins of the dark cult, he liked to move through the pattern in the early morning and at sunset on days when he wasn't working a mark. At thirty, there weren't any males in the organization who fought hand-to-hand combat as well as he did. Fighting, of course was only a small part of the arts of the assassin. If the death-dealing job was done right, there should be no need for battle with others around the body of the mark.

Two assassins dressed as Tindel cloth merchants ran into the catacomb. One carried a sack. They moved quickly to the center of the chamber and waited at attention for Callum.

Callum knew the pair was standing there. He was

aware of every person in the huge chamber. Currently, he has seven more twists of the pattern to finish. These last twists were each deadly attack moves. They were his favorite part. Years ago, he had purposely used each of these twists in the assassinations of very important lords in the city. Each day, as he went through this exercise, his mind reviewed those long-ago kills with a great deal of satisfaction. At the same time as he moved through his daily exercise, his assassin's mind constantly evaluated the catacomb. It didn't really matter to Callum what bad news these two were bringing to him. Bad news, it must be. Normally, those experienced and trusted assassins who posed as Tindel cloth merchants would never come down into the cult chambers. The greatest secret of the cult was the Tindel facade.

Ten voices shouted out, "Talka!" at the exact same time as they finished the pattern. Callum was the only one not covered in perspiration. He wasn't even breathing hard.

"Cloth merchant Anol, cloth merchant Stevens, what brings you to my dark lair on such a busy sales day?" Callum Darksoul knew these assassins and their real names. Darksoul chose to force them to remain in character as his way of telling them they had made a grave mistake in coming down in the catacombs and not asking others to send Callum to them.

Both men clearly showed their agitation in their body language.

Con-sun, as the head merchant of Tindel house, spoke for both. "Three bodies were thrown on our merchant house doorstep. They were assassins Aldersall, Tamer-alt, and Sorbell. I had their bodies quickly covered and taken to the shrine for spirit questioning. At the same time, as a diversion, our cloth warehouse is burning to the ground. The fire was not an accident."

Callum paced around the two, wanting them to be nervous. The three assassins mentioned were the ones sent to kill the wizard's mark, that Corbyn Cauldron fellow. Their deaths told of another failure in the attempt to kill Corbyn Cauldron. Aliesha had gone to supervise the killing of that man. Callum briefly wondered if she was dead as well. For the last five years, Callum Darksoul had wanted to lead his cult but had waited his time, learning from Aliesha. Maybe she had finally made the mistake Callum hoped for. Through his long years of service to her, he had always wished for the chance to permanently lead the cult. If she were dead, this Corbyn Cauldron would receive a reward and not die by the cult's hand.

"What's in the sack?" he asked the question softly.

Beral spilled out the six hands. Each hand had some strange type of marking in the palm. The same mark was on the expensive leather bag. Callum knew that mark from somewhere.

"I'm positive we've lost all the cloth in the warehouse. The fire was so intense the warehouse would be a total ruin in an hour. Nothing the firefighters can do will put it out," the cloth merchant explained.

Callum bent down to carefully inspect one of the hands. "Return to your store, gentle merchants. You know that nothing is so important that you should be breaking your cover. You have much to do in rebuilding your poor destroyed warehouse. Jakar, would you please bide a moment? All the rest of you return to your duties."

The two merchants left. Eight of the other men went to lead other assassins in their daily practice sessions. Callum tossed one of the hands and the sack to Jakar.

All the while, Callum was inspecting every aspect of the hand he held. He could tell the cut was at least three days old. He shook his head at that because the cult clerics would be getting nothing from the spirits of the dead bodies. Spirits always left their bodies going to the right hand of the cult's god within two days of their death.

The enchanted shadow-hiding rings were still on the fingers of three of the hands. Although the rings looked mundane, normal killers would surely have taken them off. The fact the rings were still on the hands was some sort of statement, as was the rune burnt into the flesh of each of the hands.

"Jakar, is that rune what I think it is?" the leader asked.

"I'm not sure what you are thinking, high assassin. But if you believe it to be a dwarven rune of the royal house of the dwarves, you would be correct." Jakar was the cult's only expert on things dwarven. In the thousand-year history of the cult, there had only been eleven attempts to kill dwarves. The King of the empire had ordered each of these. It was a little-known fact that only one of those eleven missions was successful. Naturally, the other failed ten resulted in the death of the King who ordered the assassinations. Dwarves seemed to be unusually hard to kill.

Callum thanked the dark god that dwarves lived very far away, or they did until now. "Is there anything else you can tell me about this rune?"

"Well, it can only be used by some royal head of a dwarven clan. It's a symbol of their family authority. Normally, the chop appears on treaties and state papers. The fact that it's been pressed into this bag and those hands and that the bodies were thrown on the doorstep of our supposedly secret entrance is highly significant."

"Why is that, Jakar?" the leader asked, already knowing the answer to his question but wanting to see if Jakar was as smart as everyone thought.

"Well, it's impossible to tell without asking the dwarf, but there are things we can tell from the actions of today. The fact that the royal chop, they call them chops, not runes, was used on this bag says the royal dwarf didn't consider the matter very significant. They didn't consider the matter significant because the chop appears on perishable objects. If they thought the matter serious, the chop would have appeared on stone or metal. So, I don't think dwarves will attack the cult any time soon. Now, if they would have put the hands in a stone case, that would. . ."

"Please, just tell me what you know about the chop," the leader said, growing tired of the conversation.

"Yes, of course," Jakar answered. "The fact that the chop marks the hands of our assassins is important. It is supposed to say to us that if we interfere in dwarven matters again, this severing of the hands will happen to all of us."

"Is this a dwarven declaration of war?" Darksoul asked.

"No, I'm sorry to say, they don't think we are important enough for such a declaration," the lesser assassin answered a bit timidly. "Then there is the throwing of the bodies on our doorstep. That last is telling us they know where we live and can strike at us at any time but have chosen not to. That's all I know for sure."

"Jakar, that's a lot. As always, I'm impressed with the depth of your knowledge. Don a Tindel house uniform and talk to our contacts in the stonemason's guild. I would have our new warehouse built of northern stone, maybe even from dwarven quarries. We will be sending a large contingent of our followers that way on a little exploration mission. I know dwarves seem difficult to kill, but warnings need to go both ways. Let's study our strong little friends for a year or two, shall we?"

"Your word is law, master Darksoul." Jakar bowed and left.

Many new thoughts flowed through the master's mind. He'd just finished two hours of grueling exercise. As he thought about the new developments, his body began anew, the first twist of a thousand twists. All the while, Callum thought of the possibilities if Aliesha was dead, if Corbyn Cauldron wasn't dead, if a certain wizard needed killing now or later, and if dwarves should be allowed to think so little of the greatest assassin's cult in the world. Yes, much needed thinking on.

———

Miles from SouthSword fortress, to the west at the edges of elfin lands, the human military road ended in a large open glen. Years ago, huge trees filled this area, and now only ugly stumps covered the ground for several hundred yards around the road edge. Brush of all types had grown in the area. Humans and elves had left this part of the forest to do as the vegetation wished.

Well-hidden deeper in the forest, reaver horses slept. Those beasts enjoyed many hours of cropping succulent grasses. Their front hooves held cavalry-style hobbles, slowing their movement to a crawl.

Standing on the very edge of the military road, Ash reviewed his actions of the last day. He hadn't left guards to watch the forest. He knew elves wouldn't be bothering him, and his men needed all the rest they could get. Ash planned to stay awake, all the while moving up and down the ambush point. He'd be able to warn his men if trouble came.

They'd followed the lancer troops and kept well away from the fortress. Ash's experience with the empire's infantry allowed him to predict where other infantry might be hiding. They didn't run into the hidden troops at the top of the fortress valley.

Ash saw the strangely dressed trooper mirror-signaling the fortress. No doubt, the trooper was informing the fortress of Cauldron's arrival. His reavers moved at the edge of the woods and rode past the fortress. From his years of experience in the army, Ash knew all military roads going into enemy territory held several bivouac areas along their way. Knowing Corbyn and his men would be heading out at sunrise or earlier the next day; Ash positioned his troops at the end of the military road in the forest to the east of the fortress. His men were well-fed and sleeping at their posts. There would be no action until the early morning. Ash's trap was fool proof. For the tenth time that night, he brushed the feather amulet, allowing he and his men to move through the edges of elfin territory with the permission of the day elves. There would be no stopping him now.

"Ahem."

Ash spun toward the voice, knowing he and his men were going to die.

Glowing in the darkness was the elf Ash had seen talking to Cauldron several days ago. Ash faced the same dark elf that twisted his quarterstaff and left him helpless. A luminescent purple mist wreathed the elf's body from head to foot.

"That amulet you wear doesn't work for all elves," the elf lord sighed. "We thought our words to you were painfully clear. You really shouldn't have followed Corbyn Cauldron and his men."

Ash screamed at the top of his voice, "Alarm!"

"Noble. Your race has its noble elements," said the elf, slowly coming toward Ash. "We can't imagine doing what you just did. Knowing you are as good as dead, you still tried to save your men. Let's look at those brave reavers of yours through magical eyes." Lord Cimmerian Nix lightly tossed out purple spores over the head of the reaver leader.

Ash blinked, and the darkness turned brighter. He could see everything in a purple haze. Elves stood over the bodies of all his men, bloody knives in their hands. They were moving the bodies of his men out of their ambush points and throwing the dead on their stomachs.

"We briefly thought of burying the men, but then our dueling partner couldn't see all the work we went through on his behalf. In the best of elfin worlds, those bodies would be rotting in the ground on their bellies, with their spirits never seeing the light of day again. But this isn't a gift for me; it's a gift for Captain Corbyn Cauldron of the King's Own 25th Lancers." The elf bent over double in laughter with tears running down its long, elfin face.

Ash struggled to move, to do anything.

"Oh, sorry," the elf exclaimed. "We were lost in the moment for just a heartbeat. Please let us continue; as a present, you should really know how you serve the needs of the Fey court. You and all of your dead men are a special gift we are giving to Captain Cauldron. You might not care about that, but you might care to know how you stand, frozen in place. The silver mirrors you humans wear are effective against elfin spells. There are, of course, many styles of magics that aren't spells. The spores holding you in place right now are just such an enchantment. Our dear mother, who doesn't like us much right now, more is the pity, taught our royal selves the use of them as we sat on her bended knee ages and ages ago."

Lord Cimmerian Nix walked around Ash,

looking him over from head to toe. "Well, that's nei-ther here nor there. It's our plan to make you a gift to our close friend, Corbyn Cauldron. We've found him a wonderful fellow of many talents."

Laughing again, the elf stroked the now frozen cheek of the reaver. "Captain Cauldron has already given us a fine gift, though he didn't know he did. Nevertheless, the spirit and the letter of the dance have been preserved. Now, it is our intention to give you and your unmoving reavers as our first gift back to him. We know you aren't splendid. We realize we could have done better given more time, but the forms must also be observed. He presented his gift to us, and we must quickly give a gift back. Let's you and our court bide here for a while until the good Captain rides up. We are willing to wager he arrives before the sun does. Oh, that's right, you can't speak for a while. That's all right, we'll assume you want to wager with us."

Blind terror filled Ash to his soul; he couldn't move. His body turned toward the west, and the night was lit up in his frozen eyes.

11

THE FORTRESS BEFORE DAWN

"One of the secrets of life is not to avoid gambling, but to do it with skill while enjoying whatever fate deals you."

— LORD ANWARDENTINE

NINETEEN SOLDIERS QUIETLY WORKED THEIR horses, preparing them for the day's hard ride ahead. Sergeant Wise finished working his horse an hour ago. It fell to him to watch the others at their task. He walked among the men, giving advice and waking them up a little more in this early hour. "It wouldn't do at all to have one of my fine lads fall on his ass with a broken cinch now, would it troops?"

"No, Sergeant," the nineteen men all mumbled together.

"This old Sergeant can't quite hear the mumbling going on in the King's stables. Cinches Checked?"

"Yes, Sergeant!" The shout from the nineteen throats was adequately loud as nineteen hands went to check their cinches. Two of the men had to tighten theirs quite a bit.

"Weapon's checked?" Sergeant Wise was in rare good form that morning. He actually looked forward to the ride into enemy territory, where several thousand elves had a good chance of using him for target practice.

No matter what the men were doing at the time, from brushing their mounts to looking at horseshoes, they stopped what they were doing. Each drew their horse saber, checking the blade and the sheath. Each then inspected their lance, checking the fitting of the lance head to the shaft and then checking the shaft for nicks or other weaknesses. Private Stone shouted, "Checked and double-checked, Sergeant," but all the others followed with their confirmation that their weapons were ready for battle.

The night before, the horse handlers of the fort had looked at horseshoes and the condition of each horse's withers. This didn't matter a bit to men whose lives depended on the quality of their mounts. The troopers only relied on their own observations on their mounts. Hoof checking started the process; every piece of horse tack received inspection before it went on the mount and was double-checked after settling on the animal.

Every pair of men inspected the single remount they were assigned and the supplies those horses carried. The ten remounts of the troop were just as important as every man was to the success of the company.

Seeing the work finished, Wise took a small barrel out of the hay. "Get your tin cups out, my fine fellows; we'll be drinking to lady luck this morning." He began pouring out the rum, quite against the regulations. Rum issues to the men happened legally in the evening, but they'd come in too late for the fort's nightly ration.

"I know most of you missed your ration last night. What's the good of being a Sergeant, I says to myself, if you can't ask a few old friends for a helping hand? This little toast to lady luck is from the Sergeants of the seventh regiment of infantry, with their compliments."

"What are you drinking to this morning, Sergeant?" Corbyn entered the stables with his usual energy. He was expecting his troop to be ready early and smiled to see his expectations fulfilled.

"Ten shun!" Wise shouted to the rest. All stood ramrod straight at the order of their Sergeant.

"As you were men, as you were." Corbyn went to his black stallion. A quick check told him Wise had done his usual good work on the mount.

Wise kept pouring, but his body hid the barrel from his Captain's eyes. "We're just drinking a little of the fort's well water to lady luck, as it were, Sar."

As the last of the men got their cups filled, Corbyn reached over and took the almost empty barrel from Wise. "Where's your cup, Sergeant?"

Wise knew he was in trouble. Two other times, he'd lost his rank for drinking on duty. He offered his Captain his tin cup, figuring he might as well get a good drink for his effort before the Captain was forced to bust him down to private again.

Loud enough for everyone to hear, Corbyn said, "Boys, our Sergeant here has gotten the darkest well water I've ever seen. As he wants us to drink to lady luck, and she was with me last night, we won't comment further on the vintage of this water. To lady luck!"

Corbyn took a big swig of the rum, finished what was in the barrel, and tossed it in the hay. Sputtering, the Captain moved to his horse. "They make mighty smooth water in these empire forts."

"That they do, Sar, that they do," said the happy Wise.

"Mount up!" Twenty-one boots hit twenty-one stirrups at the same time. Corbyn and his men mounted in the large stable and rode their mounts into the still-dark parade ground. Standing in the middle of the area was Major Stonewall.

The troop rode up to the Major, and the Captain and his men saluted the Commander of the fort.

The Major saluted back. He went up to the mounted Corbyn and shook his hand, speaking softly so only Corbyn could hear. "Don't think these elves you're facing today are the peaceful types. You're on a fool's errand, but a King's Commission is a King's Commission and not to be questioned by King's soldiers. Such things can make a man or break him into little parts. You make sure all your parts make it back to the fort."

"That's my intention, Major. Thank you for the thought, sir," Corbyn said, saluting once more.

"Since I don't see the Ranger with you," the Major quipped, "I'm guessing her lily-white ass is still in bed. I'll boot her awake sometime soon and send her off after you. I won't hurry with that effort, knowing how you feel about Rangers and all."

"Once again, the Major has proven why he should have command of the King's troops. Dan, I hope to see you in two or three days," Corbyn said, releasing his salute.

"If the gods be willing and the creek don't rise, I hope you're right, old son," Dan said, saluting back.

Corbyn and his men rode out of the fortress,

heading to the east on the military road. The stars of the night sky provided plenty of light.

Riding at a brisk trot out of the fortress valley, the men were all pleased as a large white owl flew across their path. All the troopers touched their foreheads and whispered, "Luck to me."

Such owls were signs of great fortune, and Corbyn's men were used to lots of owls following and marking their trails. Wise and the Captain traded glances of pure pleasure. This day would be a good one; the owl sign assured them of that. Troopers of every army had their luck signs. Some liked crossing running water before the sun was at high noon. Others liked to see red birds before a battle. Some generals kept white owls as pets and flew them on the mornings before a battle. The wild owl flying free in front of them was good news for everyone that day, and they all knew it. There weren't many beneficial signs of luck, but white owls were at the top of most everyone's list.

Two miles down the road, a lone figure appeared up ahead in the mists of the forest. Corbyn didn't stop the troop as he watched the Ranger Slash turn to match his pace at the head of the Captain's lancers. She'd obviously ridden out ahead of them, as Rangers are wont to do.

"I've scouted the road five miles ahead and found nothing unusual. The Rangers of the fort tell me that the road only goes ten miles into the forest and then stops at the edge of elf territory, Sir."

She added this last as an afterthought and excessively late to Corbyn's thinking. Rangers were all alike, no matter how pretty this one appeared to be.

"No more scouting unless I order it," Corbyn barked. "You're a support troop by order of the King, and I decide how you support my troop."

Red Slash tensed at Corbyn's harsh words. "Understood, sir; I'm at your every service, sir."

Corbyn's face twisted in confusion by her words and tone of voice—*she couldn't be trying to seduce me, could she?* He'd just dressed her down and tried to put her in her place. Her words were militarily correct, but there was the barest suggestion of sexuality in them if Corbyn understood what he was hearing. He ignored her as they rode on.

They'd ridden through the last of the night, almost the ten miles to the end of the road. With a raised fist, Corbyn stopped the troop. He made a chopping motion with the same hand to the left and right. The two columns of ten men became two lines of five men across the road. Corbyn's hand signal caused his men to take their lances out of saddle holsters. The men readied their weapons for a charge.

"Ranger, you move that impressive steed on my right. It wouldn't do for a King's Ranger to get in the way of lancers at the charge if you get my meaning." Sergeant Wise gave the instruction with a light tone, but the Ranger got the message and moved to the new position. Her short bow was out and strung as she moved. She knocked an arrow and guided her horse with her feet.

Snap!

Corbyn used his magical abilities to cause a body, not fifty yards ahead, along the edge of the road, to glow with a soft white light. A broken bow suddenly gleamed with what appeared to be moon light.

The men of the troop were all experienced soldiers of several elf wars. They recognized the signature killing by an elf when they saw one. Elves, with time on their hands, would break the bows of those they killed. An elf-killed body was always placed face down. This was so the light of the sun couldn't shine on the dead man's face. Elves deeply resented humans using the primary elf weapon of choice.

Far ahead, in the distance, they all saw the barest hint of a purple glow.

"Lord Cimmerian Nix," Corbyn muttered to himself as he waved his troopers into a canter. There was no way he and his men could go around. The elf lord was dueling with Corbyn, and the cavalry Captain knew what he now faced was the next step in the duel. The purple glow could only mean the royal elf was going to give Corbyn his first gift, no matter if the Captain wanted it or not. To refuse the gift would get the entire might of the fey elves down on Corbyn and his men. This dilemma called for boldness. Corbyn knew his puny group of men wouldn't effectively charge into a large force of elves. He just wanted to make his own statement of bravery. Besides, he thought to himself, there's nothing like a good charge of lancers to stiffen a trooper's spine. All his men needed to be brave in front of this new and deadly threat.

Riding on, in a charge of thundering horses, the squad passed more bodies of reavers and their broken bows. Corbyn and his men knew if the dead archers had loosed their arrows at his troops, he and his men would all have been dead.

Corbyn's hand signals stopped the troops. Another signal ordered them quiet and told them to sheath their weapons. Clouds of dust rose up as the horses slammed to a halt.

Not fifty yards away, a man stood wrapped in a purple glamour. A tall man, dressed in typical reaver's clothes, Corbyn noted the military mirrors on the cuffs and shoes of the man. The purple spell lighting the captured man up became magnified and brighter by those mirrors. Corbyn was more than impressed, as he didn't have the control to do that type of magic.

Off the road, among a large patch of brush, was the real source of the purple glow. Sitting on a throne of vegetation, Fey elf Cimmerian Nix smiled his royal smile. Corbyn couldn't help but be impressed. Few mortals had ever lived to see a vegetation throne. Corbyn, in his youth, had seen many of them. The plants and the brush of the forest would sometimes magically recognize the power and royal nature of an elf. When this happened, the branches of the brush and trees of the area would mold themselves into a regal throne for the elf's pleasure and use. Such manifestations were a sign of nature's respect, and only the most royal of elves gained this effort on nature's part. Nix was clearly as powerful as Corbyn suspected.

"My fine-looking Ranger, put away your bow as the good Captain ordered." Nix never stopped smiling, looking into her eyes with an air of cold command.

Corbyn turned on his horse to see the Ranger aiming a shot at Nix. Wise would handle the matter, but Corbyn needed to show Red Slash just how much trouble they were in. Raising moon magic, he snapped his fingers, spreading magical energies out into the forest.

Over a thousand elves came alight in moon colored glows, even though there was no moon in the sky. In every direction, members of the Fey elf court revealed themselves. Just seconds ago, they were invisible to human eyes. Hundreds of the elves had drawn bows. Others held magical rods and staves of obvious power.

Many of the elves gasped at their appearance to the humans. The illusionary spells they used to hide their forms weren't supposed to be subject to human anti-spells. Some canceled out Corbyn's effect instantly with magic of their own, but most couldn't remove the glow and wouldn't be able to until the sun's light touched their bodies.

His troopers and the Ranger saw the desperate situation they were in. Red Slash unstrung her bow.

"Marvelous, simply wonderful. You never fail to amuse us." Cimmerian Nix rocked back and forth on his purple throne, roaring in glee. "Please, my good Captain, approach us and receive our first gift to you."

Corbyn dismounted and ordered his mount to stand still. Many things ran through his mind. He knew he couldn't outright attack this Fey elf. There were thousands of elves all around their position. Corbyn wouldn't have minded the risk of trying to rush past a section of the attacking elves, but he doubted his small troop would survive such a charge. No, he would have to play this out and get these elves to leave. His elfin heritage told him he couldn't get a brooch from one of these elves. They gave up their brooches when they left high elf society. He knew they would be gone at daybreak, and false dawn was just a few minutes away. He graciously bowed low, lowering his eyes to the ground in respect for his royal foe.

"My gracious Lord Nix, you surprise me."

"We surprise you, sir?"

"Yes, I only gave you my first gift mere days ago." Corbyn still shuddered at the trickery causing him to present the Fey elves with his child, but he wasn't about to mention any of that. "I thought maybe you would allow the gift to develop a tad before replying back."

"Oh, that wouldn't do, wouldn't do at all. You impress us, and so, too, we must strive to impress as well. Toward that impressing end, we present the leader of an insignificant band of reavers. We don't know its name; we believe it's called cinders or dust or something like that. Being human, no one cares what the monkey creature calls itself. What is important and what we believe is the true worth of the gift appears on display down the trail. The seventy-five dead followers you see royally presented for your inspection along this less than quaint road were put there at no little effort by myself."

At the direction of Nix, Corbyn looked back down the road. He could see his band of very nervous troops. Lining the road for several hundred yards were the bodies of many men. Corbyn didn't bother to count them. He was sure there were seventy-five.

"They wished to kill you and yours," Nix said, smiling in obvious glee. "We believe they would have been entirely successful at killing you and yours. It's our hope you will agree and accept our humble gift for what it is. No less than your life, which we know doesn't mean a great deal to you but means much to us now that we have started this dance. Are you pleased?"

Corbyn ticked off in his mind all the possible responses and results. Not being pleased would anger the elf; they would fight, and his men would die. Not taking the gift would anger the elf with the same result. Belittling the gift and the elf must end in the same result. As he saw the situation, there was only one possible response.

"Lord Nix, your gift far outshines my own humble first effort." The Captain bowed low once more. Corbyn noticed the first rays of the eastern sun peeking through the trees. "I can see my second gift to you will take a great deal of thought and planning. Even though I'm a humble Captain in the King's cavalry, I must do my best to surpass this astounding effort of yours."

"Excellent, excellent. We await your pleasure. Enjoy our gift." The throne and the elf faded into the ground.

Corbyn knew this last act of magic was a deadly peril for the SouthSword fortress. A magical fade like the one he'd just witnessed meant there was a faerie mound nearby. He'd heard of the mounds of the Fey elves but had never seen one. That's why the forest easily bent to the elf's will and made him his throne. If the Fey elf ruler lived in that faerie mound, that and not the power of the fortress were the reasons there hadn't been battles in this area in years. The news of the mound and its importance would have to get back to Dan if Corbyn could manage to survive the task ahead.

"Sergeant, you and Donont see if you can rouse the reaver. We've got to get some information from him before we can proceed."

"Sar, yes, Sar. Shall I make a burial detail?" Wise asked.

Corbyn sighed, knowing he couldn't bury the dead men. "David, each of these dead bodies is a gift to me from the Fey elf Cimmerian Nix. Anyone who touches those bodies besides me in the next twenty-four hours dies. I don't have the time to personally bury them and complete this King's Commission. We will leave them and press on."

In the next half hour, trooper Donont used all his clerical spells and knowledge and couldn't get the reaver unfrozen.

Wise tried some of the smelling salts of the medic kit and a few hard slaps, and that didn't do anything.

The reaver was now lying on the ground in the stiff position with his arms and legs unbending from when he was standing.

Corbyn had his men set up a quick camp. He ordered them to boil water for tea.

The Ranger moved beside Corbyn. Keeping the proper military distance, there was something seductive about her stance. "Captain Corbyn, permission to speak."

"Ranger Slash, while we are on duty together, you should feel free to speak to any of us as needed. What do you want?" Corbyn snarled.

"I want many things, most of them I can't have at the moment," Slash smiled in response to Corbyn's anger.

She looked at Corbyn with laughing eyes. She was making him uncomfortable. He briefly wondered if she knew what she was doing to him.

"I would like to try and help your Sergeant revive the reaver if that's acceptable to you," she said.

"Revive away, Ranger," Corbyn replied. "If you have any other skills useful to the troop, be sure and tell me about those as well."

"I have many skills, and the use of each one of them is entirely in your hands," she said, almost purring.

She swayed away from him. Once again, her words were correct for the situation, but the intent was seductive. She had to know Corbyn didn't like Rangers. He'd done nothing to try to entice her. Yet there she was making every man in the unit, watching her walk away, want to throw her down on the ground and enjoy her obvious charms.

Ranger Slash went down on her knees beside the reaver. She looked his entire body over. Getting close to his face, her nostrils flared as she took in his scent. She made a grimace as if smelling something bad.

"Ranger," Wise laughed at her facial expression. "I know he hasn't taken a bath in a few days, but I didn't think he smelled that bad."

She looked up at the Sergeant. Batting her eyes, she smiled prettily for Wise. "Sergeant, would you bring me over a bucket of the hot water the men are preparing on the campfire? There's something I want to try."

"Right away, Ranger Slash, right away." He went to get a collapsible leather bucket, and he personally filled it with hot water from several cooking pots. He handed it to the Ranger.

"I think I'm smelling the extract of a mushroom on the reaver's eyes," she said. "The fungus only grows in the deepest regions of certain caves. If I'm right, the hot water should do the trick."

She took the bucket of hot water and dashed it in the man's face.

He sat up, clearly unfrozen and sputtering from the water down his windpipe.

Obvious to all, Ranger Slash wasn't just a pretty face.

Corbyn and Wise had already noted the silver mirrors on the man. Those showed the robber had some type of military training. The dead men all had mirrors on as well. The broken bows came from military storehouses.

"Ranger Slash," Corbyn ordered. "Take five men and search the woods in that direction. With luck, you'll find the horses of this group. Bring the beasts back here. Try not to quarrel with elves if you find them."

"Yes, sir." She moved out with the men Wise assigned.

Hands roughly tied behind his back, Ash Greenwood was a broken man. He'd seen the death of all his brave band of reavers. His plans undone by a powerful elf; he hadn't even been able to attack this cavalry Captain once. He just wanted to die.

Corbyn sized the man in front of him up for what he was. There was much of the beaten dog in the man. "You've seen military service. I need military information from you. Will you talk?"

Ash was tired of it all. The normally bold man hated what fate had recently given him. "My name is Ash Greenwood. That's all you're getting from me. Just kill me and get it over with. I don't serve the foolish King anymore."

The man was pleading for death. If Corbyn didn't give him some hope, he wouldn't be getting any information from him. Unknown to Ash, Corbyn didn't know how the elf Nix would take the death of this man or his imprisonment. Normally, a reaver would go into the King's prison and serve hard labor until they died. Cimmerian Nix considered Ash Greenwood a royal gift. It was possible a new elf war could start, just from how the Greenwood fellow was treated. Corbyn couldn't take the chance.

"Stand up, act like a man." Corbyn forced himself to speak in a commanding voice, trying to make this deserter think past the death of his men. He cut the man's bonds.

In spite of himself, Ash stood up straight. A tall man, he was still a head shorter than Cauldron.

Corbyn continued in his commanding voice. "There'll be no talk of killing in my command. I'm on a King's Commission. You tell me what I need to know and willingly serve me for the completion of this commission. If you do this, I'll see you get a King's pardon for your efforts. As the King's Commissioner, I have the power of life or death with the voice of the King. You know that's true, don't you?"

Ash didn't believe what he was hearing.

Sergeant Wise used the back of his hand to smack the man across the face. "Fool! You never got the chance to kill my good Captain. Now answer his questions and save your fool neck from the headman's axe, where it could be in a day's time if the Captain doesn't like what he hears from you."

"Who wanted me dead?" Cauldron asked.

"It was a wizard," Ash replied.

Wise raised his hand again but didn't strike.

"I don't know the damned spell caster's name," the reaver blurted out. "He was a spectral wizard. I could tell that by the way he ported into and away from camp. He used ghosts to help him with his magic. I was paid ten gold bars to find Captain Corbyn Cauldron on his King's Commission and kill him. I was then to get ten more bars of gold. I wish, by all the gods, I'd never laid eyes on the little bastard.

"I scouted your camp the first night you left the capital. I saw you talking to that elf, and he warned me not to follow you. I didn't pay heed to the warning." Ash sobbed this last at the thought of all his brave men dead.

Wise looked at his Captain. The Sergeant was surprised Corbyn hadn't told him about the elf's first visit.

"Your troop escaped two other ambushes I set up," Ash went on. "I thought this one was foolproof until the elves killed my men."

"How did you get a token of Arn from the elves?" Corbyn looked at the magical amulet on the right shoulder of Greenwood.

"It's a long story," Ashe replied. "I did something to save a few captured elves. They appreciated it and let my reavers and me camp in their borderlands. Let me live, and I give you my word you won't regret it. I'll help you in this commission, whatever it is, for the chance of seeing that dark elf die on your sword."

"Don't trust him, Captain. He's a reaver and a bad un if you ask me." Wise didn't like the look of the man, and no one appreciated a deserter from the King's armies.

Corbyn knew the elf magic of the token of Arn was making Corbyn like Ash. Elves were supposed to find it impossible to resist the wearer of the token. It was a rare gift, and Greenwood must have done something very special to merit the token. Such a human wearing such a token could help Corbyn on his mission.

"Ash Greenwood," Corbyn put out his hand. "If you do what you're told and bide with my men and me through the completion of this commission of mine, I'll see you a pardoned man, free to do as you will. Do I have your word on your helping me?" Greenwood took it, and the look on his face spoke volumes. The heavy weight of guilt and the fate waiting for him as a deserter lifted from his shoulders; he would live and be free. "I swear I will do what I can to help you and yours until this commission is over. I won't be going back to the capital with you if I'm truly to be free."

"That's not necessary," Corbyn said. "Just stay by my side and follow my orders, understood?"

"Yes sir, understood."

Wise wasn't pleased but took his Captain's parole of the man for granted. If the Captain wanted this reaver free, he had his reasons. "Follow me, Greenwood; I'll introduce you to the men. The Ranger and the others will be bringing in your equipment. You'll be expected to follow my orders as well as the Captains."

"Yes, Sergeant, I've followed many orders from Sergeants in my day." The man's voice was sarcastic.

"Sergeant," Corbyn said.

"Sar."

"Break out my personal colors and have Cleric Donont display them on the march."

"Yes, Sar!" Wise shook his head at the order. Personal colors were a very rare thing for an officer to order displayed. Regimental colors everyone understood. The colors showed friend and foe alike and lessoned confusion in the swirl of battle. The flags also rallied troops in the heat of the conflict. Regiments were very protective of their colors and it was the greatest of sins to lose them in the action of battle. The 25th Lancers had their proud colors, and a great many battle ribbons flew from those flags. Corbyn's current small troop of twenty men was too small a detail to carry their regimental colors. Only a full command would fly them as they moved into battle. Several generals from old military houses would fly house battle colors as they marched into battle. Wise knew Corbyn to be the only officer with the rank of Captain to fly his own war banner. It wasn't against the rules, but it was highly unusual.

"Private Donont, front and center," Wise bellowed!

"Sergeant," Private Donont was also the troop's cleric.

"Unfurl the Captain's colors and post yourself at the head of the column when on the march."

"Yes, Sergeant," Donont replied.

The men of the 25th Lancers were very superstitious about their Captain's colors. Donont took the battle flag out of its special sheath and went to the east end of the camp. When the flag was unfurled, it was always to be on the side of camp in the direction where the enemy was supposed to be waiting.

Five years ago, as Corbyn became the Captain of the lancers, he'd presented Wise, then a private, with this battle flag. Wise now watched Donont roll out the flag with the proper military method.

The black cloth of the flag never ripped, burned, or got wet. No one had the courage to ask the Captain where he got it. As the flag unfurled, the white unicorn emblem appeared with a full moon over the head of the unicorn. In the five years Wise knew his Captain, this flag had only been

unfurled three other times. In each of those times, the regiment of lancers had little chance of surviving their next battle. In every one of those times, they faced and overcame incredible odds. The bearer of the flag was supposed to go into action using the flag as their lance. Blood stained the spear shaft at the top of the banner. Corbyn had given specific orders never to clean or sharpen that lance head. The flag itself was never stained with the blood the spear generated in the heat of battle.

Private Kaledon came up to Donont, all smiles. "I love to see that banner unfurling."

"Are you daft, man?" Donont's hands shook as he holstered the unfurled banner on his mount and moved the horse to the edge of camp. "This thing means we're riding into deadly peril. How can you like it?"

"Deadly peril, you say cleric. We're ridding into elf lands with twenty men. There were thousands of elves, just a minute ago, wanting to fill us with arrows or turn us into toads for their pleasure. Moreover, mind you, that was when we didn't have this grand banner flapping in the wind. No, this banner means we have a chance now. You weren't at the other battles where it flew. Every mother's son of us knows when this banner flies at the Captain's side, the Captain is serious about the death he plans to bring to the battle. It's the symbol of his house. He might not act like a royal or show royal airs, but there's something majestic about our good Captain. He's very king-like, don't you know. You're holding his honor done as a battle flag. Mark my words, my fine cleric. I pity the poor elf facing my Captain with that banner flying. I don't care if it's the great King of the elves and ten thousand more behind him; our chances of living have gone up several notches, and don't you be forgetting it."

Wise listened to Kaledon's little boast. The Sergeant agreed with every word. Wise knew a little more about the magic in that banner. Flying it now was special to his Captain, and it made Wise very proud to be serving his officer.

Minutes later, seventy-five horses and their reaver's gear walked into the camp. Corbyn really wanted the Ranger and another man to take them back to the fort. That many mounts were an important resource. Corbyn could tell most of them were cavalry horses. Sending the Ranger off wouldn't be the most political thing he could do, as her orders came from the King. Corbyn also knew that numbers of men weren't important to this commission. He could just as easily get this mission done, if it was accomplishable at all, with ten men as twenty.

"Sergeant Wise, have privates Jelston and Gateway take these mounts back to the fortress. Have them also inform the Major that he has a faerie mound somewhere in the area to deal with. The Major will know what to do from there. Allow Greenwood the time to pick out his horse and a remount."

"Yes, Sar," Wise answered.

"Good job, Ranger Slash," Corbyn said.

"They were right were you expected them to be, sir," Slash answered back. "Would you mind telling me how you know Fey elf royalty?"

"It's an unfortunately long and boring story," Corbyn replied.

"I have as many nights as you do for the telling," Slash smiled back.

Corbyn turned away from her and started checking his horse. She was doing it again. He didn't like Rangers in general. This one was being deliberately provocative. "Maybe later if we survive this little commission. Wise, mount up the rest of the troop."

"Sar, yes, Sar!"

12

COURT OF THE HIGH ELVES IN ARN

"When rolling dice with the gods, try to remember to use your own dice as god dice are always loaded."

— CLERIC DONONT

DEEP IN A FOREST WITH TREES PURPOSELY planted when the world was young lay the heartlands of the elfin nation. The elves nurtured the life in the wilds as no other race on the planet. The elemental forces of nature loved the elfin race in turn and nurtured them as the elves worshiped and supported everything of nature.

The court of the high elves presented a grand spectacle to court officials and ambassadors from other lands and dimensions. Thousand-year-old trees were encouraged to grow their limbs and trunks, forming the architectural marvels that were the walls and arched domes of the elf palace chambers. Every wall of the many miles-long structure was alive. Talking oaks supported arched chambers decorated with constantly blooming roses and beneficial herbs. Giant walking trees stood guard at the palace gates and in the throne room as well as the King and Queen Chambers. Deadly poisoned vines wrapped themselves prettily around many of the doors, able to strike killing thorns into elf enemies, but choosing to present delightfully pleasant blooms to elves and their friends. Naturally, flowing brooks and springs watered the palace. Flowers not seen anywhere else in the world grew on the walls of bedchambers and presented healing and comforting scents to the sleepers there.

Ambassadors from many different races, including centaurs, pixies, and merfolk to cloud giants, andols, and spritefolk, all greatly enjoyed their dealings with the elves and their official positions at the palace. A peaceful relation with other nations was a hallmark of the elfin monarchy. Their allies were in awe of the temperate actions of the elves, considering the recent invasions of the humans into elf territory. All outside races thought the elves could easily destroy the human race but had hesitated for unknown reasons of their own.

A million elves lived, ate, and loved within the confines of the palace. Most of the forest of Arn, the oldest forest in the world, made up the grounds of this majestic center of power. In all the uncounted thousands of years of history surrounding the elfin kingdom, no human had ever set eyes on their capital. One pair of half-elf, half-human eyes had lived there for a short time, and the court was still reeling from that indiscretion.

The first rays of the sun's dawn light saw the King and Queen on their throne and the happy court assembled around them. King Aik, at 1,238 years of age, ruled in the prime of elf life. Eight feet tall, he was unusually broad-shouldered for an elf. The Aik elf clan produced many large elf males, and their skill with military weapons was legendary. A competent spell caster, his lovely Queen showed real talent for spell use. Queen Arn gained fame in her early years as a highly innovative wizardress. Skilled in the summoning of all manner of demons and devils, her greatest talent allowed her to work with all things of water. Her ocean conclaves brought intelligent sea creatures to her call every winter. In the time of her joint rule, she pacified the sea trolls and water giants due to her efforts in understanding their needs. The queen's ability to heal with water magics made her beloved by all at the court. She naturally favored very unelf-like blues in her daily garments, and at 998 years of age, her stately beauty was as renowned as was her gentle kindness to all her happy subjects.

This day, the entire court showed its happiness save for Queen Arn's only daughter. When the Princess entered the court that dawn, Aesc was once again dressed in the white gown of sadness. She wore this traditional gown of mourning for a loved one she thought out of her life forever. Everyone at court felt her pain, and her mourning touched most, as court lords and ladies knew the cause of her despair. She sat beside her parents, as was tradition. Usually, she presented herself as the perfect daughter; there was only one indiscretion marking her life. Whisperers around the court were full of the talk of her departed son, the prince.

Lord Pharadon and Lord Tackeldon entered the court from the Arch of Dreams, both noted Aesc's dress.

Lord Pharadon ruled over the elves of the northern elf clan conclaves. As leader of the Pharadon clan, he would be expected to rule the elves if some accident claimed the lives of the royal household. Behind the scenes, he had been very disapproving of the birth and development of Prince Sawal. Although the tolerance for life was common to all elves, Lord Pharadon had been unusually vocal in his distaste of the Prince.

"What is our good princess mourning today?"

Tackeldon asked. "I've heard no news of a death in the royal family?"

Lord Pharadon found Tackeldon's need for court news to be a tad boorish. On the other hand, this news pleased Lord Pharadon more than he could say. "Oh, you hadn't heard, my dear cousin. It seems the Unicorn Lord, her son Prince Sawal, has entered elf lands and has had dealings with the Fey if you can believe that."

"No, you don't say," Tackeldon replied. "That's why she's in mourning. The Princesses bastard half-cast son has suddenly appeared after turning his back on his family. You don't think he's coming back to court, do you?"

"Oh my no, the Unicorn Lord's return to court can't be allowed. Many of my clan of Pharadon won't put up with that evil spawn ever setting foot in the palace again. If you'll recall, the Unicorn Lord rode with the humans in the minor skirmishes to the north at that ridiculous stone fortification of theirs," Lord Pharadon spoke in hushed tones. "It was my clan bearing the brunt of those less than enjoyable little prancings as the humans invaded clan territory. Several times, I almost faced the Prince in the heat of battle. With this new violation of tradition, I will take Prince Sawal's fate into my own hands."

"What can you possibly do? You know the King and Queen love their daughter. If Princess Aesc begged for her son's pardon, they couldn't refuse her." Lord Tackeldon found himself repelled by the hate his cousin was showing for the royal prince and, at the same time, attracted to the deadly words of Pharadon. Tackeldon looked around, making sure none of the talking oaks could hear their conversation. Other court elves politely kept their distance as the two appeared caught up in conversation, and it would never do for others to accidentally hear part of their talk.

Elves at court knew Lord Pharadon and his kin had been very unelf in their dislike of the Unicorn Lord while he was growing up at the palace. Traditionally, elves nurtured life, and the most prized of treasures were elf children. Princess Aesc, having a half-human child, displayed very poor form, but the court, bound by tradition and revering all life, recognized the half-elf, half-human baby as a Prince of the realm.

"Bah," Lord Pharadon became agitated at his cousin's words. "There is a simple way to end this farce of love for anything even partly human. The Princess has been in mourning for over a hundred years. I will seek to end her pain caused by the actions of her son. Tradition forced our hands when the Unicorn Lord grew as a dark changeling in this court. There are other traditions we can use to our advantage now that the devil spawn has grown and rejected his mother's race by going to live with humans."

Wrapping himself in an emerald green glow of

court enchantment, Lord Pharadon announced to the court that he would like a moment of the King's time. Others moved to the front of the court with the same glow. The traditions of ten thousand years allowed court elves to seek the attention of their King by marking themselves in a green glow. In his time, Lord Pharadon came to the attention of the King and approached the throne.

"It has been too long since you have been at court, Lord Pharadon," the King said warmly, viewing the respected elf. "We are most glad to see you and yours." The King stepped off his dais holding the arm and hand of Lord Pharadon. This gracious move on the part of the King allowed him to sense a note of tenseness in the body language and the muscles of Pharadon. When beings like the elves lived thousands of years, they learned words could be meaningless. The feel of a speaker, his body language, and even the firmness or lack of firmness in his muscles could speak volumes to one attuned to looking at the spirit behind a person's words. The King was an expert in noting such things and knew he wouldn't like what he was about to hear.

Lord Pharadon bowed, with his eyes downcast to his King. He knelt to the Queen as well, and she put her hand out and allowed the Lord to kiss her fingertips. Queen Arn didn't favor Pharadon and his clan, but she respected his courtly grace, and her hand let him know she appreciated his style.

His lips briefly and properly touched her fingers. He rose and stepped back to allow his words to flow over both of them.

"I came as soon as I heard the disturbing news, my King," Pharadon said.

"I know of no disturbing news; what do you refer to?" the King asked.

"The Unicorn Lord has stepped onto our lands. I would be your tool in this matter," Lord Pharadon replied.

Princess Aesc heard Pharadon's words, and tears filled her eyes, but she didn't allow herself to look up. At only six feet tall and four hundred years of age, the Princess was young in elf years and considered little more than a child. Long white hair twisted in a warrior maid's braid down her shoulder revealing to all who knew the signs that she had warrior skills. While her body was slim, she had the inner strength common to members of the Aik elf clan. Until she had her baby, she was the leader of the deadly elf moon maids. The moon maids were a mystical army of elf females used as the first line of attack in important battles on elf borders. Leading this unit was an earned right, and her mother and father were very proud of their daughter when she was able to gain the rank of leader of that unit. With the birth of her child, she resigned her commission, but elf traditions had her continue to dress and wear her hair in the warrior-maid fashion.

Considered one of the greatest beauties of the empire, she hadn't even thought of taking an elf husband or lover since her son left. The normally lively court was constantly looking for ways to make the sorrow-filled Princess happier. Since she was so young, many pardoned her for the terrible indiscretion of bearing a half-human child. Some, like Lord Pharadon pardoned the lovely Princess but wanted to end the life of the dark child she brought into the world.

The King knew of Pharadon's hate of the grandson their daughter brought to them. Queen and King had talked many nights over the fate of their grandson and were secretly relieved to see him away from court. Prince Sawal was two hundred years old when he left court to learn more about his father. The Prince had known then that he could never go back to the court of the elves. Considered little more than a boy when he left, he was safe from those at court who disliked him because of his age. He was now three hundred years old and, by the traditions of court could now be challenged by other elves as he was considered an adult now.

The King sat back on his throne, stiff in irritation. Knowing of Pharadon's dislike of tradition forced him to continue this conversation "What would you have the court do?"

"My King," Pharadon said bowing. "It's clear to me that the traditions must be observed. I think an ambassador from your court must stop the Unicorn Lord's movement further into the empire. Your court must know what your grandson wants to best judge how to act. Tradition dictates that any ambassador you might want to use not be of clan Aik in a matter where your grandson is involved. I offer my own humble services."

"My Lord, can't we let our grandson come to us?" The Queen spoke the words she knew her daughter wanted to say.

Princess Aesc kept her head down and her hands folded in her lap. She was always the humble daughter and knew her place. Her son had chosen to leave the empire over her objections when she wouldn't tell him the name of his father. In her heart, she had one spark of hope; she wouldn't voice that hope.

"Lord Pharadon, you have clearly thought deeply and wisely over this matter," the King saw the possibilities here and knew the true metal of Prince Sawal. "I will accord you full ambassador status. You do know what tradition dictates of you if I charge you with that post?"

"I am at the service of you and the empire," Pharadon replied. "I know my duty to you, my King. May I go and meet the Unicorn Lord as your ambassador?"

The King thought of all the alternatives. He didn't want the law of the land forcing him to kill his own grandson if the child foolishly rode into the city of the elves. Making Pharadon an ambassador would stay the ambassador's hand in most ways, so Prince Sawal wouldn't be in too much danger in a face-to-face meeting. After all this time, the King couldn't help wondering why the boy would come back. Elf tradition dictated that someone not related to the boy must meet him.

King Aik drew his troll killer sword. "Kneel, Lord Pharadon."

Pharadon went to one knee.

"I make you our ambassador, with full rights thereof. Go and do our duty and report back as soon as you may." The King touched his sword on the head of Pharadon and sheathed the weapon.

Lord Pharadon walked away without saying another word. All who looked could see a deadly sneer of glee on his face.

"My King, might you have acted in haste?" The Queen put out a hand to her beloved.

"Prince Sawal's appearance forces our action. You know he's fought against our kin in the north. I don't know what he's up to, but someone had to be sent, and the lad will not trust Lord Pharadon. Maybe he'll be cautious enough to survive the encounter. He's made his home with his human kin and must stand up for himself."

"He's just a boy. Boys make mistakes," the Queen pleaded in her tone.

"Yes, they do. Aesc, where are you going?" the King asked.

Seeing Lord Pharadon made an ambassador, the princess watched him leave the court. As he vanished through an arch, she rose and left as well. The Princess was of a different generation than her mother and father. Her mother's intuition told her Lord Pharadon meant to kill her son. Seeing cousin Dalbergia among the members of the court, she ignored her father's question and rushed to her cousin's side, asking him to walk with her away from the court.

In the garden of Hope, the two talked in low voices.

"My Lord Dalbergia, I would ask a favor of you." The normally shy Princess forced herself to be bold in the time of her son's need. "I don't know why my Sawal has come back, but I fear he's in great danger if Pharadon finds him. Would you go to my son and discover why he rides this way again? Maybe you can also find a way to help him?"

Lord Dalbergia loved Princess Aesc. His affection for her continued, even through the time when she walked the palace heavy with the child of a human male. He knew his love to be doomed as he wasn't of high enough station to wed her. This didn't stop him from standing as her champion. Lord Dalbergia couldn't refuse a request of his lady and they both knew that. Besides, he quite liked the young Prince and wished him well.

"Let me see what I can do," Dalbergia said. "We won't tell the King and Queen of this. Your father has already sent out the official emissary. Against tradition, I'll try to find the young Prince first, nature willing."

"Nature willing, my Lord." Princess Aesc knew Dalbergia loved her. She didn't feel worthy enough to allow herself to respond to that love. Her hope was that this clever elf, who was fond of her, could find some way to save her son. Deep in her heart, she held the slim desire for something more for her son but didn't dare utter it to anyone, even herself.

———

A day's ride past the edge of the military road, Corbyn and his men made their camp and spent an uneventful night. The Ranger woke unusually early and slipped from camp. Tense, she needed to work off some of her frustration. She moved past the guards, a very unRanger-like shadow in the night. Several hundred yards away, she stood in the middle of a vale, confident she'd escaped the notice of the guards.

Unknown to her, she had moved through several of Corbyn's magical wards.

Ranger Red Slash was angry with herself and her

situation, and her exercises worked off some of the anger she felt. She wore a thin, dark one-piece shift, not at all military issue. After thirty minutes of hard stretching and mock attacks, the silken shift was damp and clinging to her toned form. In the early morning predawn light, she didn't move through the thousand twists of the pattern she normally liked to follow, but she worked her assassin muscles as she thought about her mark. Aliesha had used her Red Slash guise many times before. King's Rangers could go into many places that normal citizens of the empire couldn't.

Her palm swept out and cracked apart a young sapling. The image of the Captain became that broken limb, and three other lightning quick strikes cracked the springy wood even more. Normally, the movements would have calmed her, but her thoughts were far from calm right then.

I can seduce almost every man in this camp; why does this mark have to hate Rangers? Moreover, what happened to the three assassins I sent ahead?

Her mind worked over the problem as her foot high-kicked into another sapling, bending it over double for a fraction of a second with the strength of her kick.

The reaver she couldn't seduce. He was dead inside from the shock of seeing his men slain at the hands of that Fey elf. That elf's arrival on the scene was the wizard at work; it had to be. Disingen must have somehow contacted those elves and paid them as well. The stupid wizard had three different attacks, at least, aimed at this Corbyn Cauldron, and so far, none of them had been successful. She would be ordering the spectral wizard's death when she got back to the capital. The Death God only knew what trouble Fey elves would be in her taking out her mark. Moreover, killing Captain Corbyn Cauldron was something she was reserving for herself if at all possible.

Somersaulting to her military cloak, she reached into its folds, drew two knives, and threw them perfectly into the center of the cracked tree, thirty feet away.

Clap! Clap! Clap!

She spun to see Cauldron standing behind her. *How long had he been there?*

She hid her anger at being found and tried one more time to seduce him. Briefly, she wondered if she should kill him at this instant, but was a bit afraid while the sun wasn't up that the Fey elf lord might be able to interfere. She gave him her best seductive smile and swayed her hips toward him. *If I can bed him, I'll poison him and be gone before his men even wake up.*

"That was an impressive display of the martial arts." Corbyn was barely able to ignore her seductive charms as he deliberately walked past her and inspected the sapling he had watched her destroy with her hands and feet. He didn't think he could have done the same. "Your exercises are very hard on the local plants, but I'm sure your opponents fare even less well than this tree when they stand rooted in front of your charms."

"Oh, I rather enjoy working with hard things. Hopefully, that doesn't displease you, my Captain?" She could see the answer to his pleasure growing as she asked the question.

"Ranger Slash, while I sympathize with your need to keep fit," Corbyn admonished. "I can't have you leaving the camp to exercise. You have become my responsibility. We will only be two or three days in the elf lands; suspend your activities until you get back to the fort."

She stood at attention, knowing full well how her body looked in the thin shift.

"All my activities, sir?"

"Quite. Get dressed Ranger. I'll stand guard while you do."

"I can see you are at the ready, sir. As you wish." Aliesha noted the stony look on the face of the Captain and knew her best seduction effort wasn't working. From the other men, she had heard of the Captain's interest in ladies. It was a total mystery why he wouldn't take her when she was offering, and he was clearly physically interested. She dressed and left the glen in a huff.

Corbyn hated Rangers. The entire lot of them claimed to know of elves but knew nothing of them, really. He pulled out the two nonmilitary throwing knives from the tree, noting the unusual depth of penetration of each blade into the hard wood. The Ranger was beautiful, but there was more too her than that. She was offering herself to him, and being a Ranger had stopped him from taking that offer in the beginning. As he looked at the damage she had done to the sapling with her bare feet and the unusually fine quality of the knives in his hand, he knew there was more stopping him than just her being a Ranger.

13

THE FOREST RECOGNIZES ITS OWN

"Love of battle is so universal and exciting that it must be evil."

— LORD ANWARDENTINE

THE PRINCE HAS COME BACK. THE OAKS rustled their summer branches, passing the word from tree to tree through the forests in a joyous abandon of clicking tree limbs and rustling leaves, as Corbyn Cauldron, also known to his elf mother as Prince Sawal, came into the elfin-controlled lands. The aura of the Prince was easy for any elf-nurtured life in the forest to sense as it was magically very strong, with a significant texture about it.

Magic innate to elves allowed them to sense the feelings and intelligence found in every plant and creature living in their forests. Elves spent a great deal of their lives enhancing the aura and energy of woodland vegetation and animal life, with wisdom exchanged both ways in the process. This life's work of the elves filled their lands with intelligence not found in other empires and made the elves stronger as well.

In the exchange, many of the older types of wildlife gained the aura-sensing ability of the elves. This allowed the forest to warmly recognize the magical life energies of the Prince and respond to his coming back to the land of the elves.

The Prince is back. Long live the Prince! The Challem vines and the Teka roses threw their scent messages onto the summer wind with hundreds of other flowers, proclaiming their happiness at the return of the High Elf Prince Sawal.

The forest along the path of Corbyn's troops, both in front and past their position, grew visibly thicker and filled with opening blooms. With the nearness of the Prince, plants seeded earlier than normal at a magical speed. Creatures of the forest went into heat faster than was usual, breeding and calling out their lust in chirps, howls, and roars. Enchanted creatures from other dimensions and other places in the woods all found the Elfin land the Prince traveled through, and other elves had long nurtured, better to lair in than their old dens, and moved to find homes along the Prince's path of travel.

Corbyn found himself growing increasingly uneasy by the forest's attention. His concern was for the Ranger noticing the growing forest changes and wondering at their cause. There were questions about his past and his elf nature that he didn't want to answer, and Rangers were the first to ask these questions from his past experiences with them. Corbyn knew if his human leaders discovered he was only half human, they would kill him for his elf heritage. It was a secret he'd been able to carefully guard for over a hundred years. Those closest around him knew he was oddly gifted, but there were many humans with strong magical gifts, and he was considered part of their number.

Songbirds in unusually large clusters twittered on branches along the trooper's trail.

That morning, when the fool Ranger broke through Corbyn's magical wards, he'd woken to a wreath of flowers having grown up in the night all around his bedroll.

The forest was becoming unusually pungent with fresh summer smells of flowers, spores, and other musky scents. All of those odors carried messages of joy on his return, and Corbyn's aura-sensing abilities took in the message. Although he was worried about the Ranger's reaction, Corbyn found it impossible to be unaffected by the happiness filling the air around him. *It was a pleasure to be coming back home, even for just a little while.*

"It's happening again, isn't it, Captain?" Sergeant Wise rode beside his Captain and grinned way too widely at Corbyn's uneasiness.

Corbyn could hide little from David Wise. In forming the 25th Lancers, Corbyn took special effort to fill the lancer ranks with city men, men not used to nature and its ways. In addition, all the lancers of this twenty-man troop, although picked because of their fighting skills, were also the sons of city merchants and had no forest skills. They didn't notice the change in the forest when Corbyn rode into elfin lands.

Corbyn looked back at Ranger Slash. She was smiling and chatting with Cleric Donont. The turn of her body and the fool grin on Donont's face seemed to show her tempting even the good cleric. *No surprise there; she's almost elfin lovely under those muscles of steel.*

Not wanting to respond to Wise's question, Cauldron issued his man an order. "Sergeant Wise, take my banner and go to the head of the column. Donont could use a rest at that duty if you please."

"Sar, yes, Sar!" Wise knew when he'd overstepped his bounds; he'd made the mistake of asking about the changes in the forest. *The Captain was touchy about the magical effect he had on woods in general.* It *really didn't matter. Some people just had certain magical talents and callings. His Captain was uncommonly talented with plants and animals.* Wise could remember many times when his Captain grained information from a forest creature or read amazing amounts of detail from forest paths telling him if the enemy had passed that way and in what numbers.

Turning his mount, Wise rode down the line of men to the middle of the column where Donont and Ranger Slash rode. He moved to Donont's left side and reached for the banner pole. "I'll be taking the banner, Private. You need a break from carrying our Captain's war standard in this stiff wind."

The breeze had picked up, and there was a great deal of moisture in the wind.

"The banner is impressive, Sergeant. Private Donont has been telling me of the banner and the good Captain." Ranger Slash purposely spoke in a husky, sultry tone of voice. She gave Sergeant Wise one of her best smiles.

"Ranger," Wise said. "I'm thinking you're chaffing a might under the Captain's orders. He has his ways and has never liked sending out scouting parties in elf lands. Repeatedly, we've seen good men die to elf arrows when they go riding off by themselves. Your arrival came as a surprise to us, as this task isn't one for Rangers and complex planning. This troop isn't an army with support troops bashing and slashing its way into enemy territory, bold as brass.

We're a lightning strike into elf lands, with us leaving just as quickly. It would be a shame to lose anyone on this King's Commission." He didn't give her a chance to answer as he took the banner pole from Donont. Kicking his own horse into a gallop, Wise moved along the line of men to the head of the column.

"Sergeant, let me join you." Ranger Slash rode on the other side of the column, up to where Wise stationed himself.

Sergeant Wise was of two minds about the Ranger. On one hand, he didn't share his Captain's extreme dislike of Rangers. He'd seen them do good work on and off the battlefield. He'd also never known his Captain to dislike anyone or anything without a damn good reason. As he respected his Captain above all men, he felt the need to take on his Captain's attitude toward Rangers no matter how good-looking they were.

Looking back, Sergeant Wise saw his Captain talking to the reaver, Ash.

"You don't have to worry about the reaver. He's a broken man, not like you, my big muscled Sergeant." Ranger Slash, in riding up to the front of the column with Wise, had positioned her bootleg to rub pleasantly against Wise's leg.

Her appaloosa stallion was as large as Wise's unusually big Talendon stallion, and neither horse liked the other. Both riders were masters of their mounts, however, and didn't allow any nipping or body jostling.

"When do you think it's going to rain? I've never minded getting wet in a summer storm; how about you, Sergeant?" Red Slash made it a point to pleasantly banter with all the men. She was trying to win friends quickly, knowing she wouldn't be with the unit for any length of time. Friends allowed her to move through the men and get them to do what she wanted in a future time of need.

"Hard telling in these elfin parts; this stiff breeze and the darkness from the clouds sure do suggest a storm," Wise said, looking up into the tree cover that completely hid the sky. "On the other hand, there's something about this standard I'm holding that might not let the storm happen. I've only seen this great bloody banner of the Captain's out four times in the five years I've been in this lancer regiment. Each time we fought under, it was a deadly battle where it looked grim for us, but every time it unfurls, the clouds clear in front of it, and we pull through the fight. In the last battle, we were in," Wise stopped when he saw the Ranger not paying him any attention and looking about. "What is it?"

"Nothing, I can tell for sure," the Ranger said, looking about. "The land here feels a bit odd. I suppose it's the touch of the elves in these woods. The Captain's banner is quite remarkable. Did you know the royal elf house uses a unicorn, much like the one on the Captain's banner, for the royal household standard? The royal elf house battle flag is white with a field of stars covering the banner, and the unicorn on that flag is black."

"Get away with you now," Wise said. "That war standard isn't anything like this banner. My Captain's flag is black, with the full moon above the unicorn. The unicorn on this flag is white. Even a daft man or Ranger can see there is nothing alike between this banner and that one."

"This daft Ranger thinks they're alike." Still smiling, she turned and rode back to Ash's position in the line. The reaver didn't even look at her as he rode with his shoulders slumped and his face grim. Corbyn, on the other side of the reaver, was ignoring her as well.

———

Lord Pharadon of the Ironwood forests checked his war equipment one last time as his squires readied his unicorn war stallion. The demon-handled sword at his hip had been a war weapon used in his family for five generations of Pharadons and was eighteen thousand years old. The demon lord trapped in the blade of the weapon still raged over its captivity, even after all its centuries of forced service. Pharadon had taken the time on several occasions to summon up the spirit of the demon out of the sword just to taunt it.

The elf Lord found creating more anger in the spirit trapped in the blade made it an even more effective weapon.

Elves were able to trap demons and other enchanted creatures into specially prepared magical objects. The life force of the creature gave the object enhanced magical energy and mystical properties. Pharadon greatly enjoyed contemplating the helpless nature of the demon every time he strapped on the sword.

"Attach the King's con to my back," Pharadon ordered.

A squire brought out the ambassadorial con and fixed it to a special brace at the back of his Lord's armor. "It's a shame you can't wear your house con on this mission, Lord."

Lord Pharadon looked at the rectangular banner over his head. Such cons were made of extremely light materials. The elf cons marked important individuals on battlefields or in processions. The placement of the con at the small of the back of the wearer kept their hands free, allowing the banner to rise up above and behind the wearer. Even on windy days, the light construction of the con banner wasn't a hindrance.

This con banner was emerald green with the black unicorn at its center. An oak tree image in the upper quarter of the rectangle proclaimed him a King's ambassador with all the rights and privileges of that office. The elf's face bunched up in a sneer at the thought of the King and House Aik. *The house of Aik is weak. Imagine letting human blood taint the line. When I get back from killing the stained prince, I really must further my plans for clan Pharadon's rising to its true importance in this the most glorious empire of the world.*

The Lord mounted his giant unicorn. He looked at his squire and other king's elves in the stable. "It's an honor to fly the King's banner. I'll meet with the Prince, find out what he needs, and then send him on his way. Attention to duty has always been clan Pharadon's way."

"Hail Lord Pharadon!" His squire was first to shout praise to his lord. As Pharadon moved from the stables to the street, more of his clan and others seeing his ambassador status picked up the chant. "Hail Lord Pharadon!" Their cries of support and praise filled the Lord's ears, and he found them pleasing. Although this was a personal vendetta on his part, life was even sweeter knowing others thought he was doing good works for the empire. He slowly moved through the palace grounds, enjoying the praise. After a few minutes, he snapped his fingers activating the magics of his mount's horseshoes and the enchantments in his saddle. Suddenly horse and rider became a blur of tremendous speed, elfin magic allowing them to move at a fantastic pace.

The forces of nature didn't praise the elf Lord.

The wildlife could sense the deadly intent of Lord Pharadon. The Lord could mask his feelings from other elves but not the wildlife of the forest. The magic innate in the wild things of the woods unconsciously caused dark clouds to move high in the sky over the elf. No matter what speed the elf moved, the sun's light along his path hid behind clouds full of nature's tears. The very earth under the giant hooves of his stallion turned soft and slowed down the speed of the unicorn. This was a minor act of defiance as the elf magic in Lord Pharadon's equipment allowed elf and unicorn to move in a blur of motion, but nature had its duty to its Prince, and that duty was carried out. Lord Pharadon rode on, not caring what nature or anyone else wished. In hours, he would find the Unicorn Lord and kill him. The fact that orders by the Unicorn Lord's grandfather allowed him to do this deed under the guise of royal authority tasted sweet on the tongue of the elf empire's newest ambassador.

———

Dim twilight filled the forest paths, even though it was high noon. Heavy wind battered forest and troopers alike. The men knew there must be dark rain clouds above their heads from the feel of the air, but the thick forest cover made it impossible to see the sky. The heaviness of the air and the strong, moist wind told the men they were going to get wet soon. The column of troopers moved forward uneasily as the forest paths became narrower and narrower. None of them had ever been this far into elf lands before.

"I'm not going to give that reaver my rain gear when it starts to pour," Private Eastland spoke his current fear to Private Cook.

In any given body of military men, there was always one complainer. Private Eastland was the grumbler of this troop; although he never had a good word for anyone, he was excellent in wielding his lance and displayed unusual courage on the battlefield. The Captain and the Sergeant could always tell him to shut up, but they kept him in the regiment because they liked how he fought.

"Are you daft man?" Cook asked. "Who told you to give up your gear? You're right about one thing it's going to rain any minute now." Private Cook partnered with Eastland on this trip. Also a somber man, he had a hard time understanding his troop mate's attitude.

"You and I both know what's going to happen," Cook whined. "It's going to rain, and the Captain is going to ask one of us to volunteer their rain gear for the reaver." Eastland hushed his tones so that only Private Cook could hear. "Then that great lump of a Sergeant is going to come up to me again and tell me I've volunteered my things. Suddenly, the blasted female will be warm and dry, and I'll be forced to use my ground cover to keep the rain off."

Ranger Slash rode up to the two. "Boys, when the Captain finally figures out we should be stopping for lunch, please sup with me. I haven't had the chance to talk to you yet and I like to learn more about the men I serve with."

Surprised at being asked to share their food with the lovely Ranger, both of them just nodded their heads like loons as she smiled at them and rode to the back of the column.

"Private Eastland, if that's what the Rangers are mustering out, I'm transferring to their ranks the second we get back," Cook sighed.

"Private Cook," Eastland snorted, "let's get back alive first. At least we have something to look forward to as we get wet."

"What's that?" Cook asked.

"I bet that Ranger looks even better wet than she does dry," Eastland snorted again.

Corbyn watched the Ranger shift position for the tenth time that morning. He knew she wanted to be scouting ahead and to the sides of the column. That wasn't going to happen under his watch. Looking at the laughing Privates Eastland and Cook, he did appreciate her lifting the spirits of the men. If he could have had it his way, he would have gone into elf lands without this troop behind him.

They came to an opening in the tree cover with a

large brook cutting through the forest. Corbyn raised his hand and ordered a halt to the column.

Sergeant Wise took his Captain's horse. "I'll order the rain gear out. Will we have time to cook some hot food; it'll do the men good if they have to ride in the rain this afternoon?"

"They can set up some cookfires. It's not going to rain today." Corbyn said this while dark clouds boiled overhead.

Wise looked up through the thin covering of trees and saw lightning spark through the wet-looking sky. Thunder roared, and bolts of lightning were cracking down into the land all around them. He did note that he didn't see the backs of the leaves in the trees as the wind shifted things around, but it sure did feel like it was going to rain. *If the Captain says it isn't going to rain, it isn't going to rain.*

"Place my banner in the center of that flat clearing over there and tell the men to set up their cook fires under the trees on the other side of this brook. I need them to keep clear of the banner. There could be a chance lightning will strike it."

"Sar, yes, Sir! Cook, Eastland, collect some fallen wood and make cook fires. Mind you, don't go cutting any limbs from these trees, they just might cut back. Ranger Slash, it's not going to rain. Put away your rain cloak and be kind enough to help with the preparing of the meal. Cleric Donont, you're on tether duty."

The men went about the making of their camp. Horses were watered and tethered, two large cook pots came out, and the Ranger was able to catch fish from the brook with her bare hands to add to the pot's contents.

An unusual amount of fish seemed to be swimming through that part of the stream, everyone remarked on it.

Corbyn kept away from the water, still uneasy with the effect he was having on the woods. Wildlife gathered to get a look at the Prince of the elves. Fish swarmed the stream; birds flocked the tree branches, and deer and bobcats came into view, nodded their respect, and bounded off.

Corbyn knew the cloudy weather was a warning for him alone. It wasn't going to rain because he was going to fight today, and nature's subtle efforts at helping him in the forest of the elves wouldn't let the ground under his feet become wet. Corbyn didn't know who his attacker or attackers would be, but he suspected an elfin patrol. His banner and the amulet of Arn on Greenwood's arm should be able to stop outright confrontation, but the nature-sent weather said otherwise.

Corbyn carefully went over the lay of the land around his banner. He moved in an ever-widening circle, looking for rocks or roots that could trip a man in battle.

"Help!" Wise screamed terror in his voice.

Corbyn and the other troopers came running to the Sergeant's call. Stopping, laughter filled the camp at the Sergeant's expense. There, at the edge of the brook, the good Sergeant was half in and half out of the shallow water as one arm and his legs struggled with thin, wet vines. The vines were trying their best to pull the Sergeant into the water. Straining his massive muscles, Wise was doing a good job of resisting as more and more thin vines came out of the water to grasp the arms and legs of the Sergeant.

"Stop laughing your heads off and give your Sergeant a hand!"

Corbyn knew his man was in no danger. The Gronal dragon vine was common in elf streams but didn't grow in the lands of humans. The water vine grabbed prey from the edge of streams and pulled it into the water. This time, the plant grabbed prey far too large for its pulling abilities. There wasn't a chance in the world the watery dragon vine could hurt David.

The Ranger deftly tossed fish guts into the maw of the plant. What looked like lily pads in the middle of the stream were actually a set of sucking maws. With tasty fish parts filling its mouths, the plant let Wise go. She helped him climb out of the mud.

Corbyn was impressed at the Ranger's trick; few knew the ways of the Gronal.

"You've saved my life, Ranger, and I thank you."

"She's saved the plant, more likely," Corbyn teased his Sergeant. "What were you doing?"

"I was checking the perimeter, as my Captain knows is my duty, when this bloody thing reached out and grabbed me." Sergeant Wise brushed away the fussing hands of the Ranger and scrapped together what dignity he could. "With the Captain's permission, I will finish my scanning of the forest."

"Carry on, Sergeant," Corbyn ordered. "Don't bother putting out guards. If the elves wanted us dead, they would have killed us by now."

"That's a pleasant thought; how can you be so sure of that?" The Ranger had given up her attempts at Captain seduction. She asked an honest question this time.

Coming back, Wise broke into the conversation of the pair. "Sar, there is a monastery dedicated to Arcania, the white goddess, several miles to the north and somewhere along this brook. Judging by the taste in the water, it hasn't been there more than a year or two. I just thought you should know Sar." He walked away, leaving the mystery of how he knew about the monastery for his Captain to solve himself. *The Captain wasn't the only one who could tell things on the wind and in the water.* Wise had found a broken wooden bowl with the holy symbol of Arcania on it. Such bowls appeared in monasteries dedicated to the goddess. Such a place had to be upstream, only a few miles away.

The breeze picked up strength, and the clouds grew even darker. Lightning strikes shook the land within just a few miles of the camp.

Ranger Slash raised her voice, making it heard over the wind. "Are you sure it isn't going to rain? The storm keeps growing in intensity."

Corbyn didn't need to raise his voice; knowing his half-elf ways allowed him to be heard when other voices lost their force in the noise of the storm. "It's not going to rain. We're going to have deadly company soon. Try to get something in your belly. We're going to need food and rest before this day is done." He turned to check the camp and once again ignored the Ranger.

In the next hour, Corbyn ate sparingly of the excellent stew of fish. He couldn't refuse the offering sent by nature to feed him, but he didn't want eating too much to slow him down. The size of the storm clouds overhead told him the coming battle would be a serious one.

The men had eaten, and the campfires were put out; Wise was about to order the troops to mount up when his Captain put his hand on Wise's shoulder. "Don't bother David; we have company coming."

Crack!

Lightning struck Corbyn's banner, filling the glade with deafening noise. Thereby, the still intact banner, the largest black unicorn any of them had ever seen, reared its challenge. Its rider was an equally huge elf, all in green armor.

"Coo we! I didn't know they made them that big!" Private Cook shouted, showing the surprise all the men were feeling as he drew his saber.

The storm stopped just that quick; the weather had done all it could to warn Prince Sawal. The gloom caused by the clouds vanished, and the sun's light highlighted the powerful magical armor of the rider. The experienced troopers recognized elfin war magic when they saw it. All the men checked the mirrors on their cuffs and boots and reached for steel-tipped lances or their steel horse sabers, knowing the metal and the mirrors were the only protection they had from this obviously powerful elf.

"Sheath weapons!" Corbyn watched Lord Pharadon dismount. "This is an ambassador from the King of the elves. He will be accorded the respect his station deserves."

In quick motions, the Ranger strung her short bow, ignoring Corbyn's command, and she selected a very special arrow from her quiver. Blowing on the enchanted arrowhead, an orange Caliginous fire sprung from the metal tip. She didn't care what Corbyn wanted; if the elf attacked her, he was going to die.

Lord Pharadon slapped his mount away and told it to wait for him out of the glade. Speaking only in high elfin, the Lord looked to Ash first.

"Oh, we really can't have an amulet of Arn influencing our diplomatic talks." He snapped his fingers, and the ancient amulet, a sign of respect from the elves to the wearer, turned to dust on Ash's arm. Ash grabbed his arm in surprise.

"Unicorn Lord," Pharadon sneered, "as a court ambassador, I can cause such amulets as your man wears to end their usefulness. Let's get on with this business, shall we? I have been sent by the King of all the elves to discover why you have entered the lands you abandoned. For myself, I don't care what your reasons are, but I'm overjoyed you've returned to die in your homeland."

The elf was speaking too fast for Ranger Slash to pick up on the conversation. Her puzzled look and the magic arrow in her bow appeared strangely comforting to the Captain. Corbyn couldn't help wondering where a Ranger could have gotten Caliginous death god magics as he noted the color and type of arcane flame on the arrow fitted to her bow. He'd have to ask her where she got the arrow if he survived this encounter.

Corbyn understood the traditions surrounding ambassadors. He was more than willing to extend those rights to Lord Pharadon, even knowing the elf Lord hated him. While Corbyn was growing up in the elf court, all of the Pharadon clan made their distaste for Corbyn clear in their every thought and deed.

"If you don't care, Ambassador Pharadon, why have you come all this way?" Corbyn asked, standing to talk or withstand an attack. He stood near his war banner, drawing special magics from the shadows of its protection. He motioned to his troops to stand well back. He'd already cast what invisible magics he could about the area and his banner was capable of absorbing many of the types of battle magics the elf Lord might use against him. Corbyn purposely positioned his men on the other side of the running water. Casting battle magics over running water, greatly reduced the damage such spells inflicted.

Lord Pharadon drew his dark demon blade, ignoring the Unicorn Lord and his banner. The elf began casting a spell. Walking in a large circle, the tip of his blade worked demonic-enhanced elf magics. The weapon made a cruel hissing sound, and the grass burnt away as a bubbling line of earth melted at the magical action of the blade tip.

Corbyn's men tensed and prepared to charge. Once again, Corbyn used hand signals to make them back off. He shouted to all of them, "As long as the con of the Ambassador of the elves flies above his head, none of us will attack. Do you understand that, Ranger?" Corbyn looked directly in the eyes of the Ranger. She held her bow at the ready, not lowering it. He had no idea what magics was on that arrowhead, but he noticed its target was him, which was interesting. He moved to view both her and

Pharadon. Arrow dodging was a skill he learned early on in the service against armies of elves, as elves loved the use of the bow. He doubted a short bow arrow could come fast enough for him to not be able to dodge the strike. He was, however, just a bit busy with the elf as well. He shot a look at his Sergeant and motioned toward the Ranger.

Sergeant Wise, seeing the direction of his Captain's gaze, noticed the Ranger for the first time. "Here now, lass, you don't want to be sending magical arrows into diplomatic doings." He moved to her side with surprising quickness for a man his size; deftly, he grasped the arrow out of her bow. "Whew, this thing smells something awful. When my Captain says put away your weapons, you put away your weapons. Is that clear, Ranger?"

She watched, astounded, as he threw the still-burning arrow down and put out the blaze with his boot. The magical energy of the Caliginous arrow should have exploded that offending limb of his leg. Instead, the arrow appeared crushed as the Sergeant went up closer to the circle, still staying on his side of the brook, clearly ready to back his Captain's play. *How in the world did that lump of a Sergeant not die at the touch of the death magic in that arrow?* Aliesha, the Ranger imposter, moved behind her mount, ready to use other deadly pieces of equipment found in her open saddlebags or run, whichever was indicated by the actions of Corbyn and the strange elf.

Corbyn waited by his banner as Lord Pharadon completed three circles around him. As the Lord sheathed his weapon, he snapped his fingers in a casting gesture and started walking in the reverse direction as elfin magics flowed from his hands. Corbyn snapped his own fingers, drawing magical energy from his banner and clearly warning the ambassador. "Bide a moment, Lord Pharadon; although I must respect your diplomatic status, I won't let you complete the circle of three, no matter what your newfound rank. Why have you really come?"

For the first time, Lord Pharadon smiled. Pointing his hand at Corbyn, he spoke in the human tongue, making every word seem like he was spitting something foul from his mouth. "You have stopped an ambassador to the King in his sworn duty from accomplishing his appointed task in finishing this circle and starting negotiations. Let it be known from your actions the time for diplomatic protocols is over!"

Clapping his hands, a demonic mist flowed up from the land and hid the two from the rest of the troop. The mist completely wrapped itself around the circle in a blanketing swirl that hid the rest of the world from the view of the two.

Lord Pharadon reached back and lifted the King's con from its holder and carefully placed it beside Corbyn's banner. "Only one of us is leaving this circle." The menace in his voice clearly told of the elf's intent, and he once again drew his sword.

Private Eastland was the first of the men to reach the black circle. He began probing the blackness with his lance.

"Fool, get off," Wise's arm battled the lance away from the darkness. "If the Captain is at this edge, you might be cutting him with your bloody lance! Think man!"

"Oh, right, Sergeant. What should we do?" the worried trooper asked.

Wise didn't have any idea, but there were a few things he could accomplish. "You men with lances spread yourselves around this black circle. If you see that elf, charge, I don't care what the Captain might say. If you can, cut the damned elf down where he stands. You others get some rope; we'll try sending a man into the blackness. I'll need a volunteer; Eastland, strap a rope around you."

"I'll be going in to save the Captain," Ash spoke up and walked calmly over to the Sergeant's side of the circle. "I know a little about elf ways, though I suspect this is a demonic-inspired darkness."

"Donont," Wise said, "if this spell is demon's work, try some of your holy water and anything else you can think of to end a demon's spell,"

Ash Greenwood stood, sword in hand, looking into the darkness. He didn't want this Captain of lancers to die because Cauldron was the only chance he had of ending the life of the Fey Elf. Nix killed his men, and Greenwood wanted to be there when the Captain put his sword in that dark elf's heart.

In seconds, the reaver was fastened by his waist to several sections of rope. He fearlessly jumped into the blackness. Four troopers, with Wise holding on at the back, were pulled toward the darkness as the entire weight of Ash's body dragged down the rope as it went from waist-high to falling to the bottom of the inky darkness at ground level. The men pulled Ash out.

Ash struggled for breath, croaking his fear. "There's no ground. I swung in emptiness, feeling nothing around me as you all pulled me up. I smelled brimstone but nothing else. The blackness is terrible; how long was I in there?"

"Just a few heartbeats; we pulled you out the moment you fell," Cook handed the shaken Ash a water canteen.

"It felt like I was in there for hours," Ash sobbed. "I screamed my lungs out. Whatever that barrier is, we aren't getting past it until that elf wants us to."

"Our Captain is well and truly in the deep end of things now," Wise said. "We'll stand guard around this bloody blackness until he comes out of it, or we die of old age. If any of you have a better idea that doesn't have us turning tail and running, speak up."

No one spoke. All of them, at one time or another, had their lives saved by the Captain. They would support their Sergeant in whatever he wanted to try right now.

The Ranger felt unusually good about the blackness. There was more than a fair chance the big elf was doing her work for her.

Wise positioned the men around the circle, and they waited with their weapons at the ready.

———

In the demon circle, Corbyn was glad Pharadon's magic cut them off from his troops. Corbyn didn't want the elf revealing any princely secrets to his human followers. He'd drawn his steel sword and waited for the elf to make his play. Corbyn was an excellent swordsman, but he knew he didn't have the thousand years of skill with a blade like the one Pharadon possessed. Corbyn planned to keep on the defensive until the right moment happened.

Lord Pharadon stood on the other end of the circle. Protective magics wrapped his body. His stance was that of a fencer, with his right foot forward and his left at an angle behind him, balancing his straight frame. Drawing his famous family longsword, the weapon moaned a heavy sigh at the possibility of shedding elf blood.

Corbyn kept his tone light; he was as prepared as he could be. "Your weapon is a bit premature in its voicing of blood lust, don't you think, my lord." The

Captain had carefully selected the place to plant his banner. While his troop made camp, Corbyn walked the area around the banner, noting stones and the lay of the land. The knoll they were on was flat and rock hard, with ankle-tall grass all around. At that moment, Corbyn stood over a large gopher hole hidden in the grass. *One never knew what might come in handy during a battle,* Corbyn thought as he took up his swordsman stance. He also noted the cross guard on his opponent's weapon was unusually small. Corbyn's own bell guard was a large affair with razor-sharp bends of steel worked into the bell guard. The Captain doubted his foe would let him get close enough to smash one of those razor steel edges into flesh, thus killing the elf, but it was worth considering as they dueled.

Lord Pharadon noted the magic inherent in the Unicorn Lord's banner and put aside any thoughts of throwing spells at the half-elf.

"My King wanted to know why you would come back. I don't care why you're here. After I have the extreme pleasure of ending your life, I'll be telling your grandfather, the King, you were brought dead to the forest with your head cut off by the humans who must have found out you were an elf. I might even bring back your head."

Sword held in front of him, at the guard position, Lord Pharadon advanced a step at a time toward Corbyn. The Captain began circling to the left,

making it slightly more difficult for his foe to successfully lunge at him as more of Corbyn's blade was always facing Pharadon's blade than Corbyn's body.
The two of them moved in a deadly dance around
the circle, each trying to gauge the speed of their
opponent.

"The Queen," Pharadon sneered, "your grand-
mother even wanted you allowed into the palace.
Naturally, once you left the empire all those happy
years ago, my clan couldn't let you come back with all
the silly human sentiments you might have
picked up."

The tips of their blades touched for the first time,
and the larger elf, standing five feet away from Corbyn, knew he could now lunge with his greater reach
and have a good chance of piercing the Unicorn
Lord's body. Lord Pharadon's demon sword roared
out its battle cry and sent a mist of darkness at the
head of its foe. Corbyn's steel blade dispelled the
magic long before it could blind him.

Pharadon let his blade throw deadly magics at
Prince Sawal. None of the potent battle spells would
probably get through to the body of his foe, but they
might distract him long enough for the tip or the razor-sharp edge of his weapon to make a killing blow.

"My Lord Pharadon, there is something you
should know before your blade finds my all too
human heart."

Demon sent, black lightning erupted from the

elf's blade, only to be nullified by Corbyn's steel sword. The powerful magic turned to dust as the Captain backed out of range to make sure he finished what could be his final words. "As much as I'm enjoying our little dance here, you should know that Fey Lord Cimmerian Nix and I are dancing the dance of three gifts and have each exchanged our first gifts. There's also a certain old witch at a very good inn, a few days ride into human lands that thinks I'm going to be around for a while. Imagine that, my Lord."

Now Lord Pharadon retreated to the far edge of the battle circle, visibly blanching at Corbyn's words. "Well, it seems you have even more powerful foes than my humble self. Since I didn't come here to be diplomatic, I won't allow myself to care. Once you're dead, I'll worry about Fey elf lords and their displeasure."

The elf Lord once again came at Corbyn. A grim look of determination filled the elf's face. "I couldn't quite manage your death when an army of humans or the love of your Princess Mother protected you. I'll manage it now, no matter what a human witch might believe. Enjoy these few fleeting breaths, Unicorn Lord, for they are your last."

Moving to striking distance, the elf and Corbyn lunged at each other in a blur of blades. The elf sword was a longer and a heavier wedge of razor-sharp metal than Corbyn's saber. Constantly beating back Corbyn's blade, the demon spirit in the magical weapon roared out its blood lust.

Corbyn's fencing style used a much lighter touch as he stood his ground and quickly parried the demon blade to the left and then the right of his body. His horseman's saber was a thinner blade, but the threat of any cut killing the elf in front of him kept his foe further back and allowed Corbyn more time to defend against the powerful blows.

Each fighter moved about the other, feeling their foe's rhythms and testing their sword arms and skill. Lord Pharadon was head and shoulders taller than Corbyn Cauldron, allowing the elf fencer to keep the Captain further away as the elf's demon weapon licked out repeatedly in attempts to get past Corbyn's guard.

Blade tips touched first to the left and then to the right as both sword masters tried feints and half lunges.

The demon blade constantly cried out in frustration as its wielder pulled it back from the elf flesh it craved. None of its deadly magics could travel down the length of Corbyn's steel blade to strike at the wielder. Constant flows of black lightning moved from the hilt of Pharadon's sword to the tip, only to stop there by the magic dulling steel of Corbyn's blade.

The strength of Corbyn's wrist and the quickness of his feet were constantly challenged as he beat back the heavy attacks of his foe and danced back, always moving left around the circle of blackness.

The battle moved round and round the glade. At one point, Corbyn's half-lunges forced the elf back to the center of the circle. Pharadon took a huge cut at Corbyn's war banner. The banner stood rock solid and deeply nicked the demon blade as the magic of the banner repelled the longsword. Corbyn took a chance, lunging at his foe, but Pharadon recovered and parried the blade away.

Both fighters' breaths were coming faster.

Sneering again, the elf lord advanced and said, "I'm surprised you chose the symbols of your elfin family for your war standard. Did you intend to mock your mother?"

"I intend to have humans and elves living in peace," Corbyn answered. "That can't happen as long as you lead your clan. I'm just as glad to see you as you are to see me. Your death will further plans of my own."

Pharadon was surprised to realize the Prince had an agenda besides leaving the lands of the elves. *Peace with the humans, that would never do.*

The land was doing what it could for its prince. The grass deliberately turned from Corbyn's boots, making him able to slide his feet quicker in any direction he wished. Nature did just the opposite for the elf's movements, but the battle magics of Lord Pharadon prevented the hindering grass from having any effect. Lord Pharadon knew nature would be on the side of the Prince and prepared his defensive spells accordingly.

Feint, parry, and feint again; the dance of the blades moved back and forth, often with blinding speed.

Both weapons could kill with their tips or their razor-sharp long edges. Several times Corbyn tried lunging into an attack, but the elf was too canny a blade user and turned the tip and edge of the steel sword every time.

Neither opponent thought about their sword strikes, as thinking about their blades slowed down their responses to the actions of their opponent. Each mind plotted attacks and defenses far in advance of what their hands were doing, much like chess players thinking ten moves in advance of their current move.

Corbyn's parries became wider and wider as his foe worked out Corbyn's fighting style. The wider parries were necessary as the elf was able to come closer and closer with his strikes as he learned how Corbyn moved with the many different attacks he faced. A lunge to Corbyn's head, and he usually moved to the right. A lunge to Corbyn's leg, and he most often shifted backward. Corbyn never did the same thing three times in a row, but repeated attacks allowed Pharadon to learn the Captain's patterns of combat.

Cauldron changed his tactics and often exchanged human-learned sword point attacks with elf-edged blade tactics. Corbyn's maneuverings did little good, and Pharadon's sneering grin became wider and wider as both fighters knew Corbyn couldn't keep up his defense much longer. The elf's ages of skill forced the Unicorn Lord to become wilder in his defense. Corbyn knew his thrusts and parries should be smaller and nearer to his body, but the weapon work he faced forced a more dangerous set of acts on his hand and sword.

Corbyn's defenses barely kept the elf's deadly blade away from the Captain's head and body. In one passage of blades, a short parry allowed Pharadon to slice his longsword all along Corbyn's unweaponed arm. The elf clearly intended to cut Corbyn's limb entirely off. The only thing saving Corbyn's arm was the hidden enchanted dagger in its spring sheath on his forearm. The hidden blade surprised the elf, allowing Corbyn to back out of reach as the elf's weapon edge scraped, harming nothing off the sheath's side.

Up to this time, both warriors had saved their breaths for battle. Pharadon thought he knew enough about his opponent to taunt him. "Hidden weapons, how very unelf-like. Your human masters have taught you boorish tricks."

"My human ma. . ." Corbyn lunged, hoping the

elf would think Corbyn would finish his sentence before attacking.

Pharadon leapt back and raised his blade out of guard. "Please, Unicorn Lord, finish your thought, and then I'll kill you."

Corbyn knew Pharadon had found his measure and might easily be able to get past his guard with a lunge. With one last trick in mind, he backed up with a mock bow and positioned himself ready for his foe's next attack. "The least of the humans I've met has more honor than what I sense in your aura today. Kill me if you can." Corbyn's tone was as provoking as he could make it.

Lord Pharadon moved in quickly, his face not showing the anger he felt. He beat the tip of Corbyn's blade away with a feint left and lunged in a perfect-beat attack that would have found the Prince's heart. At that instant, Lord Pharadon's right foot found the gopher hole Corbyn had seen hours before. Falling to one knee, he was still blade master enough to mortally slash his sword deep into Corbyn's side in a killing blow, cutting the Unicorn Lord wide open and burying his blade to the hilt in the Unicorn Lord's bloody side.

Corbyn, for his part, knowing himself a dead man, leaned into the blow and let his spring dagger fall into his hand. With his last bit of strength, he plunged the steel dagger into the eye of the very surprised lord Pharadon.

With the Lord dead, Pharadon's circle magics vanished.

———

One second, there was a black circle in the middle of the forest glade. The next Wise and the rest saw Cauldron and the elf locked in death grips.

"No, no, no, this isn't happening." Wise rushed up to see his dying Captain.

Five troopers thrust their lances into the already dead elf and ripped his body away from their Captain.

Corbyn's guts spilled out of the huge gaping wound in his side. The elf's weapon, still buried to the hilt, made horrible blood-sucking noises. Wise pulled the blade out and flung the bloody weapon far away as others tossed the dead elf aside.

"Ranger, mount up and scout this brook to the north. Somewhere along its length is a monastery. Warn the friars there; we're coming with a half-dead man needing their attention. Go!" His tone didn't allow the Ranger any room for argument.

She mounted and rode out.

"Shields and lances, men," Wise ordered. "You know the drill. The Captain needs a litter, and he's getting one. Donont work your healing, man."

Earlier, the cleric had laid out his healing kit of potions and creams. An experienced healer, he knew a death wound when he saw one. "David, our Captain's dying. There isn't a thing in the world I can do but send him blessed to his maker."

"Wrong, Private Donont," Wise barked. "You can give our Captain some time. We'll carry him to the monastery, I sensed, and we'll do it right quick. Give him an hour of life with your skills now, and the friars of the goddess Arcania will do the rest."

The great gash was pumping out Corbyn's life's blood. The good cleric could stop the flow, but nothing he had could close the huge wound. The flesh was already turning black from the action of the demon blade. Donont gave his Captain what comfort he could as the others placed him on a shield stretcher held together by lances, shields, and blankets. The private doubted his Captain had an hour left in him.

14

LIGHT AND DARKNESS JUST DON'T MIX WELL

"The elf who invented the magic sword was bright, but the human who invented the army was a genius."

— COMMANDER JANON

ALIESHA, THE ASSASSIN TURNED RANGER FOR this mission, rode her horse hard into the north along the small stream. She paid no attention to the direction, letting the brook be her guide. She'd heard the Sergeant say the holy place was somewhere along the flowing water and took him at his word.

The master assassin thought carefully about her options in the coming hours and what she'd witnessed in the last few days. The Fey elf lord giving Corbyn a gift of death was frighteningly odd. Aliesha could sense the power of Cimmerian Nix and any creature that could kill seventy-five men all at once and ordered about an underground kingdom of elves commanded her respect. She'd heard all the legends surrounding Nix and knew the Fey to be immensely powerful. If Cimmerian Nix found out an assassin of Caliginous killed the object of his current interest, the entire cult might find itself wiped out before the sun rose again.

Just as disturbing was the recent attack by an ambassador from the King of the elves. Ambassadors didn't usually come to attack; they came to talk. For that elf to single out Cauldron and duel him to the death in honorable battle, there had to be something very unusual about the lancer Captain. There were too many questions and surprises around Corbyn Cauldron.

The wound she saw on his body should be the death of him. By her extensive understanding of such things, it was likely he was dead right now. She'd inflicted such wounds on marks in her time. In any other man, a gash like that caused instant death. She'd seen his breathing come in ragged and strained bursts, and bubbles of dark blood seeped from his slack mouth. His face had taken on a deathly pallor from loss of blood. On the other hand, in the magical world they lived in, powerful clerical healers existed who could negate the damage of such a wound as if the cut had never happened.

She'd seen Corbyn's liver and intestines spilling out of that wound. "Maybe the ride up to this monastery will kill him. One can only hope," she muttered to herself.

On the wild chance that Corbyn survived the trip into the holy friar's gentle care, Aliesha made her own plans. She thought about the many possibilities.

Maybe I could poison the healing salve used on the Captain. Or I could always offer to stand vigil over his healing body and thrust a slim needle into his brain while he sleeps. I've always enjoyed that type of offering to the bloodless god Caliginous, but with those kills, Cimmerian Nix might still find out I did them.

Riding a little higher on the saddle, the death cult leader made a mental note to add more riding into her weekly routines. Her toned calves were telling her, in no uncertain terms, by their chaffing, that they didn't like riding so much or so fast.

Turning over in her mind the ways of Arcania, the white goddess, the assassin thought she remembered the clerics made a very good sparkling wine.

I'll poison him a little at a time with Arcania's own vintage, which other people serve to him. He'll grow weaker and weaker and pass away no matter how well they heal the wound. I'll kill that big Sergeant of his as well; his crushing of my arrow into the ground should have never happened. The magical ef-

fect of the Caliginous death spell on the arrow should have had the Sergeant die at a touch of those flames. Only clerics of lawful orders were able to withstand the touch of Caliginous and live; that big lummox didn't act like a cleric.

In less than a half hour from the time she started, the cult mistress slipped into a cleared area to see the white monastery of Arcania several hundred yards away. *Corbyn's men would be there far too quickly.*

She rode to the front of the monastery with several lies, ready to move the clerics to action. At the open barbican entrance, a lone monk dressed in white robes waved her into the monastery. A white friar's hood hid his face, but there was something odd about his waving hand.

Her horse shied away from the entrance, and the man, Aliesha suddenly knew why. *That wasn't a man; that was a zombie!*

Aliesha, mistress of 9,999 assassins, wasn't a cleric of her death cult, but abilities came to her as gifts given by Caliginous, the bloodless death deity. Aliesha could spot undead essence in a creature if she was looking for it; she just hardly ever looked.

Forcing her horse to her will, she moved around the castle gate, trying to draw the zombie friar away from the entrance. Her plan was to quickly ride inside, scouting if there were more zombies, and just as quickly ride away. The zombie just stood at the entrance, waving her inside. Aliesha wanted to scout the confines of the holy place but wasn't ready to try riding down the zombie. In her mind's eye, she saw such an attempt as dangerous. The zombie was easily capable of clinging to the belly of her mount and ripping its guts out while the horse tried to trample it. Only the taking of the zombie's head would kill it and stop it from continuing its attack.

She rode along the wall to the corner tower, noting there weren't any friars or nuns visible on the wall above. Dismounting, she took out special climbing hooks and fastened them to her palms. Scaling the wall was an easy task for one of her skills. Reaching the top in a few heartbeats, there were no zombie guards along the wall or on the tower top. Looking inside the monastery, she could see several monks and quite a few nuns walking the area with the mindless gate of zombies. Zombies clearly controlled the entire complex. She didn't know how it happened, but she knew how to take advantage of the fact. When the troopers came, she would be ready for them. *Their horses mustn't give away Arcania's new secret. Maybe I can talk them out of their weapons as well.*

Knowing the way of zombies created from the bodies of holy clerics, she knew these undead would be unusually intelligent. She'd make a pact with them, offering them many living bodies to feast on if they could wait until the lancers entered the central tower. If Corbyn weren't dead when he got here, he would be after the zombies were through, tearing the life out of his men.

————

The Elf Lord Dalbergia moved with a purpose through the palace to a section of the metropolis where his relatives lived. A minor noble, he had no squires to help him gather equipment and ready his mount.

Dalbergia used far different magics from the spells and arcane devices employed by Lord Pharadon. Dalbergia's people were more in tune with the enchanted creatures of the sky. Although Dalbergia couldn't move with magical speed through the forest, he could fly. Cloudbreaker, his griffon friend, had been part of his family for six hundred and twenty years. A huge member of the species, it stood on four lion feet, and its giant eagle head and gold feathered shoulders were ten feet off the ground. The griffon's wing feathers were sun-colored, and his breast and tail feathers were of the purest white. The beast flew using enchantments of its own, as it was as heavy as a massive lion and couldn't rise into the air even on its sixty-foot span of wings if it just depended on the forces of wind to allow it to rise. The half-lion and half-eagle creature was devoted to Dalbergia, and one of the elf's greatest pleasures was taking to the air on Cloudbreaker's back. Other elf clans learned to tame and ride winged horses and hippogriffs, but Dalbergia relatives had always been able to converse with griffons. They didn't tame their steeds; they became friends with them.

Dalbergia could tell his griffon things he'd never say to others, griffons being very closed-beaked creatures.

"Our Princess wishes you and me to help her son. This is, of course our pleasure because Prince Sawal is a worthy elf, no matter what his father's parentage."

Dalbergia cinched the light saddle on the back of his griffon, and the beast lowered a wing to help its companion up onto its back.

"This quest is made doubly pleasant because we love that fine lady, his mother, and anything we can do to draw attention to ourselves in her thoughts is a good thing."

The beast could tell its friend was in a good mood and didn't know if it should purr or chirp at the warm sound in Dalbergia's voice. At the squeezing of Dalbergia's legs, Cloudbreaker launched itself into the air in a flurry of wings.

Dalbergia used his elfin brooch to project his spirit energy into the forest below, letting nature know he was looking for the Prince, and the elf forest began guiding him in the right direction. Messages flowed out faster than the griffon could fly or Lord Pharadon could magically ride as birds chirped, insects buzzed, and branches rubbed one another with the urgency of Dalbergia's quest. The forest life was only too happy to help its Prince, and the elf flying over the forest looking for the Prince.

———

Sergeant David Wise of the King's Own 25th Lancers deliberately stopped looking at his Captain on the litter after the tenth time. They had been moving north for over an hour. David had used every healing trick of salves, potions, and clerical magics he and Private Donont possessed to hold back the dark hand of death.

He ticked off in his mind all the things they had done; trying to think if there was anything else they could try to keep the Captain alive. *I used spider's webs to stop the bleeding. It was amazing how many thick stands of webbing they found to use in the glen. I made him swallow the healing potions. Those were military issues and not made to fix that great bloody wound in his side, but they gave him some strength. Donont cast the healing magics he knew. If the Captain lives, I swear, Donont becomes a corporal. Six men are carrying the litter at a brisk trot. Horses could have done the carrying faster, but their rough gate might do the Captain in. No, the men carrying him are the way to go. Exchanging each trooper, every half-mile was also working smoothly. They didn't even stop moving as a lancer dismounted and took position against one of the litter lances while the former litter carrier mounted up. These men, the best in the 25th Lancer Regiment, would trot themselves to death for the Captain.*

Wise and his troops moved through the tree line and found the monastery to Arcania ahead.

Ranger Slash was there waiting at the forest's edge for them. She made sure her words were loud enough for all of them to hear.

"All but the Abbess have taken a vow of silence in there. I talked with her, and she's ready to heal the Captain. She demands that you all leave your weapons and horses outside the monastery. She wants you all to go to the main tower and help pray for the life of the Captain. I'll watch the horses. You are all to go to the center keep, taking the Captain upstairs to the inner chapel."

"I know where the inner sanctum is, Ranger. Do they have the Abbess ready for the healing?" Wise asked.

The group closed the three hundred yards to the barbican entrance.

"Yes, they do," Slash answered. "But remember, none of you can take a weapon in there, or their healing spells might fail."

Wise briefly wondered where that thought came from but wasn't taking any chances. "You heard her. Stack your weapons, including your holdouts, hurry. The Ranger, here, will be minding the equipment and horses. Double time now, for our Captain's life."

Ranger Slash smiled; *soon, Sergeant Wise, you will know just how right you are.*

All the men rushed in, and she busied herself with the horses.

When the last of them was through the killing ground of the barbican towers, she calmly walked into the outer courtyard. The last of the zombies was able to restrain itself and not attack as the troopers went past it into the tower. It followed them closely and closed the door. Aliesha thought she heard the shifting of a large gate bar going into place behind that door.

Telling the zombie of her plan had excited the gate guard. The creature had gone to tell the others, and great numbers of zombies had entered the center tower to wait for the victims to come to them. Aliesha looked in the door of one of the barbican towers and didn't see what she wanted. She used spikes to seal shut that door. She didn't want possible troopers getting out of the center tower and escaping through the gateway. She went to the other door and found the chamber with the gearing controlling the inside barbican portcullis. Aliesha broke the gate mechanism. Leaving the tower, she used two spikes to prevent that portal from opening. The assassin moved through the entrance and out of the monastery as the inner portcullis slowly fell down into place. The broken lifting chain was quite out of the reach of any trooper who might escape in the first rush of zombies. There would be no raising the portcullis before they became a meal for the undead.

She dusted her hands at a job well done. *It's too bad I can't do the killing, but it looked like the mark, her dear unwilling to be seduced Captain, was already dead. A hundred-odd zombies against weaponless men should do the trick if she was any judge of deadly things, and she considered herself the best judge of such matters.*

Briefly, she thought about checking her work and waiting there a few hours. However, considering all the zombie mouths needing to be fed, there wouldn't be anything to check. She rode for the capital, not worrying at all about the Fey Cimmerian Nix, who would be very angry at a horde of very well-fed zombies.

———

"Donont keep blessing the Captain; he needs all your holy power right now," ordered Wise.

They rushed the litter into the tower of light. White-robed monks with their hoods shadowing their faces opened the doors for the lancers and pointed up the stairs to the right.

"I'm doing what I can, but I was forced to leave

my spirit mace outside. My holy symbol only grants me so much power, you know," Donont advised.

"Less talk, acting Corporal, and more blessing." Wise saw his Captain still breathed, but the saving of his life would be a near thing. The Sergeant knew the layout of an Arcanian monastery well; he led the way past other cloaked nuns and friars to the stairs. He went up the steps two at a time; sure, his men would try to keep up in order to save their Captain's life.

Wise heard some kind of chanting he didn't recognize coming from the holy people at the bottom of the stairs. He wasn't familiar with the tone, but he hoped they were starting prayers for Corbyn. Leaping onto the stair landing, he noted the corridors of Life and Light to the right and left. These corridors were common to all Arcania monasteries. Wise knew this as he had served in such places all of his young life. David went straight ahead through the long hall to the inner shrine. He could see the portal open and the holy light of Arcania filled the inner shrine and spilled out into the hall. From the holy glow of the shrine, David knew the Abbess must have been the last person working in the inner sanctum dedicated to the Goddess. There wasn't a better place to try to heal his Captain in the entire world. Moving ahead, he glanced briefly at the floor, noting a large stain on the whitewashed stone, but he didn't have time for that as he ran to the inner chapel door and threw it wider for the litter to get in.

Looking inside, he shook his head, sad to see the chamber empty.

"Clerics of Arcania, we need your headmistress!" Bellowing along the corridor, he knew his voice carried down the stairs even with the strange chanting he was hearing grow in intensity from the monks behind his men.

Only four men with the litter could fit in the inner sanctum. Wise had them gently lift the still-breathing Corbyn off the litter and onto the table in front of the altar.

Suddenly, there were screams in the hall!

Wise looked out, wondering where the Abbess was. His height allowed him to see the corridor filled with friars and his men struggling with the holy men. He gasped in horror; that wasn't holy chanting; the friaries were growling. Cowls pulled back in the struggle revealed zombies! His unarmed men were fighting for their lives against supernaturally strong undead.

The horror of the trap-filled his mind with terror. He turned to the increasing glow of holy light on the figure of Arcania in the center alcove. The power of the goddess Arcania, his goddess since the day he was born, pushed aside his fear of death. Suddenly, the holiness of the inner shine held his mind and body and gave him hope and a certainty that all would be well.

The men around him were screaming as they saw

their deaths in the terrible eyes of the undead ripping and tearing at the men in the corridor.

Ash Greenwood hadn't panicked; he stood quietly by the Captain, clearly ready to use his body as a shield.

"Calm down, take these weapons!" Wise used his loudest parade ground tone to calm his men. Mentally, he begged his goddess' forgiveness for needing to shout in her holy shrine. They hadn't taken the time to strip Corbyn of his weapons. Wise knew his Captain to be a walking armory when he rode into battle. "Pass these up!"

The two lances making the edges of the litter and Corbyn's many blades, from his sword to his boot daggers, went up through the mass to the front of the melee, where they had an instant harmful effect on the undead monsters.

Ash Greenwood picked up Corbyn's saber. "I'll kill and hold off as many as I can, but you better be quick in whatever you plan on doing." The reaver pushed his way through the press of men feeling in his soul the Sergeant would be able to do something to change their situation.

The monsters hesitated as blades and lances struck out at them. Suddenly, the creatures weren't as sure of success as Ash and others licked out to sever stretched talons and unwary zombie heads.

"Shields, now, these will keep them back!" shouted Wise.

The four shields of the litter passed to the front of the struggle through the press of men.

"Hold them off for a minute; I'll get us more help!" The Sergeant's words calmed the men. Even though they were battling for their lives against terrible odds, his commanding voice assured them everything would be all right, and the troopers believed him. No one knew where more help would come from, but if Sergeant Wise said more help was coming, then it was clear that help would arrive.

Grim soldiers bellowed to their mates to part ranks, and the men down the corridor fighting for their lives, ducked and moved to the sides of the hall.

The white shields with the holy symbols of Caliginous and Arcania blazed brightly, causing blindness in the packed ranks of zombies. Each shield responded to the undead essence in front of them. The lances, saber, and daggers began doing their work on exposed zombie necks and extended talons. The two lances lunged out and struck off the heads of two zombies wrestling on the floor with two troopers. The entire zombie mass drew back, howling in pain as the blessed light of the shields burned their eyes. The desperate men grew more hopeful, choosing to believe even with the masses of zombies fighting each other to rip and tear at the troops.

The holy energy from the shields worked to keep the zombies away from the men. Then, one of the shields burnt out and turned to dust in the hands of the trooper. Another started pulsing, working its magic and then blinking off, useless.

Sergeant Wise turned away from the corridor and stripped off his lancer armor. He calmly raised his face to the statue of Arcania and fell to his knees in supplication. His voice, now in subdued tones, begged for the aid of the goddess. A look of holy adoration on his face reflected what he felt in his soul.

"I have always been yours to do with as you will. I know, goddess, I haven't been the best of followers. I bless your name for the many gifts of luck and life you have given me over the years."

A gentle thought intruded on all the things Wise wanted to say. *Not now, my holy warrior, we have my work to do this day. Take my blessing, heal your Captain, and lay the bodies of my followers to rest.*

Wise's memories of his long-ago past came flooding back, and he rose moving to the altar and the holy bowl of light always found there. He washed his bloody hands in the oils dedicated to the goddess. The proper prayers of the supplicant flowed from his lips. David remembered them even though he hadn't uttered those words in ten years. The blood and dirt fell from his hands, but only pure oil dropped into the bowl as the death and dirt of the material world turned to dust and vanished before it could defile the holy bowl. In this, the inner sanctum of the goddess, her attention and holy power, was flowing through

David now with the act of pledging himself totally to her.

"I make the second promise of light and joining, as you knew I would."

Wise shook his head, amazed at the power of the goddess. Years ago, as a young cleric, he left the service of Arcania feeling he was unworthy of her light. As he stood in her holy chamber, needing her holy aid to survive; clearly, she obviously disagreed with him about his fitness to serve her. He felt her clerical energy flowing through his body, giving him great strength and filling him with divine wisdom.

Never hurrying, knowing the goddess wouldn't want that, he raised the cup of light to the deity's image, and a blaze of light entered the golden cup. The empty chalice filled with light, and Wise, now a sanctified cleric of Arcania, increased his commitment to her order.

"I make the third promise to serve you in the light. Know goddess that I also serve my Captain, but he'll share my time with you." Drinking from the goblet of light, he tasted the amazing gift of the goddess. With the first sip, he knew her wraith at what happened in this, her monastery. An image formed of the two demons that walked these halls, turning good friars and nuns into the undead.

The deity's plan for him and the power she was giving him transformed David into her holy warrior of retribution. Wise became a fighting cleric of Arcania, the white goddess. His mind filled with healing spells and spells to put the tortured bodies of the zombies to rest.

He pressed a secret pressure plate on the side of the altar. Seconds ago, he gained the knowledge of its hiding place, as well as the hiding places of all things in the monastery. Inside the recess were the vestments of Arcania and a white mace. He put on the vestments and took up the mace to become one of only three living symbols of the enforcer of light and her will in the world.

With the mace at the ready to aid in his clerical spell casting, he bent low over his Captain. David's hand passed over the blackened wound, and the holy power of the goddess in her inner sanctum flowed through him and into the terrible gash. Corbyn's blackened flesh turned pink, and the wound closed with the spider webs ejected from inside the body cavity. Life and energy filled Corbyn's Cauldron, allowing him to take his first easy breath. He opened his eyes.

Bathed in a white glow was his Sergeant. Corbyn discarded the thought that Wise could be an angel. The Sergeant was inappropriately dressed in a very nonmilitary clerical vestment.

David smiled down at him. Standing up in his glowing, holy robes, he walked away from Corbyn. Trying to rise, the Captain realized he was healed but still weak as a kitten. Falling into a dreamless sleep,

Corbyn knew his sergeant would have some explaining to do when Corbyn woke up.

The long corridor was still a boil with frightened troops and raging zombies. Only one shield remained functioning, and it couldn't keep all the zombies away from the men in the wide corridor. The light of the shield could keep away some of the zombies, but even being used in the middle of the corridor, some of the creatures could rush by at the corridor walls. Once a zombie was grappling one of the men, the shield could do nothing to stop the creature. The zombies attacked by wildly flailing away with their talons. They sought to grab an arm or body and pull that victim into their mass of zombies at their end of the hall, to rend them to pieces and suck the energy of life out of their prey's living bodies. Five lancers were already dead, and three others fell to the floor, sorely wounded.

The troopers at the front turned to see their Sergeant in white robes with a holy glow about his body. Some didn't know which was more of a surprise, to see zombies in a monastery or to see their earthy Sergeant cloaked in clerical robes. The lancers fell away from him, giving him as much room as the corridor would allow. None of them knew if he was an angel or what. All of them knew a glowing Sergeant just wasn't natural.

The zombies growled in pain. They hated the light cast from the body advancing toward them.

Their response to the light was a mass rush with as many zombie bodies as possible.

The holy mace of Arcania flicked out, and every zombie it touched turned to dust. Sergeant Wise somehow knew each of the names held by friars and nuns while they lived. As his mace swung out, touching zombie flesh, the power of Arcania's holy might and David's spells turned the undead things to the dust of the long dead. As the bodies fell, David blessed them. He knew their spirits were already standing at the side of Arcania, helping her to do good work in the spiritual realm. Ten zombies rushed in, and in a heartbeat, ten piles of black dust fell to the bloody stone floor.

Zombies continued rushing the now holy Sergeant. Troopers with lances and their Captain's blades took up guard positions, preventing zombies from going around the deadly Sergeant to attack his sides and back.

The undead creatures of evil couldn't fight back the compulsion to suck the life out of David. He also worked under an even stronger compulsion to lay to rest the bodies of the servants of the goddess. The confines of the corridor and men behind and on each side of Wise stopped the mass of zombies from circling and tearing at the Sergeant. For his part, the Sergeant kept swinging the holy weapon of Arcania. With each strike and a word of prayer, zombie bodies disintegrated.

The battle moved slowly down the corridor and then down the stairs. There were many crazed zombies willing to do anything to tear out the throat of Sergeant Wise.

———

Flying over the forest for many hours, Dalbergia landed Cloudbreaker in a large glade at the scene of a battle. The forest, with its many auras of creatures and plants, led him to this spot, but the unicorn standing over the body of Lord Pharadon attracted the Dalbergia's attention first.

Elf, my master, is dead, killed by Prince Sawal in fair combat. Would you help me get Lord Pharadon back to his clan for burial?

"Of course. I'll tie him to your back with his con and sword, but I trust you to tell his daughter the honorable way in which he died. You know, as an ambassador to the King, he should have never fought the Prince."

I expect the blood feud to increase, no matter what I say. The sword rests by the stream. I must take the dark thing back with the body.

Dalbergia used tall grasses to bring the demon blade to its sheath. He didn't want to touch the dark artifact of death with his bare hand. The magics in such a blade could easily cause an elf to turn from honor and the ways of the righteousness.

As he raised the enchanted blade, it howled with hatred. "Curse all you elves to the seven hells. The proudest day of my life was when I took the life of the Prince. Take me up and know godlike power elf and. . ." The blade ceased its oaths as Dalbergia put the weapon in its proper sheath on the dead body.

I will report the truth in all that happened to his clan. You will tell the story to King Aik?

"Easily done, noble unicorn, easily done. If the Prince is dead, where is the body?"

The demon blade sorely wounded him. His followers put him on a stretcher, and they went north up that brook. They said something about a human monastery close by.

"Ah, yes. King Aik, encouraged by the clerics of the elf goddess, allowed the shrine's building. It seems our goddess and Arcania, the human goddess, are one in the same deity. The building of that monastery was to represent the first steps in gaining peace with the humans. They go there to heal him, you say."

Dalbergia penned a note to Lord Pharadon's relatives and wrapped the body and the note in protective magics. *The Lord's clan didn't like Prince Sawal, but maybe with the clan leader dead, there could be peace.* He sadly shook his head; *no, that wasn't going to happen.* Dalbergia remembered the Unicorn Lord had led part of the human armies into Pharadon lands in the last few years. *Grudges were something both races held in common.*

The unicorn and the body vanished as the steed mystically entered the outer dimensions. It could arrive at the palace of the Pharadon's clan much more quickly by that path.

The elf Dalbergia walked to Prince Sawal's war standard. Placing a hand on the pole, he used his elfin bracelet to mix his aura with the magics of the standard. The magical war banner held a part of the soul of the Prince and magnified the Prince's power when the banner was unfurled. Dalbergia could sense many things from the banner's connection to the Prince.

The Prince is alive and healed! That's good news.

In Dalbergia's inner mind, he could see the Prince sleeping on a table in an altar chamber of the white goddess Arcania. Looking further about, the troopers in the lancer unit dressed the wounds of their mates as if they were just in a battle. An extremely powerful cleric, filled with the light of Arcania, worked to heal several men badly chewed up by some type of creature. There was a rare power in that cleric, as if the goddess herself favored him.

An elf of action, Dalbergia took his distant cousin's war standard and mounted the griffon once more. *The Prince must answer some questions; his mother is going to want to know everything, and won't it be pleasant to bring bad news to her.*

The last zombie rushed the Sergeant, turned to dust at the touch of the holy enchantments David cast, and received the same holy blessing all the other zombies received. With the goddess power flowing through his body and mind, Wise knew that all the zombies were now gone from the monastery. He turned to heal those men wounded in battle. With her revenge taken, David felt the strength given to him by the goddess of light quickly ebbing away. Exhausted in mind and body, he moved as speedily as he could to use what energy he had left to heal his wounded men.

Laying hands on the wounded, Wise healed them one by one. With the last man restored David slumped to the floor, exhausted. He sadly looked at the bodies of the dead. He could do nothing for them. The holy glow faded from his body, and Wise was just a man again.

"Sergeant Wise, what's wrong?" Cleric Donont knelt beside him, looking for injuries.

"The zombies are all gone from this place. Acting Corporal Donont, there's nothing wrong with me; a little rest couldn't cure." Wise looked back to see most of the troop standing behind him. "There better be four men guarding the Captain, or you're all going on report."

Wise's face was pale from his recent exertions.

His hands shook as he tried to get up; fatigue wasn't stopping him from performing his duties.

Donont gently kept him down on the floor as he offered him a canteen of water.

"We left three troopers with the two lances and the remaining working magic shield in the shrine with the Captain. With your permission, now that the zombies are gone, I'll send some men out for our horses and equipment."

"You do that, and well done acting, Corporal Donont. Help me to the inner shrine and the Captain; I'll rest easier seeing he is all right."

The Sergeant leaned on Donont, and they slowly climbed the blackened stairs to the inner shrine.

15

A MEETING OF OLD FRIENDS

"What are the stakes?" the young warrior asked.

"Top sirloin, I hope," the old warrior said dryly.

THE CAPTAIN AND HIS SERGEANT SAT IN THE kitchens of the Arcanian tower, sharing a meal together while their men worked around them. The monastery portcullis would be fixed in just a few hours, the horses were being gathered, and at the same time, weapons were being passed out to their owners. Lookouts stood watch on top of the center tower and at the barbican towers.

"David, what's the butcher's bill for the fight here?" As Captain of this troop, Corbyn's duty had him assess the losses after every battle. He would be contacting the families of the fallen men. There was a fund gathered by all the troopers of the regiment to give to wives and children of the recently fallen.

"Five dead here," Wise tiredly answered. "I was able to completely heal the other wounded. I won't be able to do much of that in the future. I was made a warrior cleric in the service of the white lady, and my holy skills are more in keeping with the damaging of foes if you understand my meaning."

David and Corbyn watched Ash Greenwood pounding away at a fire-hot cog needed for the fixing of the portcullis. Ash appeared to be a talented blacksmith as well as an able warrior.

David Wise noticed where his Captain was looking and wanted to give Ash Greenwood the benefit of a doubt. "That reaver took up your saber and did a fine job fighting the zombies. He stayed by my side through the whole battle. I'm starting to trust him a little more. He also took his turn carrying you the miles we had to go from the camp to this place."

Corbyn tiredly plopped his wooden spoon into the half-filled trencher of soup on the table. The good food was helping him gain back his strength. "He's still a reaver, David. I think I have to keep him alive and out of jail so Nix doesn't force my hand. That Fey elf thinks of Ash as sort of a gift to me. If I depreciated that gift in any way, Nix and possibly the entire realm of the Fey elves would come after me.

I'm going to pardon him using the rights of the King's Commission. I'll let him go from here, or he can stay with me. If he stays, I'll test him some more to judge if he's been tamed or not. I've gotten enough out of him to realize he thinks I'm the only one who can kill the Fey elf. Maybe that will be my leverage with him."

"How hard is it going to be to fight that Nix creature?" Wise asked. "I've seen you take on amazing foes and win."

"I'm putting that battle off for as long as I can," Corbyn said with a new wave of tiredness overcoming his body. "Knowing my clever foe, I'll be fighting him sometime in the years to come. I just don't know when. Although he looks like any other elf, he's five thousand years old if he's a day. He's the most powerful spellcaster of all the elves and he's been fighting humans all his long life. Speaking of fighting, when were you a cleric of the goddess Arcania?"

Wise grinned, a little embarrassed. He'd taken off the clerical robes Arcania gave him and placed them and the holy mace back in the altar recess. Now, he was back in uniform. "Long ago, when I was a boy, I heard the calling of the goddess. I worked in her service until I discovered I liked earthly pleasures a little more than I should. I guess I wasn't through sewing my wild oats back then, and I'm still not." He broke some bread and put some more of the hearty soup in his trencher and in his Captain's. "In order to save us, I had to promise to serve Arcania more faithfully. I'm going to have to act as a soldier cleric like Donont. It's going to cause some problems, but I still want to serve in the lancer regiment and with you."

"The empire, as far as I know, has no problem with clerics in the ranks," Corbyn said. "We'll leave more talk of your clerical ways until later. How in the world did the Ranger make this zombie trap happen?"

"She didn't exactly," Wise replied. "She just took advantage of what was done earlier. When the goddess, her name be forever blessed, filled me with her holy power I received memories of what really happened here. Two demons walked these halls, and the Nevil demon changed all of this monastery's friars and nuns into undead. I sent the Ranger up ahead to prepare the friars to heal you. Ranger Slash came upon the zombies and worked her evil to trick our troop into the main tower and into the zombie clutches. She told us to shed our weapons, allowing the zombies to have a better chance of killing us. She also knew horses wouldn't come near the zombies, so she tricked us into leaving them outside. We'd all be dead if I hadn't been a cleric to Arcania in my youth so that the goddess, may her name be praised, could use me as her vessel for vengeance." David made the sign of the goddess on his forehead.

"I had to promise to serve her for the rest of my

life. I hope you know I can still be a cleric and your Sergeant. But I'm going to need to take time to leave the regiment and bring back clerics to restore this place to Arcania's service," David said.

Corbyn shook his head at the change in his Sergeant. There was a softer, more considerate man across the table from him now. "I'll use my King's Commission to make your coming back a King's order. You and a troop of lancers will be required to come back here and restore order to this place. Take the time you need, just so long as you know I want you back with the lancers when you can arrange it. This monastery is one of the bright spots in the empire's chances of making peace with the elves, and we need to do that.

"In my things, I still have the Ranger's orders," Corbyn said. "Baron Arullian is going to want to investigate the Ranger's forged documents. Those King's seals are supposed to be proof against forging. I'm wondering if the wizard that paid to have the reavers attack didn't also hire this fake Ranger. You saved my life again. Is that the tenth time or the eleventh?"

"Oh, and that saving was my pleasure, Sar," Wise laughed. "It was the tenth, and I think I still owe you three more to make us even in the saving of lives. Can you tell me why that elf on that huge black unicorn came to attack only you?"

"My war banner was unfurled in the hope of that

not happening," Corbyn said. "We're deep in elf lands, but. I thought I could talk my way out of fighting with the first band of elves we met. That elf was High Lord Pharadon, leader of the elves we fought last year up north. There was nothing I could say to avoid that battle. He clearly thought he had a score to settle with me."

"This strange wizard, snipping at you behind the bodies of others, do you know any wizards angry enough to do this?" Wise asked.

"I haven't a clue who it could be," Corbyn said. "When we get back to the capital, we'll have to have the King's wizard guards look into finding this spectral wizard. Until we get to the bottom of that little magical mystery, others will be coming for me, and right now, I couldn't defeat a kitten in a pitched battle."

Finishing the soup in his trencher, David offered his Captain the ladle, but Corbyn pushed it away. "I'm full. That was a good meal. Our King's Commission is unchanged; we still have to get into the woods and find an elf to talk to about his brooch. Besides my war banner, is there gear to be collected at our other camp?"

David looked a bit sheepish, thinking he had failed his Captain. "The only thing we don't have here is your banner. The camp gear was packed away when the elf came to attack you. I should have grabbed your standard, but there just wasn't time, what with that gapping huge wound of yours bleeding your life away. I can only hope your banner is still there when we ride back. Finding the spot won't be a problem as all we have to do is follow that stream south."

Trooper Heartstone rushed into the room. The youngest of the lancers, his fresh boyish face, showed amazement as he came to attention and saluted Cauldron. "Sir, an elf carrying your war standard and mounted on a bloody huge griffon has landed outside the gates. He's just sitting there on his monster creature with your battle standard stuck into the ground at his side. Men on the walls are loading the ballista and catapults right now. It will take a few minutes, but they'll get a shot at the bugger real quick like."

Corbyn's face lit up in a smile for the first time in a day. "Calm down, trooper, we won't have to fight this one. He wouldn't have brought my war standard back to me if he wanted to do us harm. If he's riding a griffon, I think I know him of old, uhm, from the first time I fought with the elves. Heartstone, run ahead on those young legs of yours and tell the others not to kill the elf. They are to hold their fire until I command an attack."

Corbyn slowly got up, still very weak from his healing and near-death experience, but the food gurgled happily in his stomach. The rest of the men in the kitchen rushed out to see the new visitor and his magical steed.

Slowly, David and Corbyn walked out of the tower and to the barbican. Planking held the inner portcullis open as the chain couldn't work the opening and closing mechanism. The outer portal was open as well as it seemed to be totally destroyed before the lancers came to the monastery. Through the barbican killing ground, Corbyn and David could see the elf, griffon, and Corbyn's banner outside in the distance.

"David, you go and calm the men down. I don't want to be talking to this elf and have a catapult stone land in my lap."

"Sar, yes, Sar!" David spoke in his parade ground voice, but he moved slowly toward the tower door and the long stairs up to the walls, exhaustion still having a grip on him as well.

Corbyn thought he knew just how David felt. Every bone in his own body ached, and he couldn't even feel his wounded side. He was wishing he had a crutch with him to help him walk. Renewed energy did carry him forward, as he knew the elf in the distance and was looking forward to talking to him.

After a few minutes, he reached the pair. "Cloudbreaker, you wonderful creature, I see you're still taking care of our High Lord here."

"Prince Sawal, you should tell your men it's unusually difficult to hit a griffon with a rock, no matter how well it's thrown." Dalbergia dismounted and gave his Prince a courtly bow.

Cloudbreaker chirped a happy greeting and lowered its huge head for the Prince to stroke it.

"There'll be no rock throwing or large spear casting while I'm out chatting with my favorite cousin and his most excellent steed," Corbyn replied.

"Prince Sawal, a certain demon sword said you were dead," Dalbergia said, smiling back at the prince of the elves, now turned human soldier. "Funny, you don't look dead. Some who knew you would say you are walking a trifle slow, however. Do you feel dead?" Dalbergia's expression was one of relief at seeing his distant cousin, and there was a sly grin on his face.

"There will be no Prince this and Lord that, cousin Dalbergia," Corbyn ordered. "You bounced me on your knee when I was young and were always my favorite distant relative. Have you married my mother yet?"

Dalbergia's face tightened a bit, and his smile went away as he sadly shook his head in mock contrition. "Your mother has so far managed to avoid my clumsy advances. Our King didn't have any choice in sending out Lord Pharadon. Someone had to find out why you're in our lands. I hope you know your grandfather would have never sent Pharadon if he knew the Lord volunteered for the task merely to try to kill you. The court, your mother, and I are all very curious about why you would ride this way again.

Oh, and killing Pharadon in a duel probably wasn't the most politically wise thing you could have done in the long run."

Corbyn continued to preen the huge feathers of the griffon. From old, he knew such creatures loved having their feathers scratched. "Cousin, diplomacy and I are very distant kinsmen. Dueling an ambassador of the High Elf King wasn't the best choice for me in the long run, but it was the best thing for my health in the short run. He gave me no chance to talk or explain my intrusion into elf lands. That demon sword of his almost did me in. I'm sorry I didn't break that blade in half when I had the chance. Was it still screaming its rage in the mud where it was thrown?"

"Pharadon's steed guarded it and his body when I arrived on the scene," the cousin replied. "Yes, it was screaming all sorts of demonic wailings. I penned a note to Pharadon's clan of your innocence in the duel, even though I had no idea if you were innocent or not. I had the very great joy of sheathing that nasty sword and forcing it to shut up. My message, the sword, and the body are even now traveling back to his clan on the back of his unicorn. I followed the proper traditions even though his clan won't believe my note. You and clan Pharadon having the recent history you have experienced together, I imagine you'll be seeing that sword at least once more if you chance to pass up north again," At the very least, the blade will be a tad disturbed thinking you dead and discovering that you are not. Maybe the clan will have the good sense to store that odious weapon in some dark treasure hoard where it belongs." The elf began furling Corbyn's war banner. He handed the enchanted device to his cousin. "Lord Pharadon's daughter is said to be an able moon warrior; she'll do a better job of ruling the clan than he did. Best you watch out for that female, I think."

"From acorns grow very large and often dangerous trees. How is my mother?" Corbyn had to ask, as his family was important to him.

"She greatly mourns your loss, even after all these years," the elf replied. "She stopped wearing mourning clothes just two months ago. Now, with news of your return, she wears them again. As mothers who love their gone forever sons tend to do, she fears some bold elf lord, much like our dead Pharadon, will feel the need to take your life." Dalbergia noted the look of growing concern on his cousin's face and changed his teasing tone. "She's well enough, cousin. Just why did you come back here without an army at your back?"

With that question, it was Corbyn's turn to cease grinning. "Our good King Hamel, the thirteenth ruler of the human lands, wants to give the most amazing gift to his daughter, our Princess, on her birthday. It's a very quaint custom the humans have, this birthday business. They remember from year to year the actual day in the year when they were born. Believe it or not, they give presents to each other on that day each year. I have been given a King's Commission; we won't go into how important such a thing is considered among humans to bring back an elfin brooch for her celebration. Oh, and you really won't believe what I've been given to help expedite the matter and convince an elf, any elf, mind you, to give up their brooch. Open this, but try not to drop it in your surprise at the stupidity of the humans." Corbyn tossed the soft bag of gems into the hands of his cousin and continued grooming the head of the griffon while the huge beast purred its pleasure at the treatment.

Wonder filled the elf's voice as the emerald-colored gems spilled out into his gloved hand, "Sharn stones, Prince, does your King realize how much more powerful he's making the elfin empire with these holy gems?"

"He doesn't care anything about that, even if I did tell him, which I won't," Corbyn replied. "Place one of the stones yourself, cousin. I can't think of anyone I would rather see use one of them."

The elf made a magical pass on his forehead, saying a brief prayer to the goddess of nature, and an emerald floated from the pile in his hand and embedded itself in his flesh. Instantly, Dalbergia magically changed, growing thicker and more muscular all over his body. Dalbergia's eyes changed color from light green to a deep emerald hue. The emerald, called a Sharn stone by the elves, acted as a focus of arcane energy, changing the elf into a more powerful version of himself. All of his natural abilities were now enhanced manyfold. In the entire realm of elves, there were only a few thousand using the power of the Sharn stones."

"On you cousin, it looks fine. Use its power well." Corbyn reached out to shake his cousin's hand.

"My Prince, you do me great honor." The timber of Dalbergia's voice deepened, and there was a new vitality showing through his eyes. "After this princely gift, I would be happy to grant you my aura brooch for the human Princess. Will you tell her how the magic of the brooch must change her?" The elf handed over his aura brooch.

Corbyn placed it in the magical bag the emeralds came from. "No, I think I'll let the brooch do its work. In a few eye blinks of elf time, this King will be dead of old age if nothing else kills him first, and over the intervening years, your brooch will have done a great deal toward uniting our two peoples. The humans do many things wrong, but I'm finding the longer I live with them, that their traditions have merit as well as the elf traditions my mother taught me. I miss the elfin court and people like you. I'm also glad I've never had to face you and Cloudbreaker here in battle."

"As are we, my Prince," Dalbergia replied. "May you never come south again to war."

"That's my wish as well, and this foolish brooch idea of the King's just might make that wish come true," Corbyn answered. "At least let us keep that thought in our hearts."

Corbyn took a small cameo out of his belt and handed it to Dalbergia. "I was hoping someone I knew from the high elf court, who didn't want to instantly kill me, would find me so we could have this talk. Please take this cameo carved in my likeness to my mother with my love. I know I've embarrassed her by joining my father's race, but that doesn't stop me from loving her and her ways or my grandparents. I would also have you plead to have her stop wearing mourning gowns. Tell her I'm well and doing fine and send her my best. Use the rest of the Sharn stones any way the elf court pleases, just as long as the magic they carry isn't used to strike me down."

"Prince, one last thing," Dalbergia cautioned. "Pharadon had news that you were consorting with Fey elves. Such a thing isn't true, is it?" There was a look of concern on Dalbergia's face with the question.

"Cousin, I haven't given up all my elf ways," Corbyn replied. "On this quest of my King's, I camped the first night, and Lord Cimmerian Nix came to my camp. We sparred with words for a time, and before I knew what he wanted, he kindly, to his own way of thinking, I believe, offered the Dance of Three Gifts to me. I'm sure he was there to kill me out of hand. In that heartbeat, my choice was to enter into a magical battle with Nix and lose my life and undoubtedly the life of all my men or accept his challenge and delay fighting the most powerful Fey elf in the world. I don't think I had much choice. I accepted his kind offer as graciously as I could."

"You are dancing the duel of three gifts with the ruler of the Fey elves!" Dalbergia's words revealed his shock and amazement.

Corbyn's face showed he was equally as amazed as his cousin. "At the time, it seemed necessary to agree to the challenge. I never planned to give any gifts to the Fey elf. I realize that's very poor form on my part, but what choice have I? He's thousands of years old in experience, a necromantic spell caster of immense power, and has the resources of all the Fey elves at his instant call. I've already been tricked into giving him a son of my own foolish making as my first gift to him, and he's saved my life and the lives of my men for his first gift to me."

There was a look of utter disbelief on his cousin's face.

"I know, I know. It should have never happened. Now, he and I duel to the death and I can't back out. Even living with the humans, my own sense of honor prevents me from begging. I know of no way now to stop the dance of death. Maybe I can keep from giving more gifts and not have to fight him for several hundred years."

"Why do I doubt that cousin?" Dalbergia said in stunned amazement. "Patience is not a virtue the Fey Elf ruler Cimmerian Nix cares to cultivate. The traditions of the duel will stay his hand in many ways, but he won't wait on your pleasure forever. You certainly do attract more than your fair share of royal attention."

"With this King's Commission finished," Corbyn said. "I should keep well away from elves for a time. Maybe Nix will take up more interesting matters."

"Enough talk of Fey elves," Dalbergia said. "There will be many new elf lords made from these stones, and each owner of one of these Sharn stones will know they owe you a great debt, as do I now. May you smile with every dawn, Prince Sawal."

"Cousin, I will, and may my mother's heart soften when you return to her. Thank you for my banner." Corbyn now used the furled banner for support as he was growing very tired after the struggles of the day.

"Think nothing of it, cousin," the elf replied. "Try not to have it lead an army this way again."

"I constantly endeavor not to be trying, cousin." Corbyn bowed a very royal bow. "Farewell."

The elf, knowing humans watched, waved goodbye instead of hugging his cousin. He mounted

Cloudbreaker, and the beast rose into the air on a flurry of wings, giving a lion's roar in its pleasure at winging back to the palace. In seconds, they were gone from view, high in the clear blue sky.

There was a lighter tread to Corbyn's step as he walked back into the monastery amid the cheers of his men. The lancers thought he'd talked his way out of not fighting the elf and the griffon. Corbyn's mind was miles away, thinking about wizards attempting to kill him, demons making zombies in the wilds along his path, and a certain Ranger who selected him out for death. With the brooch in hand and a hard ride ahead, at least he could get back with his commission accomplished. *I hope that a dragon doesn't decide to try to eat my troop on the way back to the palace.*

16

PLANS REALLY AREN'T COMING TOGETHER AS EXPECTED

"Don't complain about your luck if you refuse to cut the cards."

— LORD ANWARDENTINE

DALBERGIA LANDED CLOUDBREAKER ON THE palace grounds and left the griffon to attend to its own needs. In this quarter of the palace, there were many members of Dalbergia's clan who would gladly help the griffon companion. Dragons, hippogriffs, Pegasus, and many other winged creatures were kept and groomed in this section of the palace; there was no end of visitors, and groom-elves ready to help any creature needing tending.

Dalbergia's thoughts were totally on Princess Aesc and the need to see her before he talked to the King and the court. While the entire court would want to hear what he had to say, his beloved had sent him on this quest, and he wanted to tell her his news first.

With the fullness of the moon, he knew where she would be. There was a special little park where Teka roses bloomed all year round. The flowers purposely bloomed there, trying to cheer the Princess up as she mourned for her son.

He found her there. She looked so sad in her clothes of mourning as she sat on the bench in front of a huge display of red roses. The dark green dress seemed to press her lovely shoulders down with the weight of the world. Even the sparkling gems on her head and shoulders marking her rank as Princess of the realm were dull now as if responding to her sadness. A dark handkerchief sopped up her tears as she silently sobbed, and the vegetation of the park drooped in response to her mood.

"Princess Aesc, I have returned." He stood at the park entrance with his slim hands high in the air, a light tone to his voice.

She turned, and her lovely face filled with the brightest of smiles. "Dalbergia, I was so worried. I feared Lord Pharadon. . ." Rising, she didn't get the chance to come to him as he raced boyishly to her side.

He didn't let her finish. "Let's not speak ill of the recently dead." He kissed both her cheeks and had her sit back down on the bench. "I would tell you amazing news, but I can't." There was a teasing way in the gleam in his eyes and in the tone of his voice. He sat beside her and turned his head in mock sadness.

Hoping for the best, she picked up on his playful mood. *Surely, now that Dalbergia was back, he must have good news of her son.* "Can't, why is that my Lord?" Knowing how he felt about her and returning some of that feeling, she placed a gentle hand on his cheek and turned his head toward her eager face.

Dalbergia's heart and mind were filled with the beauty of his princess. All of the enthusiasm and energy he was feeling drained out of him as his love for her responded to her touch. His next words were slower and held a gentle tone. "I can't because you are in clothes of mourning. My news is amazing, not the least of which is, as I'm sure you can see, I'm wearing a Sharn stone." She dropped her hand in surprise. The powerful gem in his forehead matched the one in hers. He continued before she could remark on it. "Before I can tell you more, you must put on your happiest gown. You will require a dress shouting to the world of your newfound pleasure in what life has brought you. I will wait patiently here for you to change. I'll amuse myself with these thirty

Sharn stones your son gave me." It took all of his willpower to take his eyes off the face of his love. He faked an absent-minded, downcast look, fingering an empire's worth of emeralds that would be used to create thirty arcanely powerful elves when the stones were given as princely gifts by the hand of the King.

Dalbergia started whistling the tune of Gloryanth. It was an elfin song with hundreds of verses about two young lovers and their grand adventures in other lands.

Princess Aesc beat Dalbergia's chest in mock frustration, picking up on his teasing mood; she suddenly wasn't worried about the life of her son. She didn't care about the power of the stones at that moment, either. "Don't tease me. Tell me of Prince Sawal."

His eyes never left the stones. "Not a bit of it, my lady. As you are well aware, I went to considerable trouble to find your son and send him your words of greeting and enduring affection. I faced deadly humans who wished to throw huge war spears and giant rocks at my valiant steed and me. The price for Prince Sawal's words back to you and an unusually thoughtful present I have to give to you from his very hands," he patted his belt pouch and continued, "is your change of mood and clothes. I'm a tool in the hands of your Prince and son and must do as I'm bid and nothing less."

Princess Aesc was well aware that she wouldn't

hear anything of her son until she changed her clothes. Knowing he was alive and probably well caused her to throw traditions to the winds. Without looking back at him, she leapt up and lifted the heavy folds of her mourning skirt to run as fast as she could back to her chambers.

Dalbergia watched her fleeting form and found her movements quite unprincess-like but extremely pleasing to view.

———

The largest faerie mound in the world lay just a few miles from the site of the duel between Lord Pharadon and Corbyn Cauldron. The underground court of Cimmerian Nix gathered in that mound and slept the day away; his court became active and filled with life as the sun set.

At the instant dusk came to the land above the mound, the Fey Lord Cimmerian Nix liked to hear news of his lands from a Knowledge devil he commanded for that purpose. The summoned creature was a foot tall, with night black, scaled skin. A forked tail sported a poison sting while its skull displayed tiny horns marking it to those who studied such things for the devilish creature it was. The elves of the day were masters of summoning demons of all types. Naturally, the Fey elves, traditionally wishing to be far different from their dayside cousins, became experts at enslaving devils. This particular devil was the personal slave of Nix and had the ability to roam far and wide during the day in the lands above the faerie mound. It noted the comings and goings of elves and other creatures that would interest Nix and reported to its master with the setting of each sun.

Tiny devil claws raked the flesh of the living throne Nix sat upon. The Fey elf King's magic created a throne made from the bodies of humans Nix had encountered in his long history. Each human, magically frozen in time, wouldn't age, and their living bodies stayed bent into a useful posture by Nix's magics. There were twenty human bodies making his throne. Some of them had stayed frozen in their postures for a thousand years. Nix didn't care if the devil supped on the flesh of the royal throne. The Fey elf knew the little devil caused pain to the human clawed up, but it wasn't as if the human could scream and disturb the pair's conversation, so Nix didn't care. The magic forming the throne regenerated the flesh and blood lost in the devil's payment for information related to its master. The magic put into the creation of the throne was a trifle difficult for Nix to maintain, but he thought it well worth his time.

"You say Lord Pharadon and my Captain Corbyn Cauldron had a duel to the death this morning?" Nix asked.

The little devil's face splattered in the blood

and flesh of the human it dined on stopped its pleasant meal to try and answer its master. The creature couldn't fill its stomach fast enough but knew the penalty for not answering a question. "Yes, great Lord, noble Lord. This one, at your order, saw the honor duel." This was the third question answered, and it only had three more to go before it could escape the gaze of its summoner. The devil started ripping and filling its fanged face again.

"Are you sure Lord Pharadon wore the con of an ambassador of King Aik?" Cimmerian Nix couldn't believe what he was hearing and planned to make the devil suffer if it was mistaken. The elf knew from the casting of his summoning spells that the devil couldn't lie, but there were many ways to fool devils, and it could easily be mistaken.

Between slurps of gore, the little devil bobbed its body up and down. Its voice was far greater than its body would suggest. In a deep timber, it said, "No mistaking the black unicorn and oak tree on the con. However, Lord Pharadon took off the con before he started the duel. He also formed a demon circle to keep out Cauldron's followers; he did." The fourth question answered, it continued its mad rush to fill itself with human blood and flesh.

Nix grabbed the small creature and squeezed its body, deliberately causing the devil pain. The little monster regurgitated its meal and used its still free hands to grab parts of the lost gore to put back in its mouth when it could breathe again.

"Vile little devil, you will never call our Captain by his name again. From now on, if we let you live, you will speak respectfully of that person as the Unicorn Lord. Do you understand?" The elf gave the summoned creature a shake and allowed it to continue feeding and talking.

A look of hurt and pain filled the devil's face. This didn't stop it from tearing up more strips of flesh. "Yes, mighty Lord. As you say, I understand your will perfectly." Five questions answered, the devil waited to answer the sixth question and then it could leave.

"We must see this battle for ourselves; let us away to the very spot. Come, my friends," Nix waved to those in his court. "We will go to the location of a death duel between Lord Pharadon and our Captain." Cimmerian Nix transformed into his massive white wolf form, bounding out of the mound with hundreds of transformed wolves behind him.

The devil stood on the arm of the throne, waiting for its last question. No one was there to give it orders. The devil leapt with glee as there were forty eyes it could eat. Chortling to itself, "My master never lets me eat the eyes of his throne." The devil moved to the first human face, talons outstretched. It had nothing to do until its master came back.

In a matter of moments, the Fey ruler came to

the dueling ground. His wolf senses took in the odors of people, horses, a unicorn, and an elf lord who moved about the camp during that day. Nix changed back into his true form, "Duke Tornalal, bide with us a moment."

A huge gray wolf came to his ruler's side and transformed into Duke Tornalal. "Lord, I'm ever at your service."

"Tornalal, did you sense our gift? That reaver human is still alive and serving our Captain Corbyn Cauldron of the King's 25th Lancers?" Cimmerian Nix asked.

"I did, my lord, well done that. It's always so satisfying when a gift is given and so clearly appreciated by the receiver of the gift." Tornalal hid his smile behind his hand. "Of course, one would expect nothing less from a gift given by you, my Lord."

"Tornalal, you are too kind, too kind by half. Right, of course, but you're too kind. Please do us a favor and use your keen magics to set up a viewing of the duel that transpired here." Cimmerian Nix said. "We would like to see it from start to finish and maybe a little more after that if you can manage. While you are setting up the spell, we want to search more of the camp. We think the humans actually cooked food in iron pots if you can imagine that."

"Of course, I will work the spell in just moments. Iron pots, you say, the ways of humans are truly odd and freakish." Tornalal bowed and moved about the dueling circle, preparing his gray spells of enchantment.

Other court Fey elves moved about the camp in wolf form or in their true forms as the court watched their ruler and Tornalal study the camp. In an hour, Tornalal was ready.

"Lord Nix, my spell is prepared. Are you ready to view the duel?" Gray threads of magical energy flowed out of Tornalal's body and fluttered in and around the dueling circle, Pharadon made hours ago.

Nix left the sight of the campfire and walked regally over to the battle circle. He waved his hand to begin the magic.

Tornalal snapped his fingers, and the interior of the battle circle filled with more gray strands of magic. The strands shaped themselves into the form of Corbyn and Lord Pharadon, the Unicorn Lord's banner, and the con of the ambassador of the High Elf King. The figures began moving just as they did many hours before. Many in the court gasped at the magical energies spent in the casting of the spell. Few could have duplicated the complex arcane power, causing the past to reveal its secrets.

"Look at the con; Lord Pharadon is truly an ambassador of the High Court." Cimmerian Nix's voice showed the excitement he was feeling as he watched the scene unfold. Nix entered the circle and moved around the gray magiced pair, watching their every expression and move.

The Fey King's entering into the circle caused tremendous difficulty for Tornalal, as the Fey elf Lord strained his inner resources to maintain the spell his liege was disrupting. Naturally, he never would have said anything to stop his master and thus make his efforts easier. His liege could do what he willed and Tornalal made it his duty to aid in his King's activities no matter what the personal cost to himself.

The scene continued to unfold before the eyes of the court. When the image of Lord Pharadon removed his con, the entire Fey court, standing around the large circle, gasped at the breaking of elf tradition.

"Naughty, naughty Pharadon. We are sure the King won't be amused when he hears of that action." Nix hid his smile behind his hand, and the rest of the court laughed at their ruler's quip.

The gray Lord Pharadon drew his weapon; the gray Unicorn Lord already had his steel sword drawn.

"Oh, this is the part we most want to see. Tornalal, cause the duel to run at half the speed it has run so far; we would get a feel for our Captain's swordsmanship," Nix ordered.

"Yes, Lord." A straining Tornalal painfully snapped the fingers of both hands, and the two gray characters slowed down in their motions as they performed the same actions as the real bodies had done earlier during the day.

Nix kept up a running commentary for his court as the battle unfolded. "Cheeky bastard, that elf, very cheeky to fight our Captain. We are wondering if we should break convention and tell the High Court they must leave our Captain Corbyn Cauldron alone?"

His people shuddered at their leader's thought. Never dealing with the day court was the main pillar of Fey elf life and tradition. They were all amazed that Nix would even consider such a thing.

Lord Nix waved his people's reaction with a brisk motion of his hand. "Yes, yes, we know, we know. However, it's intolerable that one of those boorish elves could end our dance. This Captain is ours, we tell you, and we won't give him up easily. Nevertheless, you are all correct; if he dies, he dies. Oh, look!"

Nix waved at the duel as Lord Pharadon swung at the war banner, and Corbyn lunged at him.

"Foolish elf, he should have known not to cut at the banner, even with his demon blade. The banner is clearly a gift from a very powerful relative of our Captain's. We can feel the residue of its living magic. It won't be long now; we don't care how good a sword-elf Pharadon is. Now, the magics of the banner can aid and even strengthen the good Captain. Our Corbyn will kill him."

The battle scene continued to the end. The demon sword cut into Corbyn's side as Lord

Pharadon slipped on the hole, and Corbyn killed him with his hidden dagger.

"Look at that, Tornalal; hold that image," Nix commanded.

Tornalal did as his master bid him, but observers watched as the elf Lord was straining visibly. The muscles on his arms and face revealed cords of tension. The gray images stood motionless.

Nix walked round and round the pair, marveling at the image. "Our Captain has taken a death wound. Not caring in the slightest or even showing the effects of the demon sword, our good Captain causes a hidden weapon to appear in his hand. Oh, how very human. Then, and this is the amazing part of our thinking, he thrusts this formerly hidden dagger into the eye of his foe. Naturally, the foolish humans didn't know it, but the banner kept Captain Cauldron alive until they could magically heal him."

The court marveled just as Cimmerian Nix did. Elf tradition held that even in death, elvish bodies desired nothing more than to look on the sun. The dagger in the eye took that ability away from Lord Pharadon. The attack was something a true elf would never do on purpose.

The pregnant Fey elf Leaf spoke up with some alarm in her voice. "Is your Captain dead, my Lord?"

"Leaf, attend us." Knowing what would happen as a second Fey elf entered the dueling circle; Cimmerian Nix took over the maintaining of the imagining magics with a snap of his own fingers. Suddenly, the gray images turned bright purple and glowed far more brightly than the gray images did. This was a testimony to the greater magical skill and power of the Fey elf Lord. Tornalal slumped down, exhausted to the ground. His liege caused a purple high-backed chair to appear under his follower. "Tornalal, well done this, by the way.

"Don't worry, dear Leaf. Our magics sense that the good Captain is healed and fine. His, let us see, what do they call them? Serpent, no Sergeant, yes, his Sergeant took him to the goddess' abbey. Our Captain is well. Maybe we should reward the good Sergeant for his efforts on our behalf. What do you think, Leaf?"

Leaf approached and knelt in front of her ruler. Her lovely dark hair perfectly framed her head and shoulders. The new life growing within her gave her a glow, making her even more stunning. "He's human, my Lord, and only fit for your scorn. If he's given you any pleasure at all, letting him live is reward enough, in my humble opinion."

Nix laughed, "Well said. By the way, how is Corbyn's first gift to us?"

"Well, my Lord. He will be a male you'll be proud of in his time."

"Of course, of course, let's all go back to court and sup. We've had such fun here in the early darkness. Tornalal, please make a moving tapestry of the duel. We must hang it in our chambers and have the fun of watching it over and over again."

"Yes, my Lord." Tornalal would have stood up and bowed at his liege's command, but he didn't have the

making of the magical tapestry, pleased at being able to serve his ruler.

———

The west gate of Sanguine was busy as it filled with a constant stream of people coming into the city and leaving. Guards in the upper towers took note of the royal con advancing toward the gate in the distance. The images and colors on the banner made it easy for the guards to determine who wore the heraldic device.

"Lord Cortwin, ruler of the Rill Lands, approaches the gates!" The lookout on the tower bellowed the arrival to his Captain. The Captain, in turn, sent a message to the palace. Reports went to the palace as any royal personage entered the city. Such men were easy to spot when they wore their colors and carried their symbols of heraldry on their shields.

A mile away from the city gates, the Lord joined the throng, entering the capital. Normally, riders had to contend with uncaring travelers walking and jostling the rider's mount in their hurry to move along the King's road. This crowding didn't happen with Cortwin's mount. The huge war stallion had an aura of menace around it, which even the most insensitive human could pick up. Four twenty-pound hooves pounded the crushed stone of the road and deeply marked the surface with every strike, making enough noise in themselves to warn of the power and possible danger of the beast. Even humans ahead of the rider sensed something odd behind them and turned, noticed the oversized war charger, and got out of the way.

Lord Cortwin greatly enjoyed the effect his demon horse had on the massed humans around him. "Don't eat the farmers, Challenger!" He said this aloud, smiling as people rushed to get even further out of the mount's way.

Immediately, fifty yards worth of people in front of the horse scurried to the sides of the road, stopped, and warily watched the beast and rider go by.

A very irritated Allen the Net demon transformed into the war charger, furiously thought to his current master, *Challenger? Where in the nine hells did you get that name? You know I only answer to the name Allen.*

Still speaking aloud, Lord Cortwin smiled to the onlookers. "Challenger, I don't care what you want. You can eat enemies of the realm later. On Challenger!"

Allen, the Net demon, could do nothing but

obey the commands of its summoner, but the demon hated every second of its forced servitude. *On Challenger, he says. He's posed as a human for less than two of their years, and already he's acting like one and enjoying it. His behavior isn't very demonic if you ask me. Take on their ways and rue the day, I say. Of course, no one cares what a little Net demon thinks.*

The Nevil demon in the form of Lord Cortwin greatly enjoyed not only the whining thoughts of his demonic mount but the look of fear in the eyes of the humans he rode past. He would attend court, and for the next few months to a year, he would have more fun trying to start another war with the elves. Today, he would check in personally with the stupid wizard Disingen. The demon planned on tormenting the human spell caster a bit and then returning to court and his mission to keep the elves and humans apart. *Hopefully, Corbyn Cauldron would be dead by now or, at the very least, be entertained by a surprising number of zombies.* The Nevil demon, in the human form of Lord Cortwin, loved it when a plan came together.

Special magics of detection wrapped around the Nevil demon and his mount. The demon's own defenses became aware of the magical searching and easily caused the hidden wizards to see what they expected to see; an important Lord of the empire just riding through the gate.

In the catacombs under the city, Aliesha had just arrived. As she entered her quarters, she couldn't quite decide if she should make public her removal of the mark or if she should keep the knowledge to a select few. *There's an advantage in keeping myself mysterious to the rest of the cult. I have to weigh that advantage with making it known that I'm powerful and still very capable of killing any mark I please.*

Speaking to the air, Aliesha ordered Callum to her quarters. One of the constantly attending shadow guards moved from the shadows and went to summon Callum Darksoul. The wishes of the Mistress were orders to everyone else.

As she was stripping off her Ranger uniform, Callum silently entered and knelt before her. "I have news, grand Mistress of Death."

"I also have news." In her dark, clinging sheath, she circled the assassin. Her hands gently stroked his throat and heart with every turn she made around his kneeling form. To an outside observer, such actions appeared as if she were flirting with her subordinate. Callum knew each of her touches caressed pressure points in his body. She could end his life with any one of the dozen touches she gave him.

Knowing she had the power of life and death over all assassins, he started speaking so that she would know what he did in case he was about to die.

"I must report that dwarves killed the three of our brothers. The ones you sent to kill the mark. Considering our history with dwarves, I've sent a large expedition of rock cutters and stone merchants to the edge of dwarven lands. They are to stay there for as long as it takes to learn more about the race of dwarves."

Aliesha stopped her twirl of death around Callum Darksoul. "Death is our way and our goal."

"Death is our way and our goal," he repeated back to her.

Aliesha spoke next, "I organized the death of the mark our three brothers failed to end. True, a band of hundreds of zombies actually did the killing, but I'm pleased with the result, nevertheless. After we are finished here, tell Rothal to inform the wizard the mark is dead. After the wizard understands this information, Rothal is to release the soul of the wizard."

"Finished here, Death Mistress?" Callum didn't understand what she wanted.

Aliesha moved to the bed, "Yes, I have other needs requiring your attention, your close and undivided attention. We will give the Wizard a few more hours of life before you are able to contact Rothal. Attend me."

The appetite of the Death cult Mistress after she made each one of her many kills was legendary among the men of the cult. In the many years of service to Aliesha, Callum never had this type of invitation from his leader. Her posture left nothing to the imagination, and Darksoul was up to the challenge.

————

Disingen paced back and forth in his chambers, clearly dithering over nothing. Hours before, he'd finished cadging three vampires. As a spectral wizard, he was very talented at handling the undead, and the task would have daunted many other types of wizards, but for Disingen, it was quick work. He would be using one of the vampires in his sacrifice to cause his spectral crystal ball to work again. He'd regretted his anger and spell use of many days before and really wanted to look in on his various projects again.

The bell of his door rang; knocking on that same door would have resulted in the intruder cursed into ant form.

"Apprentices, that's what I need, servants to answer the door so that I don't have to bother. I must get special servants since my spectral companions keep eating the mortal ones I hire. I'm a spectral wizard, for dark gods sake; I shouldn't have to answer my own door." Disingen was thinking about the times he'd tried having others serve him and do the menial tasks about his chambers. Each time, those servants, no matter how powerful, had been eaten or drained of life by some spectral creature of one type or another Disingen had summoned for various tasks. He shook his head at the thought of puny servants, unable to stand up to even the weakest of ghosts. Finding good help was so hard in this day and age.

Absentmindedly, he cast spectral magics, and an image of Rothal, the assassin, appeared on Disingen's side of the door. Disingen waved his hand, and the door unlocked and opened. "It's you Rothal. Did you bring me more demon tomes?"

The large killer slowly walked into the room, looking to see if the wizard had placed any more magical wards in and around his chambers. "No, no great wizard. I bring very good news, however. The mark, Captain Corbyn Cauldron is dead."

"No

, he's still alive." Disingen said this in a very distracted tone as he went back to scanning scrolls and tomes at his human bone table.

"Wizard, I have it on very good authority that. . ." Rothal stopped his words as the wizard's skeletal talon of a hand pointed to a heartbox on a shelf at the other end of the chamber. Pale spectral magics caused the box to glow, making it clear which box Disingen meant. The assassin knew enough of magic to be aware that heartboxes could hold the life of a wizard or gauge the life of another if the proper spells and body hairs were worked into the magic of the box.

"I was able to gain some of the lancer Captain's hair from his quarters. An interesting redheaded woman gained them for me for a small cost. When the spectral heart in that box stops beating, your mark has died. I just looked in the box not ten minutes ago. See for yourself."

Rothal walked to the box, lifted the lid, and peered within. First, he noticed three heartrings in small recesses on the side of the box. He palmed one of them. A heartring made by Disingen could prove highly useful. At the center of the box floated a black heart. The construct pumped regularly with a heartbeat. The outer veins of the magical heart throbbed with life, showing power and vitality. Rothal noticed the blond hairs making up part of the heart's surface. Knowing Disingen's skill, he was sure this spell showed Cauldron still alive.

Rothal tried to think clearly as the truth of Cauldron's life struck him. *The cult mistress was wrong in her claim of the mark's death. In the traditions of the cult, an assassin making a false claim of death on a mark had to die. Callum Darksoul will become the leader of our order. Should I still kill this wizard? I must report this news before anything happens to the wizard.*

Suddenly, Disingen clutched at his chest and fell to the floor, screaming in pain. Rothal rushed to his side. A red glow pulsed to a faster and faster heartbeat on the spectral wizard's exposed chest. Rothal pulled wider the black wizard robes, noting the scar. *This wizard had placed his heart in a heartring like the one in Rothal's palm.*

The magical door burst open, and through a cloud of brimstone, Lord Cortwin of the Rill Lands strode in, clutching a heartring and twisting the ruby stone at its center.

Lord Cortwin stopped, clearly surprised at finding Rothal there. The assassin rushed to kneel in front of the Rill Lord.

"Great and noble lord, I would touch your ring in all honor and supplication." Rothal tried to sound as respectful as he could.

The Nevil demon, as Lord Cortwin, still had a lot to learn about human customs. It didn't have the slightest idea what the assassin was asking, so it stopped torturing the wizard and put out its ring hand.

The kneeling human lowered his head over the hand of the Lord, touching his own fingers and lips to the ring using a surprisingly firm grip for a human.

Rothal spoke first, "Whatever this lowly servant can do for you, Lord, you have but to ask."

Quite used to claims of service by all sorts of menials, adding an assassin to that number didn't matter a bit to the posturing demon.

"You can leave. I have royal matters to discuss with the wizard," ordered the Lord.

"Yes, great Lord, as you wish, noble master," the assassin replied.

Rothal rushed out of the room as if his feet were on fire. Hurtling at top speed, he raced down corridors, and it wasn't until he was out of the palace that he dared to look at the newly acquired heartring he'd slipped off the finger of the demon, replacing that ring with the empty heartstone ring from the heart-box. Rothal knew of demons and knew that they had little sense of touch and feel in their human bodies. The assassin watched the demon twist the ring on his finger, and Disingen suffered from that twisting action.

Rothal knew what the answer would be when he handed this ring to his new lord and master, Callum Darksoul. There would be no killing of the spectral wizard now that the assassins were in control of Disingen's heart.

———

The wizard lay on the floor, the pain having driven him to the ground. "My master, please, I beg of you; I won't be able to finish your quest if I'm too weak to move."

Lord Cortwin stood tall over the body of the wizard and refrained from twisting the ring on his finger. "How go my plans?"

"The assassins have just reported Cauldron dead." The wizard knew the assassin was wrong, but he wasn't about to tell the demon that. "Naturally, I will be checking their facts, and I expect to present a body to you shortly." Grabbing the bones of his table, he struggled up on his feet. Moving deeper into his chambers, he sought to get as far away from the evil presence of the demon as he could.

"I do wish to see the body. Even dead, there is a chance that the brooch may come into the King's hand. What of that?" The anger in the huge face of Lord Cortwin seemed to swell his head to a larger size. When the demon noticed this, it got a grip on its emotions and used illusionary magics to return to a more human appearance.

Nervous at the thought of more spikes of pain shooting through his body, Disingen started babbling, saying anything to keep the pain away. "Of course, contingency plans are what we need. I will send word to the gate guards under a King's order to have the lancers take the brooch though the Sanguine corridor to the throne room. Rarely do any, but the most royal members of the court use those dark marble steps. I will transfer the control of the Door Golem there to you and myself. When Corbyn's troopers take the brooch up those stairs, spectral magics can summon us both. We will meet those men and kill them with none the wiser. The brooch will never reach the King."

The Nevil demon was delighted with his wizard's plan. Not seeing any flaws in the idea as laid out, it smiled at the wizard and allowed some of its huge fangs to show through its illusion of humanity. "You have done well. Continue in my service and great power will be given you." The Lord walked out of the chamber, and the portals slammed shut behind him.

"I have all the power I need, demon, and soon you will know my wraith!" The little wizard limped, still in pain, over to several caskets. He lifted the lid on the gold one and flipped the large skull bone chip into the air, making magical gestures in the process.

The bone began to float, and underneath appeared the ghostly form of King Hamel the Twelfth in the robes he was buried in seven years ago. "How may I serve you, master?" The words came in a slow whisper.

"Prepare four copies of a royal decree going to the four outer city gates. Order Captain Cauldron or any members of his troop, as they come to the city on their King's Commission, to come immediately to the palace up the Sanguine stairs to the throne room. They are to talk to no one until they reach the throne room. Only one of them should bring the brooch. When you've finished writing out those orders, port them into the daily order dispatches going to each gate commander. Notify me when you have accomplished this task."

"As you wish, master." The ghost took quill pen in hand and began making the royal decree using secret codes known only to the military and those of royal blood.

Disingen got the supplies he needed to spectrally

subvert the Door Golem to his will. The enchanted mechanism would seem to serve both the wizard and Lord Cortwin, but if the wizard were any judge of this Captain Cauldron, the wizard's demon could be in for a few deadly surprises. If Cauldron couldn't kill the demon, the Door Golem would have its chance as well.

17

THINGS GENERALLY WORK OUT
FOR THE BEST

"I've never seen anyone worn out carrying the gold they tried to take from me."

— COMMANDER JANON

THE THRONE ROOM IN THE CAPITAL CITY OF Sanguine teemed with its normal bustle of Dukes and Earls. Elsewhere, the king took the air of the gardens with several pleasant court ladies, allowing all of his ministers to get some of the empire's work done. Each corner alcove of the grand chamber had its share of empire officials attending to the day-to-day workings of the human nation.

The real power behind the throne, Lord Anwardentine, moved from Sars mirror to Sars mirror, collecting information from every corner of the realm. The magical mirrors, created centuries ago by a mystical method now lost to modern wizards, allowed instant communication between two speakers no matter how far apart the mirrors were. At the moment, Anwardentine talked with Major Stonewall of the SouthSword fortress over the matter of the ridiculous King's Commission. "You say there are forces at work trying to kill the Captain over this elf bauble for Princess Talyn's birthday present?" Anwardentine's face showed the bewilderment his mind experienced.

"Those forces haven't stopped Captain Cauldron so far," the Major answered. "If it pleases my Lord, not an hour ago, I sent the Captain and his remaining men on fresh mounts up the road to the Capital. He should make the journey in plenty of time to accomplish his mission if left alone by outside influences. I wanted to advise you that strange forces were at work in regard to this matter." The Major stood ramrod straight in front of his Sars mirror; an image of his body magically appeared in front of Lord Anwardentine as if he were facing the master of the Exchequer.

"Quite right, Major, quite right," the Lord answered. "Please list those forces again for me?"

"Assassins tried to kill him twice," the Major replied. "There's a wizard sending at least one group and possibly more out to stop the troop. Reavers, led by Ash Greenwood, failed three times to ambush the troop; those reavers are all dead except for Ash, whom Corbyn has given a King's Commission pardon for information, which Ash turned over to him. Zombies filled a monastery and attacked the troops when Cauldron came there wounded. Oh, yes, and an ambassador from the elves, ignoring his station as an ambassador, challenged Cauldron to a death duel. That last might not have anything to do with the brooch. It seems the ambassador was the leader of the elf clan our empire has been warring with in the northern territories." The Major was handed several scrolls and waved his adjutant away from the mirror, continuing his report. "There is a false Ranger with credentials using the King's seal mixed up in this as well. Corbyn remembered seeing garrote calluses on her hands and thought she might be from the assassin's cult as well. I have men checking into her whereabouts from this end. We'll send sketches of her appearance along with my report. I want you to know I checked her credentials myself, and they look fresh from the King's hand. She's riding a distinctive horse; maybe we should check for it at the gates of the capital."

"Yes, yes, when I get your report, I'll take care of that," Anwardentine advised. "Why didn't you send more men with Cauldron? It seems to me that he might be needing more aid if all this attention is being paid to his King's Commission." Lord Anwardentine looked to see if others listened to their conversation. No one was close or approached him. He made a mental note to erect chambers around each of these mirrors. Too much secret information could be heard in the way they functioned now.

"The Captain and I discussed assigning him more troops," the Major replied. "Both of us agreed the faster he traveled to the city, the better. More troopers would take more supplies and slow him down. I've given him spare mounts, the best this fort could offer. He's well on his way and knows the terrain. He should be there in three days or less if I'm any judge of men." Major Stonewall's face showed the confidence Anwardentine felt as well.

The Lord started thinking about the dozen other matters he had to take up before the King came back. "I don't know why this difficult-to-get-brooch is causing such a ruckus. With the help of the Captain and your resources, maybe we can sort it all out. Put any conjectures you might have in your report and send it to me immediately. If you discover other news of our good Captain, send it by Sars mirror at once, day or night."

Major Stonewall went to attention and saluted. "Understood, my Lord. Luck to the empire."

"And all who live under her banner," Anwardentine said, turning to walk slowly back to the North alcove. Deep in thought over so many hands turned against the lancer Captain, he contemplated sending out more lancers to cover Corbyn. "No, that's not going to work," he said to himself. "They could easily miss each other as there are several routes he could take back."

The Lady Marsh and the Countess Andiv were arguing again; that meant people weren't being paid today, and that would never do. Anwardentine hurried his pace to the pair.

———

In another part of the city, hundreds of yards under the earth in the assassin's catacombs, Callum Darksoul stood with the wizard Disingen's heartstone ring in his hand. With great relish and personal pride, Rothal had just finished telling Callum of the scene in the wizard's quarters.

Upon hearing the news, Callum called others in, gave special instructions, and sent those same people away. The pair now slowly walked to the training catacombs, where they expected to find Aliesha.

"Well, you're right, Rothal," Callum said. "There's only one thing to do if Cauldron is still alive. I'll take those steps only if we know for sure he still lives. This heartchest you spoke of, is there a chance the magical heart doesn't represent Cauldron's?"

Rothal thought carefully before he spoke. "The

hairs came from his room. There is a slight chance they could be from someone else, but few in the capital have the blond hair Corbyn sports. Disingen was convinced his spell displayed the heart of the Captain, and the wizard was powerful. You do realize Aliesha expects me to report the wizard's death?"

Callum waved Rothal's last question away with a gesture. "The way of our cult is clear if Cauldron does live. I will tell Aliesha the wizard needed to stay alive a bit longer. We will proceed as traditions dictate. Our roles are fixed in this action, and your coming to me with this ring was well done."

"Thank you, Master Darksoul, I. . ."

Callum interrupted, "Not a bit of it. Attend me as we talk to Aliesha and the others now. Your star rises with mine. The wizard can be an important tool in our hands. Death walks with us now."

They moved into the largest training catacomb to discover Aliesha teaching the first-year assassins. Callum noted the nine other assassin guild masters within hearing distance of Aliesha and her charges, as he had requested of them. Each occupied themselves with an activity allowing them to hear the discussion of Callum and Aliesha. An additional ten shadow guards with special instructions from Callum now guarded Aliesha, unknown to her.

He waited until she finished demonstrating one of the blurring moves of the thousand-twist pattern.

"Death Mistress, I have a favor to ask," Callum

spoke loud enough for the entire class and all of the other listeners to understand him.

She waved him to continue, smiling seductively.

"Rothal has just come back from talking to the wizard. The demon was there. I would have Disingen kept alive a trifle longer until our demon experts can learn more about the creature that commands the wizard."

Looking stunning in her tight black cult wear, she raised her hand for attention. "Assassins, in the case of the Wizard Disingen, he requested our services in slaying a mark. Then he went on to use other means as well as ours to kill this Corbyn Cauldron. I took care of slaying the mark personally, but the wizard needs punishing for his insolence. What is the only punishment our cult meets out?"

"Death," all of the assassins in training spoke the word at the same time.

Callum spoke up, "and what is the punishment for an assassin failing to kill his mark?"

"Death," the young assassins said again.

Startled, Aliesha didn't have the slightest idea why Callum would ask that question. "As long as the wizard dies in the next three days by Rothal's hand, I have no problem with your request." She stood there in a challenging posture, wondering if there was anything Callum was trying to subtly suggest. Up until this point, he had been a faithful follower. She didn't think having a relation with him would change that.

Rothal and Callum bowed and walked away. The master assassin had set forces in motion with the brief interchange. If Corbyn Cauldron appeared in the capital, Aliesha would die, and he would take over the cult. *Many things will change when that happens.*

————

In the throne room, among hundreds waiting for the evening and the royal ball to begin the two-week-long celebration of the birth of the Princess, the Lady Cordellia, dressed in her most revealing court gown, chatted with the Lord Cortwin of the Rill Lands. She didn't know why others thought him a country bumpkin and a bore; she quite liked the man.

"Are they all big and strong like you in your Rill Lands, my Lord?" She stroked her gem-encrusted fan over the vast amount of flesh she enjoyed putting on display for the world to see.

The demon Talonten really couldn't understand what the fuss was about the human males he'd talked within the last few weeks concerning this Lady Cordellia. *True, the pair of feeding sacks she supported on her breathing cavity was quite large for a human, and the red hair was interesting, but she never stood still.* "Lady, you are too kind. No, I'm considered quite average among the men of my court. You, dear woman, would shine as a rare gem in my humble castle. You really. . ." Lord Cortwin stopped. A hundred yards away, the Lord of the Exchequer talked to some officer. The demon's ear tufts easily picked up on that conversation, and he didn't like what he just heard.

'. . .If it pleases my Lord, not an hour ago, I sent Captain Cauldron and his remaining men on fresh mounts up the road to the Capital.' There was more, but none of that mattered to the demon.

Suddenly, it felt a sharp tapping on its human face. The Lady Cordellia was hitting it with her fan.

"My Lord, normally, men are thinking about me when they are lost in thought. I don't think that is the case with you. Do you find me so uninteresting?" She shifted her body and arched her back to best display her perfect form; surrounding men couldn't help themselves, conversations stopped all around her in admiration.

Her pouting lips made an expression on her face that the fake human couldn't identify. Talonten thought maybe she was trying to be seductive. The very idea repulsed the creature beyond measure. For the thousandth time, the demon wondered why human mating rituals had to be so difficult. *Why couldn't they just eject their eggs and allow males to cover them in reproductive fluids as other civilized beings did?*

The demon was in turmoil over the news it just heard. "My lady, I could converse with you all day, but I really have some pressing issues to attend to. Matters of state, you understand, don't you?"

She stamped her pretty foot. "Not a bit of it. Why do men constantly seek to leave my side with matters of. . ." She didn't get to finish as the Lord left in a rush. In a tizzy, she looked for Janon. *I'm going to have a huge argument with my fiancée, and then we are going to have great makeup sex. It's the only thing for it.*

Lord Cortwin moved as quickly as fashion allowed through the throng in the throne room. Some of the Lords there commanded his attention, and he bowed and made polite conversation with each of them. All the while, his mind wrapped round and round the problem of the hellish human Cauldron. Unknown to him, he had started muttering under his breath as he voiced the problem. "The wizard's plan seems sound, but I don't like waiting until Cauldron enters the palace. I could go out and face him on the road, but if I missed him in the darkness or if he took another way to the capital, he'd arrive, and that damned brooch would get in the King's hands. That brooch is just another bad step causing elves and humans to grow peacefully together. By all the black gods in hell, haven't my people suffered enough at both race's hands?"

Going to the side door, the fake Lord wanted to inspect the trap Disingen set for the lancer Captain. The demon threw open the portal. Unknown to it, that door design was purposely made too heavy for a human to open by himself. On this side of the door, one was supposed to knock, and Thomas, the Door Golem, would open the door. The demon's strength had no problem moving the massive portal. No one was paying the demon any attention in the throne room, or there might have been consequences for its rash act. The demon closed the door after itself and inspected the golem.

"My lord," the guard golem bowed stiffly. "It's a rare man who can open my portal by themselves." The golem's attempt at under statement was completely lost on the demon.

Lord Cortwin looked the construct over from head to toe. Demonic senses took note of things no human could see. Magical energies outlined the golem. At eight feet tall, the enchanted power of the animated statue was evident. Wisps of spectral energy covered its head. Disingen had clearly been at work here. The statue's massive spear would make it a deadly foe, even for the demon in its true form. "Raise one of your legs."

Normally, the guard statue would have ignored such an order. It raised its leg.

"You will do whatever I say?" the demon asked.

The stiff expression on the golem's face never changed, but there was an almost amazed tone in its voice. "I don't want to, but it seems I must. What would you have me do?"

Pleased, Lord Cortwin smiled. "What are your orders from the wizard?"

"When a lancer Captain comes up these stairs, I'm to stop him and wait for you and the wizard to appear. You will give me more instructions then."

"Excellent, put your foot down," ordered the demon.

An inspection of the black marble stairs revealed many spectral runes. There was no way to climb those stairs without stepping on one of the invisible runes. The magic of those runes would call to the wizard and demon. *The plan was perfect. I must reward the wizard for his acts here. I think I won't torture him again until, no, that's no good. Spare the rod and spoil the larva, I always say.*

———

At dawn, a day's hard ride away from the capital, Corbyn and Ash stood by their mounts as the rest of the troop broke down the camp. The sun was just rising in the east. The day was sharp and clear.

Corbyn still didn't trust the man, but he did respect the reaver's efforts on his troop's behalf in the recent days. In the back of Corbyn's mind, there was also the problem of the reaver existing as a gift from the Fey elf. Corbyn knew he couldn't allow the reaver to go into the King's dungeons. Elf traditions didn't allow for imprisonment of any type, as death was preferable to an elf's way of thinking. Putting Greenwood in the dungeon would be a slap in the face of Nix, which would bring instant trouble to Corbyn.

Corbyn kept his tone of voice purposely brisk and businesslike. "Ash Greenwood, this letter I'm giving you pardons you from the King's justice for all your past acts against the empire. You can ride from here a free man or come with me to the capital, where we'll be trying to find that wizard who hired you."

"I want to be with you when you plunge your sword in that black elf's heart." Ash could see Corbyn's face when he said those words and noted the doubt in the Captain's expression. "That's not going to happen any time soon, is it?"

"I don't like saying this, but I'm putting off that fight for as long as I can," Corbyn replied. "I know of no one who has a chance of facing Cimmerian Nix and living in a fair fight." That was the first time Corbyn had voiced that thought. It made him extremely uneasy. Corbyn was a fighter, and he didn't like to think there was anyone or anything he couldn't defeat in fair combat. He'd just made the realization, himself, that Cimmerian Nix could be the death of him. Part of him wanted to rush, weapons drawn, screaming his defiance at his tormentor. Another part wanted to do anything to avoid the battle and live a little longer.

In the last twenty-four hours, Ash stood taller and looked people in the eyes again. Some of the old inner fire was back in the reaver. Corbyn had treated him well since the fight at the monastery. Ash reached to shake Corbyn's hand. "If what you say is true, you should seriously consider making it an unfair fight. I think nothing less of you for being so open with me. With your permission, I'll take my leave now. There are a few men left in my camp, and I'll make a new start with them somewhere else. I'll make sure you won't be sorry you pardoned me."

"I'd be wary of your old ways if I were you," Corbyn said. "The Fey elf Lord considers you a gift to me. If you go back south, he might very well capture you again and send you my way. That act could cause me problems. I sense no taint of the elf on you now, but his magics are powerful, and he could find you if he really wants to. Nix can find anyone he's interested in by working his magical spells."

"Oh, I'll be staying away from elf lands for the rest of my life," Ash said. "The world is wide. Some places don't cotton well to elves. I'll get by. Thank you, Captain, you've been damn decent to me, considering I started out trying to kill you."

Ash tied his remount's bridal to the pommel of his saddle and mounted up. He rode north and didn't look back at Corbyn and the troop. Head held high; there was none of the crushed spirit in evidence now. A few days rest and Corbyn giving him the pardon had put new hope in the man.

Sergeant Wise walked up, watching the reaver

leave. "Commander Janon is going to want to know why you pardoned that very wanted, former regimental Captain of the King's infantry."

"Yes, I suspect you are correct again, Sergeant," Corbyn replied. "I've got an entire day's hard ride to figure out how not to tell Commander Janon that a certain legendary elf would take it very hard if I threw his present in the capital's dungeons. We have a King's Commission to finish, and it's just a day's ride from being done."

"If the creek don't rise and the goddess is willing," Wise replied, smiling and mounting up on his own charger.

———

In the heart of a dark, gnarled forest, where even the elves rarely roamed, a grove of walking oaks, the oldest of their breed, guarded an ancient stone gateway to another world. Not used for thousands of years, the location now served as a tradition-bound meeting place for elfin royalty. The gray light of predawn didn't touch the center of the grove, but the time was important to High King Aik as he swirled purple summoning magics, putting out a call he never thought he would have to make. The elf dressed in the rich, kingly green robes, his normal magical equipment he'd placed on a low altar at the side of the grove. Such equipment wasn't proper to wear in the presence of the gateway, considered the most holy of places for the elves. Long ago, the elves of another world came through that gate; the memory of their sacrifice in reaching this world was remembered with respect by all the long-lived elves thousands of years later.

A dark portal opened up on the other side of the glade, and the smell of brimstone and death filled Aik's senses. Cimmerian Nix stepped through the portal. The newly arriving elf bowed in honor to the ancient stone gateway. Not even looking toward the other elf, he moved to the same side altar where King Aik's equipment lay. Nix stripped himself of the amulets, weapons, and magical devices he constantly carried. He'd only been to the gateway twice in his long life but knew the traditions as well as any elf.

King Aik, leader of all the elves in the world, knelt on one knee and bowed his head, "Cimmerian, elder brother, thank you for coming."

"Rise Sharnen, we are kin after all and must have no formalities between us. It doesn't matter that we are your older brother. You surprise us by this summoning. What would the tradition mongers say to the meeting of the King of the Fey elves and the King of the elves of the day?"

Rising, King Aik's face filled with concern. "Cimmerian, we just heard that you are dueling the duel of three gifts with the Unicorn Lord. Please, say it isn't so."

A brief look of shock marked the face of Nix. "Oh, but it is so and most diverting. We don't remember when we've had so much fun. Surly, a mortal couldn't cause your summoning. He's of no consequence."

"He's my grandson." The look of anguish on King Aik's face spoke volumes.

Cimmerian stepped back, truly surprised, "he's not an elf. How could this be?"

Aik pressed his palms together, and his entire body showed nervous tension. "Princess Aesc, in youthful folly, mated with a human King she found worthy. Naturally, when we discovered this, we killed him ourselves, but the damage was done. Their union created Prince Sawal, known to the world as the Unicorn Lord. Brother, please, while he's only half-elf, he has a noble spirit. We don't wish his death at my older brother's hand."

"A half-cast elf is an abomination." The calming influence of the holy ground Nix walked on did nothing to halt his rising anger. "He must die. The Princess should have become Fey from this terrible act of hers. What type of kingdom are you running?"

King Aik reached out his hand to calm his brother. "Surely you understand the folly of youth. You should be the ruler of our people. Yet, you stand here having made just one mistake of the heart. Even with that mistake, the Queen mother still loves you."

Nix turned his back on his brother and faced the

portal. "We care nothing for you day elves, but your grandson, my nephew, is now both our problem. You must marry your daughter to an elf, and she must bear more royal heirs. If the Unicorn Lord should. . ." Cimmerian shuddered at the very thought. "This half-cast creature could destroy the world as we know it. If the Queen, your wife, you, and your daughter die, the upheaval of his ascending to the throne would be terrible to see. We had planned on playing with this Unicorn Lord for centuries; now, your foolish daughter has forced my hand."

"No, brother, we know you love me and our mother; we are begging you to stop the duel," King Aik asked.

Cimmerian Nix turned in rage on his brother. A cold look of defiance showed in his face and stance. "None of that. We give you fifty years. If your daughter hasn't married and made another heir in that time or if you haven't born a son, the Unicorn Lord must die at our hand. Do not cause us to come again to this holy ground for this reason."

The Fey elf ruler raised his hand, purple magics summoned his equipment, and they and he slipped through the black oval portal.

The King of the elves of the day stood there longing for past times before he assumed the throne. King Aik knew his older brother was stronger than he was; he'd always been a better elf. Aik expected Nix to be more sympathetic since love caused his downfall two thousand years ago. Nix was right, of course; Prince Sawal could never rule the elves. Dalbergia was a likely suitor; maybe he should force his daughter's hand. That thought was less repugnant than having to deal with his brother for killing a beloved grandson.

18

DEPENDABLE GUARDS ARE HARD TO FIND

"Those who don't believe in luck have never drawn a sword in anger."

— COMMANDER JANON

Sixteen tired lancers rode exhausted horses to the east gate of the capital city of Sanguine. Gate guards stopped the troops.

Ten halberd troops backed the Corporal of the guard, and he stepped out to stop the lancers. The tall infantryman held his halberd at parade rest. He shouted his question at the obvious leader of the troop of lancers in front of him. "Captain, would you be Captain Cauldron?"

Sergeant Wise wasn't in a mood to accept the tone of the gate guard. "Captain Cauldron is on a King's Commission and doesn't have time for your attitude." The Sergeant barked his words, expecting their force to move the infantry guards out of the way.

The Corporal stood his ground as the throng of people wanting to get in and get out were forced to wait on the finish of the interchange. "My Captain has King's orders for yours, and you can go anywhere you damn well please after I've given this Captain of the King's lancers his instructions."

Corbyn put a reassuring hand on Wise's shoulder and spoke to the guard. "Carry on, Corporal; we'll wait here for the orders."

Not saluting, the man moved at a brisk trot to the gate tower.

At the same time, and unseen by the guards, a lovely young woman named Cybal Smoothhand slipped through the crowds around the gate and raced for the merchant's quarter. Cybal was an up-and-comer in the assassin's cult. She thought her orders very strange when she got them with a small painted image of Corbyn Cauldron from the hands of her journeyman master. She was to sit at the gate until relieved, or until this Corbyn rode up to the gate. If he appeared, she was to report immediately to Callum Darksoul. She wasn't looking forward to her first meeting with him. She knew what her news meant. The Death Mistress had announced to everyone that she killed Cauldron. Since he was obviously still alive, the Mistress would have to die. Cybal's important information made her proud to be an assassin. She kept repeating to herself, "Death walks with me now. Death walks with me now."

Still at the gate, the two lancers sat their mounts, brushing the dust of the road off with their riding gloves. "David, he's just doing his job. I know we're beat right down to the ground. I know our horses are about ready to drop. It did no good to bark at the man. He was only doing his duty."

"Begging your pardon, Sar," Wise replied. "Troops of lower rank will keep a civil tongue in their heads around you, or I'll know the reason why."

"That's fine and appreciated, but . . ." Corbyn didn't finish as he started reading the orders handed up to him by the Corporal. He read them quickly. "That's a trifle odd. I'm to take the brooch up to the throne room by the Sanguine stairs as soon as I enter the city."

"Why is that odd?" the Sergeant asked.

"Normally, I would expect to report to Commander Janon at the barracks grounds. "We're two days ahead of schedule; I wouldn't think there was a need for orders commanding haste in this matter." With his instructions in his hand, Corbyn gave a mock salute to the still-waiting gate guards. "Men, carry on; I have my orders and intend to carry them out." The guards moved away, and traffic began flowing in and out of the gate again. "Sergeant, take the men to the barracks and stand down. After I'm through reporting to the King, I'll come back and tell you how it all went."

"Sar, yes, Sar!" Wise saluted. "Reporting to the King, now that's grand if you ask me. I'll keep a tankard of wine handy for your return." Wise and the troop turned right down the street of Dreams.

Corbyn kicked his horse in the direction of the Lord's Way and the side of the palace where the Dukes and Earls of other parts of the empire had their residences while they were at the capital. Dog tired, the grandness of his surroundings didn't impress him at all as he ached to finish his assignment and get some rest.

The palace loomed large above him on its hill. Over the years, it had grown huge with expansion after expansion. As a military officer, Corbyn was able to gain entrance at the first of many walled gateways by stating his business. Dismounting, he handed his horse off to a castle groomsman. "Do you have a horse brush handy? I'm to report to the King, and I don't want to look like a street urchin with all this road dust on me."

"You'd be amazed how many times we brush down travelers before they see the King," the tall groomsman laughed. "Let me help you." From a basket, he took two long brushes and gave one to Corbyn.

"That's much appreciated," Corbyn said as he brushed the thick dust from his arms, legs, and front while the groom did the same to his backside. "While I'm away, water my horse and give him a little grain, but don't take his saddle off unless I'm not back by sunset. I could be with the King ten minutes or ten hours."

"Understood, Captain," the palace groom said. "We'll take good care of your mount while you're gone. If you aren't back by late tonight, I'll see that the mount is sent to your billet."

Corbyn tossed the man a silver piece and walked briskly to the next gateway. There were three other gates to pass and walled enclosures to navigate through before he got to Lord's Way road. He thought about getting something to eat before reporting to the King, but the orders he held in his hand were very specific, and he knew the definition of the word, 'immediately.'

———

The Tindel and Son's merchant house had hours ago closed its doors to the public for the day, but far below ground, the business of assassination and the practicing of assassinations was going strong.

The early evening was the busiest time for the

assassins and their leader. Every night at this hour, Aliesha, in her regal black robes, sat on the golden throne of death. The assassin's hood of judgment draped over her head marked her station as the undisputed arbiter of ending life as she heard and commented on the actions of the cult. Tindel Merchant House matters took over an hour to manage; three marks were in the process of careful scrutiny before dying; there were the plans for the high holy death day, which would see ten important people of the city slain in sacrifice to the death god.

The death chamber held over nine hundred assassins waiting on the will of their cult mistress. A soft buzz of many conversations filled the area but never grew so loud that everyone failed to hear the words of their leader.

Into this crowd, Cybal rushed to give her news to Darksoul. She whispered the arrival of the mark to her leader.

"Very good, Cybal. Please go to my quarters and await me there. We will talk of a suitable reward for your actions this day." He admired her slim figure as she slipped back into the crowd. Looking at her pretty backside was his way of putting off the inevitable, but he knew there was no putting off his next action. From his own robes, he withdrew a hood of judgment and placed it on his head. The many assassins near him responded to this action by clearing a large circle around his spot. A judgment hood, especially put on in the chamber of death, meant there was killing to do in the name of the god.

Raising his hands for attention, his action caused ten specially placed shadow guards to ready their weapons.

"Death Mistress, I must have your attention!" Darksoul called out.

Aliesha looked to her new bed companion, marking the judgment hood he'd just put on. She wasn't concerned as the donning of such a hood wasn't uncommon in her chamber of death. "Callum, who must be judged?"

"Death Mistress, what is the penalty for lying about the death of a mark?" Darksoul asked.

"Callum, you asked me that earlier," she answered. "My answer is still the same, death."

"Know at this hour that the mark Corbyn Cauldron just rode into the city." Callum chopped his arm down and pointed his finger at Aliesha.

To her credit, even in her heavy robes, she managed to dodge four of the missiles shot at her heart and head. She also struck three others away with her quick hands. Two more bolts punctured her eyes, and another entered her heart. Dying, her god turned her body to black dust instead of green. If her dust had been green, her death would have been in error. All in the chamber knew Aliesha's soul had gone to the assassin's hell for all eternity, cast there by the judgment of the death god for her mistake. The dust swirled away in a god-given wind and vanished into the shadowed darkness of the chamber.

Callum sat on the throne of death, "No one should mourn her passing. She committed the vilest sin of all. Also, no one may take revenge on this Corbyn Cauldron mark. I wish to study him in my own time."

The new leader of the assassin's cult flipped the heartstone ring to Rothal, who stood as the second in command now. "Put this ring on your finger and go to our little wizard and tell him of its new owner. Everyone else, go to your duties. I have matters to attend to in my quarters and do not wish to be disturbed." Callum rose from the throne, musing on the question of why killing a deadly adversary always made one crave physical pleasure.

———

The black stairs of the Sanguine entrance to the throne room caused Corbyn to hesitate. He was tired and not trusting his senses right now, but there was something odd about the wide staircase. Looking up and down and all around, using every sense he had, Corbyn couldn't feel anything but the cool marble of the stone. He reached down and touched the first step and used his sharp nose to sense that few ever came this way. He knew that many of the royals didn't like using this entrance because of the black of the stairs. He shook his head, thinking the color of the stone was barely a reason for not stepping on the stairs. The wide corridor he stood in led to residences of Lords for hundreds of yards in either direction. The corridor was empty save for his presence.

Just yards away from completing a difficult assignment, he shrugged his shoulders and started up the wide staircase. His first step up the black marble staircase touched on an invisible spectral rune. Unknown to him, he'd activated spectral magics he wasn't able to detect.

Ghostly spirits flew invisibly from the rune and, in a second, reached the positions of Disingen and Lord Cortwin, telling the pair of Corbyn's arrival into the trap. At the same time, Thomas, the Door Golem, moved from his guard post and placed his huge pike across the door to the throne room. This prevented anyone from magically opening the door and possibly coming to the aid of the Captain.

The golem tried shaking his head to free himself of commands he knew were wrong. The spectral magics of Disingen were just too strong. The golem obeyed the instructions from the wizard. His huge body started descending the wide stairs.

Corbyn hadn't climbed the stairs high enough to see something was amiss with the barred door to the throne room. The golem coming down the stairs was a tad strange to the Captain. He'd seen many of these special guards, but they usually didn't move from their posts unless there was danger.

The golem moved past Corbyn, seeming to ignore him. The Captain continued climbing the stairs. Suddenly, huge, stiff hands grabbed him from behind, pinning his arms to his sides. "What the. . ."

"You will be held here until the wizard Disingen and Lord Cortwin appear. I wish to apologize for my actions to you, Captain, but the wizard controls me now, and I must follow his orders." The golem sounded almost sad as it held Corbyn in its clutches.

Corbyn's legs were both free; he rose up with his body and smashed both boots against one knee of the golem. His own body took the punishment as it was like slamming against a rock wall.

Corbyn knew the fear of desperation as he felt his life measured in heartbeats. Snapping his fingers, he called up his most potent magics. Lightning flowed from his hands and poured into the body of the golem, burning the animated statue.

"You have power, Captain. I think you will find that I'm sadly proof against most spells of destruction. Although, that one shook me up a bit. I will have to go to Baron Arullian for some patching after your very probable death at the hands of the wizard. It is my belief Baron Arullian will be proud of you when I tell him how you attacked and hurt me."

The golem spoke of death far too calmly for the

Captain. No twists of his body, no magics from his hand, worked to free him. *What was left to try?*

"Golem, what are your orders?" Corbyn shouted.

"Right now, I'm to hold you until the wizard and Lord Cortwin appear," the golem calmly stated. "Normally, I'm to guard the throne room from intruders. I'm to be especially watchful of demons and devils attacking the throne and King. Look, the pair arrives at the top of the stairs."

The ghostly forms of a wizard and the Lord of the Rill Lands appeared at the top of the landing and became solid.

Not knowing if it would do him a bit of good, Corbyn used the last of his magical reserves to snap protective moon energies around his body. The golem still held him in its vice-like grip.

Lord Cortwin's face showed the pleasure he felt in seeing this Captain of lancers helpless in front of him. He rushed down the stairs and didn't even notice that Disingen remained on the landing. "Finally, little human, you have no idea how hard I've tried to bring about your death." The Lord was wincing at the blazing light Corbyn emitted toward its demonic senses. The glow from the protective moon magics around the human's body appeared ugly and bright to the demon's eyes. "Where is the elfin brooch you bring to that fool of a King? I don't sense it anywhere on your person."

Unknown to Lord Cortwin, large spectral hands

floated behind him. Disingen, at the top of the stairs, manipulated the hands with spectral gestures of his own. Brows set in deep concentration, the wizard's plans for freedom hatched on the stairs below him.

"You have me at a slight disadvantage, my Lord," Corbyn groaned. "Could your wizard order the golem to free my hands? Naturally, I will tell you where you can find the brooch." Corbyn sensed things were happening around him. The wizard at the top of the stairs must be the one trying to kill him. It didn't take much to realize the Lord in front of him was very probably the mastermind behind all the actions to stop the brooch from reaching the King. Corbyn could see the floating hands behind Lord Cortwin, but the man facing him couldn't.

"Disingen does what he's told, and so will you," Lord Cortwin replied. "I will suck the life out of you and learn where you hid the brooch. I don't require your freedom to kill you and make you my zombie." Lord Cortwin transformed into his true demon form, and huge fangs dipped toward Corbyn's neck.

"It's a Nevil demon! Golem you must stop it!" Corbyn tried to get the golem to let him go. The grip on him shifted in response to his words, but he still couldn't move.

The fangs of the monster touched Corbyn's magics, and the demon's head shot back. Its lips charred from the moon magic.

"Attend me, golem," Disingen spoke softly at the

top of the stairs.

The golem looked up to see the wizard signal to free Corbyn's right hand. The golem let the arm go, keeping his grip on the other arm.

Contained in its elf-made sheath, the demon couldn't sense the Nightwing Dirk hidden behind Corbyn's steel sword. Facing the demon, the half-elf remembered the words of the witch at the inn. He drew the weapon with his free hand and plunged it into the body of the demon. The magical weapon tore at the spirit of the demon.

From out of the handle of the dirk, freed human spirits killed by demons in the past came pouring out. Spirit hands gouged out the eyes of the demon. Spirit teeth tore at the flesh of the demon. In heartbeats, the vengeful spirits held so long in the handle of the dagger pulled off the Nevil demon's arms and legs. As the demon ripped apart before Corbyn and the golem's eyes, the spectral hands of the wizard's spell worked to take the heartring from the demon's hand. The ghostly hands grasped the ring and flew back to the triumphant wizard.

The demon turned to dust along with the Nightwing Dirk. The vengeful spirits vanished to their final rest in the spirit world.

"Grab his free arm again, Thomas." The wizard walked down the stairs but kept far out of reach of Corbyn's feet. All the while, he admired the heartstone ring on his finger.

Held tight, once again, Corbyn couldn't believe his bad luck.

"What now wizard?" Corbyn asked. "It seems I've done your dirty work. Am I to die now as well?"

"Captain, I wouldn't dream of killing you now," Disingen answered. "That dirk of yours was most extraordinary. Vengeful spirits wrapped in a weapon is a wondrous idea. I'm surprised I never thought of it. I was hoping you would have something of the sort what with Nevil demons being so hard to kill and all.

"No, I can't end your life, even though I'm sure your spirit could serve me very well," the wizard chuckled. "I'm feeling unusually generous, what with my newfound freedom. I'm leaving now; let's not expect me to be so generous if we ever meet again."

"Quite, do you think you could get your golem to. . ." Corbyn watched the wizard slowly fade in spectral magics.

"Did I hear your name was Thomas?" Corbyn craned his neck to see the face of the golem. Painted with a white, childlike visage, its body was far different from that of a white giant.

"Yes, that is my name," the golem answered.

"Well Thomas then, I'm Corbyn; please let me go." Corbyn didn't have much hope for his request.

"I can't do that, Corbyn," the golem sighed.

"What can you do?" Corbyn asked.

"I can easily hold you here until I'm given other

instructions," said the artificial door guard.

The thought of being held for centuries didn't please the Captain. "Who gives you instructions these days?"

"Well, it used to be just the Lord of the Exchequer and the King. Either one can tell me what to do. There seems to be some unusual magics playing around my head allowing the spectral wizard Disingen to command me as well."

"Could one expect the Lord of the Exchequer or the King to appear any time soon?" Corbyn tried to hide his frustration; after all, he mused, it would do no good to show anger toward a two-ton animated statue.

"I've never seen the King come this way," the golem said. "I know of him, of course. The Lord of the Exchequer will be here tomorrow morning, most probably. It's his wont to come past my post almost every morning."

"Great, now I can look forward to being held here for just twelve more hours or so." Corbyn's dry wit was lost on the golem. "Thomas, did you know I was given a King's Commission?"

"Really, Corbyn," the golem sounded surprised. "Those are very important commands. Even we golems know of the serious nature of a King's Commission. Daniel, the door golem on the north portal, helped with a King's Commission once. When do you think you will accomplish your commission?"

"Roughly twelve hours from now, it would seem," Corbyn grunted out this answer, trying to struggle free, but the golem's grip was like steel. "Thomas, I have a thought. How would you like to help me finish my commission?"

"I would like nothing better," answered the eager guard. "The chance for a door golem to help in such a quest would be a great honor."

"Well then, let me go," Corbyn ordered.

"No, I can't do that," sighed the golem.

"Well, that's quite understandable," Corbyn's sarcastic tone was completely lost on the magical golem. "Is it necessary to hold me only at this spot?"

"That's a very interesting thought," said the bemused door guard considering the question. "As I review my orders, I think I can hold you anywhere. Why do you ask, Corbyn?"

"I was thinking since you left your post anyway, that I could be held in the throne room as easily as on the stairs," Corbyn said. "I could then finish my King's Commission. Could you take me to the throne room?"

"Yes." The golem started moving ponderously up the stairs.

Corbyn steeled himself for the remarks he would be getting from the Lords and King when he appeared in the throne room carried like a rag doll. Duty to King and country was often a hard burden.

19

THE KING'S COMMISSION ACCOMPLISHED

"You can count on your luck changing, usually for the worse."

— LORD ANWARDENTINE

SWOOSH, BANG! THE BIG PORTAL, FORCED open by the foot of Thomas the door golem, slammed into the wall. Thomas, carrying Captain Corbyn Cauldron of the King's 25th Lancers outstretched in its hands, strode boldly into the throne room. Thomas had never been in the throne room in the hundreds of years of his guarding that portal. The enchanted door guard had no idea what would happen if it did walk in.

Magical alarms sounded, of course.

All over the palace, enchanted gargoyle statues shrieked alarms of danger. The tones of the shrieks declared there was serious trouble in the throne room. Every military trooper in the palace and the city around the palace ran to their combat stations.

The thousands of cooks, servants, and people in all of the many royal towers took cover wherever they could from the deadly danger they knew would strike the palace any second. Their thoughts were that if the heart of the palace, the throne room, was under attack, their positions would be next.

Records would show that nine months later, an unusual number of births occurred, but there was so much work at the birthing of so many babies that few people had the time or the inclination to note the fact.

The massive gates at twenty-seven different barbicans all around the palace and in the city closed shut under the protests of thousands of people who didn't want to be on whatever side of the gate they found themselves when the alarms sounded.

The King, at the time of the alarm, was enjoying himself on his throne in conversation with several Lords about the upcoming festival of lights the King was sponsoring on the weekend of his daughter's birthday. That ended as his dragon throne animated, and the King became protected in the metallic coils of the dragon as it moved its head to strike out at anyone who might come near to try and kill the King.

The guardian Lords with their Nightwing Dirks drew their demon-killing weapons and stood all around the coils of the throne, the only ones the dragon allowed near.

Lords and Ladies ran this way and that in terror, trying to figure out the best place to hide in a huge chamber with no objects to hide behind. Many bounced against doors, as suddenly outside door golems wouldn't open doors at the chance of letting in more enemies of the empire.

Other golems in the throne room all raced to place themselves between the King and Thomas. The big, eight-foot-tall creatures made loud thudding noises as their equally large feet repeatedly slammed against the marble floors.

Out of the masses of struggling people trying to flee strode Commander Janon. The good Commander didn't care if untold thousands of demons walked through a hell portal to get at his King. He was the man who would lead the charge to stop the deadly rush. If his life ended in a swirl of demon talons, so be it. No monster was going to attack his King without stopping to taste Janon's blade. His magical armor glowed golden with an inner fire. His huge enchanted sword blasted out a song of battle and death, inspiring the other guards in the chamber to lay down their lives for King and country.

Troopers started following behind their commander, and Lords and Ladies bounced off the determined troopers and fell to the floor in a very unlord and un-ladylike fashion.

Empire wizards started popping into the air high above everyone's heads. They knew they couldn't transport onto the floor of the throne room, so they had prepared flying spells to appear at ceiling level. Death energies crackled in their hands as they, too, readied themselves to protect the King and stop the invaders to the throne.

Through all of this, Corbyn could only hang in the grasp of the golem, hoping palace destroying magical energies didn't rip him apart before someone realized he'd come to report on his King's Com-mission.

Lord Anwardentine looked up from his scrolls in the North alcove. In less than a second, he rose and moved toward the disturbance. Not a fighter, he had some battle skills imparted to him from the arcane devices he always wore. He was of a mind that there was a high percentage chance that this was a false alarm.

Anwardentine noted his King. The proper guards, enchantments, and the animated throne all worked to the plan he'd set up many years ago. The Lord nodded in appreciation of that job being well done. He saw Janon headed toward the cause of the alarm. The Chancellor of the Exchequer pitied the poor interdimensional creature that would be first to face Janon. Then, the Lord saw the head of Thomas above the rushing mob. The door golem shouldn't be there, and more importantly, it shouldn't be grasping a Captain of the King's lancer's in its hands.

Using a spell his family had designed centuries ago for times such as these, Anwardentine magically shouted, "Cease!" Waves of calming energies spun out in circles around the Lord of the Exchequer. Alarms, located in the throne room proper, stopped caterwauling. Lords and Ladies still screamed, but his magic spun out in wider circles through the chamber, changing those shrill cries to whispers. The only thing not silenced was Janon's sword. The sword's song was in refrain and now seemed extremely stupid, considering the nonfoe standing just past the Sanguine portal.

"Hearts stop beating with Janon's every stroke!
Brave men repeating that hero's okey-doke!
Janon, the destroyer, the man who will not die!
Janon, the redeemer, the man, makes ladies sigh!"

"Okey-doke, Commander Janon, while that weapon of yours might mean the death of your enemies," Lord Anwardentine walked through the now still masses of court officials toward the golem. His voice, clearly heard over the whispering den of the hundreds of others who continued to mill about, Anwardentine's words continued in calm tones aided by the force of the family-calming spell. "That terrible verse could possibly be the death of me. Sound the all clear; this is the matter of one errant golem and its prisoner."

An embarrassed Janon sheathed his still-singing sword and clapped his hands twice. Gold magics flashed all over the city, a signal that everything was all clear and the King was no longer in danger.

The throne dragon once more turned into its valued and much-needed position as a throne. The King continued to hide behind its coils, peaking out to look at the door golem and its charge, a hundred yards in the distance.

The five knights with the Nightwing Dirks didn't leave their posts; no matter what Commander Janon ordered, they would now be standing guard for the next twelve hours with their weapons drawn.

Janon and Lord Anwardentine calmly walked in front of the golem. Janon was the first to speak.

"Captain Cauldron, what in the world are you doing in the hands of. . . "

"Janon, if you don't mind," Anwardentine commanded silence, and Janon obeyed with a bow.

"Thomas, why are you holding this Captain of the lancers?" the Chancellor asked.

Corbyn appreciated the fact that the Lord of the

Exchequer didn't order the golem to drop him. Although he wasn't a dangerous enemy, the Lord didn't know that.

"I was ordered to hold him, Lord." Thomas' voice held a metallic quality. There was the barest note of pleading in the tone.

"Umh, you don't say. I didn't order it. Did the King order it?" Anwardentine walked round and round the golem, inspecting its body and the body of its charge.

"No, my Lord, Disingen, the spectral wizard ordered it," explained the golem.

"If I may, my Lord?" Corbyn was now beat red as more and more of the court gathered around to hear why the golem was in the throne room.

"No," Lord Anwardentine waved Corbyn silent. "I think we will let the golem explain things in its own words for a few moments more. Men can lie, but in theory, golems can't. At least up until now, they couldn't." Anwardentine trusted the golem and its view and knew little about the Captain except he was the one sent on the recent King's Commission.

One of the guardian wizards flew lower, just over the heads of the crowd around the golem. The spectral King's wizard, Endulal, noted the magics playing around the head of the golem and knew them to be invisible to any but a spectral wizard. He sprinkled the ash of a cleric on the head of the golem. Dark swirls of spectral magics revealed themselves. "The King could still be in danger from this one."

"Janon, you know what to do." Lord Anwardentine's tone was commanding.

"Quite right," Janon waved his men into action, and the King, surrounded by hordes of troops, rushed from the throne room and out of harm's way. The court Lords and Ladies thought it was a good idea to leave as well. The now unalarmed door golems opened doors on all sides of the throne room to the insistent knocking.

Lord Anwardentine watched the royal court leave. Looking at the alcoves, he was pleasantly surprised to see his own people getting back to work. All of the other alcoves were empty, but the finances of the empire were still being maintained. He smiled, knowing his people knew he would tell them if they had to leave. *They were good folk.*

The ten throne golems still encircled the Captain and Thomas. Anwardentine kept the wizards flying above as well. If something dangerous was going to happen, it would be handled quickly.

Lord Anwardentine respected the skills of those around him and knew no fear. "Wizard Endulal, could you please explain what's been done to Thomas."

"Certainly, Lord." The wizard flew closer to the golem and gestured. A ghostly form could be clearly seen with its hands on the head of the golem. The head of the ghost seemed to be stuck in the head of the golem. "The position of the specter clearly shows the control the specter and its summoner now has over the golem. My understanding of golems is sparse, but I can tell the specter controls part of the magics, giving the golem its intelligence and life. Disingen, the wizard casting this spell, is quite powerful. It should be no surprise that his specter allows him to give orders to Thomas. There could be several other orders given to the golem that we know nothing about."

"How do we remove this creature from our once loyal guard?" Lord Anwardentine.

The wizard floated close to the head of the golem. "Oh, it's still loyal. It's just under the dark magical control of this Disingen. It would continue to guard the throne room as normal if we let it. Naturally, we don't want others besides yourself having that control. The touch of a holy symbol by a cleric with faith will dispel this specter."

Looking around, no one was surprised that all the court clerics were gone.

"I'll get one," Corbyn said from his fixed position. The humor of the statement broke some of the tension.

"Thomas, please release our Captain," the Chancellor ordered.

The golem let Corbyn go. Corbyn dropped

lightly to the floor, rubbing his arms to get the feeling back in them. "Thank you, my Lord."

"I'm hoping you have good news to report, but that must wait a moment still. Will one of you up there please go fetch Commander Janon and a court cleric?"

Several of the floating wizards flew to the doors to the north and east and went to fetch the proper people.

"Thomas," Lord Anwardentine said, "lay on the floor with your hands behind your back until instructed otherwise. The rest of us will wait by the throne until the proper people arrive."

Minutes passed by, and door golems let in Janon and several clerics.

"Commander, I trust the King is well and safe?"

The Commander came huffing at a run. "Yes, my Lord. I have him eating in the kitchens with several different circles of guards and court ladies surrounding him."

"Well done, Janon. I'd promote you for that excellent act, but you're already the highest of military rank." Anwardentine was feeling some relief at not having to defend the empire from magical attack.

"Think nothing of it, Lord. Duty to King and country is my life," Janon said humbly.

"Quite," lord Anwardentine agreed. "You clerics, please go over to poor Thomas there, and the Wizard Endulal will instruct you in the ways to fix the golem.

While you are there, discuss how to prevent this deadly act from ever happening again. It just wouldn't do to have our golems turn against us all at once. I will expect your report tomorrow morning."

"Yes Lord," the clerics said together and hustled over to the golem.

"Captain," Anwardentine turned to Corbyn.

"Yes, my Lord." The Captain stood to attention.

"None of that, Captain; at ease, young man," the Lord waved him at ease. "I don't know which question to ask you first. There are so many interesting things for you to report. Janon, you are going to be amazed at this young man's military quest. I imagine you, and I are going to be talking about it for weeks, if not months to come."

"Really?" Janon didn't know what to make of the light tone of the Lord of the Exchequer. "Captain, what have you gotten yourself into?"

"Well sir, it's a bit hard to explain," Cauldron stammered. "The most important part is that I have accomplished the King's Commission. Here is the elf brooch I was sent to secure."

The magnificent jade brooch lay in his hand. Each of the facets of the brooch glowed with inner magical fire.

Lord Anwardentine shook his head as dark thoughts now filled it. "Does anyone have the slightest idea what this magical elf brooch will do to the Princess when she puts it on?"

"I'm sure it won't hurt her, my Lord," Corbyn tried to sound reassuring. "The elves use theirs to commune with nature."

"If you say Captain, if you say." The commander didn't sound as sure as the Captain did.

"Janon, I know you, and I will be reading this soldier's report tomorrow," Andwardtine said. "Please take that brooch to the King so that he can give it to his daughter. Sometime today, we need to get on with the business of running the empire."

"As you order, my Lord." Janon saluted and marched off with the brooch in hand.

"Captain, is there anything else I should know before I read your report?" the Lord asked.

"Well, Lord, there is the trifling matter of my thrusting a Nightwing Dirk into the heart of Lord Cortwin, ruler of the Rill lands, just a few minutes ago," Corbyn stammered again. "It seems the Lord was actually a Nevil demon in disguise. I imagine the Rill lands will have to be notified."

"Really?" now Lord Anwardentine showed his surprise.

"Also, that wizard, Disingen, is somewhere about. He was there on the steps with Lord Cortwin. When I killed the demon, the wizard took a ring from the demon's finger, taunted me a bit, and vanished. I think I've seen the wizard around the palace and at court functions."

"Tell the palace guard commander to organize a

search with court wizards protecting the squads of troops. If this Disingen can subvert one of the door golems, he can do that to living guards as well. I'm also ordering you and your men to not help in that search. You've accomplished enough this day."

"Yes, my Lord, immediately." Corbyn ached all over and wished nothing more than a warm bath after he saw to his men.

"One more thing, Captain," Andwardtine said. "The finishing of a King's Commission, even one as silly as this one was, is an important act to the crown. I'm sure Janon will place medals on you and your men's chests. That goes without saying; I just want you to know that I appreciate your effort. You now stand in my favor. If you have a need in the future, come to me, and we will see what we can accomplish on your behalf. Understood?"

Captain Corbyn Cauldron of the King's Own 25th Lancers came to attention once more, "Understood my Lord."

"Once you have eaten and washed the dust of the road from your hands, begin working on your report on the commission. From what I hear from the Major at SouthSword, your report will be lengthy and great reading. Dismissed."

Corbyn saluted and walked away, wondering how to best leave out details like ancient dark elves wanting to duel him, conversations with griffon riding elves, and possession of a Nightwing Dirk when only King's guards were supposed to have them. *It's possible the bloody report will be more work than the entire quest.*

———

King Hammel, thirteenth in his line, was truly a stupid and insensitive man, let alone a ruler of millions. Although he had lots of bad features and habits, one of his redeeming qualities was the love he bore for his daughter.

Twenty minutes before he reached his daughter's chambers, his court servants announced his coming to the Princess and her smaller court of hangers-on. A miniature copy of the adult court, the teenage lords and ladies were irritated that the King was coming as it would ruin their fun for the entire day.

The Princess sat on an oak throne carved into the form of a dragon. She was one of the great beauties of the empire. Long red hair framed an exquisite and pretty version of her father's continence. Her figure was full but very womanly. Princess Talyn was reported to have a temper matching her great beauty. Never having to work a moment in her life, she lived in an environment quickly, turning the Princess into a carbon copy of her father once she took over the throne.

Most of her dear friends left when the news came that her father was coming. Tight-lipped and extremely vexed at having her fun for the day spoiled, she sat waiting for her father to come. Her hope was he wouldn't stay long.

A crowd of twenty Lords burst into her chamber, announcing the arrival of her father. There were an unusual number of military types with him this time. The Princess was sure that was because of the alarm a few hours earlier. She had been surprised to see the hidden guards and young Lords who she never knew were ordered to surround her in times of danger. She hadn't liked being forced into hiding while the alarm rang on and on and on.

The King huffed and puffed up to her, and she stood up and knelt on one knee. "My King."

"Rise, daughter, I have an early birthday gift for you."

She stood, and the King went around to her back and placed a jade brooch around her neck. Everyone in the room gasped at its luster.

"Daughter, no human in the world but you has an elf brooch to wear."

Her anger at his coming vanished. The magic of the brooch subtly touched her mind and soul. "Father, your gift is amazing." Her slim hand went to the brooch and felt its warmth. The item started pulsing slightly with her heartbeat.

"Think nothing of it, daughter. You are worth every sacrifice the kingdom could make."

Uncharacteristically, the Princess slumped into

her chair and grasped her father's hand. Tears started rolling from her big eyes.

The King stood for a moment, thinking his gift had pleased her so much she was crying in joy. Never able to stand his daughter's tears, he patted her head and left, pleased with her reaction. He found himself choked up at her wonderful reaction. *Damned good idea, that. It will be a long time before I can top that one.*

The few remaining courtiers clustered around the crying Princess, wanting to see the amazing brooch. She waved them away, asking them all to leave.

The Princess continued crying as the magic of the brooch reflected her true nature back to her mind. She didn't like what she saw. She cried for all of the heartless things she'd done in her lifetime, recognizing for the first time the petty evils she had committed as a spoiled child and young adult. The enchantment of the brooch forced her to become sensitive to the feelings of others. The empire was destined to change drastically as the Princess started working to make everything better around her. She had to, as the magic of her birthday present wouldn't allow anything less than her best efforts. She'd never take off the brooch and in the next generation, when she ruled, a time of enlightenment would make the empire a very different place to live.

20

LOSE ENDS ARE NOT GOOD THINGS

"Chance fights ever on the side of the prudent."

— EURIPIDES

IN THE CHAMBERS OF THE WIZARD DISINGEN, many types of dust flew everywhere as the wizard rushed to pack his things before the palace guards and wizards turned out to chase him down.

Talking to himself, the wizard wished he'd been better prepared, "All right, I could have done this escape thing a bit better."

Scooping up important skull bones, he tossed them in his spectral satchel.

"Note to self to be a little more prepared for escaping in the future. Also, maybe I've acquired a bit too much stuff over the years. Maybe I'll spend some time researching levitation spells; they certainly would come in handy right now."

The little wizard looked for the tenth time at his casting pentagram. The two vampires were roosting nicely in the spectral sacrifice energies. At any second, he could walk between them and teleport away as their undead essences powered the spell. "Yes, yes, this plan has worked out nicely." For the hundredth time, he looked at the heartring on his finger. Getting it back pleased him right down to his missing spectral soul.

"Disingen, bide a moment."

The spectral wizard leapt around, deadly magics erupting on his fingertips.

Rothal stood in the chamber with his arms folded, dressed for the first time in assassin black.

Disingen smiled, not at all afraid of the assassin now. The wizard admired the effort it took to enter his chambers. He knew of the deadly and massive spells now activated and circling even the thick palace walls about his chamber. No one, no wizard, no magical creature, or assassin, should have been able to get into this room.

"Well done, Rothal. You have impressed me once again. I won't kill you if you tell me how you got in here." Just in case the assassin could do something to harm him, the wizard nonchalantly placed his now full satchel and his other large case of magical items in the teleport circle. He noted Rothal kept his distance, but a wizard couldn't be too careful these days. If he had the time, there were still some scrolls he wanted to gather, but he wouldn't let those stop him from escaping. Rothal's presence there unnerved the wizard a bit.

"Disingen, leaving, I see. Perhaps a change of location would be a good idea," Rothal said.

"Exactly," never taking his eyes off the assassin, the wizard scooped up the pile of scrolls on his bone desk and threw them into his spectral cloth of missive holding. The shroud absorbed the scrolls, and the wizard donned the spectral garment. Breathing a sigh of relief, he allowed himself one last look around as he edged nearer to the teleport circle. "I shall miss our talks, Rothal. Are you going to tell me how you managed to get in here?"

"Oh, one learns things as an assassin. I'm unusually good at what I do. Like noting those wonderful Fetchins on your shoulders, for example. I think those little beauties are the first thing I will be commanding you to turn over."

"My Fetchins, you can see them?" The wizard stepped into the circle, not liking at all the direction of the conversation.

Rothal stood unmoving in the alcove, the same alcove he'd waited in for several days and prepared with his own enchantments. His own protective magics surrounded him, and it was nearly time to end this session. The assassin strongly suspected there would be searchers coming soon for the wizard.

"No matter," the wizard said, still filled with glee. "I've won this day. Now, nothing can stop me. I'll explore some tombs I've wanted to search out for a long time now and continue my studies." He raised his ringed fist to Rothal. "No one will ever order me about again!"

Rothal smiled indulgently and twisted the heartring on his own finger.

Disingen fell to the floor, silently screaming in much the same way as the two vampires agonized several feet away.

———

A thousand miles from the capital of Sanguine, the caravan reached its destination. Unusually large flatbed wagons came to a halt at the order of the caravan master. The stonecutter Tarnold shook his head for the thousandth time at this foolish quest. Two thin men came to him weeks ago with bags of gold and a silly request. They wanted him and half his people to take a caravan to the dwarven lands far to the north. The men told Tarnold he could buy as much of the dwarven marble as he could carry away at their expense. The two men wanted to pay for the marble and for lessons in stone cutting along the way to those same dwarven lands. Lessons for fifty men so that they could appear as stonecutters when the caravan arrived at its destination was more than enough reason to refuse them outright.

At first, Tarnold had sputtered, laughing at the strange request. More bags of gold appeared in his warehouse. He still refused, not liking the thought of going to dwarf lands and feeling he was too old for the trip. The mound of gold grew until, finally, he couldn't refuse their golden request.

The gold would keep his family for the lifetimes of even his grandchildren. He took on the task, and it was a marvel from the first day to the second he arrived at the dwarven quarry.

The fifty novice stonecutters he and his people trained quickly learned the techniques of cutting and shaping stone. All of the trainees were unusually strong and kept their cutting tools sharp.

The caravan set up huge tents every night, and late into the night, those same men would exercise in fantastic ways, which were a marvel to the simple stonecutter and his followers.

In the second month of the trip, a large band of robbers swept down on the column. Such foes clearly wanted to pillage any riches the caravan had and escape into the night.

Tarnold and his other stonecutters never got a chance to protect themselves. The robbers came at the caravan like a wave and met a wall of death. In eye blinks, all of the riders faced attackers dressed as stonecutters. The stripped enemy bodies went into a nearby gully. Their weapons and their horses joined the pack train at the end of the caravan. The two thin men, merchants they claimed, reassured the stonecutter that all was well. Tarnold wasn't so sure.

The third month out, dwarven patrols stopped them at the edge of dwarven lands. The dwarves nodded appreciatively at the Sanguine blocks of granite the stonecutter brought along to trade. Gold passed hands often as constant inspections happened frequently in the next three months of travel. Every time the dwarves waved them on as they appeared to be simple stonecutters only interested in dwarven quarry stone. The dwarves seemed genuinely pleased to have human stonecutters interested in trade.

Used by these two men, Tarnold knew there were several mysteries on this trip that needed solving. He just didn't know if he wanted to solve them. On several of the nights, he glanced into the tent of the leaders of the fifty. The two men talked into the oddest mirror he'd ever seen. Some other voices talked back to them. Each time, he was politely shooed away from the tent before he could hear much of anything. Magical talking mirrors were unusual. In fact, he'd only seen the seven in the throne room of the palace. He really wanted to think he could be part of a secret empire quest, but his own common sense didn't let him believe that for a second.

Tarnold feared for his safety, but what could he do? He knew his family was now rich beyond his wildest dreams. *Fate would bring him what fate wanted to bring.*

———

Corbyn sat at the edge of his bed, wanting nothing more than to lie down and go to sleep. The quill-writing feather floated just above the parchment at his writing disk, working its magical scribing at his every word.

"Repeat back to me what I've just written," Corbyn ordered.

In his voice, the enchanted quill floated back and forth over the words just written on the parchment. "Upon reaching the capital, orders commanded me to come immediately to the throne room by way of the Sanguine stairs. Upon reaching those stairs, I was seized by the door golem. Lord Cortwin and the wizard Disingen appeared above me on the staircase. Lord Cortwin turned into a Nevil demon and attacked me. The wizard allowed one of my hands to become free of the golem, and I killed the Nevil demon with a Nightwing dagger."

"Scratch that last sentence; that will never do. Write this, 'with one hand freed; I used magics to kill the Nevil demon. The wizard commanded the golem to seize me again, and he vanished, taking a ring the Nevil demon wore. I talked the golem into taking me to the throne room and the rest, you know.' Sign it, Captain Cauldron, King's 25th Lancers. I'll reread it in the morning. Put yourself away."

The quill and ink promptly obeyed their master's command.

Corbyn had no idea how his report would be received. *The fact that Cimmerian Nix was part of the report could be a problem. If he were in command, he wouldn't want the world's most powerful elf interested in one of the empire's Captains. Corbyn had positioned his cousin's appearance as an elf scout checking the troop out. He was sure his commanders would believe a king's ransom in emeralds could buy the elf brooch, even though that wasn't really the case. He'd wanted to avoid discussion of the Wild Hunt, but he'd made the mistake of telling his friend Major Stonewall.*

He put his boot in the groove of the boot puller at the foot of his bed. The clamps seized on his heel, and he pulled his foot out. Unclamping the loose boot, he put his other foot in the boot puller and left that boot there.

Still dressed and not caring, his head hit his pillow. He knew he would be wide awake in just an hour or two as the crescent moon reached its zenith. Briefly, he wondered if he should try to stay awake until then. He could get something to eat as his stomach rumbled up at him. Then sleep took him, ending all of his problems until the moon rose.

THE END

Milton Keynes UK
Ingram Content Group UK Ltd.
UKHW050434230324
439902UK00014B/368